NATALIE'S ART
A FRANK RENZI NOVEL

"Art is a jealous mistress."

-- Ralph Waldo Emerson

I0664081

SUSAN FLEET

Music and Mayhem Press

Natalie's Art is a work of fiction. All names, characters, museums and events are either products of the author's imagination or used fictitiously. Any resemblance to actual persons, living or dead, is entirely coincidental.

ISBN-10 0984723579

ISBN-13 978-0-9847235-7-7

Cover photographs used with permission from Fotalia:

Chinesische Mafia Gangsterbraut © Haramis Kalfar

Cornice grigia con fondo bianco © Giuseppe Porzani

Postage stamp France 1982 The Lacemaker, by Vermeer © laufer

Back cover photo by Pete Wolbrette

Printed in the United States of America

Praise for Susan Fleet's Frank Renzi series

ABSOLUTION

Best Mystery-Suspense-Thriller — 2009 Premier Book Awards

"A New Orleans killer thriller." — Jan Herman, Arts Journal

"Relentless tempo . . . sharp writing." — Kirkus Discoveries

"Creole-flavored suspense." — The Attleboro Sun Chronicle

"Far above the ordinary whodunit. Bravo!" — The Florida Times-Union

DIVA

"Fleet takes us inside the head of an obsessed stalker as he lusts after his victim." — Tom Bryson, Too Smart To Die

"Great character development [and] an absolutely fascinating ending ... a very suspenseful book!" — Feathered Quill Book Reviews

"Fleet subtitles Diva, her new thriller, a novel of psychological suspense. That's an understatement." — Jan Herman, Arts Journal

NATALIE'S REVENGE

Best Mystery – 2014 Feathered Quill Book Awards

"An amazingly great read, fast paced, well written and extremely challenging to put down." — Rebecca's Reads

"Fleet's superbly drawn character, Natalie, pursues revenge for the murder of her mother, when Natalie was ten years old. Another excellent read from Susan Fleet." — Tom Bryson, Too Smart To Die

"The coolest detective in literature at the moment [is] Frank Renzi. Natalie is a truly intelligent and seductive character." — Feathered Quill Book Reviews

JACKPOT

"Thrilling and gripping. The writing is tight and builds to a tense climax." -- Julia Hopkinson, Readers' Favorite

"Fleet does it again, another page-turning thriller. Frank Renzi hunts a disturbed serial killer." – Tom Bryson, Sarcophagus

"For those who love the gritty, the witty, and perfect descriptions. A tremendously great series." – Feathered Quill Book Reviews

Praise for Susan Fleet's non-fiction

Women Who Dared: Trailblazing 20th Century Musicians
Violinist Maud Powell and Trumpeter Edna White

"Fleet's insightful writing, filled with contextual information makes for a compelling introduction to this long-awaited book." -- Monique Buzzarté, trombonist and Meet-the-Composer Soloist Champion

"Susan Fleet is an expert on American female musicians who deserve wider recognition in the history of jazz and classical music."-- Matt Morrell, 'Jazz at WGBH, WGBH-FM, Boston

"Fleet's heroines were successful, artistic performers, attracting and enriching broad audiences." – Howard Mandel, editor at Billboard

Dark Deeds, Vol. 1: Serial killers, stalkers and domestic homicides
Dark Deeds, Vol. 2: Serial killers, stalkers and domestic homicides

"Haunting and educational, well researched and well written. The inner world of these killers is vividly and psychologically portrayed." -- Arthur Smukler, MD, psychiatrist

"In Dark Deeds, Susan Fleet demonstrates both her excellent journalistic and creative writing skills." -- Micki Peluso, And The Whippoorwill Sang

Dedicated to those who are still searching for the masterpieces stolen from the Gardner Museum in 1990. May they soon be recovered.

CHAPTER 1

June 18, 2010 – 1:05 PM – New Orleans

"What was he thinking?" Homicide Detective Frank Renzi said. "Steal a car and take the woman with him?" A complication he didn't need right now. He wanted to study the report sitting on his office desk about some recent European art heists.

Focused on the road, Detective Kenyon Miller gripped the wheel in his dark-skinned fists. "Gotta be a nutcase. Drive an old rattletrap that fast? A tire blows, it might flip over."

"Hey, the guy's a bank robber, not Albert Einstein. No telling what he'll do with the woman."

Hot, humid air whipped his face as their cruiser rocketed up Elysian Fields Avenue in pursuit of the beat-up blue Chevy Cavalier one block ahead of them. The carjacker, a white male in his twenties, had held up a bank in the French Quarter. Frank and Miller had been eating lunch two blocks away when their handsets erupted: *Carjacking in the Quarter, white male took off with the female driver, heading north on Elysian Fields.*

With a screech of brakes, the Chevy swerved into Gentilly Acres, a new housing development.

Miller followed the Chevy. Frank got on his handset, identified himself and said, "French Quarter carjacker just drove into the Gentilly Acres subdivision. We're in pursuit. Get some squads over there."

Fifty yards ahead of them, the Chevy's speed increased.

Then came a loud pop. One of the front tires blew. The car careened over a curb and slammed into a big oak tree. Miller slewed to a stop twenty yards behind it. Frank got out and drew his SIG-Sauer, eyes trained on the Chevy. Steam billowed out of the hood. Nobody moving inside the car. Maybe they could arrest the guy without a problem.

The car door opened and his breath caught in his throat. The carjacker yanked the woman out of the car and ran, pulling her with him, his hand clamped around her arm. She had on a bright yellow dress with a long skirt, wailing in a thin, shrill voice, "My baby!"

"Damn!" Miller said. "There's a kid in the car?"

"Stay with the child. I'll take Einstein," Frank said, and ran after them. A rangy six-foot-one, he didn't lift weights, but he ran five miles every day, a habit he'd acquired in high school when he played point guard on the basketball team.

Two-story homes lined the street, roughed-in but unfinished, no shingles on the exterior or the roof. The mother was fighting the man, dragging her feet to slow him down. They disappeared behind a house. Frank sprinted to the corner and saw the carjacker drag the woman into the next house. A boxy white van stood beside it, THIBIDEAU ELECTRIC stenciled on the side.

He crept to the door and eased inside. The odor of sawdust and fresh-cut wood filled his nostrils. Someday this would be a kitchen, studs on the walls but no sheet rock, which allowed him a partial view of the next room. The carjacker, a scrawny kid in cutoff jeans and a white T-shirt, had the woman clamped to his chest. In his right hand, he held a butcher knife inches away from the woman's throat. Red splotches stained his white T-shirt.

Frank's heart jolted. Jesus, did he already cut her?

Then he realized the splotches were from the dye-pack in the money the man had stolen.

"Let the girl go!" said a man's voice. Two men entered Frank's field of vision, the electricians he assumed, white males in their thirties, one tall and wiry, the other short and pudgy. The tall one had an electric drill in his hand, the short one held a staple gun, advancing on the carjacker and the woman. A disastrous situation was about to get worse. Way worse.

Agitated, the carjacker screamed, "Get away or I'll cut her." Eyes bugged out, he brandished the knife, then held it to the woman's throat.

Frank stepped into the room and said, "Hold it. Let's all take a deep breath and calm down."

The woman's eyes locked onto his. Her mouth opened but nothing came out. A young, light-skinned black woman, five feet tall, weighed maybe ninety pounds. She looked a lot like Halle Berry, might have been prettier but for the look of terror on her face.

Fifteen feet away from the carjacker, the electricians stopped and looked at Frank.

"Detective Frank Renzi, NOPD," he said. "I'd show you my badge, but my hands are busy." Busy holding the SIG, aimed at the floor now, but ready to use should the need arise.

The carjacker's lips drew back in a snarl. "You come any closer, she's dead."

"No need to harm the lady," Frank said. "Stay calm and nobody gets hurt." To the electricians, he said, "Thank you for your assistance, but I think it would be best if you left." He jerked his head at the doorway behind him and gave them his don't-fuck-with-me look. "Now."

The taller electrician frowned. "Well … okay. If you say so."

Reluctantly, the electricians lowered their makeshift weapons, the drill and the staple gun, and headed toward the doorway. Frank hoped they'd keep going and leave the house, but he didn't dare turn and look, didn't dare take his eyes off the carjacker.

"My baby," said the woman, breathing hard, her eyes fixed on Frank.

"My partner's with your baby. He's got kids of his own. What's your baby's name?"

"Bella," the woman said, her voice rising in panic. "She's only sixteen months old!"

Frank studied the carjacker, who was growing twitchier by the minute, eyes darting this way and that, pinprick pupils, looked like he might be on crystal meth. Bad news. Oxy and heroin addicts tended to be laid back, but meth freaks were hyperactive and unpredictable.

Dangerous.

He edged closer, twenty feet away now. "You're having a rough day, buddy. The holdup didn't go the way you planned, then you stole a car with a woman and a baby inside."

"I didn't know the kid was there!"

"Maybe not, but we need to let Mom get back to her little girl and make sure she's okay."

The woman nodded, her eyes bright with tears.

Sirens sounded in the distance. About time.

"Hear that?" he said. "More police will be here soon. Why not quit while you're ahead? Nobody got hurt. Let the woman go and put down the knife."

"No way!" The man clenched his forearm around the woman, pulling her close.

Her eyes widened, dark terror-filled eyes. "Please," she said in a strangled voice.

Frank took a deep breath to steady his heart rate, sweaty hands clamped around the SIG. He didn't want to use it, but push come to shove, he would.

Sirens whooped to a stop outside. The cavalry was here.

He got into a zone and locked eyes with the carjacker. "Listen carefully. You stuck up a bank and stole a car. Neither of those things will put you away for life, but then you took the woman. Now you're threatening her with a knife. That carries big penalties. Nobody needs to get hurt. Let the woman go, put down the knife, and we'll all walk out of here safe and sound."

"No!" The carjacker's face contorted, a crimson mask of fury, like he was about to explode.

Situation critical. A metallic taste flooded Frank's mouth. He clenched his jaw, raised his weapon and set his finger on the trigger. "Touch her with that knife and you are dead."

"Go ahead! Shoot me!" The man shoved the woman to the floor and charged, brandishing the knife, staggering now, his movements uncoordinated.

His heart slammed his chest. Shoot him, or not? Two seconds to decide.

A life or death decision. At the last instant, he pivoted and slammed the SIG against the bridge of the man's nose. Screaming obscenities, the man dropped the knife and fell to the floor, clutching his bloody nose.

Frank kicked the knife away. As it skittered across the floor a half-dozen police officers charged into the room and subdued the carjacker.

He holstered his weapon and helped the woman to her feet. She leaned against him, chest heaving, sobbing as though her heart would break.

"You were very brave," he said, patting her back. "Let's get you back to your little girl."

"Thank you," she said, wiping away tears. "I was afraid he was going to hurt Bella."

"But he didn't. You'll be fine." But not right way, Frank thought. For the next few months, she'd have nightmares about what might have happened. He should know. It had been two years since Natalie Brixton shot him and he was still having flashbacks.

Natalie, the long-legged woman with the distinctive walk. The report on his desk contained details about several European art heists. After the most recent one, four months ago in London, a witness had told the investigators he'd seen the robber leave the museum and he was positive it was a woman. Because of her long-legged sexy, hip-swinging stride.

———

June 19, 2010 – 2:55 AM – Oxford, UK

"What should I do?" said the security guard, gazing at her, his eyes wide with fright.

All he could see was her eyes. The rest of her face was hidden by a black balaclava. She took out her weapon, a Beretta 92FS with an Evo 9 Suppressor attached to the barrel.

The weapon she thought she would never have to use.

The guard raised his hands. "Please! I didn't know he was coming, I swear it! Sometimes he stops by without warning."

Maintaining a calm demeanor, one that belied her inner turmoil, she strode to the security desk. One monitor displayed video from the security camera outside the entrance. The Security Director stood outside the door, a burly older man with a Van Dyke beard. He did not appear to be armed. The security guard wasn't either. Brits were touchy about civilians carrying firearms.

"Let him in," she said. "I'll hide in the closet near the entrance."

The guard, a slight man with sandy hair and an acne-pitted face, frowned. "Then what?"

She flicked the Beretta. "Hurry up. Unlock the closet."

4

Fumbling with his key ring, he preceded her into the six-by-eight-foot foyer near the entrance. He stopped at a door on the left-hand wall and unlocked it.

"Do what you are being paid to do," she hissed. "Let him in. Act normal."

He nodded, but his eyes were full of fear.

She entered the closet, a claustrophobic space, dark and smelly. After they put on their uniforms, the guards stored their clothes here. She pulled the door toward her, leaving it open a crack. Now she couldn't see the guard. Would he do what she said? What if he didn't?

What if this was a set-up?

She stood there in the dark, her heart racing. The next few minutes were crucial. She drew in a deep breath and held it, willing her heart to slow, a trick she'd learned years ago from her Taekwondo teacher. Don't allow your body's automatic response to fear overpower your discipline and focus. She released that breath and took another, and another.

As her panic subsided she heard the guard say, "Hello, sir. I wasn't expecting you tonight."

"Why would you?" said a gruff voice. "That's the point."

The words failed to reassure her. Shifting the Beretta to her left hand, she took a steel baton out of her knapsack and waited in the darkness, tense and alert.

After several agonizing seconds, the Security Director walked past the closet. She pushed open the door, stepped forward and slammed the baton against the side of his head. The man grunted and slumped to the black-and-white tiled floor.

The security guard stared at her, horrified.

She stuck the baton in her knapsack and held the Beretta in her right hand. Her shooting hand.

"What do we do now?" the guard asked in a shaky voice.

"Tie him up," she said curtly. "Use the twine. Put duct tape over his mouth. Hurry!"

The guard took a ball of twine off the security desk and knelt down beside the Security Director.

She checked the time. She'd been here almost thirty minutes. Much too long.

Her cellphone vibrated against her leg. Her mouth went dry. Her hands trembled as she took out the phone and answered. "Yes."

"What's going on?" said a gravely voice, a voice that sent chills through every inch of her body.

Gregor. She had never met him, but she knew he was nearby. Watching.

"The Security Director paid us an unexpected visit. I disabled him."

"Kill them."

Paralyzed with shock, she couldn't speak. Kill them? No! She only carried the Beretta to intimidate the security guards. She wanted to scream, wanted to tell Gregor she wouldn't do it. But she knew this would do her no good.

"Adam didn't know he was coming," she said. Adam was the guard's code name, not his real one. When she said this, his head jerked up. He had already bound the Security Director's wrists and ankles together.

"Shoot them. If you don't, you will die, too."

She had no doubt of it. "Got it," she said, and closed the phone.

The guard rose to his feet and backed away, staring at her eyes, the only part of her face not hidden by the balaclava. "I didn't know he was coming. I didn't!"

"I believe you, but we have to make this look like you weren't involved, remember? Give me the twine, turn around and put your hands behind your back so I can bind your wrists."

Docile as a Shropshire sheep, he gave her the twine, turned around and put his hands behind his back. Bile rose in her throat. She didn't want to shoot him, but what choice did she have?

She pulled the trigger. The Beretta made a soft popping sound, and the guard fell to the floor, blood spurting from his head.

A flashback blindsided her. Shooting Tex in the back of the head in New Orleans.

Sickened by the memory, she gritted her teeth, willing the vision away. She had to get out of here, fast. But first she had to finish the job.

Kill them. Or you will die, too.

The Security Director's body was curled up on the floor. Mercifully, his eyes were closed. She stood over him, extended the Beretta, then lowered it to her side.

Shoot them. If you don't, you will die, too.

Tears flooded her eyes. Why did it always come down to this? Her life or someone else's?

But how could she kill this defenseless man?

He uttered a soft groan and his eyes fluttered.

Startled, she shrank back. This man was innocent, utterly defenseless, his wrists and ankles bound together. No way was she going to kill him.

But she had to get out fast before he regained consciousness and saw her. With grim determination, she jammed the Beretta into the knapsack, grabbed the metal container that held the Rembrandt, dashed to the entrance door and tried to calm herself.

Her heart refused to cooperate, pounding her chest like a wild thing.

Where was Gregor? Somewhere near the museum. Not close enough to hear the gunshots perhaps, but close enough to see her when she left.

Her shoulders tensed as she opened the door and stepped outside. Thick clouds filled the dusky sky, obscuring the moon. She shut the door, averted her face and strode past the security camera. Only then did she remove the balaclava.

She stuck it in her pocket and set off down the sidewalk with a purposeful stride. Walk, don't run. Running attracted attention. The last thing she wanted while she was carrying a painting worth several million dollars. The getaway car was two blocks away, a stolen Toyota Yaris. The license plate was also stolen, stripped from a different vehicle, one that would cause no problems if the police stopped her.

She'd been given a cover story in case that happened. Be prepared. Leave nothing to chance.

But the Security Director had foiled that part of the plan.

She reached the first intersection and crossed the street. So far so good. Usually, she was afraid witnesses would see her, or the police.

Not tonight. Where was Gregor?

Kill them or you will die, too.

Her breath came in shallow gasps and her neck prickled a spidery warning. She rotated her head and arched her neck. Was Gregor inside one of the brownstones that lined the deserted street? Standing in an upper window, holding a Bushmaster, drawing a bead on her head?

Gripping the metal container, she strode along the sidewalk and tried to reassure herself.

He wouldn't shoot her while she had the painting, would he?

She walked faster. If she could get into the Yaris, she'd be less of a target.

In the distance, she heard a car engine start behind her. Her heart catapulted into her throat. Rigid with fear, she glimpsed the glow of headlights behind her, closing fast, the car engine roaring.

She broke into a dead run. The headlights came closer.

In thirty seconds she reached the Yaris.

With trembling hands, she unlocked the door, yanked it open and jumped inside.

A black Mercedes passed her and flashed its lights. Gregor.

Sick with despair, she started the Yaris and pulled out of the space.

Ahead of her, the street was deserted. No cars. No black Mercedes.

But so what? Now they had a club to hold over her.

Stealing a painting was one thing.

Murdering a man in cold blood was another.

CHAPTER 2

June 19, 2010 – 3:30 AM – Southwest London

She parked the Mini-Cooper in the four-bay garage behind Pym's mansion. Safe at last. But for how long? What would Gregor do when he found out she didn't kill the Security Director?

The Beretta was still in the knapsack. She should have ditched it, but she hadn't. Intent on survival, she had driven to the garage where her Mini-Cooper was parked. No police car sirens yet, but soon there might be. She hurriedly wiped down the stolen Yaris with alcohol-soaked baby wipes. Then, sweaty and anxious, she had stowed her knapsack and the Rembrandt in the Mini-Cooper and fled.

Her jaw ached from clenching her teeth to curb the emotions raging inside her, fear and self-loathing and a rising tide of anger that threatened to boil over. She grabbed her knapsack and the Rembrandt container and strode toward Pym's three-story mansion, the gabled roof stark against the gray moonlit sky.

Gravel crunched under her feet as she entered the portico and approached the side entrance. The employee entrance for those who did Pym's bidding.

The solid oak door opened immediately, sending shafts of light into the darkness. Smiling broadly, Jonathan Pym said, "Here you are at last. I was beginning to worry."

His smile faded when he saw her grim expression. She strode past him into the mahogany-paneled library. Two crystal chandeliers cast light over a Persian rug and two leather recliners facing a low table. A bottle of champagne stood on a sideboard, chilling in a silver ice bucket. Pym was expecting a celebration, but she was in no mood for it.

She leaned the Rembrandt container against the sideboard, set her knapsack on the floor beside one recliner and paced the room, unable to quell her anger.

Pym entered the library, a hollow-cheeked older man with thinning light-brown hair, pale eyes and skin. No celebratory smile. Now he was frowning at her. "Valerie, what's wrong?"

"A man is dead! That's what's wrong."

Her words seemed to age him. Moving slowly, he sank onto his favorite recliner, the brown leather seat hollowed out like his cheeks. "What man? Where?"

"In the museum."

His eyes narrowed, a sure sign he was angry. In the two years she'd known him, she had seldom seen him angry, and never at her. "Stop pacing," he snapped. "Sit down and tell me what happened."

Waves of nausea hit her. She didn't want to tell him, didn't want to think about pulling the trigger and seeing the blood. She sank onto the other recliner. "Just as I was about to leave, the museum security director showed up. I don't think the guard knew he was coming. I told the guard to let him in."

"Did he see you?"

"No. I hid in a closet. But Gregor was watching. He saw the security director enter the museum and called me." Even now the memory of his sinister voice unnerved her. She went to the sideboard and poured herself a glass of brandy. "Would you like some cognac, Jonathan?"

"No. Tell me what happened."

She returned to her chair and sipped the brandy. It didn't help. Her pent-up rage erupted, a torrent of angry words. "Jonathan, when I agreed to steal these paintings, you said there would be no violence. But you gave me a Beretta. In case the guard got cold feet, you said. You didn't tell me I might have to kill someone!"

"Stop this rubbish, Valerie. Tell me what happened. You shot the security director?"

"No. I knocked him out with the baton."

A muscle worked in Pym's jaw. "Did you kill him?"

"No, but I shot the security guard."

"Why?" His implacable pale-gray eyes bored into her, laser-beams of rage.

"Gregor told me to kill them. He said if I didn't he would kill me!"

Pym's face grew pale, as if all the blood had drained from it. In the silence, his gaze wandered to the leather-bound volumes on the floor-to-ceiling shelves, then to the sideboard and came to rest on the Rembrandt container. He massaged his eyes with both hands and heaved a sigh. "I will deal with Gregor."

"There was no need to kill the guard! I could have tied him up, disabled him as planned and left with the Rembrandt."

Pym shrugged. "What's done is done."

His callous remark infuriated her. Easy for him to say. He wasn't the one who'd pulled the trigger. He hired others to do his dirty work—Gregor and the insider guards—and paid her to steal the paintings. Then Pym delivered them to the wealthy collectors who had ordered them and raked in the money.

She leaned forward, opened her knapsack and took out the Beretta.

Pym's jaw dropped and his mouth sagged open.

She almost laughed. Did he think she was going to shoot him? That would be stupid. Kill a well-known London businessman? She would spend the rest of her life in jail. The one she wanted to kill was Gregor. But she had already killed too many people. Tonight she had murdered a man in cold blood. Never again.

"Jonathan," she said through clenched teeth. "You don't get it. This gun killed a man tonight."

"Stop pointing that fucking gun at me. Put it away."

Shocked, she put the Beretta in her knapsack. Pym never used profanity. But that didn't change her decision. "Get someone else to steal the paintings, Jonathan. Tonight was my last."

Expressionless, he said, "Go to bed, Valerie. We'll discuss this tomorrow."

Her decision would be no different tomorrow, but why prolong the argument? She set her brandy snifter on the sideboard and left.

————

She rode the elevator up to her quarters on the third floor. We'll discuss this tomorrow. Pym would never accept her decision, and she knew how dangerous rich powerful men could be.

After entering her quarters, she shoved a steel wedge under the door. It had no lock. Not that she feared Pym would come here uninvited. They had sex in his suite on the second floor. But old memories die hard. As a teenager in Pecos, Texas, she had woken one night to find her cousin sitting on her bed. He tried to kiss her, but she fought him off. Two days later, she had made her uncle install a lock on her door.

She put the knapsack on a table in the sitting room. She hated the decor. Pym's mansion was like a mausoleum, dark and dreary, like the paintings his wealthy clients favored. Midnight-blue drapes covered a small window overlooking a park. Two Louis XIV settees with curved legs faced a teak armoire that held her sound system and a television set. An alcove held a sink, a small refrigerator and a two-burner stove in case she wanted to cook.

But other than breakfast she ate her meals with Pym.

One of her duties. Smile and make small talk. And provide sex when Pym had the energy. Be who they want you to be, a lesson she'd learned while working as a call girl in Paris. A high-class escort.

Bullshit. She was a whore.

She hated her life, hated the woman she had become.

Overcome with fatigue, she went in the bedroom. Steep slanted eaves left only enough space for a single bed, a chest of drawers and a dressing table with a frilly skirt draped over the legs. She took off her wig, placed it on one of the Styrofoam wig stands on the table, removed the pins to release her long dark hair and scratched her scalp. Wearing a wig made her scalp itch like crazy, but wigs were useful for disguising her looks.

She stripped off her clothes, sank onto the bed and massaged her throbbing temples. Every muscle in her body ached. Her mind churned, replaying tonight's ordeal. Gregor ordering her to kill the two men. Fearing Gregor would kill her. Her frantic escape. Pym browbeating her, as if the screw-up was her fault.

But that didn't change the facts. Natalie Brixton had killed again.

Tears flooded her eyes. Two years ago in Boston she had killed Oliver James, the man who knew too much about Natalie Brixton. No one, not even her lover, was going to hinder her mission to take revenge on the man who murdered her mother. But Oliver still haunted her dreams, filling her with an aching sadness and profound remorse.

Chip Beaubien was different. His father had murdered her mother, and Chip was just like him, an arrogant rich man who used women. He had driven her to a seedy motel anticipating hot sex, not an accusation that his father had killed her mother.

Even now she could picture the hatred in his eyes before she shot him. But what good did it do? Taking revenge brought her no satisfaction, just an empty feeling that wouldn't go away.

Worse, the New Orleans police were hunting for her. Homicide detective Frank Renzi, the man who relentlessly stalked his prey and usually caught them. A frisson of fear raised goosebumps on her arms.

Was Renzi still hunting for her? Or was he busy chasing other killers? She pictured his angular cheekbones, the hawk-like nose, the scar on his chin. But his dark eyes were what she remembered most, intense and penetrating.

Renzi wouldn't give up. He would continue his pursuit, just as he had pursued her into that alley two years ago. She could have killed him as he lay on the ground after she shot him. That would have been the smart thing to do. But she didn't want to kill him.

That day she had vowed never to kill another person as long as she lived. Now she had.

After she fled to Paris, her manager at the escort service had given her a new identity, Valerie Brown, and sent her to London to work for another escort service. She'd been here ever since. Far too long. For months she had been planning her escape. After Pym paid her for tonight's job, there would be two hundred thousand dollars in her bank account. Not as much as she needed to disappear forever, but she had to get out now, before they forced her to steal another painting. And kill someone else.

She had already chosen her destination, a large European city where she would be one person among six million. Every morning during her five-mile run she listened to language tapes. She wasn't fluent yet, but that wasn't her biggest worry.

Pym might tell Gregor to find her and kill her. After all, she was a woman who knew too much. She knew how Gregor orchestrated the heists, hiring insider guards, warning them not to squeal to the cops. But the guards died anyway, from muggings or suicides or drug overdoses, according to the news. She didn't believe it.

Gregor had killed them. And he could just as easily kill *her.*

11

Gut-wrenching fear exploded inside her and bile spewed into her throat. She ran to the bathroom and vomited into the toilet. Weak and trembling, she wiped her mouth and sank onto the floor. She was tired of being afraid, tired of hiding from cops, tired of being the person others wanted her to be.

The only way she would ever have any peace of mind was to disappear like a wisp of smoke. Only then could she be the person she wanted to be.

Someone who didn't have to kill people.

―――

Saturday, June 19, 2010 – 7:15 P.M. – New Orleans

The murmur of voices and jazz playing over the sound system filled the Bulldog, Frank's favorite place to relax after a long week. Best of all, Kelly O'Neil was sitting beside him. After four years he was still crazy about her. He loved her sea-green eyes, as deep as the ocean, telling him more than words ever could. Styled in a pixie cut, dark curly hair framed her olive-skinned face. She had a temper, but he didn't mind.

Placid was boring. Volatile was exciting.

Both of her parents were Italian. Franklin Sullivan Renzi was half and half. Dark eyes and a prominent nose inherited from the Italian side, an explosive temper from his Irish mother.

Nina Simone was singing an up-tempo version of "My Way," about living life with no regrets. Frank had a few regrets, but for better or for worse, he'd done it his way. In November he'd be forty-eight, but other than a few gray flecks in his black hair, he didn't look much different than when he'd met Kelly. She was forty-two, slim and trim thanks to her workouts at the gym. Kelly was an NOPD detective, too. She had a gorgeous body, curvy in all the right places, and a great ass. And she had a great sense of humor. He loved making her laugh.

After Nina Simone took "My Way" out to a rousing climax, Kelly said, "I love the way she lets it all hang out."

He leaned closer and murmured, "I'm always in favor of letting it all hang out."

"As if I didn't know. But try to control yourself. There are witnesses." She sipped her beer. "How was your week? Anything exciting?"

"Same old, same old." He didn't want to talk about the carjacking. Not the scariest moment in his twenty-plus years as a cop, but close. Not only that it had taken him an hour to write his report. He hated paperwork.

"That's not what I heard. What about the carjacker?"

"Oh. That. Some idiot held up a bank near the French Quarter, had no wheels for a getaway and hijacked a car. Kenyon Miller and I caught the BOLO and chased him. No big deal."

"Compared to what? Atticus Kroll and his gang shooting at you with AK-47s? Jesus, Frank, how come getting a story out of you is like pulling teeth?"

"A good homicide detective deflects all inquiries."

"What about the woman in the car?"

He fished a cashew out of the dish on the bar and ate it. "You heard about the woman?"

"Yes, Frank," she said, oozing sarcasm, "I heard about the woman. I also heard her little girl was in the car."

"I don't think he saw the kid. He was more worried about the dye pack that blew up and sprayed him with red dye. The woman was smart though, kept her cool."

Kelly gave him one of her patented warning looks.

"Okay, it got a little hairy after he crashed the car and took off with the woman. Kenyon stayed with the little girl. I chased the carjacker and the woman into a house that was under construction. By the time I got inside, two electricians were threatening the hijacker with—dig this—a power drill and a staple gun."

"Hey, give 'em credit for trying to save her."

"Right, but the guy was already paranoid, looked like he was on crystal meth. But it worked out okay. I got the electricians to leave. End of story." He slugged down some beer.

She looked at him, incredulous. "Frank, he came at you with a knife!"

"Who told you that?"

Her mouth quirked, a sure sign she was pissed. "I used to work Homicide, remember?"

"Yes, and when I find the guy that blabbed the details, I'll give him a dope-slap."

Kelly flashed a triumphant smile. "Morgan Vobitch told me. You gonna give your boss a dope-slap?"

He tried to picture it. Detective Lieutenant Morgan Vobitch supervised the homicide detectives in Districts One, Five and Eight. Vobitch took no guff from the politicians or NOPD bigwigs, and never from his own detectives. Frank had worked with him for nine years. Despite their occasional differences they were in total agreement about one thing. Get the thugs off the street.

"Okay, I admit it got a little tense. The guy was holding a knife to the woman's throat. But I distracted him with a few choice words."

"Like what? *Drop the knife asshole and let the woman go?*"

"I don't remember, but he let her go and charged me. I whacked him in the head with my SIG. End of story." He smiled at her. "Happy now?"

Kelly sipped her beer. He could see the wheels turning. Early in their relationship her concerns about the dangers he faced on the job had been an issue. Until he'd delivered his I-am-who-I-am speech. "Cops are trained to run toward danger. That's our job. I'm not going to change who I am. I'm a cop." He was still a cop and his attitude hadn't changed. Do what you gotta do to protect innocent people and put the scumbags in jail.

"How was your day?" he said. Kelly worked in the NOPD Domestic Violence unit. That was no cakewalk, either. Every cop knew a domestic violence call was dangerous. Could be nothing, could be a nutcase with a gun ready to use it.

She stifled a yawn. "Not as exciting as yours. Paperwork mostly, getting women and their kids into safe housing after they leave their idiot boyfriends or husbands."

"What's with the yawn?" He ran a finger over her forearm. "Does that mean you're too tired?"

She leaned closer and whispered in his ear, "Don't be a wise-ass."

He laughed. "Want a burger? You might need it. I've got plans for later that don't include sleeping."

"Sure," Kelly said, deadpan. "With sweet-potato fries. For extra energy."

After they ordered, Frank said, "I just got an interesting report from a London detective."

"What, you're chasing international criminals now? That's new."

Not new, he thought. For two years he'd been checking the Interpol website, searching for leads on Natalie Brixton. "He sent me the file on a series of art heists with a similar MO. The thieves get into the museums and walk off with a painting or two. Old Masters, he said. What does that mean?"

Before joining NOPD, Kelly had studied art in college, but she wasn't a painter. She made metal jewelry—earrings, tie clips and broaches—and decorated them with enamel paint in various colors.

"Hey, it's been years since I studied art history, so don't hang me for the dates, but Old Masters are paintings done centuries ago by European artists, Michelangelo and El Greco in the sixteenth century. And seventeenth-century Dutch artists like Rembrandt and Vermeer."

"Thanks for the tutorial. Now I won't feel like a dunce when I talk to him. The most recent heist was in London, four months ago. A witness saw the robber leave the museum and told the police he was sure it was a woman."

"Strange," Kelly said, "but it happens. Remember the woman last year who robbed those banks?"

"I do. Flashed a toy pistol at the tellers and told 'em to give up the money. She was smarter than the idiot we nabbed yesterday, had her own getaway car. But they got her eventually."

Twirling a lock of dark hair around two fingers, Kelly gazed at him with those sea-green eyes.

"The witness in London didn't see the robber's face, but he said she had a very distinctive walk."

Kelly went still like a bird dog on point. "You think it was Natalie?"

"Yeah, I do."

"But that's crazy. She killed three men here. After she got away, wouldn't she be smart enough to lie low and hide? Why would she steal art?"

"I've got no clue, but if it's Natalie, I'm going to get her."

The message in Kelly's eyes was crystal clear: Are you crazy? Quit while you're ahead. "Frank, that woman is trouble. So what if she had a tough life? She killed those men and she tried to kill you!"

"I don't think so. She could have, but she didn't."

"Bullshit. She shot at you intending to kill you and hit your leg by mistake."

He saw the bartender coming with their burgers, but now he didn't feel like eating, didn't feel like arguing with Kelly either. The bartender set down platters of burgers and fries, saw their grim expressions and left.

Studiously ignoring him, Kelly squirted ketchup on her plate, dipped one of her fries into it and ate it.

He leaned over and nibbled her earlobe. Judging by her expression, she couldn't decide whether to laugh or yell at him. "What?" she said.

"You weren't there. You don't know what she was thinking and neither do I. For two years it's been bugging the hell out of me. The murder cases are still open--three here, one in Boston. I want answers. I want to know where she went. For two years, I haven't had a single lead. Now I do. Come on, Kelly. Help me celebrate. If Natalie's doing those art heists in Europe, I'm going to get her."

She looked at him, poker-faced, as though she was debating with herself, making a decision. At last she pulled him close and gave him a hug. "Congratulations on the lead, Frank. I hope you get the answers you're looking for."

Not saying she hoped he'd find Natalie, he noticed.

He leaned over and kissed her on the lips. "You're the best, Kelly. Eat up, so we can go home and have a proper celebration." He meant it. He cared about her a lot. Most of the time they were on the same page. Not this time, but he didn't need her permission to hunt for Natalie Brixton. If she was involved in these European art heists, he intended to track her down and ask her some questions.

First on the list: why didn't she kill him when she had the chance?

CHAPTER 3

SUNDAY June 20, 2010 – 10:15 AM London

Halfway into her run, she yanked off her headset and jammed it into the pocket of her shorts. Forget the language tape. How could she concentrate on vocabulary words and verb tenses?

She had to ditch the gun and plan her escape.

Clad in white running shoes, her feet pounded the sidewalk. The sun was hidden behind thick clouds, another gray morning in London. She hated the damp, dreary weather. Not only that, you had to drive on the wrong side of the road, and the food was awful, starchy and bland. Although he employed a top-notch chef, Pym favored chops and steaks laden with thick gravy.

In the beginning, living with Pym was relatively pleasant. Private quarters, her own car to drive. Best of all, no one knew she was here. The cops were looking for Natalie Brixton not Valerie Brown, and Pym was easy to please, no excessive demands, sex once a week, often not even that. During her free time she could go to libraries or movies and maintain her Taekwondo skills at a gym in London's Chinatown.

But the Oxford heist had changed everything. Art thefts attracted a certain amount of attention, but a dead museum guard would draw far more scrutiny, details that might reach certain homicide detectives in Boston and New Orleans. Spurred by this worrisome thought, she lengthened her stride.

On the opposite sidewalk, three people were walking their dogs: a long-legged wolfhound, a miniature Schnauzer and a beautiful Golden Retriever. For them, this was just another Sunday. Take Fido for a stroll on an upscale street lined with huge mansions, go home and relax with the London Times. Would it contain an article about the Oxford heist and the murder? Theoretically, her time was her own until noon, when Pym called to ask if she wanted anything special for lunch, a subtle reminder that he expected her to join him at one o'clock for his midday meal.

No lunch with Pym yesterday. He'd probably assumed she was sleeping, but after their tense confrontation, she had tossed and turned for hours. Finally, she had gotten out of bed and compulsively wiped every inch of the Beretta with alcohol soaked swabs to erase any latent prints. Then she'd made herself a pot of green tea and considered her options.

Keep doing art heists? Or get out while she could and disappear?

But Pym wouldn't just let her go, he'd send Gregor after her, and Gregor was ruthless.

A horn tooted as a white delivery van passed her, the male driver leering at her legs and red shorts. She ignored him and kept running. She had to dump the Beretta where no one would find it, but that would require a car, and she would have to tell Pym where she was going, a requirement he had insisted upon when he'd given her the Mini-Cooper. Another problem to solve.

Pym hadn't called her to have dinner with him last night, either. Was he angry about her parting shot? *Get someone else to steal your paintings.* With Pym, it was difficult to tell.

She'd met him two years ago. The manager at the escort service in Paris had given her a new passport with a new name—Valerie Brown—and sent her to London with glowing references. The manager of the London branch was delighted when she said her specialty was art.

"Perfect," he'd exclaimed. "I've got just the chap for you, very high class, very well educated and ..." The manager waggled his eyebrows. "Very rich." His name was Jonathan Pym.

An older man, Pym appeared rather frail, five-foot-five and thin, with knobby wrists and fingers. His skin was pale and so were his eyes, a pallid gray-blue. During their first "date" he quizzed her about art. What painters did she like? Did she prefer watercolors or oils? What was her favorite art period? As if it were a job interview. Later, the reason became obvious. He wanted her to steal paintings for him.

Horns blared, jolting her back to reality. Traffic was backed up behind a moving van double-parked outside a large brick-front mansion. She turned and jogged toward Pym's mansion, the mantra in her head keeping time with her feet. *Dump the gun. Get out now. Dump the gun. Get out now.*

When she moved into his mansion, Pym had given her a cellphone and told her to keep it with her all the time, in case he wanted to speak to her. Bullshit. Dog-walkers used leashes to keep their canines in check. The cellphone was Pym's electronic leash. Registered in his name, it allowed him to monitor the calls she made and received. Last year she had befriended a Vietnamese man at her gym. Although her mother was American, her father was Vietnamese. When she said she needed a disposable pay-as-you-go cellphone, he sent her to Chen, an older Chinese man with a long white beard, the leader of one of London's Chinese Tongs. Chen had asked no questions. An hour later she had her cellphone.

Too bad she couldn't call him today, but that would be impolite. In Asian cultures politeness and respect for elders was important. On Sunday Chen stayed home with his children and grandchildren. But tomorrow she would ditch the Beretta, go to Chinatown and ask Chen to get her a new passport and a new identity. She had no idea how long this might take. In the meantime, she would concentrate on being Valerie. Be who they want you to be. Act smart, but not too smart. Be charming but deferential.

But when she got her new passport she would disappear. Her heart soared like a bird. Free at last!

She rounded a curve. Pym's mansion was two blocks ahead. Inside the pocket of her shorts, Pym's cellphone vibrated against her leg. She slowed to a walk, took out the phone and answered.

"Hello, Valerie. Where are you? Still running? I saw you leave earlier."

Spying on her, as usual. "Yes, but I'll be home in five minutes."

"Good. One of my business associates has invited us to his country estate. He's on the board of trustees for the Tate Museum, and his wife is quite charming. The limousine will be ready at twelve-thirty."

Damn! Why was he springing this on her now? "I'll need to take a shower and fix my hair."

"Right, and pack a bag. We'll be staying with them for a few days."

Shocked, she lowered the phone. A dull ache pounded her temples. Stay at a country estate for a few days? That would derail her plans and delay her escape. "But I have a dentist appointment tomorrow."

"Cancel it. I've already accepted their invitation."

"Why didn't you tell me about this before?"

"Valerie, I think you are forgetting something. You work for me. Your appointment will have to wait."

His icy tone of voice frightened her. "When will we be back?"

"Tuesday. Come along now or you'll make us late," Pym said, and ended the call.

A black cloud of despair destroyed her upbeat mood. Her escape plan would have to wait. Worse, for three days she would have to endure Pym's company around the clock. Torture.

———

7:35 PM – London

Detective Chief Inspector Leonard Stanford got the emergency call at six-fifteen. His boss never called on the weekend, so he knew some nasty bit of business was up. Worse than nasty, as it turned out.

Stanford flipped on the light in his office and draped his tweed jacket on the wooden coat rack beside the door. Six feet tall and 210 pounds, he used his imposing physique to intimidate reluctant witnesses. But his colleagues in the Art and Antiques Unit relished his wry humor and pointed jibes. To retaliate, they teased him about his prominent ears, which his reddish-brown hair failed to hide.

Littered with yellow messages slips, his desk stood in front of a window. Beyond the glass, lights from nearby buildings stood out against the inky darkness. He massaged his temples, fighting an incipient headache. Too many gin and tonics at his in-laws' house.

After dinner they'd played whist, a torture mercifully interrupted by the emergency call. His mother-in-law was lovely, but his father-in-law, a pensioner, complained incessantly. The government was corrupt and all the politicians were nutters. Stanford couldn't figure out how the man had managed to produce such a wonderful daughter. He'd married Priscilla thirty years ago and they were still keen for each other, got along better than their two Welch corgis. Priscilla was an only child and so was he.

Maybe that's why they got along, each of them busy tending their careers. Priscilla ran an interior decorating business.

With a heavy sigh, Stanford sank onto his well-worn leather chair and powered up his computer.

During the wee hours yesterday morning thieves had got into the Ashmolean Museum in Oxford, a hundred kilometers northwest of London. They'd stolen a Rembrandt, but the buggers hadn't stopped at thievery. They'd shot the overnight guard and whacked the museum security director in the head.

One dead, one in the hospital with a fractured skull.

He heard noises in the outer office. Apparently he wasn't the only one in the Criminal Investigation Division working overtime. His door opened and a head popped inside. "Hi, Len, you heard the news?"

Detective Inspector David Carpenter was a promising young detective. Stanford was grooming him to be his second in command in the Art and Antiques Unit.

"Yes. Bloody Christ, steal the goddam painting but don't start killing people. How'd you hear?"

"The BBC did a newsflash at six o'clock about a disturbance at the museum. No details. Nothing about a shooting. Figured I'd come in and see if I could lend a hand. Who did they kill?"

"The overnight guard."

"Wasn't there another theft at that museum a few years ago?"

With a nod of approval, Stanford said, "You've done your homework. Six years ago, before you joined the Art and Antiques Unit. January 2004. They stole a Rembrandt, never recovered. But nobody got shot. No one killed during any of these other heists either, but I suppose it was only a matter of time. Can you write up some sort of benign statement for the press, a disturbance at the Ashmolean Museum in Oxford, no further details presently available, something like that?"

"I'm on it," DI Carpenter said. "Anything else?"

"Yes. If the phones start ringing, which they're bound to do once the press gets wind of it, I'm not in." He winked. "Unless, of course, it's the Prime Minister. In that case, tell him I'm working my arse off."

Carpenter grinned. "Right, sir. But at least it's not on our patch."

"If it's related to these other heists, it will land in our laps anyway."

Carpenter tossed him a mock-salute and shut the door.

He punched up the number for the Detective Chief Superintendent.

"Wolfe." A curt bark. DCS Elliot Wolfe got to the point fast and expected his subordinates to do the same. His deep voice suggested a large heavy-set man. In fact, Wolfe was five-foot-six and skinny as a pencil, a pipe smoker with stern blue eyes.

"DCI Stanford, here. I'm in my office. What's the word in Oxford?"

"A bloody nightmare. Security guard reported for his shift this morning, went inside, saw the bodies and called police." Wolfe barked a curt laugh. "But we suspect he called the museum director first. He was there when the police arrived. They interrogated the guard, poor bloke was out of his mind, swore he didn't touch anything, but of course he did. Bloody fool called from the phone inside the museum."

"Anything from the security cameras?"

"Nothing useful. The cameras were shut down at two-fifteen A.M."

"An insider guard?" Stanford said. That was one theory about these heists.

"Either that or the thieves forced him to do it. Either way, we've got no video and no pictures."

"What did they steal?"

"A Rembrandt worth millions. The museum director is doing an inventory to see if anything else is missing. The Oxford detectives tried to keep a lid on it. You know the drill, in case the robbers contact the museum and ask for ransom. But twenty minutes later the bloody reporters were on it like a pack of hounds. The museum director told them there'd been a disturbance. Right lot of good that will do."

"My assistant tells me the BBC ran a newsflash on it at six o'clock."

"I saw it, and it will only get worse. A security guard dead? A missing Rembrandt? We're in for it."

"Indeed we are." Stanford had worked the Art and Antiques Unit for fifteen years, and for some reason, the public and the media, most of whom didn't care a whit about art, never tired of hearing about art thefts and the rotters who stole the paintings. "What can you tell me about the murdered man?"

"Security guard, shot once in the back of the head. Cold-blooded bastard, whoever did it."

"Any witnesses?"

"Not yet. No tongue-wags eager to dish up an eyewitness account. The Oxford police are still interviewing neighborhood residents. We'll see if anything turns up. The security director seems like a conscientious bloke. The guard who discovered the robbery said he used to show up unexpectedly sometimes, especially on the overnights."

"Maybe because of the previous heist," Stanford said. "Six years ago they stole a Rembrandt."

"Did they! Two thefts, two stolen Rembrandts? You think they're related?"

"Could be, sir. The hell of it is, there's been no ransom attempt on any of these paintings. They just disappear."

"Private collector, perhaps? Some art lover with money to burn?"

Stanford didn't answer immediately. The myth of a shadowy art collector ordering stolen art was popular with the public, encouraged by movies like Dr. No, Topkapi and a recent remake of The Thomas Crown Affair. But the facts didn't warrant it.

Most art thieves didn't give a rat's ass about art. They wanted money. Whenever a painting by Van Gogh or Picasso or Matisse sold for big bucks, the robbers figured plenty more were lying about in museums, why not grab one and sell it? Not knowing that the more famous the painting, the more difficult it was to sell. On the legitimate market anyway. Shady art dealers were different. Often when stolen art was recovered, the thieves had to settle for a small percentage of the painting's actual worth, collecting a ransom or the insurance money.

"These heists have a similar feel to them," Stanford said. "I figure it's a gang, but what the hell are they doing with the paintings?"

"Quite right," Wolfe said. "The Oxford police haven't been able to question the security director. His wife died a year or so ago. They're trying to contact his son, but he's on holiday. No luck so far. They talked to the security guard's housemate, but the first go was useless. The girl went hysterical. But here's a scrap of good news."

Stanford stifled a smile. Wolfe was known for his sarcasm, so he didn't let himself to get too excited.

"The police checked every car parked on the street within a two kilometer radius and got nothing, but they found a stolen Yaris in a parking garage three kilometers from the museum. The plate was stolen, too. The Yaris had been wiped clean, but the forensic blokes will put it under a microscope."

"Want me to drive out to Oxford and have a look?" Stanford asked.

"Yes. You know the history of these heists. You might pick up something the Oxford cops didn't. Keep me informed. If I get any new information, I'll do the same." DCS Wolfe rang off.

Stanford studied the scribbles he'd jotted on his notepad. Not much to go on, but maybe this time he'd get lucky. Sod all, he'd better. Eight art heists since 2004, including this one. He believed the same gang was responsible. Now they'd killed one man and put another in hospital.

He had to catch them before they killed again.

A tap sounded on his door and it opened. "Saw your line go dead," said DI Carpenter. "Got some lovely news for you." Judging by the twinkle in his eye, the lovely news was anything but. "Mrs. Wynkoop called. I told her you were on another line. She said she'd wait."

"Ah, yes, Sonja. Can't imagine what she wants to talk about."

Four years ago thieves had stolen a painting from the Frans Hals Museum in the Netherlands. Haarlem, to be precise. Sonja Wynkoop's husband was the security guard on duty the night of the theft. Three weeks later, Pieter Wynkoop died of a drug overdose. Sonja had been hounding him ever since.

"She saw the newsflash about the Oxford museum," Carpenter said.

Stanford massaged his temples, his incipient headache in full bloom. He didn't want to talk to her, but if he didn't do it now, she'd keep calling until he did, and the next few days were going to be hectic.

"I'll take it on line two."

"Line two it is," Carpenter said.

When the line lit up, he raised the receiver. "Hello, Mrs. Wynkoop, nice to hear from you. What's caused you to ring me at this hour on a Sunday?"

"Hallo, Inspector Stanford. I could perhaps ask why you are in your office at this hour on a Sunday, but I already know. There's been another robbery, eh? Another art theft in your territory?"

Silently cursing the media, Stanford said, "Not my territory, Mrs. Wynkoop. In Oxford. That's quite a way from London."

"And this time they killed the guard!"

Blast! So the murder was out. Not that he would admit it. "What makes you say that?"

"I saw it on the telly a half hour ago. The cable station."

The gossip station was more like it, Stanford thought. "Afraid I can't comment on that."

"Inspector, I have told you dozens of times, my Pieter was murdered! He was not a drug addict. My Pieter never used drugs. The robbers killed him!"

He'd never given much credence to her suspicions, but maybe he should talk to her. Better send a report on the latest heist to that New Orleans detective, too. Frank Renzi. But not tonight and probably not tomorrow. For the next forty-eight hours he'd be lucky to find time to take a leak. "Give me your phone number, Mrs. Wynkoop. I can't promise how soon, but let's have a chat."

"Thank you!" Sonja Wynkoop exclaimed. "I promise you will not regret it!"

CHAPTER 4

Frank tapped on his boss's door, heard him shout, "It's open," and entered the office. Hunched over his desk, Detective Lieutenant Morgan Vobitch looked up from a yellow legal pad, had a big scowl on his face, looked like he wanted to shoot someone.

Not a good sign, He needed a favor. Frank took the visitor chair in front of the desk. "What's up, Morgan? First thing Monday morning and you're already catching heat?"

Vobitch ran stubby fingers through his silvery-gray hair. "The bean counters at Headquarters think I got a magic wand, want me to solve the Rodriguez case fast and get the media off their necks. You see the editorial in the fucking local rag?" Vobitch's colorful name for the *New Orleans Times Picayune*.

"No. Enlighten me."

"Some scumbag sexually assaulted a seven-year-old girl, beat her to death and left her in a vacant house in District Five. Her mother reported her missing last Wednesday. Friday night a crackhead called in a tip about a body in an abandoned house. Christ, we get better tips from the lowlifes than from people in the neighborhood. Needless to say, the girl's family is up in arms. The usual bullshit. The NOPD doesn't care about black crime. Hell, half the murders in this town involve black people, victims or shooters, one or the other."

"And nobody's talking, right?"

"Right. And now we got this editorial blasting the D-5 cops. Not enough black officers and detectives, it said." Vobitch tapped the legal pad with his pen. "So now I gotta shuffle my detectives."

Vobitch supervised the homicide detectives in three high-crime areas. D-8, where Vobitch had his office, covered the French Quarter and the Central Business District. D-1 served the Iberville Project, Tremé, and part of the Seventh Ward. To the east, D-5 covered an even larger, more troublesome area.

"I got two pale-faces leading the investigation. I'm sending Kenyon Miller over there to talk to the family and the neighbors. Maybe he can shake something loose."

"Good idea. Kenyon's a member of the Black Neighborhood Association. He's good with the folks." To lighten things up, he said, "How was your weekend?"

"So-so. Juliana dragged me to the opera Saturday night. Wagner. I hate Wagner."

23

Vobitch had met Juliana, one of the few black ballerinas in New York, while working for NYPD. Not many people knew he was a classical music buff, a fact Vobitch had divulged one night when he took Frank out for a beer.

"Gimme Puccini any day. Those Italians knew how to spin out a gorgeous melody, right, Frank?"

Jiving him about his heritage. Vobitch was Jewish, but considered Frank a kindred spirit. When he found out Frank had worked for Boston PD, Vobitch had chortled, "Another damn Yankee, like me."

"Great melodies," Frank said, "but everybody dies in the end. Or so I've heard."

Vobitch favored him with a rare smile. "You oughta go see one. Take Kelly. She might enjoy it."

He tried to picture Kelly dolled up in a dress at the opera, mesmerized by an Italian aria. The image brought a smile to his face. Digging Dr. John at the Snug Harbor jazz club was more like it.

"So what brings you to my office bright and early on a Monday morning?"

"I need to take a trip."

Vobitch gave him a sly look. "Honeymoon with Kelly?"

Frank burst out laughing. "Honeymoon! You trying to give me a heart attack?"

"So what's this trip you need to take?"

"Last week I got a report from a London cop about some art heists. A witness saw the thief leave one of the museums and thought it might have been a woman. I think it was Natalie."

Vobitch's slate-gray eyes widened. "Be a helluva catch if it was. When was this? After poor little Natalie got done killing people in New Orleans? What makes you think it was her?"

"We know she lived in Paris for a while."

"No, Frank, we don't know she lived in Paris. All we know is what she wrote in her diary. You think a killer is going to tell the truth?"

He knew better than to answer that one. But he'd read the diary and to him it rang true. "According to the diary, she studied art while she was working for that escort service in Paris."

"Frank, the guy said he never heard of her."

True. Two years ago he had phoned the manager of the escort service. When he asked about Natalie Brixton, the man said, "No one by that name has ever worked here."

"How about a beautiful part-Vietnamese woman who speaks French?"

After a long pause, one that told Frank the answer would be a Big Lie, the man said, "I'm sorry Detective Renzi. I cannot help you."

Which had ended that short and not-so-sweet conversation.

"I think she escaped to London," Frank said, "and joined a gang of art thieves."

"Why would she do that? Seems to me she'd lie low and behave herself for a change."

"Why does anybody steal things? She needs money. The last four heists fit the time frame. Similar MO. Early morning heists, no sign of forced entry, only one guard on duty."

Vobitch tapped his pen on his desk, laden as usual with pink message slips. "An inside job?"

"Maybe. They questioned the guards, but got nowhere."

Vobitch smiled, a sardonic smile that spoke volumes about his opinion of witnesses. "Sounds like they got a bunch of Know-Nothings like we got here. Some guy gets shot in broad daylight in front of ten witnesses and nobody saw a thing. What happened to the paintings?"

"Still missing. No ransom demands, nothing. I want to go to London and talk to the witness who saw her."

"Frank, I want to catch her too. She killed three men in my jurisdiction, including Chip Beaubien, who, if you believe the tape she sent you, was the son of the man who murdered her mother. Poor Natalie, the little girl with the traumatic childhood. Bullshit. She's a stone-cold killer."

"All the more reason to send me to London."

"And don't forget the guy she killed up in Boston." A Sherman tank with a compact body, a leonine head and a mane of silvery hair, Vobitch was working up a head of steam. He smiled but his eyes were cold. "Oliver James, the former CIA agent with the racist CIA-agent buddy."

Frank couldn't resist goading him. "Heard from him lately?"

"That guy ever calls me again I'll shoot an ice pick into his ear. A gimmick I've been working on, let's you kill obnoxious people over the phone. It's not perfected yet, but ..." Vobitch shrugged.

"Morgan, this is the first lead I've had in two years."

"Yeah, well, I'm not sending you to London because some witness saw a thief leave an art museum in the dark of night and thought it was a woman—"

"A woman with a distinctive walk. Long legs, he said. Sexy."

"Frank, I can't authorize a trip based on a cockamamie story like that. The bigwigs would crucify me."

His temper flared and heat flooded his cheeks. That was Natalie leaving the museum, dammit! He rose from the chair, planted his palms on the desk and said, "Morgan, you're not the one she shot. I want her."

Vobitch blinked, then silently stared at him. At last he said, "I know you do, Frank. And I don't blame you, but I can't send you to London. Not without something to go on. Get me some evidence I can use to persuade the people at Headquarters. A solid lead that links it to the New Orleans murders."

Knowing the battle was lost, he backed off. But he wasn't going to quit. He was going to London, even if he had pay for the damn trip himself.

"Okay. But if it turns out to be Natalie, you'll owe me a fancy dinner at Muriel's."

"If you catch Natalie I'll do better than that. I'll send you to London for your honeymoon."

Now Vobitch was jiving him again, and he wasn't in the mood for it.

"Did you tell Kelly the carjacker came at me with a knife?"

Vobitch made his eyes go wide with innocence. "What could I do? She heard about it on the squawk box in her cruiser and called me."

"Well, next time she calls and asks you what I'm doing, try being a Know-Nothing."

Vobitch gave him The Look. "Frank, you're the best detective I got. Go catch some thugs."

———

Shropshire County, Northwest of London

"Tell me what you know about Vermeer," Pym said, fixing her with his pale gray eyes.

Startled by the request, she said, "The artist?"

They were having pre-dinner cocktails in their suite on the second floor of Sir Edmund Foxhill's country estate, an enormous three-story Tudor with gleaming oak floors and massive fieldstone fireplaces. She wasn't looking forward to eating another meal with Foxhill and his wife, pretending to be Pym's live-in girlfriend.

"Yes, Valerie, the artist. Surely you've heard of him."

"Of course. Who hasn't heard of Vermeer?"

"Have you seen his paintings?"

"I saw *The Lacemaker* in the Louvre. Gorgeous, and so tiny."

Pym smiled as though she'd just aced his art-history exam. "Yes. It's his smallest painting. Is that the only Vermeer you've seen?" He waved a dismissive hand. "Not some photograph in a book. In a museum."

Why was he quizzing her about Vermeer? She pretended to sip her brandy, but didn't swallow any. She couldn't afford to let her guard down, not for a second. Being Valerie every minute of the day and night was stressful. Yesterday, Pym had been uncharacteristically silent, riding beside her in the limousine, gazing out the window. To her relief, he'd said nothing about the Oxford heist.

But that didn't stop Gregor's words from playing in her mind. Kill them, or you will die too. Gregor, the man she'd never met and never wanted to meet.

26

"Well? Have you?" Pym demanded.

"No, unfortunately. But he didn't do many paintings."

"Thirty-five have been authenticated. That's what makes them so valuable."

Her palms dampened with sweat. Had one of his wealthy collectors ordered a Vermeer? Surely he wasn't going to ask her to steal The Lacemaker. The Louvre had the best security of any museum in Paris.

Pym drank some brandy and set the snifter on the Italian marble table between them. "Holland was once the most powerful country in Europe. Wealthy merchants commissioned paintings from famous Dutch artists like Vermeer." Gazing at her intently, he said, "You know van Meegeren?"

"No. Is he another Dutch painter?"

"A Dutch faker is more like it. During the 1930s he forged several Vermeers. A clever fellow, van Meegeren. He bought authentic 17th century canvases, mixed his paints according to the formulas of Vermeer's day and used badger-hair brushes similar to the ones Vermeer supposedly used."

"Did he get away with it?"

"For a while. In 1937 he painted *The Supper at Emmaus*, got some fool to authenticate it as a Vermeer and sold it for a huge sum. In 1942 his agent sold one of his fake Vermeers to a Nazi banker. The banker sold it to Hermann Goring, the Nazi art collector. After the war the Allied forces found it and traced it to van Meegeren."

Pym began to cough, an uncontrolled spasm that lasted several seconds. He took out some tissues and spat into them. He cleared his throat and said, "The Dutch authorities charged him with aiding and abetting the enemy, which carried serious penalties. After spending three days in jail, van Meegeren admitted he had forged several paintings attributed to Vermeer."

Her mind raced, trying to make sense of it. At times Pym made casual conversation, but this wasn't one of them. His demeanor was far too intense, far too emotional. "What happened to him?"

"In 1947, a Dutch court found him guilty of forgery and fraud and sentenced him to a year in prison. But he never served a day. He died of a heart attack." Pym was about to say more, but his cellphone rang.

When he answered, she rose from her chair and wandered the room. His talk about Vermeer made her nervous. The theft of a Vermeer at the Gardner Museum in Boston in 1990 had made headlines around the world. Her art-history teacher in Paris, a Frenchman with a pencil-thin mustache, had told her about it. That Vermeer was still missing. Did Pym want her to steal a Vermeer?

If she were in London she'd get on her laptop and find out where his paintings were. But she wasn't in London, and she had no privacy here. Sleep was impossible with Pym lying in bed beside her, and every muscle in her body ached from the stress of playing her Valerie role. And it was far from over. She still had to get through tonight and endure the long drive back to London tomorrow.

Pym closed his cellphone. "Dinner is served. Let's go downstairs."

Hoping for a clue that might explain why Pym had told her about van Meegeren, she said, "I'm surprised I never heard of van Meegeren. What do the art critics say about him?"

"He was a good technician, but a second-rate artist. Nothing like Vermeer. His only claim to fame was fooling the art experts and that Nazi pig, Goring. He died in disgrace." Pym waved his hand contemptuously, frowning at her, eyes narrowed, thin lips set in a line.

A metallic taste filled her mouth. Was he angry with her? Maybe not. Like many men who were short in stature, Pym was ultra-sensitive about what others thought of him. To men like Pym, a man's reputation was paramount. Even now, more than three centuries after his death, Vermeer was revered by the art world. Van Meegeren had died in disgrace. But what did that have to do with Pym? The question would have to wait, though. Now she had to be Valerie, Pym's mistress.

Foxhill and his wife, Daphne, greeted them as they entered the dining hall, a huge room with a flagstone floor, a high ceiling and a wall of windows overlooking a flower garden bordered by oak and willow trees. "Please be seated," Sir Edmund said, gesturing at a small table set with white linen, crystal glassware and fine china.

She took the chair opposite Daphne. Pym sat on her left, Sir Edmund on her right. He was older than Pym, a white-haired, ruddy-faced man with deep-blue eyes. Daphne looked at least fifteen years younger, slender with beautiful reddish hair. An emancipated woman. After they married she had kept her maiden name, Turner.

A tuxedo-clad butler wheeled in the first course, a thick fish soup which he ladled into gold-rimmed china tureens and set in front of them. Sir Edmund and Pym began discussing the road repairs that had plagued them yesterday on their way here from London. Relieved that she didn't have to make conversation, she attacked the soup with gusto. It was tasty, but rich with cream. She smiled at Daphne. "Lovely soup. What sort of seafood is it?"

"Scallops and lobster. I don't know what I'd do without a chef." Daphne flashed a smile, which accentuated the dimples in her cheeks. "I'm useless in the kitchen. How about you?"

Grateful for the girl talk, she responded with a rueful smile. "The same, I'm afraid."

"Bloody awful what happened in Oxford," Sir Edmund said to Pym. "You heard, of course."

"Yes," Pym said, spooning up his soup. "Another Rembrandt gone."

"And they shot the security guard!" Daphne exclaimed. "It was on the telly last night."

She spread butter on a roll, picturing the Beretta, hidden in her quarters. If they kept talking about the Oxford heist, she'd never be able to eat. She didn't dare ask what had happened to the Security Director.

"Yes," Pym said. "A nasty business. Have they got any leads?"

28

"I hear that chap in London is on the case," Sir Edmund said. "The Art and Antiquities chief."

Her stomach churned with acid. Who was the Art and Antiquities chief and what did he know about the heist?

"Good man," Pym said. "I heard him speak at a convention about art thefts a couple of years ago." He smiled at Foxhill. "Right about the time I met Valerie."

His jovial tone curdled her blood. Met her after he fired whoever had been helping him steal paintings. He'd given her no details about the earlier heists but made it clear that her predecessor had *fucked up*. His words. An unmistakable warning. Where was her predecessor now, she wondered. Dead or alive?

Foxhill spooned up the last of his soup and signaled the butler to take it away and bring the next course.

"A lucky break for you," Daphne said to Pym. "Meeting such a lovely woman. Please don't think me rude, Valerie, but you have such an exotic look about you. Where are you from?"

Pym nudged her foot under the table. "Tell her your *story*, Valerie."

She forced a smile. Be who they want you to be. She parroted the same fake story she'd told Pym. Given his emphasis on the word story, she suspected he knew it was fake.

"My mother was Vietnamese. My father was American, stationed there after the war. He was a captain in the army. After they got married my father left the military and they moved to France."

"Whereabouts?" Daphne said, as the butler set a plate of roast beef in front of her.

"I was born in Lyon, but we only stayed there a few years." She faked a laugh. "Just long enough for me to learn to speak French. Then we moved to the United States."

"What an interesting life you've had," Daphne said.

You have no idea. "What about you?" she said. "Are you related to Turner? The British painter?"

Daphne trilled a laugh. "I wish. Not even a distant cousin, I'm afraid. I'm not the least bit artistic."

"Speaking of art," Sir Edmund said to Pym, "There's a meeting in London on Wednesday. The board members of several art museums want to discuss these thefts. As chairman of the Tate Museum board of trustees, I feel it's my responsibility to keep tabs on the investigation. Care to join me?"

"Absolutely," Pym said. "The sooner we find the bastards, the safer our art museums will be."

His response disgusted her. Pym had called van Meegeren a trickster, but the art forger couldn't hold a candle to the ruthless art thief seated beside her. Pym was like a chess master, visualizing his game ten moves in advance. Take her out of London. Keep her with him to make sure he knew where she was every minute of the day and night. Get Sir Edmund to invite him to a meeting about the art heists so he could keep tabs on the investigation.

She stared at the slice of rare roast beef her plate, bleeding into the mashed potatoes, and flashed on the dead security guard. Her stomach heaved. She clenched her teeth to keep from vomiting.

What was Pym planning?

Two years ago, she had managed to escape from New Orleans. But the threat from Pym and Gregor was worse.

The police wouldn't kill her in cold blood, but Gregor would.

She was certain he'd murdered the insider guards he had hired to facilitate the previous thefts.

Would she have a fatal accident too? A drug overdose? Mugged on a London street some dark night? Thrown off a bridge into the Thames?

She had to get away.

As soon as they got back to London she would run for her life.

CHAPTER 5

Tuesday June 22, 2010 New Orleans

Jazzed with adrenaline, Frank gripped his cellphone in one hand, scribbled notes with the other. DCI Leonard Stanford had called to tell him about another art heist, a Rembrandt stolen from the Ashmolean Museum in Oxford, northwest of London.

"This one was a bit more complicated than the others," Stanford said. "They killed a man, put another one in the hospital with a fractured skull."

A bit more complicated? That was an understatement.

"Who'd they kill?"

"The security guard, execution-style. One shot to the head."

His heart thrummed his chest. "Sounds like the woman I'm looking for. She shot three men in New Orleans and another one in Boston. One to the head each time."

"Bloody hell, no wonder you're after her."

He was after her all right, no need to tell Stanford how badly he wanted her. He heard Stanford yawn. He knew the feeling. A big case meant no sleep for days. He glanced at the clock. Two-thirty Central Time in New Orleans, six hours ahead in London, it was eight-thirty at night. Stanford was working overtime.

"They took a Rembrandt," he said. "Just the one painting?"

"One was plenty. It's worth millions, no telling if we'll ever get it back. Two Rembrandts and a Vermeer were stolen from the Gardner Museum in 1990. Twenty years later they're still missing."

"I know. I was with Boston PD when it happened."

"You don't say! Don't suppose you were working the case . . . ?"

"No. I was working Homicide, but every cop in Boston knew about it. The Boston FBI office took charge of the case, but I might be able to put you in touch with someone who worked on it."

One hand washes the other. Give a little, get a little. He wanted to go to London so bad he could taste it. He was convinced Natalie was involved in these heists. This could be the break he needed to find her.

"That would be splendid!" Stanford said. "Ever run across that Irishman? Whitey Bulger?"

31

"Back in the day, some people figured he masterminded the Gardner heist, might be holding the paintings as a get-out-of-jail-free card. If they ever catch him." Whitey and his girlfriend had been on the lam since 1995 when Whitey's FBI handler tipped him that the State cops were about to arrest him.

"What about Myles Connor? Cheeky bloke, that one. Stole Rembrandt's *Portrait of a Young Woman* from the Museum of Fine Arts in 1975, tried to cut a deal to spend less time in jail for another art theft."

Frank smiled, aware that Stanford was demonstrating his expertise about art heists, not just in Europe but all over the world, including Boston. Which was why Stanford was in charge of the Art and Antiques Crime Unit.

"Myles Connor was in prison when the Gardner heist went down," Frank said. "I never met him, never met Whitey either, but I worked a few gang-related cases. Drug dealers mostly." Displaying his own expertise, hoping to convince DCI Stanford he'd be an asset to the London investigation. Anything to get himself to London.

"That's my theory on these heists," Stanford said. "These gangs are getting smarter. Dealing drugs brings too much heat. Stolen art is just as lucrative. These thugs are ruthless, Corsican gangsters in Marseilles, a Spanish gang working out of Madrid, Sicilian mobsters." Stanford paused, then said, "No relation to you, I 'spose."

Frank laughed. "Hey, you never know. My father's family came from Sicily. But my father's a judge. What makes you think a gang did the Oxford heist? And the others, for that matter."

"Very professional. Neat and clean, no clues left behind, in and out fast, and no dust-ups. Until last weekend. Whoever masterminds these heists is smart. Might not do the actual theft, but he's cagey enough to hire ruthless people. This was cold-blooded murder."

"You got any leads?"

"Not yet, I'm afraid. But here's another angle. A woman in Amsterdam keeps hounding me. Her husband, Pieter Wynkoop, was the security guard at the Frans Hals Museum when a Hals was stolen in 2006. A few weeks later he died of a drug overdose. His wife Sonja swears he never did drugs in his life."

"That's what they all say." Frank glanced at the clock. He wanted to go talk to Vobitch.

"That's what I thought, but Sonja called again this weekend, got me thinking. I went over my files. They hit the Ashmolean six years ago in January 2004, which may be why the Security Director popped in unexpectedly. When I checked the file on the previous heist, I noticed the security guard died a month later in a car accident. Sent up a red flag, so to speak. So I checked the other case files."

"Some of the other security guards died too?"

"Yes, under suspicious circumstances, shall we say? The car accident, Pieter Wynkoop's drug overdose, a mugging, a suicide, and a break-in at one guard's flat."

"They were in on the heists," Frank said. "They were killed so they wouldn't talk."

"That's what I'm beginning to think. Sonja Wynkoop may be right. Her husband didn't OD on drugs, someone killed him in such a way as to make it look like he did."

"So you've got five security guards who may or may not have been murdered. Plus the one last weekend. But you said there were eight heists with the same MO. What about the other two?"

"The theft at Drumlanrig Castle in Scotland happened in the daytime during a visitor tour, a man and a woman. The woman grabbed the painting, ran outside, jumped in a getaway car and away they went."

His neck prickled. "A woman. When was this?"

"May 2005."

Frank couldn't remember where Natalie was then, but he'd use the woman angle regardless. Whatever it took to persuade Morgan Vobitch to send him to London.

"In March 2007," Stanford said, "they hit the Westfries Museum north of Amsterdam overnight. No guards inside the museum, just two men on patrol outside. The robbers disabled the guards long enough to get inside and make off with a Vermeer and a Terborch."

"Any chance I could interview the woman who called you? I'd really like to talk to her."

"Sonja Wynkoop? She'd talk to you all right. Hells bells, she'd talk to the man in the moon if she thought it would clear her husband's name. As it stands now, Pieter Wynkoop's name is mud, on duty when a Hals was stolen, dead of a drug overdose a few weeks later."

Hearing Stanford hesitate, Frank sensed a problem. "But?"

"I have no problem with it, but I'd have to clear it with my superior. You know how it is."

Indeed he did. Every police department was territorial. Bureaucracy and red tape. Same thing in London apparently. "How does your boss feel about American detectives? Did he watch *NYPD Blue*?"

Stanford let out a hearty laugh. "I sincerely doubt it, but I did. Watched it on video. Good show. Try and round up that bloke who worked the Gardner heist. That might help. Cooperation across the waters, so to speak."

"I will. Speaking of cooperation, the woman I'm involved with—she's a detective too—hails from a family of cops. Her father once did a favor for a police officer in London, DI Ian Attaway. Maybe he could put in a word for us. Kelly's great at interviewing women." He'd take Kelly with him and have her interview Sonja Wynkoop.

"Good idea. Have him call DSC Elliot Wolfe and give him a nudge."

Frank heard Stanford yawn again. "Get some sleep," he said. "You've earned it. I'll be in touch."

He shut his cellphone and jotted notes, mustering arguments for his sit-down with Morgan Vobitch. One way or another he was going to London. To catch Natalie Brixton.

———

London 8:30 PM

She ate the last bite of chicken and set her fork on her plate.

"We'll have brandy in the library," Pym said to the butler as he cleared their plates.

I don't want brandy, she wanted to scream. She wanted to call her Chinatown contact and prepare her escape plan. After leaving the Foxhill estate, they had arrived at Pym's mansion at 5:45. She had no time to call Chen, had barely enough time to dress for dinner.

But Pym was in control, as always. She pushed back her chair and followed him into the library.

Pym sank onto his favorite recliner. "Sit down, Valerie. I have some news for you."

What kind of news? He'd said nothing about the Oxford heist today, either. Did he know something that she didn't? She perched on the other recliner.

"You're going on a trip tomorrow. I already have your plane ticket."

A plane ticket to where? Aware of his gaze, she maintained a neutral expression. Be who they want you to be.

"This business at the Ashmolean Museum is getting a lot of attention. That's why I got you out of London for a few days. But it will get worse. You need to stay out of sight until the heat dies down."

This business at the museum. His cavalier attitude disgusted her. One man dead, another in the hospital, but to Pym it was only business. He wasn't the one who'd shot the guard. He wasn't the one the cops were after. Still, the fact that he wanted to send her away until the furor abated might be a good sign. Maybe he wasn't going to kill her.

The butler came in with their brandy, set the snifters on the table in front of them and left.

"What have you heard about the Oxford heist?" she asked.

"It's all over the news." Pym raised the snifter and gulped some brandy. "We need a distraction. The next heist will be in the United States. That's where you're going."

The next heist? Steal another painting and have more cops after her?

"Where in the United States?" Please, not New Orleans, not Boston.

"I'll tell you tomorrow when we drive to the airport."

She wanted to give him a Taekwondo kick, put him on the floor and press the Dokko point under his jaw until he was dead. But that would be suicidal. She'd never get out of here alive.

"How do I know what clothes to pack?"

"It's summertime," he snapped. "Pack accordingly. And don't forget your passport."

Clutching the snifter in both hands to stop them from shaking, she gulped some brandy.

"Gregor will be in charge of the heist."

Her heart slammed her chest. "Gregor scares me," she blurted. "He made me shoot the guard."

Pym smiled. "A little bit of fear is a good thing."

She bit the inside of her cheek to keep from screaming. She had to get away from this evil man. Maybe she'd leave tonight, pack a few things, go to Chinatown and figure things out from there.

"Finish your brandy, Valerie. Then we'll go upstairs to my quarters and have a proper farewell."

Snuffed out like a candle, the last shred of hope died inside her. He wasn't going to let her out of his sight.

"Will I have time to say goodbye to my friends?"

He gazed at her, expressionless. "Valerie, right now I'm the most important friend you've got."

———

New Orleans 3:45 PM

"A woman was in on at least one of the heists," Frank said. "DCI Stanford called me a half hour ago and told me about it. A daytime snatch and grab. Witnesses saw her do it."

Vobitch looked at him, his slate-gray eyes skeptical. "And you think it was Natalie."

"Last weekend they killed a security guard at a museum near London. Execution-style, one shot to the head. That's Natalie's MO."

Vobitch scratched his jaw. "Okay. What else have you got?"

"The security guards in five of the previous heists wound up dead."

"What do you mean, wound up dead?"

"Suspicious causes. A drug overdose, a suicide, a mugging, a car accident, a B&E. I figure they were killed so they couldn't talk."

"Your London contact thinks these guards were in on the heists?"

35

"Yes. He says a Dutch woman keeps hounding him. Her husband was one of the security guards, died of a drug overdose, allegedly. But she says he never took drugs. I want to talk to her."

"And this London cop says a woman is involved?"

"Right. Witnesses at a castle in Scotland saw a blonde grab a painting, run outside and jump in a getaway car. Natalie wore a blonde wig when she shot Peterson, remember? We got security video of her leaving his room."

Vobitch tapped his pen on his desk. "What's the date of this heist when they saw the woman?"

Damn. He hadn't had time to check and see where Natalie was then. "In 2005. I forget the exact date."

"Well, it's something."

"You wanted a solid lead. I just gave you one."

After an agonizing wait, Vobitch said, "Might be enough. How long do you need?"

His heart surged. Seal the deal, spring the other part later. "Three days. Leave on a Friday, fly back Monday. Hey, I'll work Fourth of July weekend. I'll buy you lunch at Nathan's South every day for a month."

Nathan's South was similar to Nathan's in New York. Deli sandwiches, dill pickles and dynamite potato salad, conveniently located two blocks from the D-1 station. Frank figured this was why Vobitch had his office here. They'd already named a sandwich after him. The Vobitch: Corn beef on rye, Swiss cheese and sauerkraut.

"Okay," Vobitch said, "but you better come back with something good."

"We will."

Vobitch frowned. "We? Who's we?"

"Me and Kelly." At least he hoped she was going. He hadn't asked her yet.

"Are you out of your mind? How am I gonna talk the bigwigs into letting two detectives fly to London?"

"I want her to interview the widow of the security guard that died of a drug overdose. Kelly's great with women. That's why she's working Domestic Violence. Not only that, her father's got a contact on the London police force, remember? Ian Attaway."

Vobitch shook his head, half-smiling. "Good thing you're not going to Ireland. Kiss the Blarney Stone, no telling what you'd talk me into."

———

7:15 PM New Orleans

Frank lay on his side watching Kelly. Her eyes were closed and she had a smile on her face. Post-coital bliss, he hoped. He never understood guys who wanted to make love, roll over and go to sleep. He liked to make love before dinner, have round two for dessert. Eager to spring his surprise, he traced a finger over her flat stomach.

She opened her eyes. "Hungry? I've got leftover chicken."

He leaned down and kissed her lips. "My favorite detective was so spectacular tonight—at least an eleven on a scale of one to ten—I'm gonna take you on a trip."

Her lips widened in a grin. "Yeah? Where? Drive across Lake Pontchartrain for some Chinese?"

"Nah. How about London?"

"Get out. You're joking, right?"

"Nope. Is your passport up to date? We leave on Friday, fly back on Monday."

"Frank, I can't just take off and go to London. I'll have to clear it with—"

"I already cleared it with Vobitch. He'll talk to your boss."

Her eyes lit up. "Wow! I've never been to London." Then she frowned. "Wait. I bet this has to do with work."

"Correct. Which reinforces my decision to take my savvy detective-lover with me."

"Natalie," she said, frowning now. "You think she's in London."

He rolled off the bed and pulled on his shorts. "Come on. I'll tell you about it over a glass of wine."

While Kelly put the chicken in the oven, he poured two glasses of Chianti and told her about the latest art heist, the murder and the guards who'd died under suspicious circumstances.

"I'd love to go to London," Kelly said, "but what's the plan?"

"Stanford seems like a good guy. We got talking about the Gardner heist and I told him I could hook him up with someone who worked the case. In exchange for interviewing that widow." He raised his wineglass in a mock-salute. "Actually, I want you to talk to her. You're great with women. That's what convinced Morgan Vobitch to let us go. Stanford said he'd bring her to London to talk to us. And dig this. The London cops are just as territorial as we are. So I told DCI Stanford about your father's contact, Detective Inspector Ian Attaway."

Several years ago Kelly's father, Chicago Police Captain Rico Zavarella, had helped Attaway nab the man who'd stolen luggage from three British tourists at O'Hare Airport.

"Can you get your dad to give Attaway a call, ask him to put in a good word with Stanford's boss?"

"Sure, if it helps us get to London." Kelly wrapped her arms around his neck. "You know, you can be very devious sometimes."

He pulled her closer, inhaling her scent. "Nothing wrong with devious if it gets me what I want."

"What if we don't find anything that confirms your theory about Natalie?"

He waved a hand, as though he'd considered the possibility and accepted it. Fat chance. He felt like a bloodhound, tracking the scent, closing in on his prey. The elusive and alluring Natalie Brixton.

"Vobitch will be pissed, but look at it this way. We'll spend three days in London and we can put European Art Heist Investigation on our resumes."

Kelly shook her head, grinning at him. "Liar, liar, pants on fire."

CHAPTER 6

Wednesday June 23, 2010 London 10:15 AM

She stared out the window of Pym's limousine. Traffic was impossible, red two-decker tour buses, London taxicabs, cars and vans headed for Heathrow Airport. Beside her, Pym was calm and relaxed. She wasn't. She was frustrated and angry and, she had to admit, deeply afraid.

He still hadn't told her where she was going. It was maddening.

Usually after they had sex, she returned to her quarters on the third floor, but last night he had insisted that she sleep with him. She hated that. She could never sleep with someone else in bed with her. Well, she'd slept fine after Wilhem made love to her, but that was years ago. An unhappy lifetime ago.

While she was in the shower this morning, Pym had ordered breakfast sent to her quarters. So he could help her pack, he'd said. Nonsense. He didn't want to let her out of his sight. She should never have told him she wanted to say goodbye to her friends. But she had no friends now. Her only friend lived in Texas. She hadn't seen Gabe since she'd left fifteen years ago after she settled the score with her cousin. Gabe had gotten her the gun.

An angry horn blast sounded as Pym's driver cut off a car to take the exit for Heathrow Airport. In five minutes they'd be at the departure terminal. Why was he torturing her like this?

The wheat toast with strawberry jam she'd eaten for breakfast sat in her stomach like a stone. Where was he sending her?

As though he'd read her thoughts, Pym reached into the pocket of his suit, took out a British Airways folder and handed it to her. "Have a nice time in Boston, Valerie."

She felt like a giant hand was crushing her chest. Boston. Her worst fear.

"I hear it's a lovely city," Pym said cheerfully. "But you won't be there long. In a couple of weeks you'll be back in London with me." His pale gray eyes hardened. "If everything goes well, that is. Make sure you don't kill anyone this time."

"Killing the security guard wasn't my idea, Jonathan."

He gestured at the Plexiglas partition that separated them from the driver, a warning to silence her. "So you said."

He took a cellphone out of his briefcase. "Activate this when you land in Boston. Gregor has the number and so do I. No one else must have it, understand?"

"Yes." A sick feeling invaded her gut. She should have followed her instinct this morning when Pym was in her bedroom. Dig out the Beretta hidden in her clothes hamper and shoot him. But what would that accomplish? His flunkeys would have set upon her like a pack of rabid dogs.

"Use this cellphone only to call me. My number is already programmed into it."

Giving her orders. Did he expect her to salute? She clenched her teeth. If she wanted to escape, she had to be smart. Strong. Devious, even.

"Gregor will call you after you land, so make sure you activate the phone right away. It's about time you met him. He will tell you about your assignment."

Gregor. The name sent chills down her neck. She didn't want to meet him, didn't want to talk to him, didn't want to take orders from him. Gregor was evil.

And how could she steal a painting in Boston? The cops were already after her for killing Oliver.

"What is the assignment?"

"Gregor will explain everything."

"But I don't have his phone number. What if there's an emergency?"

Pym glared at her. "There better not be an emergency. If there is, don't call Gregor, call me."

"But you'll be in London. I need a way to contact Gregor."

After a moment, Pym said, "In an emergency you can contact him through my Global Interpreting Office. It's in Copley Square, near the public library."

Copley Square. The Boston Public Library, where she'd done her research on Frank Renzi, who wanted to arrest her for three murders in New Orleans. Two years ago he had almost caught her, and the Boston cops were after her, too. Now Pym expected her to steal a painting there, and follow Gregor's orders. The thought terrified her.

The limousine pulled to the curb outside Terminal Five, and the driver got out. A short man with a powerful build and a dark beard, he opened her door. Hot humid air hit her, flavored with fumes from idling cars. Dressed in her travel outfit, a white blouse under a black silk pantsuit, she got out and stood on the sidewalk where the driver had placed her suitcase and carry-on bag.

Smiling broadly, Pym put his arms around her. His idea of affection.

"Have a good trip, Valerie. I can't wait for you to get back."

With a supreme effort, she forced a smile. Couldn't wait for her to come back with whatever painting she had stolen. Maybe she wouldn't. Maybe she could make her escape from Boston.

To hell with Jonathan Pym and Gregor and stealing paintings.

She bent down and kissed his cheek. Be who they want you to be. "Thank you, Jonathan."

She joined the queue for the British Airways counter and checked her suitcase. When Pym wasn't looking, she had slipped her laptop into it. She shouldered her carry-on bag and passed through security without a problem.

No one was hunting for Valerie Brown.

According to the departure board, her flight was boarding in ten minutes, but if she hurried, she might have time to make a phone call first. Racing past other passengers towing suitcases, she reached her boarding gate, breathless and sweaty. The gate attendant was at the podium, announcing that first class passengers would be boarding momentarily.

She rushed back to the deserted gate she'd passed on the concourse. She set her carry-on bag on a flat table between two leather seats, unzipped it and took out the cellphone she'd hidden in one of the interior pockets. Her cellphone, not Pym's. Standing beside a window overlooking the tarmac, she dialed a number.

One ring. Then another, and another. After the fifth ring, a voice said, "Yes, what is it?"

"Hello, Chen. It's Valerie. How are you today?" Feigning politeness, when she wanted to scream, *Help me!*

"I am well, Valerie, and you?"

"I'm at Heathrow about to board a plane and I need your help."

"Where you go?" Chen said. English was not his native language.

"My employer is sending me to Boston for an assignment and I need a favor."

"Ah. Boston. What you need?"

"A contact. Someone who can help me." She paused. "You know how it is with this man I live with."

"Not a nice man," Chen said. "Boston. Hmm. I think I know a man who can help you."

A great weight lifted from her shoulders. Boston was an ocean away but Chen knew someone who would help her. Moments later she programmed a name and number into her cell, put it in her carry-on and returned to her gate.

Her head was throbbing, a relentless ache that set her teeth on edge.

She was exhausted, but she'd never be able to sleep on the plane.

Seven hours and fifteen minutes from now she would land in Boston, a city she never wanted to see again.

———

Boston 3:45 PM

Gregor Kraus glared at the waiter standing beside his table. Moments after taking his first satisfying puff on a Gitanes Brunes, the two white-haired biddies pecking at plates of lettuce at the next table had given him nasty looks, flapping their hands at the smoke drifting their way. The waiter, a skinny college kid with a snotty attitude, had told him smoking wasn't allowed in the restaurant.

But he wasn't inside the restaurant, he was in the seating area outside.

He dropped his cigarette on the ground and stared into the waiter's eyes. Saw one of his eyes explode in a mist of blood and gore. Imagination was a wonderful thing. Still, many years ago he had seen just such a thing happen. He was the one who had pulled the trigger.

"Thank you," the waiter muttered, and bustled away.

Gregor put down enough cash to cover the bill. No tip. Maybe he'd take the snifter with him, sit on a nearby bench and enjoy the rest of his Remy Martin with a fresh Gitanes. But if the waiter saw him leave with the snifter he might call the police. That wouldn't do. First rule: Do nothing to attract attention, not with the next heist only two weeks away. At the Gardner Museum no less. This would be a challenge, but well worth it.

The robbery at the Gardner in 1990 was the most notorious art heist in the world. The FBI and many others were still searching for the paintings. Some said they were worth five-hundred-million dollars.

He downed the last of the brandy, threaded his way through the tables and strode to a nearby wooden bench. The Quincy Market was a tourist magnet. Inside the massive two-story structure were specialty food shops, trendy boutiques and pricy restaurants. Outside, along a wide expanse of redbrick pavement were towering shade trees, tall poles with globe lights, and pushcarts offering souvenirs. A steady stream of people passed him. Many wore Red Sox caps or black-and-yellow Bruins jerseys or green Celtics T-shirts.

Boston was a sports-crazy city, worse than London with its idiotic soccer fans. Gregor had no interest in sports. Such a juvenile activity, grown men pretending to be tough. He took out the packet of Gitanes, lighted one, exhaled a cloud of smoke and studied the scars on his hands. Old scars, but still hideous, angry patches of red skin.

One day when he was five, Papa had taken him to the stove in the kitchen, turned on a gas burner and held one of his hands over the flickering blue flame.

Even now, forty years later, he could still remember the searing pain, excruciating pain that consumed him.

For an instant, he'd been too shocked to react. When he began to shriek, Papa released his hand and slapped his face. "Aufhören zu heulen!" Papa said in German. "Etwas schwer werden!" Stop crying! Be tough!

Sobbing, he'd stared at his hand, the skin below the thumb already blistering. Heartbroken, he wanted to say: "Papa, why did you do this?" But he didn't dare.

Gregor puffed his cigarette. Even now, on a sunny afternoon in June with a breeze wafting faint odors of the sea, the memory of that pain sent a shock-wave through him that shriveled his scrotum.

Every few weeks, Papa had repeated this agonizing ritual. One night the burns became infected, oozing pus. Papa took him to the hospital. When the doctor examined his hands and asked how it happened, Papa, staring at Gregor, had replied: "I told him not to touch the stove, but the boy never listens."

Even then Gregor knew enough not to contradict him. He began to anticipate when it might happen again, reading the signs. A grim expression when Papa came home from work. Violent cursing. Silence as the two of them ate the dinner Papa prepared. The last time Papa held his hand over the flame, Gregor forced himself not to cry out, clenching his teeth so hard one of them broke. "Good," Papa said. "You are ready." And so, a month before his eighth birthday, he had joined the London gang that Papa worked for. Papa was their enforcer.

Gregor drew deeply on his cigarette and turned, intending to blow the smoke at the two old hags. They were gone, but so what? He had more pressing problems to solve.

Nicholas Kwan, for one. The little shit was beyond irritating, questioning whatever he said. Kwan was a ruthless bastard. That's why he'd hired him to do the dirty work. But he didn't trust him. "Never turn your back on a Chinaman," Papa had said, and Papa was right. Though Gregor hated to admit it, Asians were smart. Cunning. An Asian would smile at you even as he contemplated sticking a shiv in your back.

Marta was another problem, always complaining. She'd been in Boston since January, setting up Global Interpreting, another front for Pym's shady deals. Gregor puffed his Gitanes. He knew why Marta was angry. Her apartment was operated by the YWCA, the Young Women's Christian Association, which meant Marta couldn't entertain her lovers there.

His cellphone vibrated against his chest. He took it out and checked the ID. Marta. Sometimes it almost seemed like she could tell when he was thinking about her. Especially the bad thoughts. If only he could ignore her. But that would not be wise. Marta knew where the bodies were buried, so to speak.

He punched on and said in a quiet voice, "What is it?" Even when he was angry or threatening someone, he never raised his voice. A quiet voice was more effective. Intimidating. Terrifying.

"Gregor," she said, "I need to hire another translator. Now that we have more clients, I sometimes have to work four or five nights a week."

"You have two girls. That is enough."

"It's not enough! In the beginning I had three—"

"If you had treated Ursula better, she would not have quit."

"She didn't quit! She left one night and never came back."

"Marta, people leave their jobs when they are unhappy."

"But she didn't even pick up her last check—"

43

"Stop complaining. I am busy now. I will talk to you later."

"When? Will you be here tonight?"

Gregor smiled. Of course he would. Rather than stay in a hotel and leave a credit card trail, he used the small furnished office down the hall from the reception area as his living quarters. What Marta really wanted to know was whether he would be there before she closed the office and went home. Marta was still in love with him.

"Perhaps," he said, and ended the call. Marta could piss up a rope. She was the cause of their only failure. Back then, Marta had been the one to enter the museums and steal the paintings. For a while they had been lovers, but that was over. And after Marta screwed up, Pym had found another woman to steal the art.

Valerie, code-name Scorpio. Another problem. Never trust a scorpion, little beasts that struck suddenly, stinging their prey with deadly venom to kill or paralyze them. Like Nicholas Kwan, Valerie was part Asian. He knew nothing about her ancestors, but he knew she was smart. Dangerous.

He took out another Gitanes, then put it back. He limited himself to ten cigarettes a day. Already five were gone. Thanks to the old biddies, he had wasted one. He took out his IronMan gripper and did ten reps with his right hand, ten with his left. In addition to keeping the muscles in his scarred hands supple, the motion soothed him.

The sound of young laughter drew his attention, a high-pitched giggle. Nearing his bench, a small towheaded boy, perhaps five years old, trotted alongside a stocky man in his thirties, the boy's father, Gregor assumed. Where was the boy's mother, he wondered. His mother had died before he was two. Tuberculosis, Papa said. He had no memory of her. Papa had kept no photographs of her. To Gregor, it was as though she had never existed.

He watched the man hoist the boy to his shoulders, letting the boy's legs dangle on either side of his neck. The boy squealed with delight, hugging his father's head as they passed him.

Gregor squeezed the IronMan gripper. Now the boy was unafraid. Only later, when life dealt its first cruel blow would he know fear. Americans were so soft. They treated their children like babies, pampering them with vanilla pudding pops and chocolate cookies and ice cream cones. He studied the scars on his hands. Papa was right. Children had to learn to be tough. Thanks to Papa, he had. Some might say Papa was cruel, but this was how Papa had demonstrated his love. A good thing. When Gregor was twelve, a rival gang killed Papa.

He had been on his own ever since. During those thirty-three years, he had learned—sometimes the hard way—never to leave important tasks to others. Better to do it yourself. Always be in control.

Which brought him back to Valerie.

He didn't trust her any more than he trusted Kwan.

The day after the Oxford heist, Pym had burst into his quarters above the garage, livid with rage, saying he had warned him there must be no violence during these heists. Valerie, the sneaky scorpion, had told him that Gregor had ordered her to kill the two men. But she had disobeyed him. The Security Director was still alive. Gregor didn't bother to argue with the old man. Best to remain silent and wait for Pym to calm down. Eventually he did, and told Gregor to leave London at once. Two days later, Gregor Kraus had boarded a flight to the island of Majorca.

Or so it was made to appear. In truth, he had flown to Boston using a different passport with a new name. Stefan Haas.

And now Valerie was here. After her flight landed at Logan at 2:45, she had called him as instructed. He told her to meet him tomorrow morning, but when he told her where, she said, "No, that's too public. Meet me in the back room at Larry's Restaurant, near the Boston Medical Center."

He put the IronMan gripper in his pocket. How did she know this restaurant? According to Pym, Valerie had never been to Boston. Tomorrow he would question her about this. And about why she had disobeyed his orders.

He had intended to meet her here at the Quincy Market, but if she wanted to meet in some dim-lit restaurant, so be it. In such a setting, perhaps he could persuade her to have sex with him. He was not particularly attracted to Asian women, but Valerie had a gorgeous body. Many times in London he had watched her go running in the early mornings. Shapely legs. A narrow waist. Melon-sized breasts. He couldn't wait to squeeze them.

Having Valerie satisfy his sexual appetites might make this job more bearable. This would take his mind off other unpleasant chores. This Gardner heist would be complicated. But the money was impossible to resist.

Pym wanted them to steal two Vermeers, but the old man was in for a surprise.

CHAPTER 7

Thursday June 24, 2010 New Orleans

The women were stunning. Posed provocatively, seductive curves and flawless skin, lacy bras barely hiding their nipples, long flowing hair of every hue: black, light brown, bright red and platinum blonde.

But no faces.

Frank leaned closer to his computer monitor. The photos of the bare-breasted women were cropped to conceal their faces. The rest wore fancy masks like the ones people wore in New Orleans during Mardi Gras. If Natalie was one of the women, he couldn't identify her. Nor could a London vice cop.

Elite Escorts billed itself as London's premier escort service. "Our sensuous ladies excel in the social graces necessary for high-class events." The words whore and prostitute never appeared on these websites, and discretion was their watchword: "Complete confidentiality for your peace of mind."

Forget confidentiality. His peace of mind would come when he found Natalie. For eight years she had worked as a call girl in Paris. Trained by her escort-service employer, she had used her newfound knowledge of art to entertain her clients. When she wasn't entertaining them in bed. He skimmed the Elite Escorts blurb. "Our escorts come from all over the world. Many speak multiple languages. Why not enjoy London with a lovely lady who speaks your mother tongue?"

Natalie spoke French. That could be a plus with French-speaking clients. The Elite Escorts pitch closed with an invitation.

"Ring our friendly service now and our helpful staff will find you a stunning escort for your date tonight."

He punched the number into his phone, country and city code first, and heard the phone ring. True to their word, a man answered right away. "Elite Escorts, how may I help you?"

"I'm looking for a women who knows something about art. You got anyone like that?"

After a slight hesitation, the man said, "Did have. But she's gone now."

Natalie, he thought. "Where'd she go?"

"I'm afraid I can't say."

"What's her name?"

"We never give out the names of our ladies."

The guy giving him haughty, acting like he wasn't a pimp hawking whores. Frank wanted to throttle him. "I'm coming to London for an art conference next week. I want a woman who knows about art."

"How about Eva? She's one of our most popular ladies. A lovely woman, blonde hair, blue eyes."

Frank wondered if they did phone sex. Ask Eva if she knew the woman who specialized in art.

But why waste time? He hung up and closed the website.

If Natalie was the woman who specialized in art, Mr. Haughty wasn't going to tell him, and he didn't feel like surfing any more sex-bait websites, dozens of them located in big cities all over the world. But London was where a witness had seen the woman with a distinctive long-legged stride leave a museum after a heist four months ago. Last weekend a security guard had been shot during a heist near London.

One to the head, game over. Natalie's MO.

Tomorrow, he and Kelly would fly to London. Maybe DCI Stanford would have more information by then. Kelly was excited about the trip, poring over Fodor's guide to London, saying she hoped they'd get to see some sights before they flew back on Monday.

He didn't give a damn about sightseeing. He wanted to find Natalie. Two years he'd been waiting. Where did she go after she escaped from New Orleans in 2008? Nowhere in the United States probably. Every police department in the country had a composite sketch of Natalie Brixton, wanted for murder in Boston and New Orleans.

She knew he had her diary, which meant she wouldn't go to Paris. He figured she was in Europe, a big city where she could lose herself in the crowds, a city where they spoke English. Like London.

That's where Natalie was. He'd bet on it.

His heart thrummed a slow inexorable beat that signaled his resolve, relentless and unstoppable. This time he was going to get her.

———

10:55 AM – Boston

She poured steamy tea from a silver pot into a small porcelain cup and wrapped her hands around it to warm them. A dark cloud of dread chilled her to the bone. In five minutes she would meet Gregor.

She had arrived twenty minutes early. Preparation was the key. Anticipate the worst and plan your moves, like a taekwondo competition. But this was no taekwondo match. Gregor was a killer.

The mere sound of his voice on the phone terrified her. Everything about this job terrified her. Steal a painting somewhere in Boston, the worst possible scenario.

Two years ago she had killed a former CIA agent here. She was certain the cops were still looking for her. Pym didn't know this, of course, nor did Gregor. She raised the cup to her mouth, inhaled the fumes and took a sip. Pym had said she'd be back in London in two weeks. If everything went as planned. A veiled threat.

She studied the Chinese horoscope on the place-mat in front of her. This was the Year of the Ox, a powerful figure in Chinese mythology, but her ancestors were Vietnamese. She had chosen birds and mountains to protect her. She offered a silent plea to the Vietnamese spirit gods. *Help me escape this nightmare.*

She looked up and her heart almost stopped. A man was striding through the dining area toward her booth in the back room, eyes fixed on hers. Gregor. He was even bigger than she had imagined, over six feet tall, broad shoulders and muscular arms filling his black turtleneck. He reminded her of the relentless killer in a movie she'd seen. *No Country For Old Men.* Stone-faced, eyes implacable.

Her heart pounded as he stopped at her booth. The only other booth was vacant. Looming over her, he said in the quiet voice she knew so well, "A good meeting place. No windows."

He jerked his chin at the other side of the booth. "Sit there. I never sit with my back to the door."

Without a word, she slid out of her seat and sat on the opposite side. Damned if she'd obey his every command, but she had to pick her spots.

Gregor settled into the booth with his back to the wall and studied her. "You look like a librarian. So prim and proper. Your hair in a bun, big round tinted glasses, shirt buttoned up to your chin." He pursed his lips and nodded. "Very sexy."

She put her hands in her lap and clenched her fists. "Tell me about the job, Gregor."

He stiffened and leaned forward over the table, so close she could smell his aftershave, a spicy scent. "Stupid," he said in a soft voice. "No names. Not when we are in public."

In public? No one was anywhere near them. "Tell me about the job. Where is it? And when?"

"Soon. A few days from now."

She waited for him to say more. When he didn't, she smiled at him. Be what they want you to be. "Would you like some tea?"

"I don't drink tea." He gazed at her, expressionless. "And I don't eat Chinese food. How do you know this place? Have you been to Boston before?"

Her heart drummed against her chest. "A friend of mine in London recommended it."

"What friend?"

"You wouldn't know him. He's a chef at an Asian restaurant." A lie, but Gregor wouldn't know this.

48

When she'd called Chen from Heathrow, he had given her a name and a number to call, the first thing she'd done after landing at Logan. Pak Lam had told her about Larry's Restaurant, a fine place to meet if one did not want to be seen or overheard, he'd said.

Gregor appeared to digest this, then said, "Did you have any trouble locating your apartment?"

"No. I took a cab from the airport. The place is a dump."

His expression changed, a slight relaxation of the muscles around his eyes. Despite his coarse features, he looked younger than she had expected, curly locks of light-brown hair spilling over his forehead. Maybe it was a wig. There were the crow's feet around his eyes and deep lines etched the corners of his thin lips.

"Get a room at the Ritz if you want, but you must pay for it."

"I found a dead rat under the sink this morning."

He gazed at her, expressionless. "How big was it?"

She held her hands two feet apart. "This big."

A smile tugged at his lips. "Really? Impressive. Think how much poison it took to kill it."

The words chilled her. Was that all he thought about? What it took to kill something?

The waitress, a young Asian woman with long black hair, came to their booth, smiled at Gregor and said, "Would you care for a menu, sir? A beverage, perhaps?"

"Nothing for me. My girlfriend already has her tea."

The waitress made a pleasant face, inclined her head and left.

Annoyed, she said, "I'm not your girlfriend."

"Not yet." His gaze roamed her body, a possessive gaze that disgusted her. He raised his hands and spread them palms down on the table in front of her.

She gasped. Hideous scars covered the backs of his hands, ugly red patches of skin. With his eyes locked on hers, he flexed his fingers and the red patches crinkled with white lines. Then, smiling faintly, he put his hands in his lap. If he was trying to disgust her, he had succeeded.

But never let them see you sweat. "Where is the job?"

He glanced around the room to be sure no one was nearby and said softly, "The Gardner Museum."

Shocked, she said nothing. The Gardner? Was Pym out of his mind?

"What is wrong? You know this museum?"

"I know what happened there in 1990."

He waved a hand. "This is not 1990. That brought us a golden opportunity. There *vill* be a special exhibit there. Many fine paintings on loan from important museums, including two by Vermeer."

There *vill* be … a linguistic slip. Was he German?

But forget ancestry. Pym's lecture on Vermeer last weekend was no accident. Her armpits dampened with sweat. They wanted her to steal a Vermeer from the Gardner Museum where thieves had stolen several paintings twenty years ago. Insanity.

"Security will be tight," she said.

"Yes, but I have a plan."

What is it? she wanted to scream. But if she did Gregor might slap her. Or kill her. "This special exhibit," she said. "When does it open?"

"Friday, July second, just in time for the Fourth of July. The holiday these Americans are so proud of."

"Tell me about the security."

"The security is not your concern."

She raised her chin. "It is if I have to go into the museum."

"When the time comes, you will know these details. Right now your job is to get familiar with the area near the museum. But do not be conspicuous. Many students jog on the Fenway and the surrounding streets." A faint smile. "Put on your sexy red shorts and go for a run."

Had he been watching her in London? The thought made her skin crawl. "Is the insider guard in place?"

Gregor nodded, expressionless.

"Who is he?"

"You do not need to know this now."

A jolt of anger flamed her cheeks. Gregor was a control freak. "When will I meet him?"

"You *vill* meet ..." He paused and blinked. "In good time, not now."

German, for sure. Twice he had slipped up, saying *vill* instead of *will*. Maybe her persistent questions had unsettled him. Maybe Gregor wasn't as invincible as he appeared.

"You need to learn the transportation system. The MBTA." He paused. "Unless you have used it when you were in Boston before."

The statement rattled her. But he had to be bluffing. He couldn't know she'd been here before. "Do you have my new passport?"

"Yes."

"When will I get—?"

50

"You ask too many questions. You get it when you need it. We meet twice a week to discuss the plan."

"Where?"

A suggestive smile. "At your apartment." He put his hands on the table again. Regarding her with an amused expression, he said, "Old battle scars. You have the designated cellphone, correct?"

"Yes."

"Use it only to communicate with me. No one else."

"What about . . . the man in London?"

"There is no need to call him. I am in charge, understand?"

"Ja. Ich verstehe."

He flinched as though she'd slapped him. "Do not make jokes. Do not annoy me with stupid comments." He reached across the table and touched her hair. "I like your hair. Is it a wig?"

She pushed his hand away. "No. And we will not be meeting in my apartment."

"Why not? You might enjoy yourself. More than you do with the old man."

She removed her tinted glasses. His dark eyes were pools of venom, deadly heat-seeking missiles. Like most men, Gregor didn't handle rejection well. But he needed to understand that she had no intention of sleeping with him. "I'm leaving. When do you want to meet?"

"Monday. At noon."

"Okay," she said. "Meet me outside Symphony Hall by the T stop."

"No," he said. "Stand outside the public library on Boylston Street. Near the Copley T stop."

Imposing his control. His way or the highway. "Fine. See you then."

Feeling his venomous gaze on her back, she left the booth and walked away. Intent on her mission, she hurried outside. Dodging traffic, she ran across the street to Sav-More-Drugs, went inside and stood by the window. A minute later Gregor left Larry's, went to the parking lot and got in an olive-green Saab.

When he drove out of the lot, she dashed outside and memorized the license number. A New Jersey plate, a rental probably. Maybe she could find a way to bug the car. Considering the hellish problems facing her, she needed every advantage she could get. Gregor wanted to control her, withholding details about the job. He knew where she lived, but she didn't know where he lived or what he did when he wasn't with her. Worse, he wanted to have sex with her.

Not only that, anytime she went out some Boston cop might recognize her and arrest her.

Her one consolation: Frank Renzi, her relentless pursuer, wasn't here. He was in New Orleans.

51

But Gregor wanted her to steal two paintings from a museum known worldwide for an infamous art heist in 1990. Those paintings had never been recovered and several agencies were still looking for them: the FBI, Interpol, The Stolen Art Registry, not to mention every art detective in the world, seeking the glory—and the financial reward—for recovering them.

Steal two Vermeers worth millions of dollars from the Gardner? Impossible. Security would be off the chart.

Even if she managed to steal them, how would she escape? She had no illusions about one thing. If something went wrong, Gregor wouldn't help her. Gregor would throw her to the wolves.

Kill them, or you will die too.

CHAPTER 8

Friday June 25, 2010 11:30 AM Boston

Nicholas Kwan drove his waxed-and-polished Lexus out of the car wash, continued down Massachusetts Avenue and turned onto a side street near the Boston Medical Center complex. The sleazy surroundings did not improve his foul mood: whiny panhandlers, litter in the street, overflowing dumpsters.

He'd seen rats bigger than house cats in the alleys.

His destination lay ahead, a squat building with a Day-Glo-yellow sign— LARRY'S—in Chinese-red letters. Larry bought rat and roach poison to keep his restaurant pest-free and Tums to settle his stomach at the pharmacy across the street. Sav-More-Drugs. The name must amuse the junkies, Nicolas thought sourly as he parked his car in the lot beside the restaurant.

The gutter in front of the door was littered with candy wrappers and losing lottery tickets. Nicholas clenched his teeth. Upon arriving in Boston, he had paid his respects to the Dragon Master, ruler of a powerful Boston tong and great-uncle of his San Francisco overlord. Considering his status in San Francisco, Nicholas expected to receive the respect he deserved, but the Dragon Master sent him on these shitty errands. Soon he would escape these disgusting chores.

Soon he would have enough money to leave the country. Then the Dragon Master could find another errand boy. And so could Stefan.

Nicolas removed his mirrored Ray-Bans and stepped into the foyer. Above dark wainscoting, a mural depicted Chinese scenes: a river lined with bamboo shoots, pagodas and distant mountains. Carved-wood Fu Dogs guarded each end of a ten-foot take-out counter. In the dining room, two skinny Asian girls were serving customers.

Larry Ho lumbered through a swinging door behind the counter. His head was shaved and a Hawaiian shirt hugged his enormous belly. The top button was open, revealing folds of fat below his chin. Larry rested his forearms on the counter, his moon-face wreathed in a smile, though his eyes were flat and emotionless. "Right on time, Nicholas. You hungry? I fix you some Tai Chien Chicken."

Nicholas said nothing. He would never consider eating food from this dump. He extracted a wad of bills from the pocket of his windbreaker and set it on the counter. Larry counted the money and stuck the bills in his pocket. Nicholas studied his eyes. They betrayed nothing.

"How's your uncle, Nicolas? He doing okay?"

Seething, Nicolas scratched his beard. The fat man knew he had no uncle.

Swallowing his irritation, he said, "My uncle is fine." A sudden impulse made him say, "He commends you for dealing with his most talented nephew."

Larry's smile widened. "Always happy to help out."

The fat man pretended to be jolly, but Nicholas was not deceived.

He was about to leave when a customer walked in, a skinny black woman in jeans and a purple sweatshirt with holes in the elbows. She went to the other end of the counter near the cash register, deliberately, it seemed to Nicholas.

Larry moved down the counter. "Good to see you, Jamilla. What can I get for you?"

In a low voice she said, "How 'bout the Canton Special."

"Sure thing." Larry scribbled on an order pad and disappeared into the kitchen.

Nicholas eyed her scornfully. He knew the code. She was laundering food stamps. She appeared to be in her thirties, though he found it difficult to determine a black person's age. Her skin was the color of eggplant and her kinky black hair was cropped short. Avoiding his eyes, she scratched her scalp, then her shoulder, then her arm. Coke itch, Nicholas thought contemptuously.

A minute later Larry returned with her order. Nicholas marveled at his Buddha-like bulk. Nicolas was five-six, several inches shorter than the fat man, but the fat man outweighed him by one hundred pounds, maybe more.

Larry set a take-out bag on the counter. "I put in extra fortune cookies for your son. He must be getting big. Is he in school yet?"

"Not till next year. He's only five." She turned her back to Nicholas and slipped a wad of food stamps to Larry.

The stupid bitch. Trying to hide the transaction.

Larry pulled out the bills Nicholas had given him, peeled off some twenties and palmed them into her hand.

"Thanks, Larry. You're a prince." She took the take-out bag and went to the door.

"Stop by more often, Jamilla. We miss you around here."

The woman left without answering.

"Why were you so nice to her?" Nicolas asked. "Those people are scum."

Larry removed a roll of Tums from the pocket of his Hawaiian shirt and popped one in his mouth. "She's not a bad person. She's just down on her luck."

"She's a junkie. She is lazy. Too lazy to work."

"No she isn't. She used to be a cop, walked the beat around here for two years."

"She's a cop?" Nicholas said with sudden interest.

"She was, until her boyfriend messed up her head."

"Where's the boyfriend?"

"In jail. Too bad they didn't nail him before he got her hooked on coke. She was a good cop before she got mixed up with him."

"Since when do you like cops?"

Larry shrugged. "I feel bad for her. She got caught in the jar. Second time around, they busted her off the force. She's pretty bitter about it."

Even more interesting, Nicolas decided. "Where does Jamilla Gorilla live?"

The skin around Larry's almond-shaped eyes tightened. "Why? You want to ask her out? I don't think she's your type."

He loathed the fat man's taunts and often thought of what he might do to retaliate someday.

"Forget the jokes," he snapped. "Tell me where she lives."

"Harrison Avenue, above the 7-Eleven."

"What is her last name?"

"Wells," the fat man said, his dark eyes flat and implacable. "Jamilla Wells."

Nicolas put on his mirrored Ray-Bans. "The Dragon Master said to remind you that you have not made your quota for two months."

He left before the fat man could reply.

———

Larry went to the front window and watched Nicholas Kwan return to the black Lexus he loved so much. He looked like an Italian greaser with his slicked down hair and dark beard. Why did he wear those ridiculous sunglasses? To hide his Asian heritage? Or was it his pathetic attempt at a disguise.

Larry Ho had an insatiable curiosity. Safety, he believed, lay in knowing everything that transpired in his neighborhood and overseeing every detail of his business, which included the restaurant, the food stamp scam and a few other things he had going. After Nicholas showed up six months ago, Larry had asked around. Nobody knew anything, but he persisted. A friend in San Francisco enlightened him.

Nicholas had killed two cops there. This was a serious matter. The cops wouldn't rest until they caught him. Which meant Nicholas was dangerous. What did he want with Jamilla? Larry wondered.

Up until three years ago she had walked the Medical Center beat, making sure his customers were safe, responding quickly if a drunk got rowdy. After the cops fired her, she'd clerked at the 7-Eleven for a while, but she had the boy to support. Last year she had applied for food stamps. He hated to think what else she might be doing to make money. Blacks had it rough in Boston. So did Asians.

His parents had arrived from China speaking no English. In 1950, the year of Larry's birth, they opened a small restaurant Four years later his mother died. His father never remarried. Now his elderly father lived with him. Larry's wife had stayed home to raise their two children. His son was a neurosurgeon, his daughter, a software engineer.

He popped another Tums and thought about Nicholas. Two months ago, he found out where Nicholas lived and followed him one night. Nicholas had a job, a strange one, considering he was on the lam. He worked as an overnight guard at the Gardner Museum. Not for the money, certainly. Those jobs paid shit.

The puzzle confounded him. Larry turned away from the window. Four hours from now he would get in his Lincoln Town Car, drive home and relax with a cocktail before dinner. Barbecued steak, baked potato and corn on the cob tonight. Good old American food. He adored steak. In fact, he almost preferred it to sex, except when his lovely 98-pound wife got a certain look in her eye.

Again, the puzzle distracted him. Why was Nicholas working as a museum guard? What did he want with Jamilla? Not sex, obviously. Nicholas hated blacks.

———

New Orleans 10:55 AM

"Hey, Frank, great to hear from you! Are you in Boston?"

Frank smiled, pleased by the warm greeting. His former boss, Lieutenant Colonel Harrison Flynn, supervised the Boston PD homicide detectives in District Four where Frank used to work.

"No, but next Monday I might be. After I get back from London."

"London? What's up? Vacation? Or work?"

"Natalie Brixton."

A shocked silence, then, "Wow. You got a line on her?"

Frank glanced at the clock on his bedside table. His suitcase lay open on the bed. In two hours he was meeting Kelly at the airport and he hadn't finished packing. "Yes, but I don't have time to give you the details. She might be working for a gang of art thieves in London."

"How'd you get onto her?"

"I've been haunting the Interpol website for leads, finally got one."

"I gotta hand it to you, Frank. You're persistent."

"Yes I am and this time I'm gonna get her."

"You got a law enforcement connection in London?"

"Yes, in the Criminal Investigation Division, Art and Antiques Unit." Holding his cellphone in one hand, he opened a bureau drawer, grabbed a handful of socks and tossed them in the suitcase. "A man got shot during an art heist last weekend. One shot to the head. Sound familiar?"

"Indeed it does. Now you've really got me hooked. The Oliver James case is still open. Be nice to solve it before I retire."

"Whoa! You're retiring? When? How come?"

He went to his closet and took out some shirts. His boss didn't answer right away, which seemed odd.

"In October," Flynn finally said. "My wife says it's time we visited the grand-kids in California."

"Good for you. You earned it." He put the shirts in his suitcase. "How many years you got in?"

"Thirty-five. What time will you be here on Monday? I'll save a spot for you." Flynn uttered a sardonic laugh. "My calendar is chock full, what with all the politicians wanting to visit me."

"I don't doubt it," he said, playing along with the sarcasm. "Kelly and I land at Logan at eleven AM."

"Kelly's going?"

"Yes. She'll fly back to New Orleans from Logan, but if I get a hot lead in London, I might not fly back until Tuesday. I'll try and get to your office by twelve-thirty."

"Great. We can have lunch."

"Perfect. See you Monday." He had no idea if he'd find Natalie in London, but why not think positive?

———

Boston 10:15 PM

She had the cabbie drop her off at the Chinatown Gate. Earlier, to prepare for her meeting, she had used her laptop to research Boston's Chinatown. She'd seen photos, but the massive Chinatown Gate was far more impressive up close, four stories high. Huge cement pillars supported a green-tiled two-tiered roof. Below the upper tier, a cement panel held four gold Chinese characters. On either side of the gate, two white-stone Fu Dogs with fearsome faces sat on cement pedestals.

Bounded by the Financial District, the New England Medical Center and the theater district, Chinatown housed 5,000 residents. Most were Asians whose ancestors had come from China, Vietnam, Cambodia and other Far East countries. But other Boston residents and many tourists came to Chinatown.

Tonight, enjoying the balmy weather, people strolled along in shorts and shirtsleeves. She had on her student disguise: stone-washed jeans, a Northeastern University T-shirt and a Red Sox baseball cap.

She joined the pedestrians, walking along sidewalks lined with small shops and restaurants with neon signs that flashed Dim Sum, Cocktails. Metal plaques on some buildings indicated their family affiliation. From the 1880s to the 1920s, these benevolent associations, known as tongs, protected newly arrived immigrants from discrimination. But criminals took over some tongs, profiting from illegal activities like prostitution, gambling, drug and gun running, gangs now known as Triads.

She passed several restaurants, the Empire Garden, the Dumpling Cafe, Dim Sum Cafe. Menus posted on the windows were in English and Chinese. Following the directions she'd been given, she lengthened her stride. Now the streets were dark and narrow and silent. And she was the only pedestrian. At last she found what she was looking for, a small yellow sign on a redbrick building. Royal Dragon. Etched above it were three red Chinese characters. An arrow pointed to an alley.

But a security camera was mounted on the wall. Unwilling to have her face appear on videotape, she ducked her head and pulled the Red Sox cap lower. Her heart accelerated as she entered the dark alley. Her benefactor seemed nice enough on the phone, but now that she was about to meet him, she felt nervous.

Pak Lam was an important man. Chen had spoken of him with reverence, saying he was a great leader.

At the end of the alley, twin pagoda lanterns illuminated a red door emblazoned with Chinese symbols. She took a deep breath to calm her nerves and knocked on the door. An elderly Chinese man with white hair and a wrinkled face opened the door and led her through a room with small round tables and vacant chairs. The odor of incense filled the air, and faint music was playing, a Chinese melody.

The elderly man stopped at a carved-wood door and tapped once.

A slender man in black silk trousers and a Chinese-red silk shirt opened the door. "Come in, Valerie."

He was only a few inches taller that she was, five-foot-ten perhaps, though his dignified bearing made him appear larger. But this was not the most striking thing about him. At one time his face must have been handsome. Now an angry scar bisected his left cheek from his eyebrow to his jaw.

To hide her reaction to his disfigurement, she put her palms together and bowed deeply. "Thank you for agreeing to meet with me. I am honored to meet you."

"It is my pleasure. Chen has spoken highly of you. Come sit down."

He swept his arm, indicating four chairs with gold upholstery facing a low table lacquered with black enamel. He took the chair opposite hers and studied her, expressionless, his eyes dark and flat.

She tried to estimate his age. No gray in his jet-black hair, but she guessed he might be in his fifties.

The question flustered her. To avoid an immediate answer, she said, "How should I address you?"

A faint smile softened his expression. At last he said, "Many people come here to enjoy our food and our cultural offerings, but Chinatown has a dark side, criminals who threaten legitimate businesses owners like myself. In addition to my grocery stores, I offer other businesses protection." He spread his hands. "Along with a few other services that I provide. Chen has told me you need help with a difficult employer, but if this involves drugs, I cannot help you. I will have nothing to do with drugs or those who sell them. So. How can I help you?"

"You have been raised well. My name is Pak Soon Lam. However, the leader of a Triad is known by the number 489. My associates call me Mountain Man."

She wanted to get up and dance around the room. What a lucky coincidence! Following Vietnamese customs, she had chosen birds and mountains to protect her. And her benefactor was The Mountain Man.

"But you may call me Mr. Lam. How may I help you?"

She hesitated, suddenly anxious, fearing what he would think. "I need a gun. Not for drug deals. To protect myself."

"What sort of gun?"

"A Beretta."

He showed no surprise at her quick response. "That will be no problem. Is that all?"

"Would it be possible to get some kind of bug to track a car?"

"Yes. You will also need an iPhone to use with the tracking device. One moment." He went to an elegant carved-wood desk in the corner of the room, picked up a phone and spoke in some sort of Chinese dialect. While he talked, she studied a color photograph mounted on the wall. Two young children, a boy and a girl perhaps six or seven years old, stood hand in hand, laughing. They looked so much alike, they had to be twins. A striking woman with dark almond eyes and flowing black hair stood behind them.

Lam returned and sat down. He glanced at the photograph as though he had seen her looking at it.

"Your family" she asked.

He stared into space for several seconds, his face impassive. After a moment he said, "What is your heritage?"

"My mother was Caucasian. My father is Vietnamese, born in Paris but he later came to America. I was born here. When I was two, he abandoned me and my mother."

Lam frowned. "And you never saw him again?"

"I saw him once. I would rather not talk about it." The memory of that hideous night in Paris remained etched in her mind.

"I understand." His face betrayed no emotion, but his eyes were tinged with sadness.

A tap sounded on the door and the white-haired man appeared, carrying two boxes. He put them on the table, bowed deeply and left. Lam opened one box and took out a small object the size of a Zippo lighter. "This is the tracking device. It is magnetized on one side. Attach it inside the rear bumper of the car you wish to track. The instruction booklet explains how to activate it."

Lam opened the other box and removed a small flat cellphone. "This is the latest iPhone, much better than the previous model. Slightly bigger than a pack of cigarettes, but less than a half inch thick." Lam smiled. "All my associates insisted on having one. After you set up the tracking service, the device will send a text to your iPhone whenever the car moves. On the Internet a Google Earth map allows you to enter the

GPS coordinates and map the location. Zoom in for the street view. Zoom out for the big picture."

She could hardly believe it. A tiny bug and this magical cellphone would allow her to track Gregor. "Perfect! I didn't know such a thing was possible. How much do they cost? I am happy to pay you in cash."

"As you wish. Fifteen hundred for the bug and the iPhone. I will have the Beretta for you tomorrow. You can pay me when you pick it up. One thousand dollars."

She took out a roll of bills and paid him for the bug and the iPhone.

"Is there anything else?"

The moment of truth. The Beretta and the bug were important, but the next item was crucial. Her heart pounded. It had been many years since she cared what someone else thought of her. But this dignified man with the scarred face and the melancholy eyes had moved her deeply. What would he think?

"I may need to leave the country fast. With a new passport."

Lam frowned. "From Boston?"

"No. Given the security restrictions since 9-11 that would be unwise. But I need a new passport and a new identity. If possible, one that will disguise my gender. Could you get me a passport for a male?"

Lam gazed at her for several seconds. "Where will you go?"

"Somewhere in Europe." She didn't want to tell him where.

His eyes searched her face. "I will see what I can do. You must be here on a dangerous mission."

You have no idea how dangerous. To mask her fears, she beamed him a happy smile. "As a teenager I chose birds and mountains to protect me. Now that I have met the Mountain Man, I am sure it will go well."

His expression softened and his eyes grew warmer. Now she could see what a handsome young man Pak Lam had been, before someone disfigured his face.

He wrote something on a slip of paper and gave it to her. "My cellphone number. When I answer, you must say 'Hello Mountain Man.' I will know it is you."

She rose and bowed deeply. "Thank you, Mountain Man."

He inclined his head. "Remember, the most perilous journey begins with a single step."

CHAPTER 9

Saturday June 26, 2010 Boston

Nicholas leaned against the wrought-iron fence that enclosed a small park near Boston Medical Center. At the far end two kids were playing on swings. Even at this distance their high-pitched squeals irritated him. In the center of the park Jamilla Wells sat alone on a bench surrounded by pigeons pecking at dirt. He'd followed her and her snot-nosed brat here from her apartment.

Two women pushing baby strollers passed Jamilla, but she didn't look up. When the women reached the sidewalk, Nicholas put on his mirrored Ray-Bans and strode across the weedy grass to the bench. The pigeons flapped their wings and scattered. "How you doing, Jamilla?"

Startled, she shank away from him.

"I'm a friend of Larry's. I saw you at his restaurant yesterday, remember?"

She stared at him. Her eyes were dark brown and very large. "If you say so."

He gestured at the swings. "That's a cute little boy you've got there."

She looked over to make sure the kid was okay, then turned to face him, frowning now. "What about it? Why don't you take off them shades so I can see your eyes?"

The insolent bitch. He removed the Ray-Bans and stuck them in the pocket of his windbreaker. As he sat down beside her, shrieks of laughter came from the swings.

"Jaylen," she yelled. "Be careful!"

The brats were on one swing now, one seated, the other standing. Jamilla's little monkey was pushing them. If they didn't shut up, he'd go over and belt them. "I've got a job for you. It pays good money."

"What kind of job?"

"I need someone to set up some street action."

She inched away from him, her eyes wary. "What's that got to do with me?"

"I need someone to start a ruckus outside the Northeastern dorm on the Fenway. You know all the gangs. You were a cop, right?"

Her eyes drifted away. "Used to be. Not any more."

"You still have your uniform?"

She hunched her shoulders and her knee bounced up and down in a jerky motion. "What's it to you?"

61

He wanted to slap her. The bitch was talking tough, but he knew she was interested. "If you don't have the uniform, I can't use you." He pulled three fifty-dollar bills out of his pocket.

Her eyes widened. "Yeah, I still got it."

"Good. Line up six gang-bangers for the rumble."

"I ain't about to start no rumble."

"Hsss! Not you, the bangers. You pay them fifty apiece. The leader gets an extra fifty to make sure they show up."

She took out a stick of gum, peeled off the wrapper, stuck the gum in her mouth and chewed deliberately. "How much for me?"

He made her wait, stroking his beard, hearing the distant siren of an ambulance headed to Boston Medical Center. "Five hundred."

She stopped chewing and stared at him. "Five hundred to set up a rumble? What is this, some kinda scam?" She dug at her scalp with her nails, scratching.

Why was she playing hard to get? She was desperate for money, trading food stamps for cash to buy nose candy. "Okay, forget it." He made as if to leave the bench.

"Wait." Forehead creased in a frown, she picked a cuticle on her thumb. "Okay, but I ain't talkin' to no bangers with my uniform on."

"Of course not. That's for another job."

"What other job? I don't get it."

"Just do what I said. Line up the gang-bangers. Make sure the leader is reliable." He fixed her with a hard stare. "No crackheads, understand? No junkies."

She clamped her lips together and nodded. He gave her a fifty-dollar bill. "That's for the leader. Make sure he keeps quiet." He dangled two more fifties. "These are for you."

She snatched the bills and stuck them in her pocket. "When do I get the rest? You said five hundred."

"Line up the gang-bangers. I'll meet you here in three days with another hundred."

"Then what?"

"You give the setup to the leader."

"How can I do that, I don't know what the setup is?"

His irritation escalated. "I *told* you. They start a ruckus outside the Northeastern dorm on the Fenway. You come to this park every day with your boy?"

She chewed her gum, jaw working. "Not every day. What if it's raining?"

"I will call you. Write down your number." He took out a pen and a notepad, waited as she scribbled a number. "You live alone?"

"Hey, you payin' attention? I live with my son."

"I know that. Does anyone else live there?"

She hesitated. "Not really."

He put both hands around her scrawny forearm and gave her a skin burn. She tried to pull away, but he tightened his grip. "If you lie, I will find out. I know where you live. You and your boy."

She stared at him, bug-eyed, nostrils flared, breathing hard.

He released her arm, and she jerked away. "Okay. I'll get your damn ruckus goin' for you."

He watched her run toward the swings. He'd scared the bat-piss out of her. He would tell her about taking out the cops later. Money simplified everything. He would have to get more from Stefan.

"Stefan, the mastermind," he muttered.

Stefan was an arrogant prick, but he had money.

———

To avoid the crowd of shoppers on the lower levels, Natalie took the elevator the fifth floor, the floor with the offices, one being Global Interpreting. The elevator doors opened onto a hall with embossed wallpaper and plush green carpeting. A sign opposite the elevator directed her to the offices: a real estate agency, a travel agency, a financial planning business and several others.

Global Interpreting was Suite 610. She passed a vacant office with a "Lease Now" sign on the door. Ten yards down she stopped at the Executive Travel Agency. Shades covered the glass door. Opposite it was Suite 610, Global Interpreting. No lights in the office, but no shade on the door. She peered through the glass. In the dim light, she could see a rectangular desk facing the door, nothing else. But so what? She wasn't here to see the office. She was here to find Gregor's car.

If he worked at Global Interpreting, as Pym had implied, he must have a parking space. She returned to the vacant office. The sign gave the real estate agent's name and a telephone number. She took out the iPhone Pak Lam had given her. Already she loved it. The screen was small, but she could use it to access the Internet when she didn't have her laptop. She dialed the number and waited.

After two rings, a cheerful female voice said, "Premier Real Estate, Arlene speaking."

"Hello," she said. "I'm an associate at Richardson and Son, an estate planning firm. We're looking to expand our office and I see that you have a vacancy at Copley Place."

"Yes. Suite 625. It's a lovely office, 22,000 square feet and completely renovated since the last tenant. New carpeting and new wallpaper. We offer 24-hour security, and, as you know, it's a prime location."

"Does it come with any parking spaces?"

"One comes with the lease, but for an additional monthly fee you can add another one."

"Where are they located?"

"Up one flight on the sixth floor. The space for that unit is 303."

"How much is the rent?" She didn't care, but she didn't want to arouse the woman's suspicions.

"It's a steal at 50,000 dollars a month. Your clients will love it."

"Thanks very much. I'll talk to my boss and get back to you."

She hung up and pumped her fist. If Suite 625 had a parking space in the garage, Global Interpreting probably did too. She went to the elevator, thumbed the call button and waited impatiently, visualizing Gregor's olive-green Saab with the New Jersey license plate.

The elevator dinged and the polished brass doors parted on an empty car. She hit the button for the sixth floor and the doors closed. Ten seconds later they opened on a vast parking area with a ramp in the middle. She eased into the garage and checked for a security guard. She didn't see one. No security booth either. Maybe there was one at the downstairs exit. Her ploy had gotten her the parking information, but it might not help her today. Most of the offices were closed.

She walked along the rows of diagonal spaces hunting for number 303. Halfway down one wall she found it. The space was empty. All ten spaces along that wall were empty.

Where was Gregor's Saab? She walked the perimeter of the garage. No olive-green Saab with a New Jersey plate. Then she remembered what Pak Lam had said. A perilous journey begins with a single step.

The Saab wasn't here today, but tomorrow it might be. Or the next day. Monday. The day she had to meet Gregor. At noon she would be standing outside the Boston Public Library. The library where she'd read the newspaper articles about Frank Renzi and his troubles. Problems that had driven him out of Boston to settle in New Orleans.

She pictured him in the New Orleans alley after she shot him. Did he still think about her? Part of her wanted to believe he did. The other part, the rational part, desperately hoped he didn't.

Dealing with Gregor was bad enough. She didn't need Frank Renzi hunting for her. In New Orleans, or Boston.

———

Providence, Rhode Island

Gregor parked in front of a white one-story cottage on a residential street on the East Side of Providence. Every house on the street looked like it belonged to bikers or welfare recipients. He got out of the Saab, went up the walk to the front door and pressed the bell.

A hanging plant stand beside the door held a flowerpot with wilted orange marigolds. Burt couldn't even remember to water the flowers, much less bathe himself.

Burt opened the door, a six-foot-two hulk in a sweat-stained T-shirt with piggish eyes and a hair lip that had never been repaired. Reeking of body odor, he held a can of Miller in one hand. Gregor pushed past him into the living room. It stank of cat piss, and newspapers and magazines littered the soiled beige carpet. He shuddered to think what the kitchen looked like. A worn couch faced a flat-screen television set. He would have to get rid of the TV before Nicolas came here after the heist.

"I'm going to need to use the house for a few days."

Burt frowned. "How come?"

"Someone else needs to stay here."

"When? I gotta check in with my probation officer once a week."

"What happens if you don't?"

"I get in trouble," Burt mumbled. Burt was an ex-con fresh out of prison, a pedophile to boot. His sister owned the place but let Burt live here, the perfect setup for a safe house. A month ago he had put Burt on the Global Interpreting payroll, listing him as a driver. Happy to collect seventy dollars every week, Burt asked no questions. Why would he? Sex offenders had huge problems finding jobs.

"How'd you like to get in trouble in Florida? I've got a plane ticket for you and a hotel reservation."

"What do I do for money?" Burt said.

Gregor wanted to punch his ugly mouth, but forced himself to remain calm. Always be in control. "I'll give you three hundred dollars cash before you leave. You'll only be there a few days."

With a sullen nod, Burt said, "Whatever you say, Mr. Haas. When do I leave?"

"Soon. I'll let you know." Unable to bear the stench of cat piss and Burt's disgusting body odor, he left the house and drove off. Inevitably, his thoughts turned to the heist and what failure would mean. Pym's insufferable orders and incessant demands would continue. Worse, his dream of living the good life would go up in smoke.

The Vermeers were worth millions. The others were equally valuable. Stealing them entailed enormous risks. If the heist went bad, he might wind up in prison, or dead. He took out a Gitanes, lighted it and blew smoke out the window. Nothing would go wrong as long as he stuck to his rules. Always be in control. Always take revenge. Trust no one. Nicholas was a snake. He didn't trust Valerie, either. Controlling them was exhausting, a never-ending chore.

But Burt was an ex-con. He would do as he was told.

Everything was under control.

CHAPTER 10

Saturday June 26, 2010 London

They had their first argument at 11:15 AM. After they checked into their hotel, Kelly wanted to take the Tube to DCI Stanford's office. Frank wanted to take a taxi and get there fast. To placate her, he promised her they would do the "London experience" tomorrow.

Twenty minutes later they entered the Arts and Antiques Unit office. To Frank, it didn't look much different from the District-4 homicide detective office, four desks sat in the middle, metal file cabinets lining the walls. Two men in civilian clothes were working the phones, another was on his computer. DCI Stanford was expecting them and came out of his office immediately, an imposing man with brilliant blue eyes, reddish brown hair and an engaging smile that softened his craggy face.

"Detective Renzi, we meet at last. And this must be your colleague."

"It is," Frank said. "Kelly O'Neil. Great detective and a terrific interviewer."

"Happy to meet you both," Stanford said. "Come in my office and I'll give you the latest info on the Ashmolean heist. Such as it is."

Stanford's office was small and unpretentious and smelled of pipe tobacco. Pinned to a bulletin board on one wall were fliers with color photographs of art works labeled STOLEN. Thanks to their phone conversations, Frank was already convinced that Stanford was a good investigator, a no-nonsense type with a sense of urgency about solving cases. Meeting the man and seeing his workspace confirmed this.

Once he and Kelly settled into the chairs in front of Stanford's desk, Stanford said, "How was your flight? You must be jet-lagged."

"A little," Kelly said, "but this is my first trip to Europe so I'm running on adrenaline."

"Me, too," Frank said. He took out a three-by-five card and gave it to Stanford. "Here's the contact information for the detective that worked the Gardner heist in 1990. He's retired now, but he was one of the first detectives on the scene and he worked with the FBI on the case. I told him to expect your call."

Stanford beamed. "Thank you so much! That case has confounded the experts for twenty years. Thirteen art works still missing, including Rembrandt's only seascape and a Vermeer. I'll ring him as soon as I catch a breather from this Ashmolean case."

"Have you got any leads?" Frank asked.

"Nothing solid I'm afraid." Stanford took out a spiral notebook. "Let me run down what we've done since I spoke with you last." He glanced at Kelly. "Or should I start at the beginning?"

"No need," Kelly said. "During the flight Frank told me everything he knew about the case."

"Excellent. The doctor finally let me interview the Security Director. The knock on the head fractured his skull, but he's on the mend. Unfortunately, he couldn't tell me much. The last thing he remembered was the security guard letting him in. After that nothing."

"Did the guard knock him out?" Kelly asked.

"The poor bloke couldn't even tell me that," Stanford said. "But his doctor said this wasn't unusual, happens quite often after a blow to the head. Bottom line, there's no evidence the Security Director was involved in the heist. No unusual change in his financials, no unexplained phone calls. Looks like he picked the wrong night to check on the overnight guard and wound up with a fractured skull."

"What about the guard?" Frank asked. "Anything hinky there?"

"His flat mate was hysterical when the detectives spoke with her the first day. Alicia Rathbun, age twenty-six. She claimed he had nothing to do with the theft, but two days ago I interviewed her and got a different story. By then she'd got over the shock." Stanford checked his notes. "The guard's name was Mitchell Warren, age thirty, but she called him Mitch. She said the week before the robbery he seemed nervous, got a few phone calls but if she was in the room, he'd go outside. She claimed he didn't tell her anything about the heist, and I tend to believe her."

"Did you check the phone records?" Kelly asked.

"Yes," Stanford said. "Five incoming calls from a cellphone number. Unfortunately, it was one of those disposable pay-as-you-go types, no record of the owner. But Alicia made an interesting comment. She said Mitch was the adventurous type, liked to flirt with danger."

"How long were they together?" Kelly asked.

"A bit more than two years."

"Long enough for her to get a feel for his walk-on-the-wild-side tendencies," Frank said. "Maybe he was in on the heist and wound up dead like the guards in those earlier heists."

"I'm afraid it looks that way."

"What can you tell me about the witness who saw the woman?" Frank said. "I want to talk to him."

Stanford frowned. "Well, I can give you his name but you won't be talking to him. Three nights ago he was out walking his dog and got hit by a lorry."

"He's *dead*?" Frank exclaimed, aghast.

"Yes. Not only that, it was a hit and run. The driver didn't stop."

Frank glanced at Kelly, who widened her eyes. To Stanford, he said, "You said these art heist gangs are ruthless. Maybe they killed him. Who knew about the witness?"

Stanford pursed his lips, clearly unhappy. "Too many people, I'm afraid. The London police, my squad and Lord knows who else. We didn't release his name to the media, but there was a conference about these art heists that day here in London."

"The day the witness got killed?" Frank said, his mind churning with possibilities.

"Yes. A group of trustees on the boards of several art museums put it together, art lovers and wealthy philanthropists most of them. They invited various law enforcement officials to speak about the heists. Security experts, detectives who specialize in finding stolen art, and several officers who investigated some of the heists. No telling who might have opened their mouth."

"To someone with money and a hankering for art?" Frank said.

"You think the mastermind might have been there?" Stanford said.

"We can't rule anything out," he said, deliberately using the inclusive we rather than you. He wanted in on this investigation.

"What's the story with this woman you're hunting?" Stanford asked.

"Natalie Brixton, age thirty-two. Two years ago she murdered a former CIA agent in Boston, and three men in New Orleans."

"Frank was lucky he wasn't one of them," Kelly said. "She shot him, too."

"You don't say!" Stanford said. "No wonder you're after her."

"Nothing serious," he said. "A flesh wound in my leg. But I think she's in on these art heists. Several years ago she worked for an escort service in Paris. As an enticement, they have their girls specialize in a particular area. Natalie's specialty was art."

"Guess I'd better add Natalie Brixton to my list of suspects," Stanford said.

Frank showed him the composite sketch of Natalie and a copy of her driver's license photo. "Can you check and see if she entered the UK sometime after August 2008?"

"An attractive woman," Stanford commented.

"Don't be fooled," Kelly said. "She'd as soon shoot you as look at you."

Stanford nodded. "Duly noted. Is she Asian?"

"Part Vietnamese on her father's side," he said. "Her mother was murdered when she was ten."

"Have you got a passport number for her?" Stanford said.

"No."

"Okay. I'll try to check the entry records, but with only a name and no passport, it might be difficult." Stanford sighed. "I wish I'd paid more attention to Sonja Wynkoop. It's looking more and more like she was right. Her husband was murdered."

"When do we talk to her?" Kelly asked.

"I've set up an appointment for you to see her tomorrow morning at eleven. She's flying into London sometime today, staying with her cousin tonight." Stanford's intercom buzzed. He frowned, punched a button and said, "What's up, David?" And after a pause, "Put her on."

Kelly leaned closer and whispered, "This is incredible, Frank. Million dollar paintings stolen and all these murders?"

He nodded, half-listening to Stanford, who said, "Right, luv. I'll be there in an hour or so." He replaced the receiver and said, "Sorry, that was my wife. One of our dogs is in a bad way, just had surgery at the veterinary. It's crazy how attached one gets to these animals …"

"We'd better let you go then," Frank said. "How do we contact Sonja Wynkoop?"

Stanford scribbled a phone number and an address on his notepad and gave it to Frank. "I'll call and tell her you're here."

"Thanks," Frank said. "We'll call her to confirm when and where. Thanks for your help and the new information." He gestured at the photograph on Stanford's desk, a striking woman and two small Welch Corgis. "Go see your wife and make sure your favorite dog is okay."

"Will do," Stanford said. "Let me know how it goes with Sonja."

———

London

He padded barefoot across the plush Persian carpet and sank into his armchair, exhausted. Solitude at last. No need to put on a front for his business associates and employees. His most vexing employee was in Boston. Gregor got things done, but he was difficult to control and his methods were ruthless. Even now he could barely contain his outrage.

Ordering Valerie to kill the museum guard and the Security Director. She hadn't killed the Security Director, but the death of the security guard might sully the reputation he had worked so hard to acquire.

Gregor believed that Jonathan Pym stole art at the behest of wealthy collectors willing to pay huge sums for the paintings.

True, but he was the wealthy collector. Only he knew the paintings were here in his basement museum, a twenty-foot-square, climate-controlled space. He had designed it himself, supervising the workmen as they installed cherry-wood paneling and ornate moldings on the walls, befitting the masterpieces he intended to hang there. The room had no windows, but recessed lighting in the vaulted ceiling spotlighted his beauties.

And what beauties they were! His beloved Old Masters. Rembrandt self-portraits, painted at various stages of his life. *An Officer Bowing to a Lady*, by Terborch, the lady in her finery, a low-cut silver gown with gold accents. The Virgin and Child in Egypt, an exquisite tempura-on-canvas by William Blake.

He adored the Franz Hals, a laughing boy with long curly hair, sparkling eyes and rosy red cheeks, a toddler, four or five years old. Happy and healthy. The painting brought him great joy.

It helped him forget his own miserable childhood.

Best of all was his Vermeer. *Woman in Blue Reading a Letter*. Seeing it brought tears to his eyes. The perfect stillness. The limpid blue of the woman's jacket. Her fierce concentration on the letter in her hands. What message did it contain? A mystery. Every painting Vermeer had done was a mystery, a puzzle to be contemplated for hours. Two weeks from now he would have two more. If he lived to enjoy them.

A series of coughs wracked him, a violent spasm that brought up a wad of phlegm. He peeled tissues off the thick wad he always carried and spat into them.

He studied the woman's blue jacket, the swollen mound of her belly.

Was she pregnant? Fortunately, he'd never had children. If he had, they might have inherited his deadly disease. As a child he'd always been sickly, small for his age, unable to play sports, prone to nosebleeds and respiratory ailments. He hated going to doctors, but three years ago, plagued by nosebleeds, coughing spells and fatigue, he'd made an appointment with his physician.

After a brief examination, Dr. Thaddeus Montgomery had ordered blood tests. A week later, his secretary called and asked him to come in the next day. When Montgomery entered the room, Pym could see the bad news on his face. But Montgomery put on a cheerful front.

Thanks to the test results, he now knew the reason for Pym's fatigue and nosebleeds. "You've inherited Fanconi Anemia, but you're one of the lucky ones. Some are intellectually stunted and many of them die before they're twenty. I'm surprised you weren't diagnosed before."

Then Montgomery launched into an explanation of how the disease was transmitted. Pym tuned him out. One of the lucky ones? He'd never been lucky in his life. Everything he had, every pleasure, every possession, every human contact was his because he'd earned it.

"You've already outlived most people who have this disease," Montgomery had said. "Most don't make it to thirty. You're fifty-five. If we work together, we can keep you going for a few more years."

Favoring him with a jovial smile. The bastard.

Later, Pym had researched Fanconi Anemia, a genetic disorder. A diagram with stick figures explained it. When an unaffected "carrier" father and an unaffected "carrier" mother had children, there were four possible outcomes. The child would be unaffected. Two children would be carriers. The fourth would inherit the disease.

Pym, who'd never been lucky in his life, had been unlucky even before he was born. Thanks to the cosmic lottery, both his parents had carried the gene for the disorder. Statistically, he'd had three out of four chances to escape the disease. But he hadn't. A death sentence.

He struggled to his feet, went to a sideboard and poured Louis XIII Remy Martin Cognac into a snifter. He swirled the liquid in the glass, sniffed the fumes, took a sip and felt the fiery liquor burn its way down his throat. Other than Dr. Montgomery, no one knew he was dying. Well, everyone died in the end. But his demise would come sooner rather than later.

He sank into his chair and cupped the snifter in his hands. After receiving that nasty bit of news he had gone to see his solicitor. Alistair Tibbs was a senior partner at Cartwright & Tibbs, a prestigious law firm that handled financial matters for business magnates. Without revealing his health status, he'd given Tibbs several directives to alter his will. Tibbs was privy to some of his shadier dealings, though not the art thefts. A man to be trusted, Pym believed.

Still, he'd written one directive himself and had Tibbs notarize his signature without reading the contents. A mystery, like the contents of the letter Vermeer had placed in the woman's hands.

The others were straightforward. Upon Pym's death, Tibbs was to liquidate his assets: his mansion and automobiles, his stocks and his import-export business. Twenty percent of the proceeds would go to his loyal employees: those who worked for his business and those who served him at his mansion. After much reflection, he had left twenty percent of the proceeds to Gregor. After all, were it not for Gregor, he would not have his glorious collection.

He hadn't decided what to do about Valerie. For two years, she had been a fine companion, charming and agreeable, and considerate in bed, especially when his fatigue allowed him infrequent release. He had no illusion that Valerie was in love with him, nor he with her. Recalling their farewell fuck the night before she flew to Boston, he smiled. That night he had actually performed quite well.

He leaned back in the padded chair and shut his eyes, recalling his first encounter with a prostitute.

Forty years ago, after cashing his first paycheck, the pittance he earned as a janitor, he'd worked up his courage and asked a girl for a date. Her ruby-red lips and ponderous breasts excited him. They'd met at the cheap cafeteria where he ate his meals. He took her to see La Dolce Vita, a Fellini film featuring Anita Ekberg with her incredible boobs and seductive smile. Afterward, he'd walked the girl—he no longer remembered her name—home. She let him kiss her, but when he tried to touch her breasts, she slapped his face. Humiliated, he ran away.

The next day he asked one of the other janitors how to find a prostitute. An older boy with a Cockney accent, Ron laughed. "Wot? You still a virgin? Come on then, laddy. After we get off work I'll take to you one."

That night he'd had his first sexual experience. The prostitute, not much older than the girl who'd slapped him, made everything easy. After he paid her, of course. When she put her mouth on his penis, he came right away. But she didn't laugh at him, she seemed pleased.

Pym opened his eyes and drank some cognac. Why was he thinking about those sordid days in London? Because he was going to die soon? Forty years ago, he'd been a penniless teenager, a callow, inexperienced youth of fifteen. Now he was a wealthy man.

He yawned and rubbed his eyes. He should go to bed and conserve his energy. Last week Dr. Montgomery had told him his bone marrow was failing but offered a last ditch solution. A hematopoietic stem cell transplant. The best donor would be someone in his family. Struck by the bitter irony, Pym had struggled not to laugh aloud.

His family? Montgomery had no idea who his real family was.

The last time he'd seen his father was when Mum dragged him to Winson Green Prison in Birmingham. At fifteen, he was the man of the family. Mum was an alky, buying cheap wine at the supermarket and drinking herself into a stupor every night. His sister wasn't with them. Charlotte was twelve, too young to visit a prison.

How he'd loathed that place, a forbidding brick monstrosity surrounded by a barbed-wire fence. He hated the trapped feeling when the doors slammed shut, hated the guards with their hard eyes and pistols, hated the visiting room where prisoners in leg-irons met their visitors. It stank of piss and sweat and rancid food. Most of all, he hated the look on his father's face, bleak with despair as he slumped in his seat across from them. Maximilian Beecham. Not Max-a-million, that's for sure. His father, "Max" to his friends, had been unable to support his family with his con-man schemes.

Two days later, the fifteen-year-old man-of-the-family packed his few belongings in a cardboard suitcase, left the house in the dead of night and took a train to London. For weeks he had lived in fear: sleeping in Tube stations, begging for money on street-corners, avoiding the toughs who preyed on weaker boys. Finally, he lied about his age and got a job at the Victoria & Albert Museum. One day while he was sweeping floors in the basement he saw a small painting and got an idea.

His father had once helped a man fence a stolen painting, an East German named Kraus, who bragged about stealing art from Jewish families for the Nazis. Kraus had kept one and brought it with him when he immigrated to London. Back then, Pym had been an impressionable ten-year-old. What he remembered: After Max fenced the painting for Kraus and took his cut, they had decent food to eat for almost a month.

The next time he cleaned the basement, he had stolen his first painting, a small portrait. A shady art dealer gave him two hundred quid for it—a dazzling sum in those days—and asked if he could get more. Two weeks later, when no outcry arose over the missing portrait, he stole another. But years of hardship lay ahead.

With an abrupt motion, Pym drained his cognac. Did Charlotte have children? he wondered. Did she have Fanconi Anemia? Boys and girls were equally likely to inherit the disease. If she didn't, would she agree to donate her healthy stem cells to him?

He studied the Vermeer. Woman in Blue Reading a Letter.

Would he live to see his new Vermeers?

Maybe he'd write Charlotte a letter. But what would he say?

Dear Charlotte, this is your long-lost brother, the one who's been sending you money all these years. Now I've got a fatal disease and I need your help. A wee stem cell transplant should do it. How about next week?

Rubbish. He would do no such thing. He would tell Dr. Montgomery he'd been unable to find his relatives.

Let fate decide.

CHAPTER 11

Sunday June 27, 2010 London

At 9:15 AM Frank and Kelly walked into the Jane Austin Tea Room, a small shop with a display counter, four tables and the delicious aroma of fresh-baked pastries. Sonja Wynkoop sat at a window table, an attractive woman in her forties with rosy cheeks and short blonde hair.

As they took the chairs opposite her, she said, "I despise tea, but they make good coffee here, now that I've told them how to do it. So. Would you like a nice big cup of coffee?"

A strong-willed woman, Frank thought, smiling at her. "That would be perfect."

"Three large coffees, please," Sonja called to the woman behind the counter. "Cream and sugar on the side." Then, regarding them with her azure-blue eyes, sharp with intelligence, she smiled. "DCI Stanford has sent me two detectives from America. One is Italian, the other Irish. A good combination."

Kelly laughed. "Actually, I'm the Italian. Frank's half Italian and half Irish. A volatile combination."

Forget nationalities, Frank thought. He had no time for chitchat. Their flight left in three hours and he wanted to talk to Stanford before they went to the airport. "We're anxious to hear your story, Mrs. Wynkoop. Tell us about your husband."

Her smile disappeared, replaced by a grim expression. "They killed him!"

Kelly elbowed him, a sharp rebuke. "His name was Pieter, wasn't it? What was he like?"

Stylishly dressed in a royal-blue skirt and matching blouse, Sonja sank back in her chair, lost in thought. At last, she said, "My Pieter was a good man. Hardworking and honest. Until he got mixed up in this terrible business at the museum."

"The Franz Hals Museum?" Frank said.

"Yes. He was a security guard."

"How long did he work there?"

"Almost ten years. He loved the job. It made him feel important, guarding famous paintings. But these people convinced him to do a bad thing." Sonja heaved a sigh. "At first, I didn't want to believe it, but ..."

The teashop woman arrived with a large tray and set down three large mugs of black coffee, a pewter pitcher of cream and a bowl of sugar. "Would you be wanting a pastry?" she asked.

Still lost in thought, Sonja didn't answer. Frank glanced at Kelly, who shook her head.

"No, thanks," he said. "Just the coffee."

After the woman left, Kelly said in a low voice, "Were there any financial problems, Mrs. Wynkoop? Bills for large expenses, perhaps? For your children?"

"Please, call me Sonja. No, no large expenses. Pieter and I had no children." Her mouth twisted. "You are thinking what I was thinking. Why would Pieter agree to help these robbers steal a painting?"

"Did you notice anything different about his behavior before the robbery?" Frank asked.

Sonja added cream to her coffee and stirred it with a spoon. "Yes. He would go out sometimes at night without telling me where he was going."

"Was that unusual?" Kelly asked.

"Yes. Pieter always told me where he was going. Once a week he would go to a pub with his friends, men he'd known for years. Some of them were on his rugby team. Not a professional team, a local team that played on weekends."

"How long before the robbery was this?" Kelly asked.

"Two weeks before. Maybe three."

"How often?"

"Three or four times." Sonja's rosy cheeks darkened in a flush. "I thought he might be ..."

"You thought he was seeing a woman," Kelly said.

Sonja nodded, her eyes full of anguish. She drew herself up and set her jaw. "But there was no need for him to see another woman," she said, angrily. "We were not having what you call the sex problems. None of that. Never. And so I did something I thought I would never do." She lapsed into silence.

Frank waited. He didn't want to prompt her. Clearly she was reliving events that were upsetting to her.

"One night I followed him."

"Good for you," Kelly said. "That's what I would have done. What happened?"

"He walked to a pub four blocks from our flat. I waited outside for a while before I went in." Sonja pursed her lips. "I am not in the habit of going to bars by myself, not even when I was single. But I had to find out what my Pieter was doing. So I went inside and looked around and saw him sitting in a booth near the back with a man and a woman."

"Did you know them?" Frank asked. "Had you seen them before?"

"Never. But I knew they were Krauts! I know that look. The Krauts killed my grandfather in World War Two. The bastards!"

Amazed, Frank said, "You could tell by looking at them?"

"Of course. The man had that hard Teutonic look, an angular face and thin lips. The woman's face was softer, but she had blonde hair and wore stylish clothes." Sonja waved a hand. "All the German women wear fancy clothes. Expensive."

"What about the man?" Frank asked. "Was his hair blond?"

"No. He had dark hair."

"Could you identify them from a photograph?"

"I'm not sure. The bar was dark and I did not stay long. I sat at the bar and ordered a beer, but I didn't drink it. The thought of my Pieter socializing with Krauts was too upsetting."

"Could you hear what they were saying?" Kelly asked.

"No. They were too far away. So. Ten minutes later, I left. But that was not the end of it!" Her lips tightened. "When Pieter came home I confronted him. I told him I had followed him to the bar."

"What did he say? How did he react?" Kelly asked.

Sonja frowned. "Not the way I expected. He seemed frightened. I asked him why he was out drinking with Krauts. He said he met the man when he was with his friends at a pub. Pieter said the woman was his translator. He said the man didn't speak Dutch. Pieter's English was not good."

"Did he tell you their names?" Frank asked.

"No. And then came that horrible robbery. After the police questioned him Pieter was very upset. So anxious and nervous he couldn't eat. But the next week he seemed better. He took me out for a nice dinner at this expensive restaurant that he knows I like."

With the money the robbers paid him, Frank thought

"He never told you about the robbery?" Kelly asked.

"Never. And then he was dead." Sonja's face worked with emotion. "But that is not the worst part. Now people think I married a drug addict. That's how he died. In a cheap hotel room, foaming at the mouth from a drug overdose. But my Pieter never used drugs, never! Not even for a headache!"

Kelly reached over and touched Sonja's hand. "I'm so sorry for all the troubles you've had, Sonja. We want to find the robbers. If we catch the people you saw with Pieter, maybe we can clear Pieter's name."

"I have something that may help you." Sonja opened her purse and took out a card, slightly larger than an American business card. "After the funeral, I was cleaning out Pieter's things, going through his clothes. I found this in the pocket of one of his shirts." She set the card on the table. "There is not much on it. Only a name: G. Kraus. And a phone number. But when I called this number, it was disconnected."

"May we have the card?" Frank asked. "I'm sure DCI Stanford will want to investigate this."

"Of course," Sonja said, "if it will clear my Pieter's name. But nothing will bring him back to me."

———

They took a taxi to DCI Stanford's office. Kelly didn't object. Like Frank, she was eager to tell Stanford what Sonja had said. Frank wanted to ask him about the name on the card. G. Kraus. Whose phone number had been disconnected.

When they told Stanford about Sonja's surveillance operation, Stanford said, "Doesn't surprise me a bit. The woman's relentless when she wants something."

Frank showed him the card Sonja had given them. "She found this in Pieter's shirt pocket after he died. Does the name G. Kraus mean anything to you?"

Stanford sat bolt upright in his chair. "Gregor Kraus. Must be!"

"You know him?" Frank said. His heart thrummed his chest. Now they were getting somewhere.

"Never met the bloke. Good thing, probably. Gregor's well known to the London coppers. Back in the '80s, his father, Ernst Kraus, worked for a London gang. I forget which one. Plenty of gangs in London. Ernst was an enforcer, vicious and brutal, passed his predilections on to his son. A rival gang killed Ernst in 1984. Gregor was only twelve but he was already working for the same gang as his father."

"Where is he now?" Frank asked.

"Hold on, let me call my colleague in the Gang Unit." Stanford picked up the phone and dialed a number. "He's been with the Gang Unit forever. He'll know."

Frank saw Kelly check her watch, already worried about getting to the airport.

"Hallo," Stanford said. "Len Stanford here. I need some information on Gregor Kraus. What's the bloke up to now?" He listened for a while, jotting notes on a yellow pad. "Burn scars on both hands? Right. So he's out of prison?" And after a moment, "Keeping his nose clean? Right. Thanks."

Stanford cradled the phone and said, "Okay. My colleague says Gregor was an enforcer for the Dorchester Gang during the '90s. Killed a few people and did serious damage to some others, but the cops couldn't nail him for it." Stanford smiled tightly. "Nobody was willing to testify against him."

"Sounds familiar," Frank said.

"But they nailed him for running a protection racket in 1994. Gregor was twenty-four at the time. He spent eight years in prison, got out in 2002." Stanford grimaced. "Time off for good behavior, the usual rubbish. Some British philanthropist offered him a job."

"Why?" Frank asked. "Who was he?"

Stanford checked his notes. "Jonathan Pym, a wealthy businessman. Owns an import-export business."

"Import-export," Frank said. "Sounds like a front. Who's this guy Pym?"

"Hold on." Stanford did a search on his computer. Two minutes later, he said, "Okay, this should do it. Jonathan Pym owns Global Imports and Exports. Offices in the UK and Europe. Hold on. They opened another office in Boston in January. Global Interpreting."

"Interpreting?" Frank said. "Sonja said the woman with Gregor Kraus was his interpreter."

Stanford frowned. "Here's another red flag. Pym's quite the philanthropist. He's on the board of trustees of the Victoria & Albert Museum here in London."

"Bingo!" Frank said. "Gregor Kraus works for a rich businessman who's on the board of a London art museum? That's too big of a coincidence for me. What does Gregor do for Pym?"

"No way to tell." Stanford arched an eyebrow. "I could have Pym come in for informal chat."

"No," he said. "Don't do that. It's too soon."

"Frank," Kelly said, pointing at the clock. "We need to check out of the hotel and go to the airport."

"Right. In a minute. Whereabouts in Boston is this Global Interpreting?"

Stanford checked his computer. "At the Copley Place Mall, corner of Boylston and Huntington."

"I know the area. Len, we need to get to the airport. But I'm going to stop over in Boston and check out Global Interpreting."

Kelly turned to him, frowning. "You are?"

"Yes. I'll change my ticket when we get to Logan. You can fly on to New Orleans."

"Vobitch isn't going to like it," Kelly said.

"He'll like it if we catch Natalie Brixton." To Stanford he said, "Did you check to see if she entered the UK two years ago?"

"Put in a query," Stanford said. "Nothing yet."

"Okay. Let's keep in touch. Anything else you can tell me about Jonathan Pym and Gregor Kraus would be a plus. After I check out Global Interpreting, I'll call you." A sudden realization hit him. "You know, there are a lot of art museums in Boston."

Stanford nodded, grim-faced. "Indeed there are. Including the Isabella Steward Gardner Museum."

CHAPTER 12

Monday June 28, 2010 Boston

At noon precisely, she took her position outside the Boylston Street entrance of the Boston Public Library. Not where she wanted to be. A horrible sense of deja vu crushed her. A few blocks to her left was the Prudential Center where she and Oliver had eaten dinner the night they met. Before her dreams of a romance were destroyed by his insatiable need to know more about Natalie Brixton.

A honking horn drew her attention to the street. Not Gregor's Saab, a taxi jockeying for position amidst four lanes of one-way traffic headed for Copley Square. Moments later, Gregor's olive-green Saab pulled to the curb in front of her. She got in and shut the door.

"A good day for a reconnaissance," Gregor said without looking at her. "Cloudy, but no rain."

Excellent. They must be going to the Gardner. Maybe he'd tell her more about the heist and when it would be. And she wanted to attach the bug to his bumper. The tracking device was in her purse.

He turned right at Copley Square, caught a green light at the next intersection and turned right onto Huntington Avenue. She closed her eyes, unwilling to look at Copley Place and the Marriott Hotel.

More memories of Oliver, something she didn't need cluttering her mind right now.

As they passed Symphony Hall Gregor said, "Why do you wear that silly hat? Are you a Red Sox fan?"

"No, but lots of people wear them in Boston."

He grunted but said nothing. Now both sides of the street were lined with Northeastern University dormitories and classrooms, separated by the Green Line tracks in the middle. They stopped at a red light beside the Northeastern University Student Center.

"Did you buy your Northeastern T-shirt there?" Gregor said.

"Yes. And the Red Sox cap."

"Good idea. The T-shirt lets you blend in with the students." He looked over at her. "Lots of foreign students in Boston. What are you, anyway? Japanese? Chinese?"

"None of your business, Gregor."

"No names! I told you before."

Deliberately using his name again, she said, "Gregor, we're not in public. I'm stuck with you inside your car. What does it matter?"

His jaw clenched and he stared at the red light, like an angry bull enraged by a matador's cape.

The light changed and he turned right onto Ruggles Street. At the next intersection, he turned left onto the Fenway, joining the flow of cars and bicyclists. The Gardner was two blocks away, and groups of pedestrians walked along the sidewalk toward the museum. "Can we stop and walk from here?"

"No. I do not want my car to be seen here. I will circle the museum once and tell you what to expect the night of the heist." He turned left onto Evans Way, a one-way street alongside the museum. "A squad car with a police officer will be parked on this street."

"How do I—"

"Quiet! Do not talk. Listen!"

She clamped her lips together. Gregor, the control freak, turned right at the next corner, drove past the rear of the museum and turned right onto Palace Road, another one-way street.

"A police car will also be parked at the far end of this street."

"How do I prevent the cops from seeing me?"

"My plan for this is not yet in place. When it is, I will tell you." Halfway down Palace Road, he pointed at the Museum. "That is the employee entrance. The guard will let you in."

"What's his name?"

"Nicholas."

"What's his last name?"

"You do not need to know that."

"Gregor, I told Jonathan before I left London and now I'm telling you. I will not kill anyone on this job. So don't call me on your cellphone and order me to shoot him because I won't."

"Nicholas will take care of the other two guards. You disable Nicholas and tie him up to make it look like he was not involved. Our usual plan."

"Our usual plan didn't work very well the last time."

Gregor gripped her left wrist in his scarred fist, a vise-like grip that sent pain up her forearm. "Shut your mouth and listen! Why do you act like an ignorant schoolgirl? After you take the Vermeers from the Special Exhibit, you walk out the employee entrance and I pick you up. Not in this car. A different one."

She jerked her arm away and massaged her wrist.

"Tell me you understand, Valerie, and this time do not insult me with one of your feeble attempts at German. Tell me in English. Do you understand?"

Shaken by his vehemence, she said, "I understand." Gregor had a long memory and thin skin about his ancestry apparently.

"Good. I will drive you to your apartment now."

He drove past the front of the Gardner Museum, continued to Huntington Avenue and turned right, merging into two lanes of traffic.

She sat there, cursing his control-freak behavior, disappointed that she hadn't been able to plant the bug on his car. But her dominant emotion was fear. Everything about this heist scared her. Too many factors were beyond her control. Gregor. Nicolas, the insider guard. Extra guards inside the museum, police patrols outside.

Maybe she wouldn't do it. Maybe she'd get on a plane and disappear forever. But she couldn't do that with her current passport. Gregor would hunt her down like a dog. And she couldn't stay in this country. The police were looking for her.

Gregor stopped in front of her apartment, a three-story tenement with ugly brown shingles. "Thursday night there will be a party at the museum. A private showing of the Special Exhibit for wealthy donors and other important people, political figures and so forth. I have two tickets. We will go together."

She tried to decide if this was a good or a bad thing. She didn't want to spend any more time with Gregor than she had to, but attending a party at the Gardner might be helpful. She could scope out the layout before the heist.

"Nicholas will be on duty. So you will see him and he will see you. For this important event, you need a fancy dress. I will buy you a new one, something elegant, to go with my tuxedo. Meet me Wednesday morning at ten outside your favorite T-stop near Symphony Hall." His eyes roved over her body. "Wear something nice, not a T-shirt. And no baseball cap. I don't want the sales clerk to think my girlfriend is an inexperienced college girl." He smiled. "We both know you are not inexperienced, right, Valerie?"

A haze of anger clouded her vision. She wanted to kick him in the balls and watch him writhe in pain. But that would be foolhardy. Gregor had a violent temper, and no compunctions about killing people. She gritted her teeth and said nothing.

"See you Wednesday," Gregor said. "Ten o'clock."

Fuming over his insult, she got out and slammed the door and walked away.

———

Jamilla shifted her position on the park bench. The wooden slats were killing her butt. She looked at Jaylen, playing on the swings, then at the sun, trying to figure how long she'd been waiting. At least a half hour, so it had to be after noon.

She wished she still had her watch, but she'd hocked it last month when money was tight.

Where was Nicholas? The son-of-a-bitch scared her. The mirrored sunglasses were bad enough, but when he took them off it was worse. She'd seen eyes like that before. Killer eyes.

Her scalp felt like bugs were crawling over it. No crank this week. She'd put the hundred bucks away so she couldn't get at it in a moment of weakness. Soon as she got the rest she'd split this dirt-bag town with Jaylen and start a new life. She vaguely remembered the farmhouse in Georgia where she'd lived with her mother. Maybe that's where she'd go. When she was three they moved to Boston so she didn't remember much, but it had to beat her roach-and-rat infested apartment.

She took out a stick of gum, put it back when she saw Nicholas enter the park. She tried to stay calm, but as she watched him stride across the weedy grass, her guts turned to liquid.

He planted himself on the bench beside her. He had on a windbreaker and jeans, same as yesterday. No sunglasses today, dark eyes fixed on hers. Terrifying eyes. "Are the bangers set?"

"They're set." she said, hugging her arms to her chest.

"How many?"

"Six. Like you said."

"Okay. You only talked to the leader, right?"

"Yeah." She knew the punks Zipper would use, but she wasn't about to give up their names to this creep. She swallowed hard. "He wants to know when."

"I told you. On a weekend."

"Okay, but if it's this week—"

"Not this weekend. I will let you know." He dangled a hundred-dollar bill in front of her, but when she reached for it, he jerked it away. "You still have your uniform, right?"

She wanted to scratch his eyes out, stuck her hands in her pockets so she wouldn't. "Yeah. So what?"

"You'll need it for another job that night. I need you to take out a couple of cops."

"Are you crazy?" Her voice rising in a banshee wail.

"Quiet! You want your kid to come over and hear this?"

She looked over at the swings. Jaylen was still playing with his friend. While his mother made deals with a gangster. She tried to look the bastard in the eye. Couldn't.

"Why don't you tell me what's going on?" she mumbled.

He gave her the hundred-dollar bill. "It's dark. You're in your uniform, the cop's in a cruiser. You zap him with a stun gun, drug him and he passes out."

She stared at him, incredulous. "Are you crazy? I can't do that!"

"Hssss! Shut up and listen! You do the first one, walk around the building to the cop in the second cruiser and do the same thing."

"Walk around what building?"

"Never mind. When the time comes I will tell you."

Her heart hammered her chest. Just thinking about it made her break out in sweat. "No way."

"Why not? You need money. You hate cops."

"Who told you that?" Only cops she hated were the big-shots that shit-canned her.

"Never mind. Will you do it?"

She thought about the farmhouse in Georgia. "How much? You said five hundred, but this deal with the cops? That's dangerous."

"Stop complaining. Seven-fifty for the whole deal. Set up the ruckus and put the two cops to sleep."

"Seven-fifty is shit money, do something like that. What if the cops see my face? They'll identify me later. Jesus, I'll go to jail!"

"They will remember nothing. I guarantee it."

"Seven-fifty isn't enough, I gotta do something like that."

"It's more money than you've seen in a while, isn't it? Think about your boy. He needs clothes and some decent shoes. You should buy him some toys."

A cloud of guilt descended on her like a woolen blanket. Jaylen never complained, but sometimes his eyes got a certain look when he saw the other kids with their toys. She scratched her scalp. "Two thousand."

"Fifteen hundred." He dangled another hundred.

She snatched the bill. "Okay. Fifteen hundred."

"Tell no one about this." He aimed a finger at Jaylen and cocked it like a gun. "I'd hate to see anything happen to your boy."

Fear sucked the air from her lungs. The prick-bastard would kill Jaylen in a New York minute, wouldn't even blink. She nodded.

"Good. Next week you get another hundred."

"When next week?"

"I will call and let you know."

—————

Frank sipped his coffee and leaned back in his chair. It felt like old times, sitting in Lt. Colonel Harrison Flynn's office, hashing over a case with his boss. Hank looked older than the last time he'd seen him two years ago, seemed like he'd lost weight and his skin looked sallow. But his Irish-blue eyes were the same, had lit up like high-beam headlights when he told him what he'd learned in London.

"Sounds like you're onto something," Flynn said.

"Yeah, but I still don't know where she is."

Flynn smiled. "I might have a lead on her."

He sat bolt upright in his chair. "Tell me."

"I only heard about it this morning or I'd have told you before. A State cop patrolling Logan Airport thinks he spotted her."

"Jesus! Here? In Boston?"

"Yes. Last Wednesday, the twenty-third of June. He saw her leaving the international terminal. Unfortunately, he couldn't follow up on it. Big accident in the roadway. By the time he handled that she was gone."

Frank could hardly believe it, his heart doing cartwheels in his chest. "She's here to do an art heist! Can you check the international arrivals ninety minutes prior to when he saw her?"

"I can, but what if she's using a different name?"

"Tell them to check female passengers traveling alone. If it's her, we're in trouble. There are dozens of art museums in the Boston area."

"True," Flynn said, "and a big show is set to open at the Gardner Museum this weekend. The trustees want to raise money to increase the reward for the paintings that were stolen in 1990. Currently, the reward is five million. They're looking to double it. To pack in the art lovers, they arranged to have several famous museums, mostly from Europe, lend them a dozen paintings."

Recalling Kelly's tutorial in art history, Frank said, "Old Masters?"

Flynn shrugged. "I'm not up on art terminology, but they're famous paintings worth big bucks. Two of them are Vermeers, one from the Louvre, another from the Rijksmuseum in Amsterdam."

"Last time the guards let the robbers in. What's the security setup?"

"Heavy. In 1990 there were two overnight guards. For this exhibit, three guards will be on duty overnight and two police cruisers will be parked outside the museum 24-7. The head guard has to call in a fail-safe code every hour on the hour. Same with the cops in the cruisers."

Frank scratched his jaw, his thoughts racing. Kelly had boarded her return flight to New Orleans this morning. He'd changed his ticket, figuring he'd talk to Hank and fly back tomorrow. But Hank's information changed everything. No way was he going back to New Orleans if Natalie was in Boston.

Flynn yawned and massaged his eyes. "You really think she's here to steal art from the Gardner?"

"Since she escaped in 2008, there have been four art heists in the UK, most of them near London. I think she's working with a gang of art thieves. If that State Trooper saw her, I guarantee she's not here on vacation. She's here to steal art, and the show at Gardner would be a great target."

"I'll notify the Special Operations Unit," Flynn said. "Maybe they can add some extra patrols."

"What about the guards? Who vetted them?"

"The Gardner Museum officials, I presume. Why?"

"My London contact is pretty sure insider guards were involved in some of the heists over there. Not all of them, but several."

Flynn jotted notes on his notepad and smiled at him. "Guess you're not flying back to New Orleans tomorrow, huh?"

"Good guess. I'm staying at a low budget motel in Revere." Frank checked his watch. "Right about now Kelly O'Neil is probably telling my boss why I'm not there. He's a good guy, used to be with NYPD, but he's not going to be happy about it."

CHAPTER 13

Tuesday June 29, 2010 10:12 AM Boston

Natalie took the stairs to the sixth floor and eased into the garage. Five minutes ago when she walked past the Global Interpreting office, the lights were on and she chanced a quick peek inside. An attractive blond woman had been seated at the desk. No sign of Gregor, but he might be in another room. She hoped.

Now that it was a workday the garage was full. She walked down the wall to the right of the stairs. And there it was! The olive-green Saab. She took the tracking device out of her purse, but then she heard a car coming up the ramp. She ducked into the stairwell and stifled a yawn.

Last night Pym had called her after midnight. Ten past six in the morning in London. He probably did it on purpose, hoping to wake her up. He hadn't. She'd been lying awake in bed, fretting about the heist. Without any pleasantries—no hello and how are you—Pym had asked how the plans were going. When she said Gregor wanted her to go to a party at the Gardner, Pym said, "I know. I got him the tickets. I want you to make sure you know where the Vermeers are."

That was all he cared about, his precious Vermeers. How much he was getting for them, she wondered.

"Everything else okay?" Pym had asked.

"Gregor didn't tell me much about the job." Hoping Pym would tell her when it would be.

"I'm sure he will when the time comes. I'll call you again after the party," Pym had said and hung up.

She peered through the window in the stairwell door and saw a woman with a briefcase walk to the elevator. As soon as the woman got in the elevator, she went back in the garage and trotted to Gregor's car.

It was parked in the number 306 space, nose out. Holding the tracking device in her hand, she squatted beside the rear bumper on the passenger side, placed the device inside the bumper and heard a faint click. Mission accomplished. Whenever the Saab moved, she would get a text on her iPhone. She couldn't follow Gregor, but at least she'd know where he was, and if she ever needed a car, she could rent one.

She rose to her feet and returned to the stairwell. First she would go downstairs and locate the exit where the cars left the garage. Then she'd go back to the fifth floor and scope out Global Interpreting.

———

Marta Ludwig hung up the phone, sank back in her chair and rubbed her arms. After talking to the Swedish car mogul she felt like taking a shower. Sven was a pig. The other two girls refused to work with him. Maybe she'd ask Gregor to scold him. But she knew he wouldn't.

This morning he'd barely spoken to her. After she opened the office at nine-thirty, he had come down the hall from his office and said he was going out for breakfast. He seemed distracted these days, irritable to the point of hostility. She couldn't figure out why. She had to handle all the problems. Maybe it was a mid-life crisis. Or a new mistress.

She took a mirror out of her purse and examined her face. Smooth skin, no lines around her eyes. Not bad for thirty-nine. She still attracted younger men, but most of them were uncultured idiots and useless in bed. It had been four years since she'd slept with Gregor, but she still hoped to rekindle their relationship. She would never forget the exquisite delights of his tongue. The memory made her crotch wet.

The office door opened, interrupting her sexual fantasy. A dark-haired man with a rugged build approached her desk. His sports jacket was off-the-rack, but his shoulders filled it well. He had an angular face, high cheekbones, and deep-set dark eyes with a hard look about them.

Cop, she thought. She held his gaze without speaking.

The man smiled, but his eyes were cold. "Good morning. I need a translator and a friend of mine recommended Global Interpreting."

"One of our clients?"

"A friend of a client. I need someone who speaks Dutch."

She mentally cataloged their Dutch clients. Two, but both spoke English. This man had glossy black hair and olive skin. He didn't look Dutch and his story sounded phony.

"What sort of services do you require, Mister ... ?"

He stood there, silent and still, studying her like one of those lions on a National Geographic TV show before it attacked an antelope.

"Capone," he said. "John Capone. I've got some Dutch documents that need translating."

"We don't do written translations. And we don't have any Dutch interpreters."

"What about Stefan Haas? He's Dutch, isn't he?"

Her heart thudded. Why was he asking all these questions? "Mr. Haas isn't an interpreter, he's the manager. I'm afraid I can't help you, so if you'll excuse me, I need to make some calls."

Right on cue, the phone rang. Merde! If it was a client, things could get sticky. She let it ring, hoping the man who called himself John Capone would leave. He didn't. She gritted her teeth and took the call.

"Global Interpreting. May I help you?"

"Hallo there, Marta, how're you keeping?"

She recognized the voice, one of their best clients, a British banker. "What can I do for you, Evan?"

"If I could get you to do me, I'd be in heaven. S'pose that's not possible, eh?"

"No, but tell me what you need and I'll arrange it." She looked up. The man she believed was a cop smiled at her. The arrogant bastard. She finished the transaction with the Brit and hung up.

Capone planted his hands on the desk and leaned forward, his dark eyes locked on hers. "I need a German interpreter, too. Can you give me some names?"

To avoid his relentless gaze, she studied the zigzag scar on his chin, stark white against the dark stubble on his jaw. She gave him a faux smile. "We never give out names of our employees. For their safety. I'm sure you understand."

"For their safety. Sure." He circled the office, checking out the black leather sofa and the tubular steel end tables, and returned to her desk. "I'd like to speak to Mr. Haas."

"He's not here."

"When will he be in? I'll come back." Putting an edge on his voice.

"I'm not sure. I'll have him call you." *When hell freezes over.*

Conscious of her racing heart, she opened a folder and leafed through some papers.

"Don't you want my number?"

She glared at him and picked up a pen. He rattled off a number and she wrote it down.

"Thanks. Have a nice day, Marta."

She watched him leave, her armpits damp with sweat. How did he know her name? There was no name plaque on her desk. Damn! The first few months had been lucrative, but after Memorial Day all hell had broken loose. The obnoxious Swede. Ursula quitting unexpectedly. Gregor's fits of temper. Now this. She didn't know what the man was up to, but it didn't involve translations. She was certain he was a cop.

And Gregor was no help.

Sometimes he wouldn't even answer her phone calls.

The phone rang. Merde! She hated this job. She pasted on a smile and picked up. "Global Interpreting. May I help you?"

———

Natalie studied the exit for the parking garage. No payment booth and no security. The people who rented parking spaces probably had a device to get them into the garage, but if she rented a car to follow Gregor, she wouldn't. She would have to find a place to park, someplace with a view of the exit.

Across the street a narrow alley faced the exit. She could park there, but it would be tight. She might have to park on the street. The exit road forced the cars to turn right. She walked down the roadway and scanned the street. All the metered parking spaces were full.

Damn. Parking was always a problem in Boston.

She circled the building and entered Copley Place via the waterfall entrance. An escalator took her to the second floor, a large air-conditioned space with leafy green plants and plump chairs grouped around a grand piano. She found an elevator and hit the call button. Time to check out Global Interpreting.

When the doors opened four women in business attire got off. She stepped inside, punched the button for the fifth floor and studied her student disguise in the polished-brass doors. Her Northeastern T-shirt and the Red Sox baseball cap. Gregor didn't like it, but she did. It made her look younger. Harmless. See? I'm no murderer.

When the door opened, she stepped out and turned right toward Global Interpreting. Her heart almost stopped.

Unable to believe her eyes, she gasped.

Frank Renzi was walking toward her.

Panic-stricken, she went to the nearest door, opened it and plunged into an office, heart pounding, hands sweaty. Did he see her? She had on her student disguise, but still.

Her breath came in shallow gasps and she felt lightheaded. She couldn't think, couldn't breathe.

"May I help you with something?"

Startled, she realized the woman behind the counter was looking at her. Then she noticed the posters of Rome, Paris, Tokyo and other famous destinations. This was a travel agency.

"Are you all right?" the woman asked, frowning, clearly concerned.

"I'm sorry. I just got some bad news ..." She trailed off helplessly, afraid to turn around. Afraid she would encounter the relentless eyes of NOPD Homicide Detective Frank Renzi.

"I'll get you some water." The travel agent, an older woman in a stylish mauve dress, went to a water cooler, dispensed water into a paper cup and brought it to the counter.

"Thank you," she said, gratefully. Anything to make it appear that she was just an ordinary person in a travel agency office, not the woman Frank Renzi wanted to arrest for killing four people.

She drank the water and set the cup on the counter. "Thank you," she said again. "That helped a lot. I may have to fly to Rome to meet my brother. He's there with my mother and she's very ill."

"I'm sorry to hear that. Would you like me to check the flights?"

"Yes, please, the least expensive one, if possible. I'm a student and I don't have much money."

"Of course. I understand." The woman smiled. "Let me see what I can do for the Red Sox fan." She went to desk with a computer and began tapping keys on the keyboard.

Steeling herself, Natalie turned and risked a glance at the hallway outside the office door.

No one was there.

————

When Frank got downstairs, Rafe Hawkins was waiting for him.

"Let's take a walk," Frank said, and they went outside.

The clamor of traffic assaulted them. A UPS truck roared by, then a yellow taxi, blasting its horn. Frank mopped his brow. Even now the heat was oppressive. Ten-thirty in the morning and it had to be in the eighties, the sun beating down on Copley Square.

Hoping to escape the traffic noise, he pointed at the small park between Trinity Church and the Boston Public Library. While they waited for a Walk light, Frank said, "How's the team doing?"

Rafe worked the Gang Unit for Boston PD. They'd been friends for years, a relationship that had begun when they played on the District-Four basketball team. "District-One team's got a new center," Rafe said. "Bigger than Shaq."

"Can he play?"

Rafe grinned, his white teeth a stark contrast to his ebony skin. "Takes up space in the lane, but he's got no footwork. I back him up, do my fancy moves, put the ball in the hoop. How'd it go with Marta?"

They caught the walk light and hustled across the street to the park.

"Man," Rafe huffed, "you training for the Olympics?"

"What's the matter? Can't keep up?"

"That'll be the day. Come on. Stop holding out on me. Did Marta fall at your feet in a swoon?"

Yesterday afternoon over a beer, Frank had told Rafe why he was here: his suspicions about Natalie, Gregor Kraus and his employer, Jonathan Pym, the British philanthropist who'd recently opened a new office in Boston. Global Interpreting.

"More like Frosty the Snowqueen," Frank said.

To conceal his identity, he'd given her the fake name he'd used when he worked undercover for Boston PD. He'd flash his NOPD badge later if he had to. "She stonewalled me, but sometimes the information you don't get is just as useful. When I asked for a Dutch translator, she said they didn't have one. I got the feeling she's hiding something. This morning I checked the Yellow Pages. No ad for Global Interpreting, and the office is worse than a hospital waiting room, no magazines, no water cooler, no slick brochures. Marta says they don't do written translations, just one-on-one interpreting. When I asked for names, she blew me off. She's not interested in drumming up business. Not from me, anyway."

A curvy redhead in a blue spandex running suit approached them, jogging past a flowerbed ablaze with orange and yellow marigolds. Rafe beamed her a smile. She smiled back but kept jogging. When Rafe turned to watch, Frank said, "Hey, you've already got a wife."

Rafe shrugged. "Nice scenery. No harm in looking. Did you find out anything about Gregor Kraus?"

"No. Stefan Haas is the manager, allegedly. When I asked to speak to him Marta seemed shocked. She said he wasn't there. I told her to have him call me, but I'm not holding my breath."

He figured Stefan Haas might actually be Gregor Kraus. After all, he'd used a fake name, nothing to stop Kraus from doing the same thing. He was determined to track him down. He wanted to help DCI Stanford solve the London art heists, but he also wanted to help Sonja Wynkoop. She was desperate to clear her husband's name.

He knew the feeling. He was desperate to find Natalie.

Pieter Wynkoop had died from a drug overdose, but Sonja believed he was murdered. At this point, Frank agreed, and Gregor Kraus was his prime suspect. For all he knew, Marta was the blonde Sonja had seen in the bar with her husband. No one could exonerate Pieter for helping them steal the painting, but if Frank could prove Kraus killed him, Sonja could at least have the satisfaction of telling her friends and family that her husband wasn't a drug addict. But that wasn't the most important point If Kraus was in on the European art heists and he was in Boston, it would reinforce his theory. Natalie Brixton was here to steal a painting.

"Might have an interesting tidbit for you," Rafe said.

Surprised, he said, "Yeah? Lay it on me."

"After we talked yesterday I went back to the station, did my due diligence," Rafe said. "Global Interpreting opened in February, figured I'd check the files, see what turned up. Two months ago a German exchange student disappeared, Ursula Schmidt, blue-eyed blond, age twenty-two, and …." With a triumphant smile, Rafe said, "Employed by Global Interpreting. Her girlfriend told the lead detective Ursula spoke fluent French and English in addition to German."

"The body count is rising," Frank muttered. And his sense of urgency was off the chart. An art heist was about to go down in Boston. He'd bet on it. But he didn't know where or when.

"What's the girlfriend's name and address? I want to talk to her."

CHAPTER 14

Gregor drove through an adult entertainment district on the south side of Providence. The main attraction was a windowless two-story building with a bubblegum-pink exterior. Bold black letters on the front said: CHEETAHS-GIRLS-GIRLS-GIRLS. The entrance was on a side street, sheltered by a mauve canvas awning flanked by two large signs: LADY GODIVA NUDE LOUNGE and CHEETAHS-TOPLESS-DANCING.

He parked in the lot beside the entrance and opened the car window. Whenever the door opened bump-and-grind music boomed into the sultry night air. Five minutes passed. He took out a Gitaines, then put it back. His daily limit was ten and he'd already smoked eight, but Kwan was testing his patience. The punk was late, and not for the first time.

Kwan was unpredictable, but essential to his plan. Six months ago the Gardner Museum had hired a new security guard. Nicholas Kwan, known to his employers as Daniel Leone.

A black Lexus roared into the parking lot, tires screeching. When Kwan got out, Gregor walked over to him. "You're late," he said.

"One night off and I have to drive to Rhode Island. Why do we have to meet here?"

Kwan's usual tactic: attack to deflect criticism. "I don't want anyone to see us together in Boston. Someone might recognize me."

"Why?" Kwan sneered. "Are you a celebrity?"

Gregor swallowed his anger. The punk would pay for his insolence soon enough.

Inside the club the music was unbearably loud. No overheard conversations here, just a roomful of lonely men with greedy eyes, sucking up draft beer. The air was pungent with cigarette smoke, and strobe lights raked the room, flashing on men seated elbow-to-elbow at the bar and at tables below two raised platforms.

Gregor recognized one of the dancers, Go-Go-Flo. A leggy platinum blonde with breasts like soccer balls, prancing around in red sandals with five-inch heels. Brass rings pierced her nipples. The red-white-and-blue tassels attached to them twirled crazily as she gyrated around a brass pole. When Gregor claimed a vacant table, Flo waved to him, whipping her breasts in circles.

A waitress in shorts and a halter top took their order, Glenlivet on the rocks for Gregor, Sprite for Kwan. Kwan drank no alcohol, nor did he smoke or use drugs. Kwan despised drug addicts. Flo gyrated her sweat-slicked body in an orgiastic frenzy, but Kwan didn't look up. The first time they'd met here he had wondered if Kwan was gay, but quickly discarded the notion. Kwan wasn't interested in sex, only killing, the bloodier the better. Nicholas Kwan killed for sport.

Gazing at him with the eyes of a cobra, Kwan said: "I hired someone to cause the diversion. A woman. She used to be a cop."

"Used to be. What happened? Did she get fired?"

"No. She quit."

"Why?"

Kwan guzzled some Sprite. "She is black and she is a woman. She couldn't hack it."

"Where did you find her?"

"In a Chinese restaurant near Boston Medical Center. Larry's."

He stiffened. The restaurant where he had met Valerie.

"Her name is Jamilla Wells. Like I said, she's an ex-cop, which solves two problems. She lines up the gangbangers to create the diversion and she takes out the cops in the cruisers. If she wears her uniform, they will accept her as one of their own. They will never suspect a woman."

Not a bad idea, Gregor had to admit. "She agreed to it?"

"Of course. She needs money. She has a—" Kwan scratched his beard and bared his teeth in a smile. "Don't worry, she'll kill the two cops, no problem."

"We are not going to kill the cops, Nicolas. Did you not learn anything in San Francisco? Killing cops is a mistake, and we can't afford mistakes. I told you before. She zaps them with a stun gun and knocks them out for a while with a drug."

"How do you know this drug will put them out?"

"Stop questioning me!" He forced himself to be calm. Always be in control. He set his scarred hands on the table and felt a measure of satisfaction when Kwan stared at them. "This drug will do the job."

Kwan rattled the ice in his glass. "I need more money. I gave the woman four-fifty to line up the six gangbangers. They want seventy-five apiece to get the riot going."

"Screw the gangbangers. After she knocks out the cops, kill her." He took out a Gitanes and lighted it. The woman wasn't the problem, Kwan was. He was an animal. Vicious. Bloodthirsty. That's why he'd hired him, of course. Controlling him was another matter.

The bump-and-grind music ended, eliciting whistles and catcalls as the strippers circled the platforms collecting their tips. Flo looked over, but Gregor waved her off.

"The cops outside the museum call in every hour on the hour so you don't have much time."

"How do you know this?"

"I *know,* because I have spent months planning this job."

Sullen-eyed, Kwan fingering his thick dark beard.

"I will have two-way radios for you and the woman. Have her call you after she knocks out the second cop. Then you disable the alarm and the video cameras. You know how to do that, right?"

"Yesss." An angry hiss.

"Use a garrote to take out the other two guards."

Something flickered in Kwan's eyes. "A knife is better."

"No. Think, Nicholas. After the heist, three guards go missing. They're all suspects. If the cops find blood from the other two and none of yours ..." He let the words hang in the air.

"What about my ID? Sooner or later they'll find out it's fake."

"You shave your beard, we take a photo and I get you a new passport. Once we get the ransom, you hop a plane and split." He leaned back in his chair. "Where are you going? Got any plans?"

"I'm not sure yet," Kwan said, expressionless. "Why?"

"Just curious." He sipped his scotch. "I need you to steal a van to transport the paintings. Have the woman drive it into the courtyard. Kill her and dump her in the rear compartment."

"What if the cops in the cruisers wake up? I still think it's better to kill—"

He slammed his palm on the table. "No!" A heavyset older man at the next table looked over. Gregor lowered his voice. "The other security guards and the woman know you. The cops in the cruisers won't. Killing cops would only bring extra heat."

Kwan's eyes went flat and a muscle jumped in his jaw. Hiring Kwan might have been a mistake, the one flaw in an otherwise perfect plan.

The bump-and-grind music started again, and Go-Go-Flo shimmied around the platform, stroking her breasts. She paused beside their table, pursed her glossy red lips and said, "Want a lap dance, hon?"

"Not tonight, Flo. Maybe next time." He slipped a twenty into her G-string, and she flounced away, twirling her red-white-and-blue tassels.

"After Scorpio puts the Vermeers in the van, kill her." Scorpio was Valerie's code name. Kwan didn't know his real name either. Kwan thought he was Stefan Haas.

"You didn't tell me I had to kill four people. I want more money."

Gregor stared at him, incredulous. "I have to talk you out of killing two cops, and you complain about offing the women?"

"I deserve a bigger share," Kwan said. "I'm taking all the risks."

Rage clogged his throat. Fighting for control, he waited until he was able to say, "I take plenty of risks. You forget something, Nicholas. I hired you. You work for me. After Scorpio delivers the Vermeers, kill her and dump her body in the van with the ex-cop. Then you put the other two paintings in the van."

"What happens after I split with the paintings?"

"I meet you with a getaway car and we swap."

"What about the bodies?"

"That's my problem."

"Hssss! Stefan, you keep me in the dark about everything!"

"You do your job, I do mine. I lined up a hideout. You go there and you wait."

"Where is this hideout?"

"I will tell you the night of the heist—"

"Bullshit! Tell me now!"

"Keep your voice down," Gregor snapped. "Stop arguing."

"Get somebody else to do your shit work!" Kwan jumped up and stalked away.

He sat there, stunned. After all his preparations—months of work!—Kwan was backing out on him. Consumed with rage, he rushed to the exit. Hot humid air hit his face as he burst outside and ran to the parking lot. Kwan stood at the door of his Lexus, parked nose to the bubblegum-pink wall. He sprinted to the car, put his hands around Kwan's neck and squeezed.

"You think you can back out on me, you worthless piece of shit?"

Gasping for air, Kwan clawed at his fingers. Gregor shook him like a rat, then released him.

Kwan massaged his throat. "This job sucks. You treat me like a servant and tell me nothing. I'm stuck in a rat-trap apartment with no money—"

"I pay your expenses—"

"Shit money!"

"Really? That's a fancy car you're driving. Where did you get the money for it?"

Kwan clenched his jaw. "You're not the one taking orders from those museum assholes. My boss is already apeshit about security. By the time the show opens on Friday he will be impossible."

"Thursday," Gregor said. "Don't forget the party Thursday night."

"Right. A private show for the big shots." Kwan spat on the pavement and glowered at him, dark eyes glittery with rage.

Gregor leaned closer and said in a quiet voice, "Listen carefully, Nicholas. No more questions. No more arguments. From now on, you will do exactly as I say. If you do not, I will kill you."

Kwan gazed at him, expressionless. "I need more money to make sure the ex-cop cooperates."

"How much?"

Kwan's eyes shifted away. "Nine hundred."

He took out his wallet. The punk was probably lying, but nine hundred was a pittance. Anything to keep him under control.

———

She put her iPhone on the kitchen table, went in the living room and stood at the window, staring at the inky darkness. Her apartment felt like a prison, claustrophobic, the walls closing in on her, dingy wallpaper above dark brown wainscoting in every room, infested with roaches and vermin. But rats and roaches were the least of her problems.

Frank Renzi was in Boston. Not just in Boston, at the Global Interpreting office. No one could connect her to the office, but why was Renzi there this morning? Who was he after? Jonathan Pym? Gregor Kraus? But how would he connect them to Global Interpreting?

Why wouldn't Gregor give her any details about the Gardner heist? When was it? How long would she be able to fend off his sexual advances? All these questions were driving her mad.

She went in the bathroom and studied her face in the medicine cabinet mirror above the rust-stained sink. Her eyes had dark circles under them and her face was gaunt. She wasn't sleeping, and she wasn't eating much, either. Her stomach was too jumpy.

This morning at the travel agency, she hadn't bought a plane ticket to Rome. She didn't have enough cash and she never bought plane tickets with a credit card. Now she wished she had.

After leaving Copley Place, she had walked across the street to Back Bay Station, a massive structure with a T-stop and a terminal for Amtrak trains, crowded with people, but she felt safe in her student disguise, just another anonymous traveler. Thinking she might leave Boston by train, she went to the electronic departure/arrival display. But on the bulletin board beside it, a poster leaped out at her. Bold black letters at the top: **Wanted For Murder**. Below it was a photo from her driver's license. The sight of it had made her physically ill.

She massaged her throbbing temples. The same poster was probably in the bus station. There might not be one at Logan, but the airport had its own State Police Barrack, and it might be on a bulletin board there. State Troopers patrolled the airport and the roadway outside the all departure and arrival terminals.

Stealing two Vermeers from the Gardner entailed huge risks. Now Renzi was in Boston.

A feeling of dread overwhelmed her. She had to get out now.

She returned to the kitchen, punched the phone number of her Swiss bank into the iPhone, and entered a six-digit code to access her account. She checked the balance: $98,600. A paltry sum if she wanted to disappear forever, but she couldn't worry about that now.

A series of keystrokes took her to the withdrawal menu. She entered the amount: $10,000. If she needed more she would make another withdrawal. She finished the transaction by entering the number of the business where the bank could wire the money, a UPS store on Huntington Avenue. That made her feel a better. But if she used her Valerie Brown passport to fly out of Logan, Pym might find out.

She didn't know how often Gregor and Pym communicated, but Gregor was a control freak, and Pym had powerful friends. In addition to Sir Edmund Foxhill, Pym might have other contacts, powerful men with the clout to check flights departing from Logan.

Maybe she should tell Pak Lam that her need for a new passport was urgent. Forget the gender disguise. Any kind of a passport would do.

The most vexing question returned. Why was Renzi in Boston now?

What did he know and how did he know it?

If he knew she was here, she was trapped.

Her stomach revolted. She ran to the bathroom and heaved her guts out in the toilet. When she rose to her feet, her legs were shaking and her mouth tasted vile. She went to the sink and brushed her teeth, wet a facecloth with cold water and pressed it to her face.

She heard her iPhone beep. Gregor was on the move. She ran to the kitchen, snatched the iPhone and retrieved the text, which gave the Saab's location. What was he doing in Providence? Not that she cared.

She was more worried about Renzi, but she couldn't afford to forget about Gregor. She accessed Google Earth, switched to the street view and zoomed in on the location. It appeared to be some kind of bar. No, not a bar, a strip club. Cheetahs.

No surprise there. Gregor was obsessed with sex.

Tomorrow she had go with him to buy a dress for the Thursday night party at the Gardner Museum. Gregor wanted to have sex with her. And Gregor usually got what he wanted.

Another problem with no solution.

CHAPTER 15

Tuesday July 1, 2010 Boston

"You got the feeling Ursula wasn't happy with her job?" Frank said.

Lisa Malone took a dainty sip of her black coffee. "Yes, but she didn't talk about it much."

The morning rush at Starbucks had cleared, and they were perched on stools beside a window overlooking Charles Street at the foot of Beacon Hill. Lisa groomed her auburn hair with long skinny fingers. She had baby-blue eyes, a flawless complexion, and a black halter top and black spandex pants hugged her rail-thin body. Frank wanted to buy her a decent meal, put some meat on her.

"Did she mention any boyfriends?"

"No. She could have had most any guy she wanted, but she was totally focused on her career. She wanted to be an actress. Anytime she wasn't working, she was studying books on acting and movie scripts. She only had a nine-month visa and she didn't want to waste time."

"How'd you meet her?"

Lisa flashed a smile, showing her flawless, pearly-white teeth. "At a Bruce Springsteen concert. He played the FleetCenter in February. Do you like Bruce Springsteen?"

Frank wasn't wild about him, decided it wasn't worth the discussion. "Doesn't everyone? What happened at the concert?"

"I was standing beside Ursula in the ladies room line and we had on the exact same outfit, isn't that weird?" Lisa's baby-blues went wide. "We hit it off right away. She'd only been in Boston a week and didn't know anybody so she came by herself. I made her sit with me and my friends. Later, we went out for a drink and—you'll never believe this!—Ursula's sign is the same as mine. I'm into astrology. Are you?"

Frank grinned. "Only when the newspaper horoscope says I'm gonna make lots of money and meet the love of my life."

It got a laugh out of her. "Right, but newspaper horoscopes are very general. You have to have your chart done by a professional if you want an accurate reading."

He was willing to bet his chart wouldn't help him find Ursula. Or Gregor. Or Natalie.

"What made you think Ursula was unhappy with her job?"

Lisa stared out the window at a mounted policeman clip-clopping down Charles Street, nursing her black coffee as if it were a fine cognac. "She was sort of vague when I asked about it. But every job has its drawbacks. I did a fashion shoot last August during that heat wave? Ninety degrees and I'm out on the beach in a fur coat! People think models have it easy, but it's not as glamorous as it sounds."

Weary of the chitchat, he said, "Lisa, I need help if I'm going to find Ursula. Think carefully. What did she tell you about her job?"

"She said it was boring, translating for French and German businessmen. She spoke French, too, and her English was perfect, hardly any accent at all!"

"Did she mention any client in particular, maybe drop a name?"

"Not really. She said the Frenchmen liked to eat and the Germans liked to drink." Lisa gazed at him over the rim of her coffee cup. "She liked the French guys better because they took her to nice restaurants. She went to dinner with them. For business meetings, I guess."

"Any of them hit on her? You know, give her a hard time?"

"Guys hit on women all the time, unless you're fat and ugly, and Ursula wasn't fat or ugly." She frowned. "But I got the impression something happened at the office that upset her. She said whenever she was in the office the manager would look at her." Lisa grimaced. "You know, the way guys do when they're mentally undressing you."

"When was this?"

"In March. We went shopping at Copley Place. Ursula wanted to buy her parents a gift for their wedding anniversary. When I asked if she felt safe working there, her eyes got this, I don't know, haunted look. Maybe if I'd paid more attention ..." Lisa gnawed her lip. "Ursula would never take off without calling me, I just know it!"

"The manager was bothering her? Stefan Haas?"

"Yes. But she said when she went there to pick up her paycheck once, the woman who runs the office called him by another name."

His heart sped up. Gregor. "What did she call him?"

"I can't remember," she said. "Some kind of G-name."

"Think, Lisa. It could be important." He didn't want to prompt her.

"Gary? No, that wasn't it. It sounded foreign. Gustav, maybe? Wait, I think it was Gregor."

Frank wanted to kiss her. Just as he'd thought. Gregor was working at with Global Interpreting, under a fake name. Stefan Haas. He'd better pay Marta another visit and ask her about Ursula and Gregor.

Lisa's eyes brimmed with tears. "Do you think you'll find her?"

"I hope so." But he doubted it. He wrote his cellphone number on his card and gave it to her. "If you think of anything else, anything at all, give me a buzz, okay?"

"And if you find Ursula, you'll call me, won't you? No matter what?"

Frank said he would. Got a bad feeling as he said it.

———

Nicholas paced his apartment, a shitty third-floor walk-up in Mission Hill. Compared to his San Francisco condo it was a dump, ancient appliances in the kitchen, mismatched furniture in the living room and a closet-sized bedroom with a lumpy bed.

Because Stefan wouldn't spring for a better one.

He scratched his beard. He couldn't wait to shave it off. The bristles irritated his skin.

A whistling teakettle drew him to the kitchen. He spooned tealeaves into a mug, poured hot water over them and set the steaming mug on the table. A stack of papers lay on the yellow Formica tabletop, articles he had copied when he visited the periodicals room at the Boston Public Library yesterday. He picked up the first one, dated March 19, 1990, and began to read.

$200m Gardner Museum art theft

In the biggest art robbery since the 1911 theft of the Mona Lisa, two men posing as police officers gained entry to the Isabella Stewart Gardner Museum last night, overpowered two guards and fled with an estimated $200 million worth of art.

Karen Howe, acting curator of the famous museum, said the stolen art, including a Vermeer and a seascape by Rembrandt, were worth "hundreds of millions of dollars." The art was not insured for theft, Howe said, because the cost of such a policy would have exceeded the museum's $2.8 million budget.

However, if the thieves don't have a prearranged buyer, the works may be worthless. "They're too hot to handle," said one expert. "The Vermeer and the Rembrandt will be impossible to sell." Some speculate that an art connoisseur engineered the theft. Others say this doesn't fit the psychology of owning famous art. "It's all about ego-gratification," said one. "You don't get that if you can't show it off." Others believe the paintings were stolen for use as "bargaining chips," but questioned whether law enforcement officials would agree to such demands.

Nicholas sipped his tea. Bargaining chips. Interesting.

He skimmed the next article, published one week after the theft.

Motive, recovery of art elude investigators

A $1 million reward has been offered for the safe return of the $200 million treasures stolen from the Gardner Museum. The case has focused attention on an epidemic of art heists. Soaring prices make art theft a $1-billion-a-year industry, investigators say. Art is easier to smuggle than cash, and political extremists sometimes use stolen art as bargaining chips.

Sources close to the investigation say that FBI agents and police detectives are checking discrepancies in the stories of the overnight guards, who were paid $6.85 an hour. In the early morning of March 18, one guard sat in a cramped room at the museum's watch desk, scanning four television security monitors, while the other made his rounds.

Nicholas studied the floor plan beside the article. Even now it was reasonably accurate, but this time three guards would work the overnight, and this time the cops would have no guards to question. Two would be dead and he would be a rich man. He picked up the next article.

Masterpieces, masterminds.

Ten years ago today, on a night when many Bostonians were celebrating St. Patrick's Day, two men disguised as police officers forced their way into the Isabella Stewart Gardner Museum and pulled off the biggest art theft in modern history. In less than 90 minutes, they stole 13 art works worth hundreds of millions of dollars and vanished into the rainy night.

In 1997 the Gardner boosted the reward for their safe return to $5 million, but FBI agents see no sign of a break. Law enforcement officials believe the thieves assumed the art was insured and the insurance company would offer the customary reward—5 to 10 percent of the paintings' value—but the Gardner carried no theft insurance.

"Thirteen art works," Nicolas muttered, "worth hundreds of millions." But the Rembrandt and the Vermeer appeared to account for most of it. If they stole two Vermeers, why did Stefan want him to steal two more? He had a lot to do. Kill the other guards. Have Jamilla drive the van into the courtyard and kill her.

Then he had to deal with Scorpio. She and Stefan would be at the gala tonight. To see the Vermeers, Stefan said. After she put them in the van, Stefan wanted him to kill her. This he would happily do. He could think of only one reason why Stefan was using her. Stefan didn't trust him.

But at least Scorpio would not collect any of the money.

At the last staff meeting the security chief had said each of the ten paintings in the Special Exhibit was insured for fifty million dollars. Nicholas did some calculations. If they stole four, and the insurance companies paid ten percent of the insured value, Stefan might collect a twenty million dollar ransom.

"Motherfucker!" He pounded his fist on the table. Stefan had offered him a measly half-million. Stefan thought he was too stupid to research the previous Gardner heist. Wrong.

Stefan thought he could cheat him. Wrong again.

He envisioned the exquisite pleasure he would have slitting Stefan's throat after they collected the ransom.

Maybe he'd watch a movie before he went to work. Rambo, with Sylvester Stallone. Rambo took no shit from anyone. But one term in the articles kept running through his mind. *Bargaining chip.*

He needed a bargaining chip to prevent Stefan from cheating him.

———

Revere, MA

Frank entered his motel room at 4:15 and dropped his keys on the table beside the door. He'd rented the room for a week but had told the desk clerk he might stay longer. Whatever it took to find Natalie.

He popped the cap on a Heineken and put the rest of the six-pack in the mini-fridge. Not bad for a low-budget motel, a queen-sized bed and cable TV. The rates were cheap because the MBTA Blue Line ran behind the motel, trains rattling by every few minutes. But they stopped at midnight, didn't resume until 6 AM. He was seldom in bed before midnight, almost always up by six.

And the Beachmont T-stop was two blocks away, hop on the T, he'd be downtown in thirty minutes. Plus, there was a Dunkin' Donuts outside the T-station and a liquor store on the opposite corner beside an Italian pastry shop that made espresso.

He sat on the faux-leather easy chair and sipped his beer. Only thing missing was Kelly. He felt bad that she didn't get to see any sights in London. Or Boston. She had a tight connection and had dashed off to catch her flight as soon as they landed.

He used the clicker and turned on the TV, but then his cellphone rang. He hit the mute button and answered.

"How's things up there in Boston Bruins land?" Vobitch said. He sounded annoyed. Moreover, he knew Frank had no interest in hockey. The only Boston sports team he followed was the Celtics.

"Last night at the Garden there was a fight and a hockey game broke out." The oft-quoted canard about hockey players always fighting.

"Believe it or not," Vobitch said, "we got plenty of fights down here. We got a few homicides, too."

Frank sipped his beer. Sometimes he enjoyed Vobitch's sarcasm. But not when it was directed at him.

"When are you coming back? I'm short a detective."

"Morgan, I've got a lead on those art heists, a lead in Boston. Didn't Kelly tell you?"

"NOPD isn't paying you to solve art heists. You're a homicide detective."

"Okay, but Natalie might be here." He told Vobitch about the State Trooper who'd spotted her at Logan. "If she's in Boston, she might be getting ready to pull another art heist."

"Last I heard Boston's got a police department. Let them handle it."

"If she's in Boston, I'm going to get her."

"Frank, let it go. You don't know for sure that she's there."

His irritation escalated. Vobitch didn't understand how badly he wanted Natalie. He didn't just want her; he was bound and determined to get her.

"You know, I haven't spent much time with my father lately. I've got some vacation time. Maybe I'll take it now."

"Vacation time."

He pictured Vobitch's outraged expression, slate-gray eyes cold as ice. But if Natalie was in Boston, she was here to steal a painting. And he was going to grab her before she did.

"Can you fax me the form I need to put in for vacation time?"

A heavy sigh. "Okay, but no more than a week. We got three homicides over the weekend and I'm catching heat."

"Thanks for understanding," he said, and felt a stab of guilt. Morgan was a good guy, and the NOPD brass was leaning on him.

"I'll email you the form," Vobitch said. "And you can email me your report on the London trip."

Frank grinned. Vobitch running true to form: Tit for tat. "You got it," he said. He punched off and sipped his beer. If he was going to be here for the Fourth of July, why not invite Kelly up? They could watch the Boston Pops and the fireworks on the Esplanade.

When he called her, she answered right away. "What's up, Frank?"

"Missing you, that's what's up. Can you fly up for the weekend? I'll pay your plane fare."

"I'd love to, but I'm on patrol duty Friday night. You know how it is on holiday weekends."

"Come up Saturday then and fly back Monday. I'll pick you up at the airport, show you the sights."

Kelly laughed. "You don't have to ask me twice. Book the flight and send me the details."

"Great. I'll email you." He closed his cellphone and looked around the motel room. It would look a lot better when Kelly got here on Saturday. Four days from now, but work would keep him busy.

Tonight he was going to the gala at the Gardner Museum.

CHAPTER 16

Thursday July 1, 2010 7:10 PM Boston

She clenched her jaw and stared out the window. It did nothing to quell her anxiety. Or her anger. Not with Gregor sitting beside her in the limousine. Yesterday at a boutique on Newbury Street, he had told the saleswoman he wanted to buy his girlfriend a fancy dress. He picked out three and had her model them for him, devouring her with his eyes when she came out of the dressing room. He'd chosen the gaudiest one, a form-fitting gold lamé dress with a plunging neckline and a skirt that came halfway up her thigh.

She hated it. It made her look like a hooker.

Gregor was wearing a tuxedo with a white dress shirt and a red cummerbund. And white gloves, to hide the scars on his hands, she assumed. He'd told her to wear her blonde wig, but she hadn't. She had fashioned her long black hair into a French twist.

A small act of defiance, but it made her feel better.

Their limo turned onto the Fenway. Spotlights crisscrossed the facade of the Gardner museum, and whistle-tooting police officers directed traffic around a line of limousines disgorging passengers. Across the street mounted policemen patrolled a throng of spectators.

It reminded her of the Academy Award ceremonies she'd seen on television. Outside a tall wrought-iron fence, television cameras filmed well-dressed couples as they left their limos and strolled down a red carpet. Her fear blossomed into panic.

Television cameras would film her with Gregor, at the Gardner.

Their limousine pulled forward and stopped at the red carpet. When the driver opened her door, she put on her dark glasses. Gregor stood on the sidewalk, wearing a pair of sunglasses. "You look frightened, Valerie. Don't be. You look stunning in your new dress."

"Television cameras," she hissed through a fake smile.

He took her arm and they walked down the red carpet. Heat from the television lights warmed her face. Maintaining a fixed smile, she strode past the cameras. Although it felt like an eternity, thirty seconds later a uniformed guard checked their tickets and waved them inside.

A line for the Special Exhibit extended all the way to the door. A sign for the reception pointed left.

"The line is too long," Gregor said. "Let's have a drink." When she didn't respond, he said, "No need to be rude, Valerie. This is a party. Why not enjoy yourself?"

I would if I wasn't with you. She removed her dark glasses and went to a wide archway that opened onto an interior courtyard. The garden was amazing, an oasis of calm. Mesmerized, she gazed at the lush green ferns, towering palms trees and fragrant flowers. She had chosen birds and mountains to protect her, but flowers were part of the natural world, too. The tension in her neck and shoulder muscles eased.

Gregor touched her arm. "The reception is that way," he said, pointing. Gregor, the control freak.

Annoyed, she said, "Let's go see *El Jaleo* first. It's one of my favorites." Her art history teacher in Paris had raved about the painting and she was eager to see it. When Gregor looked at her, mystified, she said, "It's by John Singer Sargent. A famous Boston artist."

"As you wish, Valerie. Lead the way."

She took him to the Spanish Cloister adjacent to the courtyard, a long narrow corridor with a tiled floor. At the far end, a high Moorish arch with scalloped edges framed an enormous painting, lit from below by floodlights. John Singer Sargent's masterpiece.

Her teacher had called it a symphony in black, gray and white. She had seen the photographs. The real thing took her breath away. Inside a dim-lit tavern three black-suited men sat in an amber cone of light, strumming guitars, their black hats casting shadows on the wall. Beside them, a man clapped his hands, eyes fixed on a larger-than-life finger-snapping flamenco dancer with a billowing white skirt.

"Looks like they're having a great time," she said.

But Gregor wasn't looking at the painting, he was gazed at her cleavage, exposed by the plunging neckline of her dress. "So am I. It is good to relax and enjoy life now and then."

Relax and enjoy life? How could she? Soon she would be here again.

To steal two paintings.

———

To avoid the traffic jam near the Gardner, Frank's taxi driver dropped him off a block away. At 7:15, he joined a line of people on Palace Road waiting to enter the museum. Five minutes later he reached the employee entrance. No sign on the door, but he knew what it was. Hank Flynn had given him a floor plan of the museum. A security camera was mounted on the wall above the door.

Would Natalie be here tonight? If she planned to steal a painting, she might. He studied the people in the line, men in tuxedos, women in their finery, none of whom looked like Natalie. He'd rented a tux for the evening, had to buy a white dress shirt to wear with it.

The line inched closer to the corner, close enough for him to see the TV cameras outside the entrance, filming the VIPs as they left their limousines. He doubted Natalie would be one of them. To avoid the cameras, she would probably stand in line with the peons like him.

The woman in front of him turned and smiled at him. "I can't wait to see Vermeers," she said.

She appeared to be in her 60s, gray hair, cornflower-blue eyes, slender and smart looking in her blue dress and lacy white wrap. "I'm retired now, but I used to teach art history. I saw the Vermeers in Amsterdam and Paris with my husband. I wish he were here to see the exhibit, but he died two years ago." Scarcely pausing for breath, she said, "Have you been to the museum before? Mrs. Gardner built it herself, you know. She was quite a gal, very adventurous for her day."

"Tell me more. I like adventurous women." And some background on the Gardner might be useful. The museum where thieves had stolen paintings worth hundreds of millions of dollars. The museum he feared Natalie was targeting for her next heist.

The woman smiled and offered her hand. "My name is Lee."

"Nice to meet you, Lee. I'm Frank. Tell me about Mrs. Gardner."

"Isabella Stewart was born in 1840. Her parents sent her to private schools and a finishing school in Paris. Then she married Jack Gardner. His family was rich, too. In 1863 they had a son, but he died in 1865."

"After the end of the Civil War." He didn't want her to think he was history-challenged.

"Yes. Mrs. Jack—that's what they called her then—was grief-stricken, so the doctors told Jack to take her on a tour of Europe. That's when she began buying art. After her father died and left her two million dollars, she became a serious collector."

Frank turned and studied the line behind him. No sign of Natalie.

"Are you looking for someone?" Lee asked.

"Just checking to see how long the line is."

Lee gestured at the limos lined up at the curb. "Those are the VIPs. We're the hoi-polloi. I got my ticket from the Mass College of Art president." She looked at him expectantly.

He smiled and said, "Tell me more about Mrs. Jack."

"Gladly! They wanted to build a bigger house for their collection, but in 1898 Jack died. That didn't faze Isabella. She bought a parcel of land on the Fenway. An architect helped her design this museum. It's similar to a palace she saw in Venice. In 1901 she moved into an apartment on the top floor. Two years later she opened her collection to the public."

Eager to get inside, Frank eyed the entrance. He wanted to check out the security arrangements, but his main preoccupation was Natalie. He wanted to see if she was here.

"When Isabella died in 1924," Lee said, "there were 2,500 objects on display here. Rare books, antique furniture, photographs and scads of important paintings. Her will stipulated that nothing be added to the collection nor sold, but it didn't prohibit temporary exhibits like this one." She flashed a triumphant smile as they reached the door. "Which means we get to see the Vermeers!"

She gave her ticket the guard. Frank handed his over and they entered the museum. "Enjoy the Vermeers," he said.

"Thank you, I will. And so will you!" she said, and joined the line for the Special Exhibit.

Frank perched on a stone bench and studied the courtyard. Enclosed on four sides, it was four stories high. Mrs. Jack's former residence on the top floor was dark, but lights were visible on the second and third floors. None of tonight's guests would see those rooms, however.

This afternoon when he picked up the ticket Hank got him, Hank told him guards would be posted at the elevators and stairways. No one allowed upstairs. If Natalie was here to case the joint, that might thwart her. Unless she planned to steal a painting from the Special Exhibit.

Frank studied the glass skylight, recalling a movie he'd seen. A gang of jewel thieves had lowered themselves from a helicopter and attached explosives to a skylight. After they blew, the thieves got inside and stole the jewels. But nobody in their right mind would try that here. Anyone looking to steal a painting from the Gardner would arrive in the dead of night. That was the MO for the London heists.

But in those heists only one security guard worked the overnight. During the Special Exhibit, three security guards would be on duty overnight. How would Natalie deal with that? Would she shoot them?

The line for the Special Exhibit was longer than before. He decided to go to the reception. Maybe Natalie would be there.

———

She could have gazed at *El Jaleo* for hours, but Gregor quickly tired of it. "We go to the reception now," he announced.

Not just a control-freak, she decided, a killjoy as well.

"How do you like my wig?" he said. Acting as if this was a date.

"It looks fine." In fact, given his dark eyes and rough features, the dirty-blond wig looked ridiculous.

"I asked you to wear your blond wig, but you didn't. Is that your own hair?" He reached over and stroked her French twist.

"Don't touch my hair!" she hissed.

He smiled and took her hand. When she tried to pull away, he tightened his grip. "We are supposed to be lovers, Valerie. Smile."

She gritted her teeth and said nothing.

The reception was in an outdoor courtyard, illuminated by large orange Japanese lanterns, fragrant with the scent of peonies, and jammed with people. They appeared to be in a festive mood. She wasn't. She wanted to check out the Special Exhibit, go home and fall into bed. Alone.

Gregor plucked two glasses of champagne from a passing waiter's tray and gave her one. She took it but didn't drink any. She needed to stay alert. The insider guard would be at the Special Exhibit and she wanted to assess his manner and memorize his face.

A linen-draped table beside the door held a two-foot high swan carved out of ice, surrounded by platters of pink jumbo shrimp. Gregor speared the biggest shrimp with a toothpick, dipped it in cocktail sauce and put it in his mouth. She was too jumpy to eat anything.

What if a State trooper or a Boston cop came in and recognized her?

Positioning herself with her back to the door, she scanned the room. Decked out in their finery, two dozen guests stood in the courtyard. Murmured conversations filled the space, wealthy patrons talking to influential politicians, she assumed. Most held wine glasses and clustered around tables laden with assorted finger sandwiches, crackers and cheese platters, or an assortment of dips and chips.

Her gaze settled on a man in a tuxedo at the far end of the courtyard. He stood near a table with his back to her. Her neck prickled. Glossy black hair. Muscular shoulders. He half-turned and she caught a glimpse of his profile. A hawk-like nose and a prominent chin.

Frank Renzi. Fear iced her veins.

"Gregor, we have to get out of here."

"Why?" he said, frowning at her.

"I just spotted a cop."

"How you know he's a cop?"

She rushed out the door without answering.

————

Frank looked up from the floor plan he'd been studying. He got the feeling someone was watching him. Alert for any telltale motion, he scanned the room, but saw nothing unusual. Then he saw a well-dressed couple leaving the reception, a woman in a gold lamé dress, medium height, short dark hair. The man was wearing a tuxedo, tall and rugged-looking, with dirty-blond hair.

A quick glimpse and they disappeared.

He put his bottled water on the table and shoved the floor plan in his pocket. This afternoon, Hank Flynn had given him a book about the Gardner Museum. Conveniently located on one page was a detailed floor plan of the exhibition rooms on the first, second and third floors, followed by descriptions of the paintings in each room. Appalled, he said, "This is like a blueprint for a heist."

Flynn shrugged. "And readily available in the museum bookstore."

He had copied the one-page floor plan and brought it with him. The Gardner was open every day but Tuesday. It closed at 5 PM, but they had extended the hours for the Special Exhibit. Between the hours of 11 AM and 9 PM, timed-tickets would allow people into the exhibit, twenty at a time. The last entry was at 8:30 PM. Those viewers had to leave the museum by 9 PM.

But tonight the exhibit would stay open until 9:30. It was only eight o'clock, plenty of time for him to see the paintings and check out the security.

———

She strode down the hallway in her spike-heeled shoes, trying to put as much distance between her and Renzi as possible.

Hurrying to keep up, Gregor said, "You have been in Boston before. What happened?"

When she didn't answer, he took her wrist and squeezed.

"Let go or I will scream." Fat chance. If she screamed the security guards would come running. The last thing she wanted. But Gregor wouldn't want that, either.

He let go, but leaned closer and said, "You lie. You keep things from me that endanger the job! Come, we must go to Special Exhibit."

No, no, no. A thousand times no! Go into a tiny room with only one exit and have Frank Renzi come in there and spot her?

"I don't need to see the exhibit. I know what the paintings look like!"

He grabbed her arm. "Slow down, Valerie. You are attracting attention. The insider guard needs to know what you look like."

"Fine. But I'm not going inside."

When they reached the Special Exhibit, two couples stood in line behind a maroon rope. A guard in a blue uniform stood at the door. He saw Gregor and gave a tiny nod. He appeared to be Asian, which surprised her. He had short black hair and a full beard, not too tall, an inch or two shorter than she was.

"Scorpio," Gregor murmured as they passed him. The man's eyes flicked to her face. His eyes were dark and flat. Killer eyes.

"Let's go," she said to Gregor. "Now."

But when she turned to head for the museum exit, her heart almost stopped. Renzi! Twenty yards away at the far end of the corridor coming toward the exhibit. "Meet me outside on Evans Way," she said and ran for the ladies' room.

———

When Frank got to the Special Exhibit, a short, stern-faced guard held a coiled rope in his hand. "No one can enter now," he said, his dark eyes flat and expressionless. "The room is full."

A nametag on his navy-blue uniform jacket said Daniel Leone. A thick beard covered much of his face and his jet-black hair was slicked back in a pompadour.

Moments later a young couple left the exhibit, and the surly guard let him in. The first thing Frank noticed: an armed police officer stood in each corner of the room. This would continue for the duration of the exhibit, but not after the museum closed. Then there would only be three security guards, two on patrol, one at the security desk. None of them armed.

The next thing he noticed was a gorgeous painting. He read the tag on the wall. *The Milkmaid* by Johannes Vermeer, on loan from the Rijksmuseum. It was stunning, light shimmering over a crusty loaf of bread, a wicker basket, and a stout woman in a goldenrod-yellow blouse, pouring milk from an earthenware jug into a bowl. Another Vermeer was also in the exhibit, *The Lacemaker*, on loan from the Louvre.

Seeing them up close, the purpose of the exhibit hit home. In 1990, the only Vermeer in New England, *The Concert*, had been stolen from the Dutch Room on the second floor. None of the stolen paintings had been recovered. To increase the reward for their safe return, Gardner officials had convinced ten museums to loan them priceless paintings and were charging top dollar for people to see them.

Ten priceless paintings. A tempting target for a gang of art thieves.

———

She stayed in the toilet stall as long as she could, but there were only three and people were waiting. She flushed the toilet and left the stall. An older woman in a frilly blue dress immediately took her place.

She went to the sink and ran warm water over her hands, hoping to warm her icy fingers. A woman in a dazzling green gown came to the other sink. "I love your dress," the woman said.

She went into deception mode. "Thank you. It's not my favorite, but my husband bought it for me."

The woman smiled. "Isn't that always the way?"

To avoid further conversation, she hurried out of the restroom. Where was Renzi? She peeked around the corner. Two people stood outside the Special Exhibit. Frank Renzi wasn't one of them.

She had to get out of the museum, but she couldn't go past the Special Exhibit. Renzi might be in there. Which meant she had to take the long way around to the exit. Every fiber of her being told her to run, but she forced herself to walk. Attract no attention. She sauntered past the gift shop, the reception in the courtyard, and the museum entrance.

At last she came to the exit and breathed a sigh of relief. Now she had to meet Gregor. She would have to fend off his advances when he took her home probably, but that seemed inconsequential now.

Frank Renzi, the hunter, was in Boston. And she was his prey.

CHAPTER 17

Friday July 2, 2010

Natalie stepped out of the shower stall, toweled off, put on her clothes and took her gym bag to the women's dressing room. Usually a forty-five-minute taekwondo workout invigorated her body and cleared her mind. Not today. Seeing Frank Renzi at the Gardner last night had shaken her to the core. Even now she felt sick to her stomach.

Last night she hadn't slept, lying in bed, her mind in turmoil. She had left the Gardner without Renzi seeing her, but then she had to endure Gregor's interrogation when he parked outside her apartment. This time he wasn't interested in sex. He had grilled her about the cop. "When were you in Boston before?" he asked. "How do you know this cop?"

She hadn't told him, of course. She'd made up a story. The cop was after her for something she'd done as a teenager, spinning Gregor a modified version of the fairytale she'd given Pym.

She took a comb out of her gym bag. Her long black hair was soaking wet and full of snarls. There were hair dryers here, but she decided to sit outside in the sun to dry her hair. She needed to think.

There had to be a solution to her predicament and she needed to find it. Fast.

She perched on a wooden bench facing the kiddie playground. The sun felt good, easing the bone-chilling fear inside her. Oblivious to the happy shrieks of two little kids playing on the slide, she assessed her situation. One fact was inescapable. Frank Renzi was in Boston.

Three days ago, she'd seen him leave the Global Interpreting office. After she recovered from her initial shock, she had rationalized her concerns. No one could connect Natalie Brixton to Global Interpreting. Renzi wasn't hunting for her. He was there to investigate Jonathan Pym. Or Gregor.

But there was no way to rationalize his presence at the Gardner last night, an invitation-only party for VIP's to view the Special Exhibit before it opened to the public. There was only one reason for Renzi to be there. He thought someone might try to steal a painting from the Gardner. The sick feeling in her stomach grew worse.

Did the London cops have information that Pym hadn't told her? Information about her? Not Natalie Brixton, Valerie Brown, the woman who had shot a man at the Ashmolean Museum.

But how would Renzi know about the art heist at the Ashmolean?

She massaged her throbbing temples. So many questions with no answers. Including the biggest one of all. When did Gregor plan to execute the heist?

The Special Exhibit had opened today, just in time for the Fourth of July celebrations. Millions of people would spend the holiday in Boston. This year July Fourth fell on Sunday. The Boston Pops would play a concert on the Esplanade followed by a fireworks display. Monday would be the legal holiday.

Gregor wouldn't dare pull the heist this weekend. Boston was swarming with cops. Which meant she had three days to escape. But she needed a new passport and new identity papers. She took out her iPhone and dialed a number.

When Pak Lam answered, she said, "Hello, Mountain Man."

———

Larry stood behind the takeout counter, chewing a Tums. His gut told him the customer in booth number four was trouble. He knew the guy wasn't a fed. The feds had an aura about them. He wasn't a plain-clothed cop, either. The cops had no reason to hassle Larry Ho. He treated them right, slipped an extra appetizer into their takeout orders, and his food stamp clients were careful to use the code.

The customer in booth four had ordered Kung Pow Chicken and a Budweiser. Nothing unusual there, but when his gut told him something was wrong, he paid attention. He leaned over the counter and eyeballed the man. He wasn't from the neighborhood, and his well-tailored suit didn't look like something a hospital worker would wear. The man snubbed out a cigarette, took out his wallet and put cash on the tab.

Larry busied himself with an order slip as the mystery man entered the foyer and headed for the door. Then, as though he'd forgotten something, the man shoved his hands in his pants pockets and strolled to the counter. "A fine meal," he said, gazing at Larry, expressionless.

His face was foreign-looking, Larry decided. Angular features, hard eyes, light brown hair curling over his square forehead. He looked like a bouncer, over six feet tall, weighed maybe two-fifty, and muscular. Not someone you'd want to tangle with in a dark alley.

Larry beamed him a customer-friendly smile. "Glad you enjoyed it. Come back soon."

"Has Jamilla been in lately?"

Larry ran a hand over his shaven head, damp with sweat now, alarm bells ringing in his mind. "Jamilla? Why? Are you a friend of hers?"

The man nodded slowly, his face impassive. "I worked with her when she was a cop."

Larry didn't believe it. This guy was no cop. Acid flooded his stomach, bringing a sharp pain.

"I'll tell her you stopped by. What'd you say your name was?"

The man gazed at him. His eyes were black ice, dark and cold. "Tell her Joe Jones was asking for her,"

After he left, Larry popped another Tums. First Nicholas wanted to know where Jamilla lived. Now this mystery man was asking for her.

He didn't know what this meant, but he was certain of one thing: the mystery man was trouble.

———

I wouldn't want anything to happen to your boy.

The words exploded in her mind like a bomb. Jamilla sank onto the lumpy cot in her bedroom.

Out in the living room Jaylen squealed, "Wheeee!" He loved the set of Hot Wheels she'd bought him, yellow plastic track with a steep hill and four tiny racecars, bright colored and edged with chrome. Every time a car zoomed down the hill he let out a squeal of delight.

You still have your cop uniform?

She eyed the closet but couldn't make herself leave the bed. Her thoughts drifted to Larry Ho. Larry had always been good to her. He knew Nicholas. Did he know about the rotten scheme the bastard had roped her into? Probably not. Larry had his food-stamp scam, but he'd never get mixed up with a creep like Nicholas. Or the crime he was planning, whatever it was.

The springs under the mattress creaked as she rose from the bed.

Out in the living room Jaylen let out another "Wheee!"

She opened the closet door and studied her clothes. Two pullovers, three T-shirts and a raggedy sweatshirt. And her uniform, encased in clear plastic.

When she stepped into the closet, her feet crunched on something.

Rat droppings, she could smell them.

She took out the uniform, cleaned and pressed at the dry-cleaners three years ago, before they fired her. She hooked the hanger over the door, ripped off the plastic and ran her hand over the blue fabric. She'd loved being a cop. The uniform made her feel important, but that wasn't the best part. She was helping people. Comforting them after a car accident. Keeping an eye on their building after they called about a prowler. But she wasn't a cop anymore. She was a junkie.

Damn Jaylen's father! She loved Jaylen, but she hated his father, getting her on the junk, turning her into a zombie.

"Wheeee!" from the living room.

She put on the uniform shirt, then the trousers, and studied herself in the grimy mirror on the back of the door. She'd lost weight, but the uniform fit well enough. Well enough for what she had to do anyway. When they busted her off the force they had taken her weapon. She wished she still had it. That scared her.

She stared into the mirror, feeling sick to her stomach. Okay, she'd do what the bastard wanted. Then she'd take the money—fifteen hundred, including the four hundred he'd already given her—and split this dirtbag town. Get on a bus with Jaylen, head south and start a new life. She'd get a job, rent an apartment, and things would be fine.

If she could muster the courage to do what the bastard wanted.

On Monday he would give her the stun gun and the drugs to knock out the cops. A shiver of fear rippled through her.

She heaved a sigh. Fuck it. She'd do what she had to do.

Then everything would be fine.

————

"I need a new passport right away," she said, sinking lower in her chair. Pak Lam regarded her silently, expressionless. She tried not to look at the long vertical scar that ran down his cheek. It made him look grim and harsh. And unforgiving.

Inside his office the silence stretched out like an endless road headed toward the horizon.

"My name is not Valerie," she blurted, her cheeks hot with embarrassment. "It is Natalie Brixton. A policeman is after me."

"Why is this policeman after you? Who is he?"

She massaged her icy fingers. How could she explain the circumstances that had culminated in violence and sent her running for her life? "It's a long story. When I was ten, someone murdered my mother. It took me twenty years to take my revenge."

His eyes widened slightly. He glanced at the photograph on the wall, his wife and two children, she assumed. Then he went to his desk, picked up the telephone and spoke rapidly in Chinese.

After returning to the chair opposite hers, he said, "I have ordered a large pot of jasmine tea to be brought to us. When it arrives, you must tell me this story, about how you took your revenge."

Forty-five minutes and many cups of tea later, she sank back in her chair, exhausted. Under the Mountain Man's gentle prodding, she had told him about her twenty-year journey. Now he regarded her silently. At last he said, "You are a brave woman, Natalie."

A great wave of relief swept over her. Contrary to her expectation, he did not look at her with revulsion. In fact, he seemed ... what? Pleased? No, more than that. His eyes brimmed with admiration.

But she could not allow this to divert her from her goal.

She swallowed the last of her tea and set the porcelain cup on the table. "Now you know why I need a new passport. As soon as possible. I need to leave Boston before this policeman finds me."

"I understand. Unfortunately, the person who prepares my passports and identity papers is in California. She is at Disneyland with her children and grandchildren. Their gift for her eightieth birthday."

An eighty-year-old grandmother was going to create her fake documents? Her face must have registered her dismay. Pak Lam went to the telephone again, spoke rapidly and returned to his chair.

"Her return flight to Boston arrives late Wednesday afternoon."

Her heart sank. It was worse than she thought. Six days from now.

"I could ask someone else to create a false passport. But you want the best papers, correct? So that your escape will be successful?"

She nodded. But she needed them now, not six days from now.

Pak Lam gave her a reassuring smile. "Then Madame Li must create your documents. She is an expert. She learned how to do this from her husband. When he died ten years ago, she took over his business. Madame Li will be tired after her long flight home on Wednesday. I will contact her on Thursday and have her make your documents."

"Thank you," she said. But that might be too late.

By then, Gregor might have ordered her to steal two Vermeers from the Gardner.

CHAPTER 18

Saturday July 3, 2010

At 2:15 Frank picked Kelly up at Logan Airport. After a hug and a quick smooch, he put her luggage in his rental car and drove her to his motel. While Kelly organized her clothes, he said, "Want to go see the sights? Or would you rather take a nap?"

Kelly gave him one of her mischievous smiles. "I've got a surprise for you."

"I like surprises. What is it?"

"You'll see." She went in the bathroom and shut the door.

Ten seconds later the door opened and Kelly posed in the doorway, one hand on her hip. The little red bikini didn't leave much to the imagination. A visceral jolt hit his scrotum.

"You like it?" she said in a low husky voice.

"I love it," he murmured, "but I like your birthday suit better."

He traced his fingers down her throat, slid the straps off her shoulders and caressed her breasts, felt her nipples hard against his palms. Already he was at half-mast. He guided her to the dresser and they gazed at each other in the mirror.

"I love watching you," he said. "Watching us."

He pulled off his polo shirt, turned her to face him and kissed her mouth. Her lips were soft and pliant and her body melded to his. He couldn't wait to be inside her. He took off his clothes and they lay on the bed. Waves of sensation washed over him, banishing any thought of art heists. All that mattered was Kelly, the warmth of her skin, the feathery touch of her fingers, her tongue exploring his mouth.

She locked eyes with him and pulled him on top of her.

Eons of intoxicating passionate minutes later they lay in bed with their arms around each other. He never tired of making love to her.

"Welcome to Boston," he said.

She gave him a lazy smile. "That was a mighty nice welcome."

He traced a finger over her flat stomach. "The beach is only a mile from here. Want to go swimming?"

"I'm not much of a swimmer. I never learned how."

"Get out. Everyone knows how to swim."

"Not me. I grew up in Chicago, remember? The Windy City."

"So? I thought it was on one of those big lakes."

Kelly smiled faintly. "Lake Superior."

"Right, Lake Superior."

She burst out laughing. "Frank, have you ever looked at the map of the United States?"

"What," he said, "you gonna make me name the state capitals now? I flunked sixth grade geography. My mother gave me hell."

"Michigan, Frank. Chicago is on Lake Michigan. And the water is very cold."

"Don't they have YMCA's there?"

"Yes, but Dad thought it was more important for me to learn how to shoot. And as you may recall, there have been a few occasions when that came in handy."

He remembered all right. When he met Kelly, she had been working Homicide for NOPD. Following in her father's footsteps. One of her brothers also worked for Chicago PD.

"But you gotta see the beach. It's gorgeous."

"Are there any restaurants? I could do with some food."

"Okay, I'll take you to Santorini's, great seafood and lots of windows facing the ocean."

They got dressed and he drove her along Revere Beach Boulevard. When Kelly saw the sandy beach and the mob of people—tiny tots shoveling sand into plastic pails, teenagers frolicking in the surf, people lying on blankets soaking up the sun—she said, "Wow! I'm impressed."

"It was the first public beach in America." He looked over and grinned. "Don't ask me when. I wasn't that great at history, either." He spotted Santorini's and pulled into a parking space. "Let's walk from here and see the sights."

As they strolled along the sidewalk, enjoying the sea breeze and the warmth of the sun, he pointed north along the coastline. "You can't see Swampscott from here, but that's where I grew up. Last night I drove up to the old homestead and took my father out for dinner."

"How's he doing?" Kelly asked.

"Not bad, but he's worried about the Celtics, says they better make a trade or they'll never make the playoffs next year."

"Sounds like my dad, but he's into baseball. He's a Cubs fan."

Kelly's mother had died when Kelly was two and she seldom spoke of her. His mother had died ten years ago. He didn't talk about her much, either, but he still missed her.

"Tell me about Global Interpreting," Kelly said.

He pointed at Santorini's across the street. "When we sit down with a beer, I will."

They ordered baked scallops and took their beers to a window table facing the ocean. While they waited for their food, Frank told her what happened with Marta at Global Interpreting. "She might be the blonde woman Sonja Wynkoop saw in that bar with her husband and Gregor."

"But why would she be in Boston?"

"To do translations. If that's what Global Interpreting actually does. I think it's a front for something else. The manager's name is Stefan Haas, but when I asked to speak to him, Marta said he wasn't there, didn't know when he'd be back. I think he's Gregor Kraus, using a fake ID. I asked my FBI buddy to get me some info on Stefan Haas. Turns out, he died two years ago."

Kelly sipped her Budweiser, processing the information. "Okay. Let's assume Gregor Kraus was involved with those European art heists. But if your FBI agent friend got you information on Stefan Haas, I assume he's American. How would Gregor Kraus know him?"

"That's what I want to know. Stefan's dead and so is his father, but his mother lives in Seabrook, New Hampshire, which is where I'm going on Tuesday." He drank some Heineken and set the bottle on the table. "I saved the big news for last."

Kelly gave him an arch look. "Don't hold back, Frank. I'm listening."

He told her about the State Trooper who'd seen Natalie Brixton at Logan Airport.

"You think she's here?"

Their scallop dinners arrived and Kelly dug into hers, marveling at the size of the scallops and the delicious flavor. While they ate, he told her about the Special Exhibit at the Gardner. "Bottom line, I think Natalie came to Boston to steal a painting from the Gardner."

"Make a helluva splash if she did," Kelly said.

"It sure would. But I intend to catch her before she does it."

———

Depressed by her dreary apartment, Natalie decided to go to a movie, a trip to fantasyland, her usual ploy to take her mind off her problems. There was a theater near Copley Square, but she didn't want to run into Gregor. She rode the Green Line to Boylston Street and bought a ticket at the theater opposite Boston Common.

But when she left the theater her mood was worse than before. The film brought back too many memories. *The Karate Kid*, starring Jackie Chan and Jaden Smith, continued a series that had begun with a remake of the 1984 film. The movie she'd seen with Gabe so long ago. The film that had inspired her to study Taekwondo.

Her eyes welled with tears and her throat thickened.

If only she could talk to Gabe. Every year she sent him an email on her birthday— April 15, tax day—and signed it IRS. Their private joke. Gabe was her best friend. Her only friend. She'd met him in high school when she joined the drama club. If only she could be that innocent teenager again. Not knowing how to use a gun. To kill people.

Gabe still lived in Texas, but she couldn't call him. He had a wife now and twin sons. His pride and joy.

Pak Lam had twins, too—or so she assumed—the boy and girl in the photo on his wall. How old were they now, she wondered. Someday she would ask him about them. But she couldn't call him either. That would be rude. On a holiday weekend, he would be with his family.

Overwhelmed with loneliness, she descended the stairs of the MBTA station and boarded a train. Unwilling to return to her apartment, she got off at the Northeastern stop and headed for the Student Center, intending to buy a grilled chicken salad. Maybe she'd buy a book in the shop around the corner and read it while she ate.

The Spy Who Came In From the Cold.

The shop wouldn't have it, of course. It was an old book. But she desperately wanted to come in from the cold. For twenty-two years, her life had been an endless series of obstacles and disasters. An empty life. No friends and no one to love her.

Then she thought, Grow up, Natalie. Stop feeling sorry for yourself.

She pictured her escape-hatch city in Italy. There she would be warm, for part of the year at least. She might even make some friends. Best of all, she wouldn't have to kill anyone.

———

Sunday, July 4, 2010 10:15 AM

"I'm taking you out for brunch," Frank said. "You need a healthy breakfast and a mimosa."

Kelly grinned at him. "Oooh, decadent. Will there be a Welcome-to-Boston party afterward?"

He loved her bawdy sense of humor. "That could be arranged."

They feasted on three-egg omelets, fresh strawberries and a mimosa, fresh-squeezed orange juice fizzy with champagne. After another Welcome-to-Boston frolic, they rode the Blue Line into Boston, got off at Park Street and strolled down Beacon Street. Kelly walked along the redbrick sidewalk, admiring the golden dome of the State House, gleaming in the sun. Frank was admiring Kelly, a luscious sight in white shorts and an aqua halter-top that set off her dark curly hair.

Traffic was heavy, people already arriving for tonight's fireworks celebration. At Charles Street they caught a Walk light. Frank hustled Kelly past six lanes of cars into the Public Gardens.

"When I worked for Boston PD, I used to do power walks here on my lunch break. All the tourists would ask me for directions to Cheers, the pub on that TV show."

"Are you going to show me the station where you worked?"

"Nah. I'm on vacation."

"Allegedly," she said, and lapsed into silence as they walked along a gravel path, surrounded by flowers, a riot of colors, pink and purple and orange. They stopped at a wide lagoon. Weeping willows drooped over the banks and white swans floated over the sun-dappled water.

"You're not on vacation," Kelly said, as if resuming a conversation she'd been having in her mind. "You're here to catch Natalie."

"True. So?"

"You think she's working for an art heist gang. A ruthless gang, according to DCI Stanford. Now you tell me Gregor Kraus is using a fake ID. How do you think he got it, Frank? You think he just walked up to Stefan Haas and asked him to give it up?"

Frank said nothing. She didn't expect an answer; she was working up to something.

"Gregor probably killed him, just like he killed Sonja's husband. And those other guards."

He stroked her cheek. "Kelly. Talk to me. What's bothering you?"

"One night my husband didn't come home. I haven't forgotten that. Have you?"

Her husband, Terry O'Neil, had been an NOPD cop, too. On his night off, he had stopped to help a motorist with a flat tire on the I-10 and a sixteen-wheeler hit him. The motorist survived. Terry died instantly. It wasn't work-related, but that made it no less traumatic.

Frank pulled her close and hugged her. "I haven't forgotten."

She pulled back and gazed into his eyes. "I don't want it to happen again. It's not just Natalie I'm worried about. Gregor's not some carjacker with a knife, Frank. He's a vicious killer."

He kissed her, long and hard and deep. "I've gone up against killers before. I'll be careful."

"I know you're careful, Frank. And I know you're a good cop. I just worry, that's all. You like to flirt with danger"

"Yup. You're gonna love my next hobby. Hang-gliding."

Kelly laughed and punched his arm. "Smartass."

That seemed to satisfy her. The rest of the day went by in a blur: window-shopping on Newbury Street, then a burger and an ice-cream cone to fortify themselves for the concert and fireworks. By now the sidewalks were mobbed with people in red-white-and-blue outfits and kids waving tiny American flags.

At seven-fifteen they arrived at the Esplanade near the Charles River. The Pops concert would start at eight with fireworks to follow at ten. They got in line at the security checkpoint. No booze allowed, so police were checking bags before they allowed people onto the Esplanade.

Kelly put her arm around him, her eyes sparkling with anticipation. "This is so fun."

"Yes, it is. I've done it a few times, but it's more fun seeing it with you."

"Years ago I used to watch the Pops on TV," she said. "I never thought I'd hear them live. You think Natalie will come here to watch the Boston Pops and the fireworks?"

Startled, he looked at her. Was she reading his mind? Or were they both pretending he was here on vacation? "If she does, we won't spot her. Almost a million people come here on the Fourth. With weather like this there might be more."

They passed through the checkpoint and threaded their way past hundreds of spectators toward the Hatch Shell, the huge half-domed structure where the Pops would perform.

———

Natalie paced her claustrophobic apartment. She felt like a caged animal. She didn't want to stay here, not on the Fourth of July, but each time she left the apartment increased the possibility that some Boston cop would recognize her. But to hell with caution. She went into her bedroom and put on her black silk slacks and a dressy white top, then put on her blond wig and a floppy wide-brimmed hat.

She took a taxi to the Ritz, a posh hotel on Arlington Street. When she entered the lobby, she heard a piano in the lounge playing "Take Five." Most people had gone to the Esplanade to hear the Pops concert and watch the fireworks so the lounge wasn't crowded. Three couples sat on high-backed stools at the bar.

Natalie took the end seat. The bartender, a distinguished-looking older man wearing a tuxedo, set a cocktail napkin in front of her. "Hello, Miss. What may I get for you?"

She smiled at him. "Something patriotic and delicious."

He laughed. "That's a tall order. A glass of wine? A cocktail?"

"A glass of your best red, please. Something dry and not too fruity."

"I've got a nice Chateau Beychevelle from 2009. A blend of Merlot, Cabernet Sauvignon and a touch of Cabernet Franc. I'll let you sample it." He moved down the bar, opened a bottle, returned with a wine glass and poured her a taste.

She inhaled the aroma, as she had been taught, and took a sip. Delicious, smooth, slightly tart and full-bodied. "Excellent," she said.

He poured more into her glass. "Would you like to run a tab?"

"Yes. Thank you."

He went to the register, returned with a slip of paper and went off to serve another customer. Now she could sit in peace. She couldn't bear to watch fireworks. Here she could avoid them. But she couldn't erase the memory. Watching fireworks in New Orleans with her mother, four months before she was murdered.

Orange fireworks bursting high in the sky, drooping like orange tears before they fizzled out. Everyone else, including her mother, cheered, but she was crying. Was it a premonition? A hint of the terrible events to come? No. She was crying because her mother had a new job, a night job, which meant Natalie had to stay home alone in their apartment. She hated it. And then her mother was dead.

She shook her head and drank some wine. Forget the past. What's done is done. Think positive and look to the future. But her future was not guaranteed. Was Renzi still here, or was he back in New Orleans? And avoiding Renzi wasn't her only problem. Today was Sunday. She wouldn't get her new passport from Pak Lam until Thursday. Four days to wait.

Her cellphone beeped. Not her iPhone, the other one. Her heart sank. Gregor. Or Pym. She didn't want to talk to either of them. She took out the phone, checked to make sure no one could hear her, and said, "Yes."

"Where were you yesterday? Why did you not answer when I called you?"

Gregor. The same quiet voice, but with an angry edge.

"Maybe I was in the shower. Or out jogging."

"I have told you. Always keep the phone with you."

Her hand trembled as she raised the glass to her mouth and took a sip of wine. The expensive wine.

"I need more money. Living here is expensive."

"Nonsense. You have only been here eleven days. The old man gave you money before you left London. Travelers Checks, he told me."

True, but she'd given half of it—five hundred dollars—to Pak Lam to pay for the Beretta. "It wasn't enough. I need more."

Silence. She pictured his dark venous eyes. Her stomach clenched and her palms grew sweaty. Now he was angry.

"Meet me Tuesday morning at ten outside the library. I will give you one hundred dollars, but no more. We need to meet on Thursday as well."

"Why?"

Another silence. She could hear him breathing.

"Have you forgotten? We have a job to do. See you Tuesday at ten," he said, and ended the call.

We have a job to do. But when? Why wouldn't he tell her? Why keep her in the dark about it?

Maybe he would tell her on Tuesday. Or Thursday.

Would Madame Li have her new passport and documents ready by Thursday?

Her hands were cold, and clammy with sweat. She had a bad feeling about this job. Worse than bad. Unspeakably bad.

She had a terrible feeling that she might not get out of it alive.

CHAPTER 19

Tuesday July 6, 2010

A burst of laughter came from the dining room, eight Boston Med-Center workers celebrating something. Behind the takeout counter, Larry thumbed through order slips and heaved a sigh. The place was bedlam today, one waitress out sick—after a weekend of partying probably—the lunch crowd busier than usual. Anyone else came in he'd have to take the order himself, give his skinny-assed waitress a break.

Right on cue, the door opened. Larry frowned, then breathed a sigh of relief. Dressed in cut-off jeans and a gray T-shirt, Jamilla Wells approached the counter.

"Great to see you, Jamilla. How about a plate of Spicy Chicken?"

"No thanks, Larry. Only got a minute."

"How's it going? How's your little boy?"

"Jaylen? He's okay." Her expression was solemn, almost grim, and frown lines creased her forehead. He hoped she wasn't into drugs again. No pinprick pupils, no droopy lids, but her eyes had an odd look about them, sad or worried, he couldn't tell which. Maybe both.

"Everything's okay then?" he said cautiously.

"I guess. Least they gonna be, soon."

Recalling the foreign-looking man with the hard eyes, Larry said, "Last week a guy was asking for you, said you were friends when you used to walk the beat. Joe Jones." It sounded stupid to him, even as he said it. Joe Jones. John Doe.

Jamilla frowned. "Don't know any Joe Jones."

"Big guy? Dark eyes, light brown hair." He paused. "A white guy."

"Don't sound like no friend of mine."

He hesitated, then said, "How about that other guy? Nicholas."

Her eyes came into sudden focus. "Don't know any Nicholas," she muttered. "I'm leaving town soon and I wanted to thank you before I go. You been good to me."

"Hey, what goes around comes around. You helped me out a few times." She wouldn't look at him, eyes downcast, edging away

"When are you leaving?"

"Soon. You're a good guy, Larry. Thanks for everything."

She turned and hurried to the door.

"Take care of yourself, Jamilla," he called, but she didn't look back.

Something was wrong. He could feel it in his gut, sitting there like a puddle of sour milk.

———

Seabrook, New Hampshire 1:35 PM

"Would you like a sandwich? I could have the maid fix one."

"No thanks, I've had lunch," Frank said as Sofia Haas invited him to sit down in her living room.

He had found her phone number using the address his FBI pal, Ross Dunn, had given him. When he called and said he was a friend of Stefan's, Sophia had readily agreed to see him. Maybe she was lonely, living in a big house with only a live-in maid for company. She was in good shape for sixty-four, slim and trim in a plum-colored dress, a handsome woman with strong features, fair skin and light brown hair.

Sofia took the chaise lounge opposite him, crossed her legs, smoothed the skirt over her knees and smiled. "I looked you up in Stefan's yearbook, Mr. Capone. You weren't in his class, were you?"

He smiled back. "No, two years behind him. My parents moved during my sophomore year." He didn't want her checking other yearbooks for his picture.

"That must have been difficult, leaving your friends."

"Not really. Most of them were boring. I heard Stefan went to Rhode Island School of Design. You must be very proud of him."

She glanced at a painting on the wall, a mish-mash of color depicting no recognizable object Frank could discern. Her eyes lingered on the painting. Then she turned to him, her eyes bright with tears.

"Did Stefan do the painting?"

Her eyes brimmed over, spilling tears down her cheeks. She plucked a tissue from a box on the table beside her and wiped away the tears. "Stefan's talent wasn't obvious to everyone, but he was very creative."

Frank decided he belonged to the "everyone" group. Only reason to hang a painting like that on your wall was if your son had painted it.

She blew her nose and put her hands in her lap, clutching the wadded-up tissue. "Stefan got in a few scrapes in high school, but my husband and I had great hopes when he was accepted at RISD." She arched an eyebrow. "It's one of the top art schools in the country."

And one of the most expensive, Frank knew. He wondered if the admissions office bent the rules for students with wealthy parents. Sofia's house, an oversized two story Colonial, had an ocean view and ADT security signs posted on the well-tended lawn.

"In high school Stefan didn't have many friends. He could be ... difficult."

"Some kids have problems in high school," he said, "but then they go to college—"

"Exactly!" she said, beaming at him. "Stefan was happy at first. He got an A in art history his sophomore year!" Her smile faded. "But his RISD friends were a bad influence. They got him into drugs." Her eyes teared up again. "When the police told us Stefan was dead, I couldn't believe it."

Police? That was a stunner. Ross Dunn had told him Stefan was dead, but not how he died.

"Three years ago Stefan moved to London. To take art lessons, he said. Johann and I were thrilled. But we never saw him again." Sofia dabbed her eyes. "That's where he died. Alone in London."

Frank sat there, dumbstruck. Stefan Haas died in London? Where Gregor Kraus lived and worked?

"I'm sorry to hear that. What happened?"

"It was awful. Two police officers came to the house. The London police had called them. They said Stefan had been mugged. Someone found him late at night in an alley near a jazz club. It took them a while to identify him. His passport and his wallet were missing. Johann and I flew to London right away and brought him back to Seabrook."

"The police didn't hold his body for an autopsy?"

"Autopsy?" she said, her eyes full of anguish. "Cutting into my Stefan's body? I wouldn't allow it. What good would that do? It wouldn't bring him back."

"Did the London police find the person who did it?"

"No. We kept calling them, but after my husband died last year ..." She heaved a sigh. "I couldn't do it anymore. It just brought it all back." Her eyes teared up again. "What kind of animal would do that to Stefan? Kill him and leave him lying in some alley?"

Frank considered the possibilities. Was it some thief with no connection to Stefan? Did someone who knew Stefan have a beef with him? Or was it someone looking to steal a passport from an American citizen. But he didn't want to share his theories with Sofia. He already sounded like a cop, asking too many questions. He'd call DCI Stanford and ask him to get the file on the case.

"I don't know, Mrs. Haas. These things happen sometimes in big European cities." Especially to rich young Americans who liked to party. "Do you have any snapshots of Stefan taken in London?"

Sofia brightened. "Oh yes, he was always sending us pictures of famous places. The Tower of London, Buckingham Palace, Big Ben."

"How about photographs of Stefan? Did he send any of those?"

Sofia smiled. "Yes, now that you mention it. The week before he died, we got some snapshots in the mail. One of them was Stefan with his latest girlfriend. Stefan always had a lot of girlfriends."

"Could I see it?"

"Of course. Wait here while I get them."

After she left Frank got up and went to the picture window. Great view of the ocean, whitecaps rolling toward shore. A big house in a prime location like this had to cost big bucks. How did Johann and Sofia Haas get the money to buy it, he wondered. Inherited wealth? Or was Johann a successful businessman with a good-looking wife and an aspiring-artist son with little or no talent.

Sofia returned and showed him a color photograph. "This was at Stefan's high school graduation."

Stefan in a cap and gown with his beaming parents. Frank could see why he had no trouble acquiring girlfriends. A handsome guy, even features, curly blonde hair. But his lips were set in a line, and his dark eyes were somber. Not a happy camper when he was in high school.

"A fine-looking boy," he said, which elicited a big smile from Sofia.

She took two snapshots out of an envelope. "This one was taken when Stefan was at RISD." In the snapshot, a slightly older Stefan, early twenties maybe, grinned into the camera. After he fell in with evil companions, and started doing drugs.

Sofia handed him another snapshot. Stefan standing beside a leggy blonde in a short party dress. It took his breath away.

The woman's face was blurry, as though she'd tried to turn away from the camera to hide her face. But she wasn't totally successful. If that wasn't Natalie Brixton in a blonde wig, he'd put mustard on his Nike's and eat them.

"Pretty girl. Did Stefan tell you her name?"

"No, but he said he liked her a lot. Why?"

"Just wondering. People tell me I've got a habit of asking too many questions." The biggest question being: was Natalie working for a London escort service? Or did Gregor Kraus get her to seduce Stefan so he could jump him that night in the alley and steal his passport?

"Could I make a copy of the snapshots? I'd love to have something to remember him by." Lying through his teeth and feeling guilty about it. "I'll send them right back to you."

For a second, he thought she was going to refuse. But hospitality prevailed. Either that or she was happy that someone thought enough of Stefan to want to remember him. "Well, all right. But could you give me your phone number? So I can call if you forget?"

"Absolutely." He slipped the snapshots into his pocket, wrote his cellphone number on the envelope and gave it to her. "Thank you, Mrs. Haas. It was nice talking to you, but I need to be going."

"I'm sorry I went on so long about Stefan," Sofia said as she walked him to the door. "I still get emotional when I talk about it."

Frank nodded gravely. "That's understandable. I'm very sorry for your loss."

He left the house and got in his car. Ten minutes later he was on the highway headed for Boston. During his hour-long drive from Boston to Seabrook, he'd thought about how much fun he and Kelly had over the weekend. Except when she got on him about Gregor. She was afraid Gregor might kill him. But she hadn't mentioned it again.

Yesterday he'd driven her to Logan to catch her flight to New Orleans. Already he missed her. In New Orleans they got together at least three times a week, usually at her house. His condo was in the French Quarter, where parking was almost non-existent.

Tonight he'd call her and tell her about Stefan, murdered two years ago in London. He was certain Gregor had killed him and stolen his identity. Maybe telling Kelly about it wasn't such a good idea. It would feed into her fears about Gregor. On the other hand, he didn't like hiding things from her. Besides, she was a great detective. He loved bouncing ideas off her.

Did Natalie help Gregor ambush Stefan, he wondered? When he caught her, he'd ask her. Seeing her in the photo with Stefan was a shock, but it validated his theory. Two years ago Natalie had fled to London. She still invaded his dreams, a taunting reminder that he had failed to capture her. He couldn't prove it, but his gut told him she was in Boston and so was Gregor Kraus, using Stefan's ID.

Stefan was thirty-two, seven years younger than Gregor, but that wouldn't matter in a passport or driver's license photo. Stefan was blond. Gregor had dark hair, but it was easy enough to dye your hair or wear a wig. Case closed. Gregor Kraus, posing as Stefan Haas, was the Global Interpreting manager.

Given the late-afternoon traffic, the office would be closed by the time he got back to Boston. But tomorrow it wouldn't.

CHAPTER 20

Wednesday July 7, 2010

She spread a dark green bath towel over the kitchen table, took a tube of grease and a four ounce container of oil out of her lube kit and set them on the towel beside the gun Pak Lam had sold her. The Beretta 92 FS felt comfortable in her hand, lightweight and compact. When she loaded it with the 9mm hollow-point slugs, it would be heavier.

A gun needed to be cleaned and oiled regularly. That's what Uncle Jerry said. When she was a teenager in Texas, she had asked him to teach her how to shoot. She didn't dare tell him why. His son, her disgusting cousin, was making his sister give him blowjobs. Natalie had put a stop to that.

With practiced efficiency, she disassembled the Beretta. But cleaning and oiling the parts didn't erase the problems that torment her. Frank Renzi. Gregor. Her doubts about Madame Li.

Yesterday when she met Gregor to get the money she'd asked for, she had mustered the courage to ask when the heist would be. He didn't fly into a rage as she'd feared. He just didn't answer her.

"Keep your cellphone with you at all times," he'd said.

Holding her hostage with the cellphone, her electronic leash.

Gregor didn't know about the bug on his car. Now she was tracking his movements. After he left her yesterday, he had driven to a residential street on the east side of Providence and spent almost an hour there. Then he had driven to the strip club he'd visited last week.

Cheetahs. To get a lap dance, probably. She'd danced at strip clubs in New York. She knew how it worked.

She checked her iPhone. Now he was in Jamaica Plain, a few miles from her Mission Hill apartment. The Saab was parked beside a pond on the Jamaicaway, a secondary road people took to avoid using the highway to get in and out of Boston. She had no idea what Gregor was doing there, but this rash of activity made her nervous.

She wouldn't get her new passport and documents until tomorrow. Madame Li would make them. An eighty-year-old woman. What if she had a heart attack? What if her flight from California was delayed?

What if, what if. All this fretting accomplished nothing, and it was driving her mad.

Annoyed, she slammed the magazine into the Beretta and took it into her bedroom. A shoebox lay open on her bed. Inside it were two boxes of 9mm hollow-point slugs. She put the Beretta in the shoebox beside the ammunition and picked up the box. It was heavy. Holding it in both hands, she went to the closet and hoisted it onto the top shelf. Not a great hiding place but she had no better one.

Now she could go to Chinatown for her Taekwondo workout. She'd gone there every day this week. She had to stay strong and maintain her TKD skills. Her secret weapon.

––––––

When Frank walked into Global Interpreting at ten-thirty, Marta was alone in the office. "Hi, Marta. Remember me?"

She looked up some papers, scowling as he approached her desk.

"I remember you, Mr. Capone."

"I thought maybe you forgot. Stefan Haas didn't call me."

Her lips tightened. "I gave him the message."

Frank went to the doorway beside her desk and looked down a long gray-carpeted hall, illuminated by florescent ceiling panels. "Is his office down there?"

She swiveled her chair to face him. "Yes, but he's not in today."

Three strides got him to her chair, looming over her, inches from her face. She recoiled, eyes wide with fear, hands raised to ward him off.

"I don't believe it. Show me."

Anger flared in her eyes. "I don't have to—"

"Show me," he snapped, and strode down the hall. Too bad he'd left his 9mm SIG-Sauer in his motel room. So he wouldn't be tempted to threaten Marta with it. At the end of the twenty-foot hall, he stopped at a wood-paneled door with a Yale lock. "What's in here?"

Rigid with fury, Marta stormed down the hall, lips set in a line. "Mr. Haas' office, but he's not in today."

"Show me."

"I can't. I don't have a key. How many times must I tell you? He is not here!"

Frank pounded the door with his fist. Waited thirty seconds. Looked at Marta. Her smug expression said: *I told you so.*

"Okay," he said, "let's talk."

When they returned to the foyer, Marta sat in her chair with her arms folded over her chest.

"Show me your client list."

A big frown. "Why?"

"I'd like some references, see if your customers are satisfied."

"Why? We have never had any complaints."

"Give me some names then. What are you afraid of?"

"I can't. We're very scrupulous about guarding our clients' privacy."

"You keep telling me Stefan Haas isn't here. I'm beginning to think he doesn't exist."

She tucked a wisp of blonde hair behind her ear, glaring at him. "What do you want, Mr. Capone?"

"What happened to Ursula?"

She licked her lips. "Who? I don't know any Ursula."

"Yes you do. She used to work here. Then she disappeared. You seem real concerned about your employees' welfare when I ask for names. Aren't you worried about her?"

She clenched her jaw and said nothing.

"How about Natalie? Does she work here?" Watching her closely to assess her reaction.

She seemed surprised. "No one by that name ever worked here."

"How about Gregor Kraus?"

Her mouth sagged open and her eyes shifted away, avoiding his.

"Put me in touch with him. Why should you take all the heat?"

A muscle worked in her jaw. "I don't know what you're talking about."

He knew he'd get nothing more out of her without flashing his NOPD badge. He wasn't ready to do that, but her startled reaction confirmed his suspicion. Gregor Kraus was Stefan Haas.

And Frank was determined to talk to him. He aimed his finger at Marta. Not as good as a gun, but safer. "Have him call me, Marta. If I have to come back, things could get ugly."

––––––––

Kwan was late. Again. Gregor took out a Gitanes, his second in thirty minutes, he realized. Unacceptable. He put it back. He'd told the punk to meet him near the boathouse on the Jamaicaway, a four-lane road lined with scrub pine, older homes and brick apartment buildings.

If Kwan didn't show up in ten minutes he'd leave.

He slammed his palms against the steering wheel of the Saab. It didn't matter how late the little punk was. He would wait regardless. He had no choice. Without Kwan his plan was useless. He had violated his code—Trust no one—and now he was paying for it.

He eyed the rearview mirror. A lime-green Toyota approaching the Saab. Not Kwan. To calm himself, he shut his eyes and pictured Go-Go-Flo, relishing the memory of her enormous breasts and her talented mouth. His reward for packing Burt off to Florida yesterday.

After he sent Burt to the airport in a taxi, he had spent an hour in Burt's stinking cottage, completing his tasks. First he called the telephone company and had them disconnect the phone. Then he called the cable company and canceled the service. Kwan would stay there after the heist and Gregor didn't want him watching the news reports. Kwan thought they were going to collect a big ransom for the stolen paintings.

When Gregor left the cottage, he had carried the flat-screen TV out to the curb and left it there. After he left someone in the neighborhood was sure to grab it off the sidewalk. One problem solved.

But Valerie was another problem, lying to him after the party at the Gardner, some cock-and-bull story about the cop. He could always tell when someone was lying.

Gregor studied the scars on his hands. As a child, he had learned to watch Papa carefully—his face and his eyes and his body language—trying to anticipate when Papa might burn him again. His ability to read people had facilitated his work as an enforcer for the London gang. People who owed you money would lie like crazy. Anything to make you believe they would pay the money tomorrow or the next day.

Valerie had said the cop was after her for some teenage escapade. Bullshit.

His cellphone rang. Thinking it might be Kwan, he answered without checking the ID. "Gregor! We have a problem!"

Marta. The last thing he wanted to do right now was listen to list of Marta's problems. "What?" he snapped.

"A man came to the office today, asking about Ursula."

He took out a Gitanes and lighted it. "Who is he? What did he say?"

"John Capone, or so he said. I think he's a cop. He came here last week, too."

"What did he want?"

"Last week?"

Rage coursed through him. Marta could be incredibly stupid sometimes. In his usual quiet voice he said, "Tell me what this man wants, Marta."

"Last week he wanted to talk to Stefan Haas. I told him I'd have you call him."

"And? So? What did he want today?"

"He knows Ursula went missing."

"I told you that girl was trouble, Marta. You recruited her. Looks like you didn't check her out very well. What did you tell him?"

"I said she ran off to New York one weekend and never came back. But—"

"Good." He puffed his Gitanes and spewed smoke out the window. "I must get back to work."

"Wait! Don't hang up! He asked to talk to Stefan Haas again. When I said you weren't here, he went down the hall to your office."

Gregor frowned. That was disturbing. But Marta had no key to his office. "Did he show you his identification?"

"No, but I know a cop when I see one. Gregor, I'm scared. He frightened me."

"You worry too much."

"Worry too much? Merde! He's an animal! And then he asked for you, Gregor. Not Stefan Haas, you! Gregor Kraus."

He took another drag on his Gitanes and sucked it into his lungs. Why was some cop asking for Gregor Kraus? Was this the cop Valerie saw at the Gardner last week?

"What does he look like, this animal you are so afraid of?"

"Dark hair, dark eyes. Italian-looking. Tall and rugged."

He tried to recall if he'd seen anyone like that at the Gardner. But in truth he hadn't paid much attention to the other guests. His eyes were feasting on Valerie. "What did you tell him?"

"I said I didn't know anyone by that name. He said if you didn't call him he would come back."

"Fine," he snapped. "I'll take care of it next week."

"Next week! What if he comes back tomorrow?"

"Marta, I said I would take care of it." He ended the call and stared out the window. No one would ever find Ursula, but these inquiries were worrisome. Especially now, when he had no time for them.

To steal four masterpieces from the Gardner many details required his attention. Not to mention riding herd on his underlings. Burt. Jamilla, the ex-cop. Nicolas Kwan. Valerie. But the paintings would bring an enormous reward, millions of dollars. Fuck Pym. The money would go into his bank account.

But the heist would draw enormous media attention. Would Marta suspect him? He would deny it, of course. Even if she didn't believe him, she'd keep her mouth shut. She had helped him steal several paintings in Europe. Not only that, she was still in love with him. Years ago he had thought her exciting. Now she disgusted him.

Still, he longed to see a woman's eyes light up when he told her about his life of crime. Not just any woman, a woman he could trust. Valerie, perhaps? He had the art heists and the murder to hold over her head. An ache stirred in his groin. They said love made the world go round. Wrong. Love was a trap. Falling in love meant losing control.

That's why he paid his blond beauties to pleasure him.

In the rearview he saw Kwan's Lexus approaching the Saab. He pulled away from the curb and Kwan followed him. At a rotary, he took the first exit and parked beside a grassy knoll shaded by giant oaks. When Kwan got out of the Lexus, Gregor motioned him to follow and walked down a grassy slope to the edge of the pond.

The punk took his time, strolling down the hill, then saying, "Why do we meet here?"

"Why are you always late? I told you eleven. It is eleven-thirty."

Kwan responded with a sullen shrug. Aching to punch the rat-bastard's mouth, Gregor clenched his fists. Took a deep breath. Forced himself to speak in a soft voice. "We are three miles from your apartment, Nicolas. What's going to happen the night of the heist? Will you be late then too?"

"Why are we meeting here?"

"This is where we switch cars after the heist."

Kwan turned and looked up the hill. "Up there?"

"No, over there." He pointed to a road that paralleled the Jamaicaway. Stately Victorians and towering oak trees lined the street. "Safe enough if I am not there too long, so don't keep me waiting."

"You think I want to hang around with four stolen paintings and four bodies and wait for the cops to show up?"

He fixed Kwan with an icy stare. "Do not be late. We meet here and switch vehicles. I take the van, you take the car. The hideout is in Providence, a cottage with an attached garage. Put the car in the garage and stay in the house. There will be plenty of food so you won't need to go out."

"How long do I have to stay there?"

"That depends on the negotiations."

Kwan gazed at him, his eyes flat and inscrutable. "How long?"

"I don't know. After Jamilla drives the van into the courtyard—"

"How does she get the keys?"

"Park the van on the street behind the museum before you go to work. Put the keys over the visor and leave the door unlocked."

Kwan fingered his beard, frowning. "What if someone steals it?"

"No one will steal it," he snapped. "Use a garrote to kill the guards. There must be no blood, understand? No evidence. Once the van is in the courtyard, kill the ex-cop and dump her in the van. This should take no more than ten minutes."

"Easy for you to say. What about Scorpio?"

With a supreme effort, he fought down his anger. "She takes the Vermeers in the Special Exhibit, *The Milkmaid* and *The Lacemaker*. You take the Rembrandt *Self Portrait* in the Dutch Room." He took two photos out of his picket, gave one to Kwan and studied the second photo, Manet's *Portrait of Madame Manet*.

For some reason her dour expression and stern eyes irritated him.

He showed Kwan the photo. "The Manet is in the Blue Room on the first floor."

"I know where it is. It's big and the frame is heavy. How do you expect me to carry—"

"Stop complaining. The Manet is our insurance. When the negotiators demand proof that we have the paintings, we give them the Manet. It is an important painting, easily verified. The others are even more valuable. The insurance companies will pay millions for them."

Kwan said nothing, face expressionless.

"Have Scorpio put the Vermeers in the van. Then you kill her and dump her body in the van."

"With pleasure. I don't understand why she is a part of this job. Why do we need her?"

"Because I say so. Take good care of the paintings. Make sure they are not damaged."

"Why are you so worried about the paintings?" Kwan sneered.

Rage boiled into his throat. "Idiot! These paintings are worth millions! If they are damaged, the insurance companies will not pay. This is my operation, Nicolas. Listen to me and do exactly what I say. Treat these paintings like the treasures they are."

He grabbed the punk by the throat. "Do not fuck up, Nicholas. If you do, I will kill you."

Kwan jerked away and ran up the slope to his Lexus.

Enraged, Gregor watched him. His hands trembled as he took out a Gitanes. He lighted it and took a deep drag to calm his nerves. Moments later he tossed the cigarette on the ground.

Always be in control. He could not allow Kwan to infuriate him. Or Marta.

Or Valerie. Gregor smiled. Tomorrow he would see Valerie again.

He was looking forward to it.

He had a surprise for her.

CHAPTER 21

Thursday July 8, 2010

Natalie hopped off the Green Line trolley, hurried across the street and jogged up Tremont Street hill. An hour-long Taekwondo workout had put her in a better mood, but she was late. She had to meet Gregor in half an hour. Three blocks later she trotted past the Mission Church, a massive beige-stone building. The huge circular window on the facade reminded her of Notre Dame in Paris.

If only she were there. Then she wouldn't have to deal with Gregor.

She turned onto a narrow side street and stopped short, horrified.

Gregor's Saab was outside her apartment building, a three-story tenement with ugly brown siding.

When she reached the Saab, Gregor got out, frowning at her. "Where have you been?"

"Working out at a YMCA. The one on Huntington Avenue." She didn't want him knowing what she did in Chinatown, or that she had a helpful contact there.

He stared at her, expressionless. At last he said, "Come upstairs. We need to talk."

"Why can't we talk out here?"

"You know why," he snapped. He marched to the front door and waved her into the foyer.

Butterflies fluttered in her stomach as she unlocked the door. Her iPhone was in her gym bag, but she couldn't remember if she'd left anything incriminating on the kitchen table. As they climbed the stairs to her third-floor apartment she tried not to think about the Beretta in her bedroom closet.

She unlocked her door, went inside and put her gym bag on the floor beside the kitchen table. Relieved that she hadn't left any telltale papers on it, she said, "What do you want to talk about?"

Gregor didn't answer. Instead, he began opening her kitchen cupboards. When he'd checked every one, he said, "You eat healthy food. You will probably live to be a hundred. Pack some clothes, Valerie. We stay in a hotel tonight."

She felt like he'd kicked her in the gut. Not tonight! She had to get her documents from Pak Lam.

"Why?"

"To prepare for the job."

A feeling of dread chilled her. "When is it? Tonight?"

"We discuss this later at the hotel."

Infuriated, she stared at him. Imagined the TKD spin more she'd practiced this morning. Saw her foot strike his head. But Gregor was big and strong and her gym shoes weren't that sturdy. If she didn't put him down with one kick, he might put her down, permanently.

"Gregor, I'm not staying in the same room with you."

He smiled, leering at her. "Why not? We could have some fun."

She reached in her pocket and took out the cellphone Pym had given her. "I'm calling Jonathan."

Gregor's eyes hardened. "Put that away. Don't threaten me. You killed a man in London. You may think I have forgotten, but I have not. I am sure the police would love to hear about it."

She clenched her teeth to keep from screaming. Just as she'd feared. Gregor was using the murder at the Ashmolean Museum to blackmail her. Keeping her under control.

"What's the old man like in bed? Is he a stud?"

"That's disgusting, Gregor."

"He's dying, you know. A month from now he'll be in his grave."

"I don't believe it. Dying from what?"

"He inherited some sort of fatal disease from his parents. I convinced the woman who works for his doctor to tell me about it."

Shocked speechless, she stared at him. Pym was dying? Maybe her escape would be easier than she'd thought. To hide her elation, she put on a sad-face. "That's too bad. He's a nice man."

"No he's not. You don't know who he really is."

"So? Who is he?"

Gregor gazed at her, expressionless. "After he's dead, you and I could continue these art heists and make a lot of money. We would make a good team."

She knew his offer was a smokescreen. If Pym was dead, why would Gregor cut her in on anything? After she delivered the two Vermeers, he'd probably kill her and the insider guard. Nicholas, the man who'd looked at her with hate in his eyes.

"Maybe," she said. "I'll think about it."

"Get your suitcase and start packing."

Damn! She had to bring the iPhone, but where would she hide it?

"I need to use the toilet." Before he could say anything, she grabbed her gym bag, went in the bathroom and locked the door. Her heart pounded. She had to hurry or he would wonder what she was doing. She took her first-aid kit out of the medicine cabinet, tore off four strips of adhesive tape and stuck the ends to the sink. She took the iPhone out of the gym bag. Her lifeline to Pak Lam. She set it to Vibrate, taped it to her abdomen, flushed the toilet and left the bathroom.

Her heart almost stopped. Gregor was pawing through the clothes in her closet. If he decided to look inside the shoebox on the top shelf with the ammo and the Beretta, she was done for.

"What are you doing?" she demanded in an outraged voice.

He held out one of her dresses, the one with the low-cut jade-green top and short white skirt. "I like this one. Bring it with you," he said, gesturing at her suitcase, which lay open on the bed.

A familiar mantra sounded in her head. Be who they want you to be.

Anything to distract him from the shoebox in the closet.

She slid the dress off the hanger, folded it and put it in the suitcase. Her blond wig sat on a Styrofoam form on the bureau. Would he let her take it? She went to the bureau, took out four sets of underwear and her black running suit and put them in the suitcase.

Gregor leaned against the door jam, watching her. "Bring the shoes you wore to the gala."

Wordlessly, she slid the spike heels into a plastic bag, put them in the suitcase and returned to the closet. The black pumps she wore for the heists sat on the floor of the closet, built for running, with reinforced-steel inside the two-inch heels. A well-placed kick with those shoes could be lethal. But when she picked them up, Gregor said, "Not those. They are ugly. Wear your gym shoes for the job."

"These are better."

"Why must you always argue with me, Valerie? Do what I say."

Mentally cursing him, she put down the black pumps and picked up her duffel bag.

Gregor yanked it out of her hands. "What is this?"

"For the job. The tin snips are in it. To cut the wires that attach the paintings to the wall. And latex gloves, so I don't leave any prints."

After a cursory glance inside, Gregor tossed the duffel on the bed. She jammed it into the suitcase. There were other things she wanted to bring. Her blond wig. Extra money. The Beretta and the hollow-point slugs. But Gregor was watching her every move.

She zipped the suitcase closed.

Gregor towed it into the kitchen and gestured at the cabinet under the sink. "You want to feed your pet rat? The big one you told me about at that Chinese restaurant?"

She wanted to kick him in the balls. "Don't make jokes. Where are we going?"

"First we do some errands. Then we check into the hotel."

———

Seated by the window in his motel room, Frank sipped espresso from a take-out container. It was 9:30 AM in Revere, 2:30 PM in London. Fifteen minutes ago he'd called DCI Stanford to tell him the latest developments. His cellphone bill was going to be brutal.

"Can you get the file on Stefan Haas?" he said. "Sorry I don't have the exact date and location, but his mother didn't tell me much. They found him in an alley near a nightclub and his wallet was missing."

"I'll have someone in the Homicide Division check the cold-case files. Shouldn't be hard to find."

"Did you get any info on Natalie Brixton?"

"Nothing yet, but she might be using a different name."

He studied the snapshot Sofia had given him. "I'm pretty sure she's the blond in the snapshot Stefan sent his mother, which means she was in London before he was murdered. Maybe they went out clubbing. Can you post some fliers with the composite I gave you in some clubs and ask people to call if they recognize her? It's a longshot, but maybe someone saw her and overheard the name."

"Will do, Frank. If Gregor Kraus is in Boston posing as Stefan Haas, he's up to no good. This Special Exhibit at the Gardner worries me. Ten priceless paintings make a terrific target."

It worried Frank, too. Gardner officials and Boston PD had instituted extra security measures for the exhibit, but that didn't reassure him. "Anything new on the Ashmolean heist?"

"No," Stanford said, "Not a peep from my underworld contacts. Almost three weeks and the bloody trail is colder than a dead fish. If I get anything, I'll call you straight away. When I get the file on the Haas murder, I'll call you with the details."

Frank thanked him and ended the call. He finished the espresso and tossed the container in the wastebasket. His cell rang. He checked the ID and answered. "Hey, Kelly, how's it going?"

"Better than yesterday. Sorry I couldn't talk, but I had to get this woman away from her boyfriend. He beats her but she won't leave. She's an alcoholic and he buys her booze. I wish I was still on vacation in Boston."

"Me, too. I miss you."

"I miss you, too, but I figure you've been busy. Did you talk to Stefan's mother?"

"Yes, and I got some useful information." He recapped his conversation with Sofia Haas.

When he finished, Kelly said, "You think Gregor killed Stefan and stole his ID?"

"Yes. Right now I'm looking at a snapshot Stefan sent his mother. Stefan and Natalie."

"Get out! Are you sure it's her?"

"Yes. In a blond wig, like the one she wore in the security video two years ago."

"The Peterson murder," Kelly said. Back then she'd been working Homicide.

"Exactly. I think she's getting ready to steal a painting from the Gardner."

"Natalie and Gregor," Kelly said. Her unspoken words being, "Be careful, Frank."

Kelly was afraid Gregor would kill him, but he wasn't going to let that deter him. "I'm positive Natalie is in Boston, but I've got no way to find her. Yesterday I went back to Global Interpreting. When I asked Marta if Natalie ever worked there, she gave me a blank stare. But when I dropped Gregor's name, she almost shit her pants. She recovered fast, though. Still wouldn't give me squat."

"Can you check the RMV records? Maybe he's using Stefan's drivers license."

"Good thinking. I'll do that. What's up for the weekend? Wanna come back to Boston?"

"Frank, I can't keep flying up there."

"Why not? We could have another Welcome-to-Boston reunion."

Kelly laughed, a low throaty sound. "Tempting, but I'm assigned to the Domestic Violence hotline. Penance for my holiday weekend escape. Have you told Vobitch your latest theory?"

"No. I figure let sleeping dogs lie. If I call him, he'll just lean on me and tell me to come back."

"True. There was a murder in the French Quarter last night, so he's probably getting heat. Have you been back to Santorini's? Those scallops were delicious."

"No. Maybe I'll have lunch there today."

"I'll be working all day Saturday and Sunday," she said. "Call me Sunday night."

"Will do." He closed his cell and studied the snapshot.

Stefan Haas and Natalie. Where the hell was she?

Somewhere in Boston. He was certain of it.

———

She sat in the Saab, fuming as Gregor meandered through downtown Boston. Traffic was horrendous, but he didn't seem to care. They passed a sign for the theater district and a sign for Chinatown.

Were her documents ready? Even if they were, she had no way to get them. Tonight, she'd be cooped up in a hotel with Gregor.

"Want to stop in Chinatown?" Gregor said, glancing at her.

Her heart jolted. Could he read her mind? Maintaining a neutral expression, she said, "You're driving, Gregor. You decide."

He gave her a peeved look but said nothing and entered the Callahan Tunnel, a mile-long, two-lane tube below Boston Harbor. They emerged from the tunnel in East Boston near Logan Airport, but Gregor followed the signs for Revere.

Fifteen minutes later, he parked outside a sprawling two-story storage facility. "Stay in the car while I am in the office," he said, giving her a stern look. "I will be watching."

Fine by her. There might be security cameras in the office. Did he think she might disappear like a puff of smoke? If only she could.

When Gregor returned to the car, he drove back the way they had come. After they crossed a railroad bridge, a sign pointed toward Logan Airport, but Gregor went straight. Two blocks later they stopped at a traffic light. On the corner, a huge sign with a racehorse on it said Suffolk Downs.

When the light changed, Gregor said, "You like to swim?"

She looked at him, mystified. "Swim?"

"Yes, Valerie," he said sarcastically. "Swim. You get in the water and move your arms and legs."

"I don't have a bathing suit."

He chuckled, a sinister grating sound that set her teeth on edge. "So? We can go skinny dipping."

He seemed to be enjoying himself. She wasn't. Leaving Boston before the heist was impossible now. Gregor was taking her to a hotel to make sure she followed orders. Steal two paintings from the Gardner, so wealthy art connoisseur could have them to himself.

They came to a rotary and the ocean appeared, deep sea-green, extending for miles. Her escape-hatch city was an ocean away. Depressed by the thought, she focused on their route. They passed a sign: Revere Beach Historical Site. On their left, cheap restaurants sold pizza and beer and sub sandwiches. To the right, a sandy beach stretched out as far as her eye could see. Happy toddlers frolicked in the surf and people lay on blankets soaking up the sun.

Carefree beach-goers on a hot summer's day without a worry in the world. She wished she were one of them.

"Time for lunch," Gregor said as he pulled into a parking lot.

Inside Santorini's the odor of fried fish permeated the air. Two dozen tables filled a large sunlit room with a wall of windows facing the ocean. She wasn't hungry but she'd better eat. No telling what might happen later. She chose the baked scallops with rice pilaf and coleslaw. Gregor ordered the most expensive item on the menu, a double lobster roll, with French fries and coleslaw.

It was only 11:30 and the place wasn't crowded. They took a table by a window. "You like seafood?" Gregor asked.

"It's healthier than beef," she said, and stared out the window. That ended that conversation.

A perky young waitress delivered their food. On her plate a mountain of fat scallops sat atop a bed of rice pilaf. She cut one in half and tried it. Delicious. Sweet and succulent and cooked to perfection. Gregor set upon his lobster rolls like a starving man. In less than a minute the first one disappeared.

He dipped a French fry into some ketchup and ate it. "The lobster is good, but the French fries are pitiful. I have eaten much better ones in Brussels. Pomme frites, the Belgians call them."

When was he in Brussels, she wondered. Did he and his previous partner steal a painting there?

Gregor devoured the second lobster roll and set his plate aside. "Where is your mother?"

The question blindsided her and tears stung her eyes.

For more than twenty years, she had thought about her mother almost every day. Every October on the anniversary of her death, she followed the ritual of her Vietnamese ancestors. She built a shrine around a snapshot of her mother—the only one she had—lit some incense and told Mom she loved her. What would happen in October this year? Would she live to do it again?

She looked out the window at a rainbow-colored kite floating high above the beach. It looked like one of those blow-up mattresses people used when company came to visit, but the kite was concave-shaped to catch the wind. She wanted to get on it and fly away.

She turned away from the window. "My mother is dead. Someone murdered her."

His eyebrows rose in surprise. "Who? Your father?"

"No. I don't ask about your parents, Gregor. Don't question me about mine."

"As you wish. We need to leave, Valerie. Finish your lunch."

How could she eat in the company of this vile man? She felt like a prisoner. And Gregor, the control freak, was her keeper. Abruptly, she pushed back her chair, strode to the entrance and went out to the car.

Gregor followed her outside, frowned at her and unlocked her door. As they drove along the beach the silence was deafening. When Gregor followed the signs to the airport, her heart surged. If they stayed at one of the airport hotels, maybe she could sneak out and take the T to Chinatown and get her documents.

But Gregor took the left-hand fork to the Williams Tunnel.

"Where are we going?" she asked.

He didn't answer. When they exited the tunnel, he got on the Expressway South and they zoomed through Dorchester past a marina, then an enormous gas tank with paint splashed over it.

"Enjoying the sights?" Gregor asked. "Or did you see them when you were here before."

She gritted her teeth. "Yes, I am enjoying the sights. I have not been here before."

To avoid his gaze, she turned and looked out the window.

Thirty-five silent tension-filled minutes later, they left the highway in Dedham and entered a rotary. Gregor took the second right. At a fork in the road, one arrow pointed to an industrial park. The other pointed to the Hilton Convention Center Hotel.

Her heart sank. Was this where they were staying? Miles from Boston in the middle of nowhere?

A curving road took them to a ten-story hotel beside a large parking structure. A large sign listed the amenities: a restaurant, a lounge, a breakfast cafe, a swimming pool and a fitness center.

All the comforts of home, except for one thing.

She had to stay here with Gregor, a man she feared and detested, with no way to escape.

No public transportation, no money and no gun.

A black cloud of despair settled over her.

CHAPTER 22

Friday July 9, 2010 1:35 PM Dedham, MA

The hotel fitness center on the second floor had top of the line equipment: ten treadmills, a two-tiered rack of weights, and Nautilus machines to tone every muscle in your body. She'd spent forty minutes on a treadmill, working up a sweat. Now she was on the rowing machine, toning her biceps and back muscles. Two conventions were here and some of the attendees were working out on their lunch hour.

A petite blond with a ponytail was on the machine beside her. What would the woman say if she told her the man in the corner lifting weights would kill her if she didn't steal two paintings tonight?

Dressed in shorts and a T-shirt, Gregor thrust a large dumbbell over his head, grunting audibly. His chest was massive and muscles bulged in his biceps and hairy thighs.

He was using a fake ID. When they checked in yesterday, the desk clerk had said, "Welcome to the Hilton, Mr. Haas!" Greeting them like royalty. When they got to their room, she saw why.

Gregor had booked a two-bedroom, two-bath suite on the top floor. There was a privacy door between the rooms. Not that Gregor gave her any privacy. Last night after dinner, he had propped it open and told her to go to bed. "Rest up for tomorrow," he'd said. "Have a good sleep."

But how could she, with Gregor in the next room? Each time she dozed off, she jolted awake, fearing he was in her room. Then she lay awake, obsessing over one catastrophe after another. Renzi catching her outside the Gardner with the stolen paintings. And she didn't trust Nicholas. Would he do his job? Her safety depended on it. What about the other guards? But her biggest fear, the one that kept her awake all night was Gregor. The evil man with the scarred hands and the sinister voice that filled her with dread.

She worked the rowing machine faster. Tonight was the night. In twelve hours it would be over.

Last night she had locked herself in her bathroom to check her iPhone. She deleted the texts from the bugging device on the Saab. She knew where it had been. She'd been inside it.

There was also a text message from Pak Lam: docs are ready. She deleted that, too. It took her a while to decide how to respond. Finally she had sent him a text: *Boss took me out of town. See U when I can.*

But would she? Tears filled her eyes. Her nerves were shot, her emotions raw.

Gregor wouldn't let her out of his sight. This morning he'd ordered breakfast from room service and made her eat with him in his room. They ate in silence. Gregor didn't do idle chitchat. When he said something, he did it to control her or needle her, sticking his nose into her personal life, asking about her mother.

She looked over at him. Now he was sitting on a bench, mopping sweat from his face with a towel. Watching her. She looked away and resumed her workout. Screw Gregor. She had to stay strong.

The most perilous journey begins with a single step.

Gregor approached her, his eyes fixed on her loose-fitting T-shirt. "We need to discuss the job."

Finally, he was going to tell her about it. "Okay, but I need to take a shower first."

"Come to my room at four o'clock. Dress for dinner. We eat early tonight. Wear your pretty dress."

She clenched her teeth. *Come to my room. Wear your pretty dress.*

What fun.

Frank finished reading Ursula's case file and put it on Hank Flynn's desk. "No leads, no suspects."

"Tough to work a murder case without a body," Flynn said. "Her parents live in Germany, didn't report her missing for ten days. And her friend Lisa didn't give us much. You talked to her, right?"

"Yes. We had coffee at Starbucks. Lisa claimed she and Ursula were best friends. I let her ramble a while, then told her I needed information if I was going to find Ursula."

Flynn's eyes widened. "She thinks Ursula is still alive?"

"I think she knows Ursula is dead. She just doesn't want to believe it. But she gave me something useful. Ursula told her the Global Interpreting manager was always undressing her with his eyes. Stefan Haas. But Marta slipped up once and called him Gregor. I figure Gregor Kraus is using Stefan's ID."

"Why would he kill Ursula?"

Frank gestured at the file folder. "Did you see the pictures her parents sent? She looks like a movie star. Maybe Gregor's a sexual predator. Maybe he hit on her and she said no."

"Wouldn't be the first time." Hank's phone rang. He picked up and listened for a while, jotting notes. A minute later, he cradled the phone. "The New Hampshire Registry of Motor Vehicles."

Hank had already talked to someone at the Massachusetts RMV. No one by the name of Stefan Haas had a license to drive in Massachusetts.

"Stefan Haas was licensed to drive in New Hampshire for the past fifteen years," Flynn said, "but his license lapsed in November 2008. He didn't renew it on his birthday."

"Because he was dead."

"Correct." Hank glanced at his notes. "But prior to that he had four DUI arrests."

"He was a party animal, liked to go to clubs and pick up girls."

"If Gregor Kraus is as bad as you say, Stefan would have been a pushover. Kraus sees him flash an American passport to get into a London club, chats him up at the bar, gets him drunk?"

"Exactly. Kraus probably hung out at the clubs in London where Americans go. Stefan Haas was in the wrong place at the wrong time."

"But if Kraus is driving around Boston using Stefan's expired DL, we might get him." Hank flipped through the papers on his desk. "One of my detectives got a tip from his CI yesterday. He said some kind of street action was going down this weekend. No specifics."

"No where or when?"

"No. My guy leaned on him but that's all he'd say."

"On the weekend?"

Hank smiled. "That's when all the excitement happens, Frank. You know that."

———

She took a shower, dried her hair and put on the dress Gregor liked, the one with the low-cut jade-green top. Be who they want you to be. But if he made a move on her, she'd kick him in the balls.

When she entered his room, he rose from one of the easy chairs grouped around a coffee table.

"You look lovely, Valerie. Please have a seat." Gesturing at the chair beside his.

He had on a well-tailored suit, Armani, she guessed, and he wasn't wearing that ridiculous wig. His dark hair was damp but neatly combed, his face freshly shaved. She could smell his aftershave lotion.

"Would you care for a drink?"

"No, thank you. Tell me about the job. What about the cops in the cruisers?"

"At one o'clock they go to sleep for a while."

"What does that mean? How do you know this?"

Gregor frowned. "Take my word for it. I know."

Take his word for it? Not in a million years.

"I have set up a diversion to keep the cops busy during the heist," he said. "A disturbance on the Fenway several blocks from the Gardner."

"How do I get to the job? This hotel is miles from the Gardner."

A brochure in her bedroom listed information about the hotel: 250 guest rooms and six meeting rooms for corporate events, conveniently located twenty miles from downtown Boston, seventeen miles from Logan Airport. It might as well be seven hundred. She had no car.

Gregor smiled at her. "A fine hotel, isn't it?"

She clenched her teeth and said nothing.

"I will drop you off at one of the apartment buildings on Tetlow Street behind the museum. You walk around the corner to the employee entrance and Nicolas lets you in."

"What time do we leave?"

"Relax, Valerie. Not until after midnight. When it's dark."

"Relax? How can I relax? You dole out details like a miser hoarding gold, a tidbit here, a tidbit there. When do I get my new passport?"

Gregor gazed at her, expressionless. "You get your new passport when you deliver the Vermeers."

"When will that be? What's the timetable?"

"The cops go down at one o'clock and the hoodlums start the disturbance on the Fenway. Nicolas disables the security system and lets you in."

"What about the other security guards?"

"That is not your concern. Nicolas will take care of them."

"Take care of them? How?"

"Stop questioning me!" he shouted.

Shocked, she stared at him. Gregor had never raised his voice to her.

A moment later he said in his usual quiet voice, "You go to the Special Exhibit, take the Vermeers and leave through the employee entrance, the same as always. I will be waiting in a car on Palace Road."

The same as always? What about Nicolas? What happens to him?

But she didn't dare ask. Gregor was giving her some of the details, but not all of them. What was he not telling her?

"You give me the paintings, I give you a new passport, and we drive away." He smiled. "Happy now?"

Not the least bit happy. "I'll feel better when the job is over."

"Let's have a drink." He went to a sideboard that held several liquor bottles. "Want some cognac? Remy Martin. Not the best, but adequate. Or some wine, perhaps? A glass of Australian Merlot?"

When she didn't answer, he poured cognac into a snifter, opened a bottle of wine, poured some in a crystal wineglass and brought it to her. She took the glass and set it on the coffee table.

"I try to please you, Valerie. Why must you be so … standoffish?"

He sat down in his chair and sipped his cognac, gazing at her. "You hate your father."

Stunned, she stared at him. "What makes you say that?"

"You don't want to talk about him?"

"No." She picked up her glass and gulped some wine.

"Why not?" Without waiting for an answer, he said, "I know why. You hate him."

A headache stabbed her forehead. She didn't want to think about her father, much less talk about him.

"Why?" Gregor said quietly, gazing at her intently. "Why do you hate him?"

Why did she hate her father? For many reasons, too many to count. An ugly scene flashed in her mind, one she would never forget. A hotel room in Paris, the night she had confronted him. But she wasn't going to tell Gregor about it.

Gregor held out his hands. When they were together she avoided looking at them, unwilling to see the hideous scars.

"My father did this," he said.

"Your father?" she gasped. And immediately thought, No wonder Gregor is so cruel.

"Yes. When I was five, I did not understand this, but now I do. He did this to make me strong. The world is a cruel place, full of dangerous people. Physical pain is nothing to me now. Even when I was five, it was not the pain that frightened me. It was the anticipation. Knowing he would do it again and not knowing when."

You bastard, she thought. *That's why you won't tell me anything.*

He sipped his cognac. "Why do you hate your father?"

"Because he abandoned me," she snapped. "Me and my mother."

"When was this?"

"A long time ago, when I was two. Eight years later someone murdered my mother."

"So you said. Who killed her? Not your father, you said."

"An evil man."

"Did you punish him for this?"

She drank some wine. "I don't want to talk about it."

Gregor studied her for several seconds, then nodded. "You did. I see this on your face."

She didn't want him reading her face, or her mind. "I'm tired, Gregor. I need to rest."

He gestured at the king-sized bed. "We could rest together."

"Gregor," she snapped, "I told you before. I'm not going to have sex with you. We need to focus on the job."

His face remained expressionless, but anger showed in his eyes.

"As you wish, Valerie. Come. We go to the dining room. A good meal will give you energy for the job."

CHAPTER 23

Friday July 9, 2010 11:25 PM

Gregor averted his face as he drove past the police cruiser on Evans Way. His black two-door Chevy was innocuous enough, no reason for the cops to take note of it, but better safe than sorry. The rain was an unexpected bonus. Not many people would be walking around near the Gardner in this kind of weather. The wipers could barely keep up with the torrent of rain slashing the windshield. But the rain and the traffic, people leaving town for the weekend probably, had delayed him.

An hour ago he had parked the Saab at the storage facility in Revere. Marta had rented it with her credit card, but if someone remembered seeing it near the Gardner tonight, the cops might trace it to Global Interpreting, and that wouldn't do. A taxi had driven him to a rental car agency near the airport. He'd rented the Chevy with the same stolen credit card he'd used at the hotel in Dedham.

He turned right onto Tetlow Street. To his left, brownstone apartment buildings faced the Gardner. He lowered his window and heard loud music. Lights blazed in several windows. Cars were parked nose to tail along the street, and two young men laughed as they ran up the steps to one building. They appeared to be college students, ready to party on a Friday night.

When he reached the corner of Palace Road, he saw the dark-brown Chevrolet Express mini-van Kwan had stolen. Kwan had found a good spot for it. He'd better make sure the Rhode Island license plate was also stolen. He stopped in front of the gate to the Simmons College parking lot on the opposite corner, not a legal space, but the guard booth was empty. He killed the headlights but left the motor running.

Rain drummed the roof of the car. He could barely see the employee entrance thirty yards away. Inside the watch room, a security guard was watching the video monitors. He craved a cigarette, but resisted it. The flare of his lighter might attract attention.

Always be in control. Focus on the job.

Yesterday he'd given Kwan the stun gun, a hand-held Taser similar to those police used to subdue violent criminals. The ex-cop would know how to use it. A 200,000-volt jolt of electricity would incapacitate the cops in the cruisers long enough for her to put them to sleep. His San Francisco contact had sent him the stun gun and four speed-injectors of Scopolamine-S. The drug would induce a sleep-like stupor and the recipient would remember nothing later. But he had to take the gangster's word for this, a violation of one of his rules. Trust no one.

He opened his leather briefcase and took out a two-way radio. Kwan and the ex-cop had the other two. Later tonight they would use them to stay in contact. The radios had 14 channels and an operating range of two miles, more than enough for his purpose, he believed, but he intended to make sure. Leave nothing to chance.

Again he felt the nicotine craving. Again he resisted. His appetite for nicotine was difficult to control. And thanks to Valerie, sex was never far from his mind these days.

He raised the two-way radio to his mouth and murmured, "San Francisco." It had amused him to designate Kwan's birthplace as their code word.

Moment's later he heard, "Yesss."

"Location?"

"Gothic Room."

The terse answer reassured him. He'd warned the punk to use no unnecessary words. For once, Kwan was following orders. "Go to the Dutch Room."

"Why?"

"Just do it," he snapped.

Thirty seconds later he heard, "Dutch Room."

"Listen carefully and do not interrupt. Take the Rembrandt Self-portrait first. It is one of the Gardner's prized possessions. Make sure it is not damaged. Then take the Manet in the Blue Room." He pictured the woman's dour face. He still couldn't think who she reminded him of, but it had to be someone he disliked. "The Manet is our proof that we have the paintings. Take good care of it, understand?"

"Yesss."

"You did well with the van. Is the plate stolen?"

"Yes."

"Stick to the time-line. Do nothing until five minutes past one. By then the head security guard and the cops in the cruisers will have phoned in their all-clear calls. When you kill the guards, use the garrote. No blood, understand?"

"Yessss."

"After the ex-cop drives the van into the courtyard, let Scorpio in through the employee entrance. After she delivers the two Vermeers, you know what to do. Don't waste time. You must leave by two at the latest. Drive directly to our meeting spot. Don't be late, understand?"

"Yesss."

He shut off the radio and lit a Gitanes. The nicotine rush calmed him. Kwan thought the insurance companies were going to pay millions of dollars to ransom the four paintings. He was desperate for money so he could leave the country. Nicholas Kwan wanted to believe, and Gregor had no intention of spoiling his fantasy.

He put the two-way in his briefcase, turned on the wipers and pulled out of the space. He drove past the cop in the cruiser at the corner of Palace Road, turned right on the Fenway and sped away.

Valerie was waiting at the hotel in Dedham, fuming probably, wondering where he was. He parked beside a fire hydrant on Huntington Avenue, took out his cell, hit his speed-dial.

She answered after one ring. "Yes."

Poor Valerie, so anxious about this job. "Listen carefully, Scorpio," he said, in a voice that cut off questions the way a sharp knife cuts off the tip of a fine cigar. "I cannot drive you to the job. The details are now in place but this took longer than I anticipated. I am near the target now. It is too late to come get you. I have ordered a taxi to pick you up at 12:15 exactly. Dedham Cab. He will drop you off at the location. Understand?"

There was a brief silence, then, "Yes."

"Dress for the weather. It is raining. See you soon." He punched off and closed the cellphone.

Judging by her terse response, Valerie was not happy. In fact, she had been angry and upset for two days. He could always tell when others feared him. Thanks to his experience as an enforcer, he knew the signs. Rapid eye movements, desperately seeking escape. Parted lips, shallow breathing, stiff posture.

But Valerie was up to something. It was written on her face and her body language was unmistakable. He didn't know what it was, but soon it wouldn't matter. He smiled, recalling her reaction when he asked why she hated her father. Gulping her wine, her inner turmoil displayed in her lovely almond-shaped eyes. What did her father do, he wondered. Try to fuck her? Why not? She had a luscious body.

He wanted to fuck her, too. A pity she had to die.

———

Nicholas prowled the dark hallway on the third floor of the Gardner. His rubber-soled shoes made no sound on the floor. He didn't need his flashlight. He knew every inch of the building. Dust motes danced in a shaft of moonlight falling through a window. Beside it, an antique chair with a cushioned seat gave off a musty odor. He hated the overnights, hated the smells and the shadowy silence. Sometimes it took all the willpower he possessed to keep from screaming.

He paused at the one object in the museum that interested him, a Christ-like figure carved from rosewood, its arms outstretched. Nails pierced its palms and feet, which were decorated with painted blood drops. It reminded him of the statue he'd seen in the church where he'd hidden after his escape from juvenile prison.

His radio bleeped, shattering the silence. Not Stefan's radio, the one the security guards carried.

He took the handset off his belt and flicked a switch. "Yes."

"What are you doing, napping? Tony's is waiting for you in the Special Exhibit. You should have been there at midnight." Charles Lawson, the head guard, was in the watch room, eyes glued to the monitors. Hidden video cameras were everywhere.

Lawson had worked here for ages and was a stickler about patrols. It would be a pleasure to kill him.

Before their shift tonight the security director had given them a stern warning. "Be extra vigilant tonight. The Robbery happened on a weekend. Those guards violated protocol and let the thieves into the museum. Never allow anyone inside, not even for an emergency!"

The fool was in for a surprise. Other than Scorpio, no one was coming into the museum tonight, but four paintings were leaving it.

"Be right there. I heard a noise in the Titian Room on the third floor, but it was nothing."

He descended the stairs to the second floor. Three strides took him into the Dutch Room. Drawn by the bright red surplice over the dark judicial robe, he studied the painting opposite the door. *A Doctor of Law* by Francisco de Zurbaran. A judge with cruel eyes, staring at him, like the judge who'd sent him to juvenile prison when he was twelve. The memory infuriated him. Older boys had forced him to do unspeakable things. Never again would he return to jail.

Never again would he submit to such degradation.

A small wooden frame stood on a table beside a window. Ten years ago the frame had held Vermeer's masterpiece, *The Concert*. Now brown velvet filled the frame. On an adjacent wall, another frame held green fabric, not *Rembrandt's Storm on the Sea of Galilee*.

The two most famous stolen paintings, worth millions. Now the thieves were living in luxury somewhere. Soon he would, too. Nicholas smiled. Maybe he'd go to Thailand. There he could live in luxury, hire servants, buy any car he wanted. He could hardly wait.

He checked the luminous dial on his wristwatch. 12:10. His pulse quickened. Soon it would be time to kill Lawson and Falcone. He reached inside his uniform jacket and touched the leather sheath that held his Nakura hunting knife. The seven-inch stainless-steel blade had a sharp point and the upper half of the blade was serrated.

His insurance, in case the garrote failed him.

But first he had to radio Jamilla and tell her to take out the cops. Would she do it? The question set his teeth on edge. He would tell her exactly what he would do to her little monkey if she didn't.

He stopped near the door to study the Rembrandt *Self-portrait*: a bulbous nose, curly hair down to his shoulders, a fancy uniform with brass buttons, a hat with a feather. The first painting on Stefan's list.

Too bad he couldn't rip it off the wall now to save time. But the security cameras were on.

He stepped into the corridor. Tonight it was darker than usual. Clouds obscured the moon, and rain drummed the glass roof above the interior courtyard. The darkness would come in handy later.

Recalling Stefan's insulting radio test, he ground his teeth. Stefan treated him like a lackey. Stefan thought he was desperate because the San Francisco cops were after him. Wrong.

Trust me, Stefan said.

But he trusted no one, least of all Stefan. The bastard was in for a surprise. Once he secured his bargaining chip, Stefan would be the desperate one. Then the bastard would come crawling to him.

———

Jittery with nerves, Natalie paced the hotel room, unable to sit still, every muscle in her body tense, her heart thumping her chest. For the umpteenth time, she checked her wristwatch. Five minutes to midnight.

For two weeks she'd been desperate to know when the heist was.

Now she knew, and she was terrified.

If only Gregor hadn't kept her prisoner in this hotel, never letting her out of his sight. Her only respite came when she went in her bathroom and locked the door. Earlier she had fended off his disgusting sexual advance. This infuriated him, though he tried to hide it, talking about innocuous topics during dinner. She'd forced down a chicken Caesar salad and two cups of coffee. Later, he'd left her alone, though he left the door between their rooms open. At 9:45 he had come in her room and said he had to take care of some details. He would be back at midnight to drive her to the Gardner.

But at 11:25 he'd called and told her a taxi would pick her up at 12:15. *I am near the target now.*

A statement that set off red flags in her mind. According to the texts to her iPhone, the Saab had gone to the storage facility in Revere at 10:25 PM. Nothing since, which meant it was still there. If the Saab was in Revere, how could Gregor be near the Gardner?

There was only one explanation. He had another car.

She massaged her temples but the dull ache didn't go away.

The red digits on the bedside clock clicked over to midnight. In fifteen minutes a taxi would arrive to take her to the job. Compulsively, she checked her duffel bag to make sure the black trash bags and the tin snips were there. Took out her wallet and counted the money. Seventy dollars. She'd have to use most of it to pay the cab driver.

If she had a gun she'd feel a lot safer.

But the Beretta was in her bedroom closet at her apartment.

Maybe she should call the Mountain Man. But what would she say?

My boss wants me to steal two paintings from the Gardner Museum and I'm afraid he's going to kill me?

After Gregor called she had pulled her hair into a ponytail and put on the outfit she used for the heists. Black running pants and a black turtleneck. Not her black pumps, unfortunately, her gym shoes.

She studied herself in the mirror above the dresser and decided the ponytail was too conspicuous. She went in the bathroom and used hairpins to fasten the ends of the ponytail to her head. She returned to the bedroom, put on her dark glasses and studied herself in the mirror.

She looked like a thug. Dressed in black, wearing dark glasses.

What would the cab driver think?

She took off the glasses, put them in the duffel bag and took the iPhone off the bedside table. No new texts.

The Saab was still in Revere. But Gregor wasn't.

Dress for the weather. It is raining. See you soon.

As if they were going out on a date. And rain was the least of her problems. First she had to deal with Nicolas. She didn't trust him. Then she had to steal the Vermeers from the Special Exhibit and deliver them to Gregor, who would be waiting on Palace Road in a car.

But how would she know which car?

Why didn't he tell her when he called?

A sick feeling gnawed at her stomach. The answer was obvious.

Yesterday he'd said he would give her a new passport when she gave him the paintings. She didn't believe it.

As soon as Gregor had the Vermeers he would kill her.

She hid her iPhone under the trash bags in the duffel bag.

That made her feel better. She didn't feel so alone.

There had been many times in her life when she had badly wanted something. With all her heart and soul, she wanted to be somewhere else tonight.

Someplace where she didn't have to worry about Gregor killing her.

She glanced at the bedside clock. 12:10.

The cab would be here soon. Time to go.

A perilous journey begins with a single step.

CHAPTER 24

Saturday July 10, 2010 12:20 AM

Wrinkling her nose at the sour stench, Jamilla pulled up her jeans and flushed the toilet. Her nerves were so frazzled she had the trots. She was desperate for a hit, anything to calm her down. "No," she said to her reflection in the medicine cabinet mirror. "No drugs."

She went in the living room and sank onto the lumpy sofa she slept on. Jaylen used the cot in the bedroom. She pushed aside a crumpled Frito bag on the TV tray, picked up the phone and stared at her alarm clock. 12:17. Jaylen was at Lateesha's apartment. Lateesha smoked pot sometimes, but what choice did she have? Jaylen loved playing with Lateesha's little boy. Jaylen would be fine.

She had to stop thinking about all the things that could go wrong. She dialed a number and waited. Zipper didn't answer right away. Her stomach clenched. After the eighth ring, an eternity, a voice said, "Yo."

"Wha's up, Zip? You set?"

"Bet your ass we set. Tell me 'bout the bucks. When's the payoff?"

"Tomorrow morning, ten o'clock."

"Fuck that! Gotta be tonight. My troops wanna party."

"Dammit, Zip, I told you! I don't get the money till after the rumble."

"We do the hoot 'n holler at one, plenty of time to hook up after."

She wiped her sweaty hands on her jeans. Zipper had made his name, and tons of money, selling guns on the street, zip guns first, then deadlier models. When Zip got a bug up his ass, he didn't quit till he got what he wanted. "Okay, but I can't meet you till—"

She bit her lip. How the hell did she know what time she could meet him? She didn't know how long the cop deal would take, didn't even know where they were. Damn Nicholas to hell! She took a deep breath. "Meet me at the 7-Eleven on Harrison Avenue at three."

"No way. Two o'clock, no later."

"Dammit, Zip, I gotta deal with The Man first! Two-thirty."

"Awright. Two-thirty. You better be there with the bucks."

"And you better make sure the rumble happens on time. Five before one. No sooner, no later."

Her T-shirt clung to her back, damp with sweat. She put down the phone, went to the window and raised the tattered green shade. Rain pelted the glass and a flash of lightning slashed the dark sky. Three stories below her, headlights from passing cars flashed over puddles and rain-filled gutters. A shitty night to be out, but it was time to leave.

Sick with dread, she went in the bedroom. Her uniform lay on the bed beside a black plastic shopping bag with rope handles. Inside were the items Nicolas had given her: the 2-way radio, the stun gun and the drug applicators. A wave of dizziness hit her and her stomach cramped.

Clutching her belly, she ran to the bathroom and vomited in the toilet. When there was nothing left, she struggled to her feet, ran cold water in the sink, and brushed her teeth to get rid of the rotten taste. She hadn't been this scared since the night she held off a knife-wielding drug dealer in a dark alley, hearing faraway sirens, hoping her backup would get there in time. They did, but after the collar went down she had puked her guts out.

She opened the medicine cabinet and took out a plastic baggie. She'd copped half a dozen Valium on the street last week to ward off the panicky feeling she got when she thought about what Nicholas might do to Jaylen. Two pills left. She shook them into her hand.

But Valium made her drowsy. She had to keep her wits about her tonight. She flushed the pills down the toilet.

In the bedroom she stripped to her underwear and put on the uniform, hearing the bastard's words. *Go to the Dunkin' Donuts on Huntington near Ruggles Street. Be there at twelve-thirty sharp.*

But he didn't tell her where the cops were, just said he'd call her 2-way radio when she got there.

She opened the shopping bag and looked at the stun gun and the four drug syringes. Her hands shook with tremors and her legs felt weak, too weak to walk to the damn Dunkin' Donuts.

I wouldn't want anything to happen to your boy.

With a low moan, she picked up the shopping bag and took it in the living room. Two suitcases stood by the door, packed and ready. Twelve hours from now, Lord willing, she and Jaylen would be on a bus bound for Georgia.

She set her jaw and left the apartment.

———

Nicolas opened the watch room door and yelled to the senior guard in the Special Exhibit. "Mr. Lawson! I see something on the monitors!"

He heard pounding feet. Seconds later, an older man, eyes wide behind his wire-rimmed spectacles, burst into the watch room.

"Look." Nicholas pointed to a monitor. Lawson planted his palms on the desk and bent forward, eyes fixed on the monitor. An angry red pimple stood out on the back of his neck. Nicholas crept up behind him, flipped the garrote over his head and yanked hard.

"Aaah!" Lawson screamed, flailing his arms wildly.

He twisted the wooden handles of the garrote, pulling the wire tighter and tighter. Lawson clawed at the wire and strangled noises came from his mouth. Lawson was stronger than he looked, wiry muscles standing out in his arms. Suddenly he threw back his head. Nicholas tried to duck, but Lawson's head cracked against his cheekbone. The bastard! Trying to head-butt him!

Nicholas kicked his leg and Lawson fell to his knees, clawing at the wire. But the wire was buried deep in his neck, digging into his throat. Nicholas yanked the handles of the garrote. Lawson's face turned crimson, mouth open, seeking the precious air that would keep him alive, his tongue protruding. He kneed Lawson's back, forcing him facedown on the floor.

A minute later Lawson's struggles ceased and his body went limp.

Winded and sweaty, Nicholas rose and studied the monitors. Tony Falcone was in the Veronese room on the third floor. The timing would be tricky. Now it was 1:04. At 1:15 Falcone would go downstairs to patrol the second floor. Eleven minutes. But he couldn't kill Falcone until Jamilla called to tell him the cops in the cruisers were in dreamland. Despite his threats, he was not certain she would do this.

A sudden stench hit his nostrils. Lawson's bowels had let go.

Grasping his arms, Nicholas hauled the body out of the watch room so Scorpio wouldn't see it when he let her inside. He dragged the body down the hall past the Special Exhibit. A closet with cleaning supplies was beside the elevator. Panting, he dropped Lawson's body, unlocked the closet door, shoved the body inside and shut the door.

His uniform shirt was damp with sweat and beads of moisture dripped from his nose. He ran back to the watch room and checked the time. 1:12. The ex-cop was screwing up his timetable.

What the hell was the stupid bitch doing?

He mopped sweat off his face with his shirtsleeve, alternately watching the monitors to track Falcone and checking his watch.

The minutes crept by, second by agonizing second.

———

Huddled in the doorway of a four-story apartment building opposite the Gardner Museum, Jamilla squinted at the cruiser parked at the corner of Evans Way. At least the cop was dry. She was soaked to the skin. Even her feet were wet, rainwater seeping into her loafers.

When she got to Dunkin' Donuts, Nicolas had called her 2-way radio and told her the two cops were outside the Gardner Museum.

Synchronize your watch. It is exactly twelve-forty-two.

She didn't dare tell him she didn't have one. She'd hocked it weeks ago.

Buy coffee and donuts for the cops. At two minutes past one, go to the first police car and take out the cop. I have a very sharp knife. If you fuck up, I will slit your boy's throat.

Jamilla shuddered. A cardboard tray with two coffee containers and a pink-and-white Dunkin' Donuts bag sat beside her feet. She'd bought two large coffees and two donuts for the cops, a small coffee for herself, and sat at a table to drink it, watching the clock on the wall. The kid behind the counter probably thought she was a cop goofing off on the job, but she didn't care. She had needed the break to muster her courage, had needed the damn clock even more.

Now she was counting the seconds in her mind.

Thousand forty, forty-one, forty-two ...

A sudden gust of wind drove sheets of rain into the doorway, drenching her trousers. Drinking the coffee was a mistake. Her bladder was ready to burst. She shifted her feet. *Fifty-nine. Sixty.*

It had to be one o'clock by now and it would take her a minute to reach the cruiser. She picked up the cardboard tray, crossed the street and trudged down the sidewalk, hearing the bastard's warning: *Make sure the cop sees your uniform. And the coffee and donuts.*

Her bowels turned to liquid. Jesus, she needed a bathroom!

She went to the driver's side door, and the cop rolled down the window. "Hey, Jamilla! I didn't know you were back on the job."

Panic hit her like a fist. Johnny Perkins, his wide ivory smile stark against his black-as-coal skin, not a buddy exactly, but she knew him. And he knew her. Her heart spun out of control like a car broadsided by a truck. How could she do this to Johnny? But she had to, had to do it fast, before he suspected. Balancing the cardboard Dunkin Donuts tray in one hand, she set the stun gun against his neck and zapped him.

Johnny's face registered an instant of surprise. Then he recoiled as if hit by a punch. His eyes rolled up in his head, and his chin sagged onto his chest. Tears stung her eyes.

Hit him with the drug, please God don't let him remember.

She set the tray on the sidewalk and pulled an applicator out of her pocket. Her hands trembled violently. The tube slipped from her fingers, fell in the gutter and rolled under the car. Frantic, she groped the bag for another applicator. A trickle of urine dribbled into her underpants.

She pulled out the applicator and turned to Johnny. Sweet Jesus!

His face was contorted and white foam dribbled out of his mouth.

She heard a moan. Jerked away. Realized the moan was hers.

———

Inside the cruiser at the corner of Palace Road, Officer David Sweeney held his handset to his mouth. "All clear, Louise. Haven't seen a soul since midnight. What fool would go out in this weather?"

"Roger that," chirped the dispatcher. "I checked off your one o'clock, Dave. Gotta go, the 911-lines are lit up. Talk to you at two."

He clicked off and squirmed in his seat to get comfortable. Six hours to go. Overnight duty sucked, but he needed the extra bucks. He and his wife had just put a down payment on an oversized Cape in Dedham. It was no palace, but it had four bedrooms, which they desperately needed now that they had two sets of twins. Rachel was a peach, but she wanted lots of kids. But kids were expensive, especially two at a time. Her family had a history of twins and …

He peered through the windshield. Who was that walking along the sidewalk beside the museum? Then he smiled. A uniform, carrying a pink-and-white Dunkin' Donuts bag.

As the officer came closer, he saw that it was a black woman.

Why was she walking the Fenway beat at night by herself? But then it came to him. She was a friend of Johnny's and he'd sent her for coffee. Johnny was a prince. He rolled down the window.

———

Shaking with rage, Nicolas left the watch room and stood in the hall, pacing back and forth. If the bitch didn't call soon, he would make good on his promise and carve her little monkey into a million pieces.

Thirty seconds later his 2-way radio bleeped.

He flicked it on and said, "Yes?"

I took them out, like you said. Jamilla's voice, shaky and high pitched.

"Good. A brown Chevrolet mini-van is parked at the corner of Palace Road. It is unlocked. Sit inside and wait for my instructions."

"Wait? Are you crazy? With two cops in—"

"Shut up and do it! Or your little monkey will be minus some fingers and toes."

He put the 2-way in his pocket and checked the monitors.

Shit! Falcone was in the Veronese Room, the last stop on his third floor patrol. In two minutes Falcone would go downstairs to the second floor. Scorpio was probably waiting outside the employee entrance, but screw her. He shut down the security system and ran to the staircase that led to the second floor.

———

With a final wail of its siren, a twenty-foot ladder truck pulled up in front of the Northeastern University dormitory on the Fenway. Seated at the wheel of his cruiser, Sergeant Neil Weaver checked his watch. 1:13. Ten minutes ago all hell had broken loose, 911-calls about a disturbance on the Fenway near the NU dorms. Pelted with rocks and bottles by a gang of rowdies, the officers in the first cruiser called for backup. The punks hid behind shrubs, waging a guerrilla-type action until three more cruisers arrived, Weaver's among them.

The rowdies had disappeared, but college kids were hanging out the windows of the five-story dorm, watching the show. Then someone pulled a fire alarm and they had to evacuate the building, kids straggling outside in pajamas or T-shirts, half of them angry, the others excited by the commotion.

Weaver called the dispatcher. "Better send another unit for traffic control, Louise. I got a bunch of college kids milling around over here. Be hell to pay if some idiot driver hits one."

A burst of rain splattered the windshield. He got out, hunching his shoulders against the rain. Now he had to coordinate with the fire unit captain to make sure the building was clear.

It was shaping up as a long night.

CHAPTER 25

Shrouded in darkness in the back seat of the taxi, Natalie pressed the stem of her watch to illuminate the dial. Almost one-thirty. She was late. Traffic on the Expressway had been backed up due to an accident, and after they passed it, cars were moving at a snail's-pace to avoid puddles on the rain-slicked highway. She hadn't heard from Gregor since his earlier phone call. She didn't know if this was good or bad.

There were too many things she didn't know.

The driver turned left onto Evans Way. She sank lower in the seat as they passed the police cruiser parked near the corner. When they got to Tetlow Street, she said, "You can let me off here."

The driver, a young guy with bushy brown hair, said, "You sure? It's a nasty night."

"It's fine." She took her wallet out of the duffel bag. "How much is the fare?"

"Forty-two dollars."

She gave him two twenties and a ten. "Keep the change."

She waited until the cab drove off before continuing down Tetlow Street. Wind-driven rain hit her face. Before leaving the hotel, she had stopped at the gift shop to buy a windbreaker with a hood, partly to keep her dry, partly to hide her outfit and her hair. The jacket was lightweight but the waterproof outer layer acted like an insulator, and her black turtleneck clung to her back, soaked with sweat. The storm had brought no relief from the heat and humidity.

Cars were parked bumper to bumper along Tetlow Street. No pedestrians, but lights were visible in some of the apartments. Behind a tall wrought-iron fence across the street the Greenhouse loomed behind the Gardner Museum. She walked faster, hurrying now. At the corner of Palace Road she spotted someone inside a dark brown mini-van. Was it Gregor? If it was, he gave no sign, no quick flick of the headlights. If it was a cop she was in trouble.

She kept walking at a steady pace. Attract no attention.

The employee entrance was thirty yards away. All she had to do was go inside, deal with Nicholas, get the Vermeers and deliver them to Gregor. Her mouth went dry and her stomach clenched.

But Nicholas was a thug and she was afraid Gregor would kill her after she gave him the Vermeers. During the cab ride, she had remembered what he'd said during their reconnaissance mission, gesturing at the employee entrance and saying: *I will pick you up, not in this car, another one.* But he hadn't told her what car he'd be driving. Still, there wouldn't be many cars driving around the museum at this hour. A flick of the headlights would signal that it was him.

She didn't want to think about what would happen then.

As she approached the employee entrance she ducked her head. She had no idea if Nicholas had disabled the security camera yet. The door was closed. She took a deep slow breath. Exhaled slowly through her nose. Counted to sixty. She couldn't wait here long. If a patrol car drove by and saw her, they would stop and question her. Game over.

———

Inside the Dutch Room Nicholas flattened himself against the wall beside the door, poised on the balls of his feet, gripping the handles of the garrote. His body tingled with excitement. Falcone would be here any minute. He drew in a deep breath. Dust tickled his nose. A sudden urge to sneeze sent his heart racing. He blew soft puffs of air out his nostrils. The urge subsided, but it rattled him.

Sweat beaded his forehead. Breathing through his mouth, he waited.

His timing had to be perfect. Falcone was dull-witted and genial, but he was built like Godzilla. He heard a soft scuffling sound. Footsteps in the hall. His hands tightened on the garrote.

Falcone stepped through the door, a hulking presence in the shadowy room. Nicholas flipped the wire over his head and yanked it tight. Falcone let out a strangled yelp and threw an elbow, striking Nicholas in the ribs. It knocked the wind out of him, but he kept hold of the garrote, twisting it tighter around the guard's windpipe. Falcone flailed his arms, fighting him.

He kicked the back of Falcone's knees. The guard lost his balance and pitched forward onto his knees, emitting a hideous raspy sound.

Die you motherfucker! The words rang out so clearly in his mind, he feared he had spoken them aloud.

Fingernails raked his face. Searing pain made him drop the garrote.

Falcone turned and shoved him away. "Leone, you stupid fuck! Get off me!"

His heart hammered his chest. Falcone had seen him! He reached in his jacket and withdrew the Nakura hunting knife. As Falcone's fingers groped at the wire digging into his neck, Nicholas slashed his throat with the serrated edge of the knife.

Blood spurted, bringing a familiar coppery odor. Falcone scrabbled away on his hand and knees, but the floor was slick with blood. Nicholas straddled his back, riding him like a bull, stabbing him again and again. But the motherfucker kept fighting him, flailing his arms.

The bastard refused to die!

161

Enraged, he plunged the sharp point of the knife into Falcone's gut and ripped it upward.

The guard's moans became a harsh rasp, a death rattle. Falcone pitched forward, face down on the floor. Nicholas grasped clumps of his hair, jerked his head up and slammed it down against the floor.

A horrible stench filled the air. Falcone's bowels had let go. A sure sign he was dead.

He grasped the guard's ankles and dragged him across the room. It was slow going. Falcone was heavier than a dead moose. Panting, he hauled the body into the hall, dropped it in front of the elevator and paused to catch his breath. His muscles ached and his cheek throbbed.

He touched his cheek, felt something wet and sticky. Blood.

Leave no evidence, Stefan had said. Stefan had told him to use the garrote to kill the other guards.

As if strangling someone was a simple matter.

He wiped his fingers on his uniform pants and slid the elevator key into the lock. The door opened on an empty car, just as he'd left it. But he had to hurry. At two o'clock there would be no all-clear calls from Lawson or the cops in the cruisers. He hauled the body inside and checked the time. 1:23.

He had thirty-five minutes. He ran back to the Dutch Room, positioned a high-backed antique chair with an upholstered seat under the Rembrandt Self-portrait and stood on the chair. But when he yanked on the frame, it didn't budge. Stefan had given him bolt cutters to snip the wires that held the painting to the wall.

Screw that. He jumped off the chair, knelt beside a chest of drawers and took out the crowbar he'd hidden beneath it. He climbed onto the chair and set the crowbar behind the frame. Ignoring the shriek of splintering wood, he pried the frame off the wall and jumped off the chair. And saw stains on the seat.

Even in the dim light he could see the footprints. Blood from the soles of his shoes. If he didn't get it off his shoes, he would leave a trail of bloody footprints. The cops would be on them like flies on rice.

He leaned the Rembrandt against the wall and scuffed his shoes on the worn carpet in the center of the room until he was certain no blood remained on the soles of his shoes.

Now it was 1:26. Falcone had cost him precious minutes. He carried the Rembrandt to the elevator and rode it down to the first floor, breathing through his mouth to avoid the stench of Falcone's body.

When the doors opened, he ran to the Blue Room and attacked the frame of the Manet with the crowbar, ripping it off the wall. The frame splintered, but the painting was undamaged.

He carried it to the elevator and left it inside. Scorpio was probably outside the employee entrance. After he let her in, she would steal the Vermeers. Then he would deliver his little surprise.

_____

She was about to abandon her position outside the employee entrance when the door suddenly opened.

"Get inside. Hurry up," said a sibilant voice.

Nicholas, the guard she didn't trust. He appeared agitated, wild-eyed and sweaty-faced. She could smell him, stale sweat and something else, a funky odor. She half-expected him to yell at her for being late, but he motioned her down the hall.

"The Special Exhibit is down there. Hurry up and get the Vermeers."

"Where are the other guards?"

"Don't worry. I already took care of them."

Chills prickled her neck. Took care of them? What did that mean? "Is the security system disabled?"

"Yesss! Get the Vermeers and take them to the Cafe at the far end of the hall. An emergency exit opens onto the grounds of the Greenhouse. A brown mini-van will be parked there with the back door open. Put the Vermeers in the rear compartment and wait there for me."

"No. I'm supposed to take them out through the employee entrance."

Nicholas glared at her, his dark eyes hard and cold. "Just do it."

Unwilling to argue with him, she turned and walked down the hall to the Special Exhibit. Nicolas reminded her of some gangsters she'd seen in London. Ruthless and vicious. Like Gregor.

Everything was different from what he had told her. Did Gregor have some secret plan that she knew nothing about? But she had no time to analyze it. She had to get the Vermeers and get out.

Inside the Special Exhibit she paused to let her eyes adjust to the dim light. _The Milkmaid_ was beside the door. It was even more beautiful than the reproductions she'd seen. A glorious painting, centuries old, on loan from the Rijksmuseum. After tonight, no one would see it again. Because some rich bastard wanted it for himself.

But she couldn't think about that now. She set the duffel bag on the floor, opened it and took out the tin snips. A sign warned visitors to stay behind the velvet rope hanging from two stanchions in front of the painting or an alarm would sound.

But Nicholas had disabled the security system. Or so he'd said.

Her heart thudded against her ribs as she went around the rope. No alarms, no flashing lights. Using the tin snips, she cut the wires that held The Milkmaid to the wall.

Two minutes later she leaned the frame against the wall and took two large black trash bags out of the duffel bag. It was raining and she didn't want the painting to get wet. She shook open the bags, slipped one over the frame of _The Milkmaid_, then the other.

If only she had time to admire the other paintings, but she didn't.

She found *The Lacemaker* and got to work.

———

Jamilla hugged her arms to her chest. It was sweltering inside the van but her teeth were chattering worse than they did in a raging blizzard. She'd never been so terrified in her whole life. Fuck the money. She wanted to run home and get Jaylen and disappear.

But she couldn't. The bastard wanted her to back the van into the courtyard of the Greenhouse.

If you don't, I will find your little monkey and carve him into little pieces.

Urine dribbled into her underpants. She was desperate to pee but she was trapped in this van like a mouse in a hole. Her eyes brimmed over and tears ran down her cheeks. She jockeyed the van out of the space and shifted into reverse. The side mirror was blurry with raindrops. She lowered the window and stuck out her head. Rain spattered her face, mixing with her tears.

She backed the van down Tetlow Street, slowly and carefully, so as not to sideswipe any parked cars. Then she saw the wrought-iron gate in front of the Greenhouse. One side of the gate swung open, then the other. The gates of hell.

Would this nightmare ever end? Would she ever see Jaylen again?

She backed up to the gate.

———

Crouched behind a hedge in the courtyard of the Greenhouse, Nicholas wiped the blood off his knife. It hadn't taken long to dispose of Jamilla. Her body was lying on the front seat of the van. Later he would dump it in the rear compartment. He would have to wipe the blood off the front seat before he drove it.

He looked up at the moon barely visible in the dark sky. The storm clouds had parted and the rain had slowed to a drizzle. He peered around the thick shrubbery and studied the emergency exit.

No Scorpio, but it would take her a few minutes to get the Vermeers off the wall. She wouldn't use a crowbar the way he had. She was too docile, following Stefan's orders, looking anxious when he told her the new plan. He didn't know how Stefan bamboozled her into doing this job and he didn't care. Now she would pay for it.

He squatted, balancing on his heels, hidden behind the thick shrubbery. Gripping the handle of his Nakura hunting knife in his right hand, he checked his watch. 1:43.

If she didn't come out soon, he would go back inside and kill her.

CHAPTER 26

Natalie slung the duffel bag over her shoulder and picked up the trash bags with the Vermeers, one in each hand. Anxious to leave, she stepped out the door of the Special Exhibit and stood in the hall. The corridor was dark, silent and still. No sounds, no sign of Nicholas.

Her neck prickled. Where was he?

To her right at the far end of the hall, dim light shone in the cafe.

On the alert for any odd movement or sound, she hurried down the hall to the cafe. Empty chairs stood around the tables. On the far wall an exit door was propped open. Cautiously, she went to the door. Beyond the slate entryway, a dark-colored paneled van was parked ten yards away, the van she'd seen at the corner of Tetlow Street. The rear doors were spread open like butterfly wings, but where was Nicholas?

And where was the person she'd seen sitting behind the wheel?

Alarm bells went off in her mind. Something didn't feel right.

But the sooner she delivered the paintings, the sooner she could get out of here. Puddles stood on the uneven slate floor, which would make it slippery. A sudden gust of wind-driven rain spattered the entryway. The trash bags would protect the Vermeers.

Should she put on the windbreaker? *No, forget the rain and get out!*

Holding a trash bag in each hand, she avoided the puddles, stepped off the slate floor onto the gravel and approached the van. It had a Rhode Island license plate. Maybe it was stolen. That was Gregor's usual ploy. Steal a getaway vehicle and slap a stolen plate on it.

She carefully placed the trash bags on the floor inside the rear compartment and felt a rush of relief. But then she smelled a foul odor. She knew that smell.

She ducked around the open door and approached the driver's side of the van. The window was closed. No light inside. She brushed raindrops off the window and peered through the glass.

Her heart slammed her chest. A woman in a police uniform lay on the front seat in a pool of blood.

She heard a faint sound behind her. Footsteps on the gravel.

Already spooked, she whirled, hyper-alert, her heart beating her chest like a wild thing.

Out of the shadows, Nicholas came at her in a street-fighter crouch, his lips drawn back in a snarl, his eyes hard and ruthless. In his hand was a vicious-looking knife.

Adrenaline jolted her into action. She yanked the duffel bag strap off her shoulder, dropped it on the ground and faced him, legs wide apart, arms by her side. Her Taekwondo fighting stance.

He lunged at her with the knife.

Instinctively, she raised her right arm to parry the blow. She felt a burning sensation on her forearm and backed away.

He came at her again, thrusting the knife at her midsection.

She spun away. If she didn't put him down fast, he would kill her.

Gathering herself, she did a spin move and launched a TKD kick with all the force she could muster. Her foot struck his jaw and he fell to the ground. She grabbed the duffel bag and ran.

Behind her, Nicholas yelled, "You bitch!"

But she didn't look back. She ran as fast as she could toward the street. The wrought-iron gate was open. She plunged through it onto Tetlow Street and ran toward Huntington Avenue, her feet pounding the sidewalk. Her arm throbbed, but she didn't dare stop to see how badly he'd cut her.

She kept running. Not another pedestrian in sight. No cars either.

A good thing. Soon the cops would know about the robbery, and she didn't want anyone remembering a woman running away from the museum. She glanced over her shoulder. No sign of Nicholas. Of course. Why bother to chase her? He had the Vermeers. She didn't know what he planned to do with them, but that was the least of her worries.

At the corner of Huntington Avenue, she stopped, gasping for breath. Her arm was on fire, burning with pain. She had to tend to it. There was a 24-hour Dunkin' Donuts a few doors down, but she didn't dare go inside. A car approached her on Huntington Avenue, driving fast. She ducked into a recessed doorway. Off in the distance, she heard other sirens, a lot of them.

The car passed her. No flashing lights, no siren. Relieved, she opened the duffel and took out the windbreaker. Standing as far back from the sidewalk as possible, she took off her black turtleneck.

Blood oozed from a jagged three-inch gash in her right arm. She wrapped her turtleneck around the wound, put on the windbreaker and sagged against the wall. Her head was woozy, and her legs felt weak. Several times she had jogged from the Gardner to her apartment, but she couldn't do that now. She would never make it up that steep hill.

Maybe she could take a cab. Would the twenty dollars in her wallet be enough to get her there?

She tugged the hood of the windbreaker over her head, put on her dark glasses and stepped out of the doorway. Not a taxi in sight. She started walking. Her legs trembled, each step more difficult than the last. She turned to look behind her and saw headlights.

A car moving fast. Was it a cop? No, it was a taxi!

Waving her left arm, she went to the curb. Mercifully, the cab slowed and stopped. She opened the back door and climbed inside.

"Hi," she said. "I've only got twenty bucks. Can you take me to the Mission Church?"

The driver, a young white man, studied at her in the rearview mirror. "Okay, that should be enough."

When the taxi drove off, she sank back against in the seat, clutching her right arm. The church was at the top of the hill, two blocks from her apartment. She felt like a wounded animal, desperate to get home. Her apartment wasn't much of a home, but it was all she had. At least she could tend her wound and get more money. And the gun.

But she couldn't stay there. Gregor knew where it was and he probably had a key. Overwhelmed by exhaustion, she leaned her head back against the seat. All along she'd known this job was dangerous.

Now it had turned into her worse nightmare.

Grunting with each step, Nicholas dragged Falcone's body out of the Cafe onto the slate floor. The slob had to weigh at least two hundred pounds. He hauled the body across the gravel driveway, dropped it on the ground beside the van and climbed into the rear compartment.

The overpowering stench made him gag: sweat, urine, feces and the coppery odor of blood.

Please don't hurt Jaylen, please. The ex-cop, pleading with him. Until he'd slit her throat. Now her body was in the rear compartment with Lawson's, but her blood was on the front seat. He'd better grab some towels in the cafe and use them to mop up the blood.

Sweat dripped down his nose and his hands were damp inside the latex gloves. He mopped his face on his sleeve. His cheek throbbed. Falcone's nails had broken the skin. He touched his aching jaw.

When the bitch kicked him, he couldn't believe it. Using some kind of martial arts move, like the ones Jackie Chan did in his movies, she had slammed her foot against his jaw. The bitch was lucky. If he hadn't been so worried about the timetable, he would have caught her and sliced her to ribbons.

He checked his wristwatch and cursed. 1:48. Twelve minutes from now the dispatcher would expect an all-clear call from the cops in the cruisers and the security guard.

Standing in the rear compartment, he bent down and grabbed Falcone's arm, yanked him upright and put both hands under his armpits. Falcone's uniform was soaked with blood. In fact, Falcone's blood was all over the museum: the Dutch Room, the second floor hall, the elevator, and the first floor hall.

When Stefan found out, he'd be furious, but by then Stefan would have more important things to worry about.

Bracing his feet against the frame, Nicholas heaved the body into the compartment, dragged it forward and dropped it beside Lawson and the ex-cop. He removed the bloodstained surgical gloves, threw them on the floor of the van, put on a clean pair and ran back to the Cafe.

The Manet and the Rembrandt were propped against the wall beside the emergency exit door. Stefan's precious paintings. Grasping the splintered frame of the Rembrandt in both hands, he ran outside and put it on the floor of the rear compartment.

The wind and the rain had died down, but the misty drizzle was just as annoying. The air was thick with humidity. He mopped his forehead on his sleeve and returned to the Cafe. The Manet was the largest painting, encased in a heavy frame. He picked it up with both hands and lugged it out the exit door.

Halfway across the slate floor he slipped and fell to his knees. A jagged shard of wood pierced his palm and he dropped the Manet. The painting skittered across the slate floor and landed in a flowerbed.

Cursing, he scrambled to his feet. The Manet lay face down in a puddle beside a shrub. He turned it over.

The surface gleamed with moisture and clumps of dirt clung to the canvas. Worse, there was a big tear in the canvas.

Stefan would be furious. "Stefan can piss up a rope," he muttered.

He carried the Manet to the van, put it on the floor beside the Rembrandt and shut the doors. Sirens wailed in the distance.

Fear jolted his heart into a jagged rhythm. Then he remembered the riot. The sirens were cop-cars heading for the Northeastern dormitory. The bitch had done one thing right at least. He wondered where her little monkey was. But that wasn't his problem.

He checked his watch. 1:54. Way behind schedule.

Meet me by 2:15 and don't be late. Too bad. Stefan would have to wait until he secured his bargaining chip.

She took two extra-strength Excedrin, gulped the rest of the water and set the paper cup on the bathroom sink. Her head throbbed and the pain in her arm was worse. It had taken every ounce of her energy to climb the three flights of stairs to her apartment.

Wearing her sports bra and black running pants, she went in the bedroom and lay on the bed. She had to get out of here fast, but she wanted to take her belongings with her. Her suitcase was at the hotel in Dedham. The duffel bag might hold the Beretta and the ammo, but not much else. When she sat up, she felt dizzy. Focus. She had to focus.

She staggered to the closet. Unable to raise her right arm, she took the shoebox off the shelf with her left hand. It was so heavy she almost dropped it. She put it on the bed beside her duffel and went in the bathroom.

Her gym bag sat on the floor beside the tub. She'd forgotten it was here. She opened the medicine cabinet. The only items inside were the first-aid kit and her over-the-counter meds. She put them in the gym bag and noticed the paper cup on the sink. Fearing the cops might use to trace her, she crumpled the cup, put it in the gym bag and looked around. Satisfied that nothing incriminating remained, she grabbed a hand towel and took the gym bag into the bedroom.

She packed the ammo boxes into the duffel, wrapped the Beretta in the towel and put it in the duffel with the ammo. All that remained in the shoebox was the cash she'd withdrawn from her bank. She stuffed it in her wallet and tucked the wallet in the duffel.

Exhausted, she sank onto the bed. The room was stifling, but she didn't dare open the window. The black turtleneck was still wrapped around her right arm, sodden with blood. She needed clothes. At Gregor's insistence, her fancy outfits were at the hotel. If the cops traced his credit card, they would find them, but she doubted they would. Gregor was using a credit card with the name Stefan Haas.

She went to the bureau, put the rest of her underwear in the gym bag and added the black pumps with the deadly two-inch heels. In the closet were two pairs of pants, her little black dress with the short skirt, and four short-sleeved T-shirts. She stuffed them into the gym bag.

Her arm throbbed. The wound needed attention, but if she went to a hospital, they would report it to the cops. Another wave of dizziness hit her. She sank onto the bed, too tired to think.

She had to leave, but where would she go?

There was only one solution, one she didn't want to use, but what choice did she have?

She took out her iPhone, punched in a number and waited.

After three rings, a voice said, "Yes?"

"Hello, Mountain Man," she said, and held her breath.

"Natalie. What is wrong? You have not come for your documents."

"I'm hurt. A man tried to kill me. He cut me with a knife, but I got away."

"Wah!" Pak Lam exclaimed. "A knife? Where did he cut you?"

"My right arm. It's bleeding a lot."

"Where are you now? I will send someone to get you."

"At my apartment in Mission Hill. I'm afraid the man will come here and find me." Gregor, not Nicholas.

"Give me the address. Wait inside. Feng will call you when he gets there."

"Thank you," she said. She gave him the address and punched off.

Tears filled her eyes. Now she didn't feel so alone.

The Mountain Man would help her.

CHAPTER 27

Gregor lowered the car window and flicked his cigarette onto the rain-slicked roadway. The rain had slackened but hadn't stopped. To his left beyond a grassy median, traffic was sparse on the Jamaicaway, sporadic cars, their wipers working against a steady drizzle.

He had been here more than an hour, an agonizing wait, the minutes ticking by slower than snails inching through mud. Now it was 2:05. Kwan should arrive soon if all had gone as planned, and there was no reason to believe it hadn't. He resisted the urge to smoke another Gitanes. A bottle of fine cognac awaited him in his quarters at Global Interpreting. He would wait and celebrate there.

At 2:10 headlights flashed as a vehicle circled the rotary behind him. A compact car, not the van. Where was Kwan?

He visualized the paintings, two Vermeers worth millions, the Rembrandt Self-portrait and Manet's portrait of his mother, Madame Auguste Manet. Her dour expression set his teeth on edge, but the Manet was an important painting, worth a large sum of money.

Rain splattered the roof of the car, and wind whipped the branches of the oak trees along the street. He checked his watch. 2:15 and still no sign of Kwan. Two compact cars followed by a red Jeep circled the rotary. No Chevrolet mini-van. Kwan would pay for his tardiness.

At 2:25 more headlights swept the rotary, a dark boxy-shaped vehicle. Gregor pumped his fist. The Chevrolet mini-van!

Without slackening speed, it veered onto the side road and passed his black Chevy. Alarmed, Gregor flicked the headlights on and off. What the hell was Kwan doing?

The van's brake lights showed red as Kwan double-parked beside a white station wagon four cars ahead of him. Moments later, Kwan jumped out and sprinted toward him.

Gregor got out and leaned against the Chevy.

"You're late," he snapped. "Do you have the paintings?"

"They're in the van. Give me the keys so I can get out of here."

Gregor studied his face. There were scratches on his cheek and his jaw looked swollen. And there were stains on the front of his uniform. "What are those scratches on your face? What happened?"

"Nothing. Give me the keys!"

He tried to calm himself. Forced himself to speak in a quiet voice. "Is that blood on your uniform? I told you to use the garrote."

Agitated, Kwan paced in tight circles, his eyes glittering dangerously. "I had to knife the ex-cop. Stop questioning me. The whole city is crawling with cops. We have to get out of here now!"

"Not until I check the paintings to make sure they are in good condition."

Kwan thrust a knife at his face and kicked the back of his legs. Stunned by the sudden attack, he lost his balance and fell to his knees.

"Don't move or I will slit your throat."

Gregor froze. He could not see the knife, but he could feel the blade against his throat, a serrated edge pricking the skin. He did not doubt that Kwan would kill him. He'd seen street punks in London with eyes like that, murderous eyes, and Kwan was deadlier than any street punk. Kwan killed for sport.

To placate him, he said, "What are you doing, Nicholas? We are partners. You take the paintings. I deal with the insurance companies and get the money."

"If we are partners, why do you treat me like a servant? Questioning me. Telling me I'm late. Where are the keys? I want to get out of here."

The pressure on his throat increased, tiny needles of pain. Kwan was out of control. "Calm down, Nicholas. The keys are in the ignition. I gave you the directions to the safe house in Providence. Go there and wait for me to call you."

"Your precious paintings are in the van with the bodies. Get the money or you'll be dead, too." Kwan shoved him away from the car, jumped inside and drove off without turning on the headlights.

Shaking with fury, Gregor rose to his feet. The nerve of the bastard, threatening him with a knife! A snub-nosed Smith & Wesson was in the holster strapped to his right ankle, but Kwan's attack had taken him by surprise. Next time he would be ready.

Kwan was a dead man and his death would not be quick or easy.

Sirens interrupted his vengeful thoughts. Flashing blue lights lit up the Jamaicaway, police cars on the northbound side racing toward Boston. He caught a glimpse of the black Chevy as it pulled onto the Jamaicaway headed south. Nicholas, hell-bent on escape. He'd better do the same.

He ran to the mini-van and climbed behind the wheel.

A sour stink hit his nostrils. Urine and feces. The dead lose control of bodily functions. But he was alive. And his audacious plan had succeeded! Four priceless paintings were in the rear compartment.

But there was still work to be done. Drive to the storage facility in Revere. Take the paintings out of the van, put them in the trunk of his Saab and hide the Chevrolet mini-van in his storage locker. Then he would drive to Boston.

An hour from now he would be celebrating in his quarters at Global Interpreting, savoring a fine cognac and a Gitanes.

———

This time when Natalie arrived at the Royal Dragon, Pak Lam threw open the door, frowning, his dark eyes full of concern. A sharp pain shot up her arm and she grimaced. Grasping her elbow to steady her, he helped her inside. Feng, the man who'd driven her here, spoke to him in a torrent of Chinese. Lam nodded and said in English, "Bring her bags to the spare room."

Five minutes later she was lying on a bed with a soft mattress and clean, fresh-smelling sheets. Pak Lam stood by the bed, his forehead grooved with worry lines. "Doctor Wu will be here soon to tend your wound. How did this happen? Who did this to you?"

The question she had been dreading. Woozy from the pain, she pointed at the water glass on the table beside the bed. Lam helped her sit up and handed her the glass. "Never mind," he said. "You don't need to tell me now. You must rest."

She drank some water and gathered her courage. It didn't matter if she told him now or later. Either way, he would think badly of her. Because of her shameful deeds.

"Tonight I stole two paintings from the Gardner Museum. My boss would have killed me if I didn't." Tears filled her eyes and her throat thickened. "I know it was wrong to do this."

Lam said nothing for several seconds. At last he said, "To steal art from a museum is indeed a bad thing. This deprives others of their beauty. But you say he forced you. He holds a sword over your head?"

She knew he didn't mean a literal sword. This was a common figure of speech in Asian cultures, and an apt description of her situation. Gregor knew she had stolen other paintings and killed a man.

"Yes." Exhausted, she sank back against the plump white pillow. She didn't want to tell him about the murder at the Ashmolean. Stealing a painting was bad enough. Stealing someone's life was far worse.

Footsteps sounded in the hall. Moments later, a tall dark-haired man in a dark suit, carrying a black satchel, entered the room, followed by a middle-aged woman in a white cotton robe.

Pak Lam bowed. "Thank you for coming so quickly, Doctor Wu. Someone has knifed this woman's arm." Gesturing at the white-robed woman, he said, "My assistant will bring you whatever you need."

Doctor Wu spoke rapidly in Chinese and the woman left the room. Then he set his black satchel on the table beside the bed, took out a pair of latex gloves and turned to her. He didn't smile, but his dark eyes were warm and kind.

"I must examine your wound. I will try not to hurt you."

He put on the gloves and unwrapped her turtleneck, her makeshift bandage. His hands were gentle as he manipulated her arm, bending it at the elbow, turning it side to side. It hurt, but not too badly.

"There are no damaged muscles or tendons," said Doctor Wu, "but I must clean the wound so that it will not become infected."

The woman in the robe returned with several white towels and a basin of water. Doctor Wu gave her a packet of herbs. "Boil them for five minutes, pour the broth into a clean basin and bring it here." Then he took a syringe out of his medicine bag. "This will numb your arm while I debride the wound."

Two minutes later, Doctor Wu, frowning in concentration, began working on the deep gash in her arm. She felt no pain, only pressure as he cleaned the wound.

The white-robed woman returned with a large basin that gave off a spicy aroma. "Soak your arm in this liquid for five minutes," Dr. Wu said. He gave the woman an envelope with a sterile gauze bandage and a roll of clear tape. "Use this to bandage the wound."

To Natalie, he said, "I will see you tomorrow."

"Thank you," she said. Doctor Wu made a nice face and left. Natalie eased her forearm in the aromatic liquid. It was hot, but not scalding.

When the five minutes were up, the woman dried her arm with a towel, bandaged her arm and left.

Pak Lam immediately entered the room. His concern was obvious, though he appeared less worried than before. In a reflexive gesture, he fingered the scar on his cheek. Not for the first time, she wondered how he'd gotten it. Had he been injured in a knife fight?

"You stay here tonight. Rest now. We talk in the morning," he said."

"Thank you, but I cannot stay here tonight."

Lam frowned. "Why not?"

She hesitated, gathering her thoughts. When Gregor found out she was still alive, he would call her, a conversation she didn't want Pak Lam to overhear. But she couldn't say this.

"I think the man who stabbed me took the paintings," she said, and stopped. She needed a better reason to convince Pak Lam that she couldn't stay here. Then, as though beamed into her brain by her Vietnamese ancestor gods, the solution came to her.

"I want to find the paintings and return them to the museum."

Another frown. "No. You stay here tonight. Doctor Wu will come back tomorrow to check your arm. And we must take photographs for your new passports. For the second one, you must cut off your hair."

"Cut off my hair? Why?"

"For the male passport."

She had almost forgotten about the passports. Maybe she could get out of Boston after all. The police would be watching the airport and the train and bus stations, but they wouldn't be looking for a man.

"Thank you, but I really can't stay here tonight. I will come back tomorrow. I promise."

Clearly unhappy, Lam gazed at her. A muscle worked in his cheek, accentuating the jagged scar.

"Please, hear me out. The man who stabbed me was supposed to give the paintings to my boss, but I'm not sure he did. If he didn't, my boss might think I took them. Could you hand me the iPhone? It's in my duffel bag." And so was the cellphone Gregor would call her on when he found out she wasn't dead.

Using the iPhone, she searched for a hotel near Copley Square. A small hotel on Huntington Avenue opposite Copley Place looked promising. She dialed the number.

When the clerk answered, she said, "Bon soir, monsieur," and launched into a torrent of French.

Pak Lam stared at her, his eyes wide.

At last she said, "Tres bien. Merci beaucoup." She clicked off and said, "I booked a room at a hotel in Copley Square. Could Feng drive me there?"

A faint smile of amusement appeared on Pak Lam's face. "You are a formidable woman, Natalie. I will have Feng drive you there, but you must use a credit card with another name. Only then will you be safe. Wait here while I get one for you. And you must come back tomorrow to see the doctor."

"Thank you for understanding. And for all of your help. I'll be back tomorrow. I promise."

———

Nicholas got off the Jamaicaway and took the back roads to Mission Hill. Three blocks from his apartment, the Mission Church stood atop a steep hill, shrouded in fog. He parked behind the church, entered through a rear door and stopped to listen. Hearing nothing, he crept up a flight of stairs and stood at the rear of the sanctuary to allow his eyes to adjust to the darkness.

In an alcove at the front of the church, votive candles flickered, casting an eerie glow over the altar. He walked down the long center aisle, eyes fixed on the crucifix above the altar. It had been years since he'd been inside a Catholic church. Mesmerized, he gazed at the life-sized figure nailed to the cross, head tilted in agony, crimson blood-drops vivid against his alabaster-white skin.

Thirteen years ago, he had sought shelter in Our Lady of Precious Blood Catholic Church. For the first time he had seen the man on the cross. He was fourteen, deemed incorrigible after his fifth arrest for a series of robberies. The judge sent him to a juvenile detention center. Bigger boys forced him to do unspeakable things. He and Bobby, his cellmate, plotted their escape. They stole two eating utensils and sharpened them. One night when a guard came to their room, they attacked. Nicholas had taken great pleasure in slitting the bastard's throat. But when they left the building, guards in the towers shot at them. Nicholas escaped but Bobby did not. For months he had roamed southern California, eating out of garbage cans, sleeping in the woods. That night in the church he had hidden inside the confessional until the sexton locked the church. Then he had curled up on a pew and slept.

"Hey buddy, whaddaya doin?"

Nicholas froze, conscious of a presence near the flickering candles. He smelled the man before he saw him, the putrid stench of body odor and rotgut wine. Dressed in a torn T-shirt and filthy jeans, the man shuffled toward him. He was six feet tall, but thin as a cadaver with a scrawny neck and rheumy eyes.

Eyes that grew crafty as he said, "Got any spare change?"

What was this wino doing inside the church? Did he know about the paintings?

He whirled and ran up the aisle to the confessional. A thick maroon curtain hung over the right-hand stall. He parted the curtain and felt a rush of relief. The paintings were still there.

The drunk sidled up to him. "Ya wanna go to confession? Ain't no priests here now. They're tucked into their nice warm beds in the rectory down the street." The wino smiled, exposing yellow rotted teeth.

Nicholas turned on him with the knife in his hand. "Shut up, motherfucker."

"Wait. Hold on buddy—"

"I'm not your buddy."

The wino backed away, but not fast enough. Nicholas slashed at his face.

"Don't! Wait!" The man put up a feeble defense, but Nicholas lunged and slashed his neck. Gouts of dark-red blood spurted.

The man's rheumy eyes registered shock, then panic.

He went in for the kill, stabbing him in a vicious frenzy. The wino slumped to the floor. Nicholas slit his throat from ear to ear, sniffing the coppery blood-scent, waiting for the death gurgle to subside. But he had wasted precious time. By now the pigs would know the museum had been robbed. He wiped the blade on the wino's trousers, returned it to the sheath on his belt and hurried to the confessional.

Three minutes later, four paintings were stacked beside the downstairs door. The rain had stopped and patchy fog swirled over the blacktop. Nicholas loaded the paintings into the trunk of the black Chevy and drove off. Stefan's directions to the safe house lay on the seat beside him, but he had already memorized the route.

Providence, armpit of the universe. Italians ran the city, even the gangs. He had no contacts there, but he had something better.

He had his bargaining chip.

176

CHAPTER 28

Stopped at a traffic light, Gregor drummed his fingers on the steering wheel. It had taken him forty-five minutes to get to Revere. In weather like this, cops had better things to do than stop speeders, but he didn't want to take any chances, not with dead bodies and stolen art in the rear compartment.

He could hardly wait to see the paintings, four of them, worth millions of dollars. Never again would he take orders from the old man in London. A triumphant smile parted his lips. Until he remembered the jolt of fear when Kwan held the knife to his throat. It had been many years since he had felt this emotion.

Fear was something he instilled in others. He took out a pack of Gitanes, noting with satisfaction that his hand was rock steady, not the slightest tremor. Kwan had threatened him but now he was in control. He put the cigarettes back in his pocket.

He had to maintain discipline. Trusting Kwan had been a mistake, one he did not intend to repeat.

When the light turned green, he stayed in the left lane and used the U-turn to drive to the storage facility. Other than security lights mounted on poles along the massive two-story building, the place was dark. Two moving vans were parked out front, dark and unoccupied.

He circled the building and backed the Chevrolet mini-van up to the storage locker he'd rented. The Saab was parked opposite the locker.

He could barely contain his excitement, his heart thrumming with anticipation. After hours of planning and weeks of work, he was about to reap the rewards.

He climbed out of the mini-van. The fresh air was a welcome relief after the sickening stench. He went to the rear compartment, unlocked the doors and swung them open. The stench of death hit him. Back here the stench was a hundred times worse. He covered his nose with his sleeve. Kwan had disabled the light in the rear compartment. Although he could smell the bodies, he couldn't see them.

But forget the bodies. Find the paintings. He groped the floor of the compartment with his hand and felt nothing. Where were they?

His chest felt as though two giant hands were squeezing it. Alarmed, he ran to the Saab, unlocked it, opened the glove box, took out a small flashlight and ran back to the van.

Ignoring the stench, he beamed the flashlight over the compartment. Farther back he could see bodies, lying in a heap.

Bodies, but no paintings. His body trembled and a red haze clouded his vision. For an instant he thought he was having a heart attack. He gripped the doorframe to steady himself. Unable to believe his eyes, he stared at the floor of the mini-van. Willing the paintings to appear, he flashed the light around the compartment. No paintings.

Bile rose in his throat and he feared he would vomit.

Your precious paintings are in the van, Nicholas had said. The miserable cocksucker!

A fulminating fury rose up inside him, rage worse than he'd felt that first night in prison, lying on his cot in the darkness, trapped and powerless. But he had used his brains and his brawn to exert his power over the other prisoners, thereby regaining control.

Control. He had to maintain control.

Steeling himself, he climbed into the compartment and flashed the light over the bodies. Two security guards in their distinctive uniforms, one of them drenched with blood. The ex-cop in her police uniform, also bloody. Three bodies. Not four. Where was Valerie?

He clenched his fists and studied the scars on his hands. Despite his efforts to control his underlings, Nicholas and the ex-cop and Valerie, someone had double-crossed him. But they would not defeat him.

He jumped out of the van, shut the rear doors and locked them. Using the key to the storage locker, he unlocked the handle and rolled up the door. Inside the enclosed space the stench would quickly grow worse, but by the time anyone discovered the bodies he would be long gone. He backed the mini-van into the locker, went outside, rolled down the door and locked it.

Blind with rage, he got into the Saab, lighted a Gitanes and took a deep drag. The nicotine did not quell his fury but it allowed him to think. Where was Valerie? Kwan had said he would take pleasure in killing her, but Valerie was no pushover, she was fit and strong.

He puffed the Gitanes and blew smoke out the window.

Did Nicholas have the paintings? The bastard had no way to sell them, didn't have the smarts to deal with the insurance companies to collect a ransom. But Valerie would. The apartments he had leased for Valerie and Nicholas were in Mission Hill, two blocks apart. Had they been conspiring against him all along? He tossed the butt out the window.

He didn't know where the paintings were, but one thing was certain.

Whoever had them would pay for their treachery.

———

When Natalie left the Royal Dragon, Feng was waiting in his car. His eyes widened when he saw her outfit, but he said nothing, just drove her to the hotel in

Copley Square. She swept into the lobby of the hotel like a movie star, decked out in her blond wig, dark glasses, her little black dress and black pumps. To the desk clerk, she said in accented English, "I 'ave called to make the reservation. Three nights, n'est pas?"

The man eyed the bandage on her arm, frowned, then fussed with the computer. After a moment he said, "I see the reservation. Could I have your credit card, please?"

She handed him the credit card Pak Lam had given her, which bore the name Albert Roberts.

To distract him, she continued her broken English routine. "This wretched airline, c'est impossible! They sent my ... how you say? Luggage, yes? My luggage they sent to California by mistake."

The clerk studied the credit card. "And your name, madam?"

"Lily. Lily Roberts." Choosing a new name was second nature to her now. She used the names of the months—April, May, June—or the names of flowers. Lily had a nice ring to it.

The clerk swiped the card, returned it to her and asked if she needed help with her luggage.

"If I had my luggage I would not need to stay here. These carry-on bags I can carry myself." The ammo and the Beretta were in her duffel. If a bellhop took it, he might wonder why it was so heavy.

She rode the elevator to the top floor, used the key card and entered her room. Justifying the exorbitant room rates, plush royal-blue carpeting covered the floor and matching curtains draped the windows. Ivory wallpaper embossed with pale-blue flowers decorated the walls. Catering to their well-heeled guests, the room boasted a teak writing desk, two blue-velvet easy chairs, a big screen TV, a mini-bar and a small refrigerator.

Exhausted, she dropped her bags on the floor, kicked off her shoes and sank onto the king-sized bed. Now she was Lily Roberts, staying in a luxury hotel. Gregor would never find her here.

The digital clock on the bedside table read 4:15 A.M. She wanted to sleep for a week, but that was wishful thinking. When Gregor found out she was still alive, he would call her. She wondered what had become of the two Vermeers. Did Nicholas give them to Gregor?

The wound on her arm still hurt, but less than before. Despite her exhaustion, she rose from the bed, went in the bathroom and studied herself in the mirror above the blue-veined marble vanity. She had to cut off her hair for the second passport photo. A drastic step, one she hadn't considered when she'd asked Pak Lam to get her a male passport. But she'd worry about that tomorrow.

A white terrycloth robe lay on the vanity beside the sink. She stripped off her clothes, put on the robe and lay on the bed. An overpowering urge to sleep hit her. She yawned and closed her eyes.

Her cellphone rang. She jerked upright and her heart began to race. Gregor. Gathering her courage, she waited until the third ring to answer. "Yes."

"Valerie, where are you?"

She smiled grimly. Gregor wanted to know where she was. So he could come and kill her. "I'm still alive, no thanks to Nicholas. He tried to kill me, but I escaped."

"Where are the paintings?"

"I don't know. Don't you have them?"

After a short silence, he said, "I waited outside the Gardner in my car but you never came out. Then I heard sirens, so I drove away. Did you get the Vermeers?"

"Yes. I put them inside trash bags to protect them from the rain. Nicholas said a van was parked in the courtyard behind the museum. He told me to put them in the rear compartment, so I did."

Another silence. "Where are they now?"

She parsed his words. If Gregor was asking her where the paintings were, he must not have them. Which meant Nicholas did.

"I don't know," she said. "Ask Nicholas."

"I am asking you, Valerie. Where are the paintings?"

"I don't know. I don't have them. Maybe Nicholas took them."

"What makes you think so?"

"He tried to kill me!"

In the quiet voice she knew so well, he said, "I think you lie. I think you and Nicholas decided to take the paintings for yourselves. This was a bad idea, Valerie. Very bad. Where are you?"

As if she would tell him. "Gregor, I don't have the Vermeers. If Nicholas didn't give them to you, he must have taken them."

Another silence. Then, "Meet me outside the library on Boylston Street tomorrow at noon. We will discuss what to do about this."

When hell freezes over. "Fine," she said, and shut off the phone.

But when she put it on the bedside table, her hands were shaking. She might be in a ritzy hotel registered under a different name, but that didn't mean she was safe. When Gregor was angry—and clearly he was angry now—he could be utterly ruthless. To Gregor, people were disposable, as easily discarded as a child's paper-dolls. And Gregor wasn't her only problem. The Gardner heist would attract enormous publicity. Police would be swarming the city, searching for the thieves and the paintings and asking for tips.

Using the remote, she turned on the big-screen TV, propped two pillows against the headboard, leaned against them and channel surfed, hunting for news. She tuned in Channel-4. The Eye-Opener News at four-thirty was just starting. A breaking news banner appeared on the screen. **Art Thieves Hit Gardner Museum Again.** A young anchorwoman said, "We have breaking news about an overnight theft at the Gardner Museum. Our reporter is at the scene. What can you tell us, John?"

The picture shifted to a young man doing a standup on the Fenway near the Gardner. "Police officials aren't saying much, just that four paintings were stolen from the museum sometime after midnight."

Natalie gasped. *Four paintings?* How could that be?

"Twenty years ago," John said, gazing into the camera, "paintings worth many millions of dollars were stolen from the Gardner. They're still missing. To increase the reward for their safe return, Gardner officials mounted a Special Exhibit, which opened last weekend, ten paintings on loan from other museums, two by Johannes Vermeer. According to our sources, both were stolen."

He paused as two police vehicles with flashing lights and loud sirens passed him. "Police won't let us near the museum, but as you can see behind me ..." The picture zoomed in on the Gardner and several police vehicles parked outside. "There is heavy police presence here. In addition to the Vermeers, a Rembrandt and a Manet were stolen from the Gardner collection. I'm told that the Boston office of the FBI will lead the investigation, assisted by Boston police. Back to you, Deb."

Natalie muted the sound, trying to make sense of it. Nicholas must have stolen the Rembrandt and the Manet after she put the Vermeers in the mini-van. She replayed the conversation she'd just had with Gregor. *Where are the paintings*, he kept saying, not "Where are the Vermeers?"

Now it was clear why Gregor had refused to tell her any details about the plan. All along he had been planning to steal four paintings, not two. That's why he'd told Nicholas to kill her. But Nicholas had double-crossed him.

She had no idea where Nicholas was, but he'd better watch his back. Nicholas didn't know how ruthless Gregor could be. Gregor would track him down and kill him.

CHAPTER 29

Providence

Nicholas attacked his beard with a pair of scissors, hacking off clumps of wiry hair and flushing them down the toilet. He glanced out the window. It was still dark. His temples throbbed with a dull ache. He had tried to sleep, but each time he dozed off, he jolted awake, drenched in sweat, his heart pounding. The familiar nightmare: armed guards and snarling dogs chasing him, drawing closer and closer.

He lathered his face with soap and shaved prickly stubble off his face. He had already shaved his head. Now he was as bald as Larry Ho. The thought amused him. Never again would he have to deal with the fat man and his obnoxious jokes. He finished shaving and studied his reflection in the mirror.

Excellent. A far cry from his former appearance.

He left the bathroom and went in the kitchen. Stefan's hideout stank of cat piss and body odor, had a shitty little kitchen with filthy appliances, a tiny bedroom and a living room with a dilapidated couch. But no radio and no television set. He believed this was no accident.

Stefan didn't want him to know what the cops were doing.

His cellphone rang. He studied the faceplate. Stefan's number.

"Yesss," he answered.

"Nicholas, you have done a dangerous thing. Dangerous and stupid."

"Steal the paintings and wait for the money, you said. That is stupid. How do I know you won't keep the money?"

"Where are the paintings?"

"You said the Manet is our insurance. I am looking at it now." He wasn't, but the Manet was leaning against the wall in the bedroom. Unfortunately, the canvas had a three-inch tear in it.

"The paintings are there? In the safe house?"

"The Manet is."

"Where are the others?"

"In a safe place. You'll find out when the insurance companies agree to the ransom. The paintings are my bargaining chip."

Silence on the other end. Nicholas could hear him breathing. Stefan was pissed. Tough. "This place is a dump and there's no TV. What are the cops are doing?"

"The Boston stations are covering the story, but the cops aren't saying much."

"What about the guards? Did they show my picture?"

"No. Nicholas, these paintings need special care—"

"Stop worrying about the fucking paintings! Get the money!"

"If you want money, the paintings must be in good condition. You can't negotiate the ransom, but I can. I know how to deal with the authorities—"

"But you need the paintings to do it."

Another silence. Then, "What happened with Scorpio? You were supposed to kill her."

Nicholas ground his teeth. If he ever saw that bitch again, he would slice her to bits. But Scorpio was Stefan's problem, not his. And Stefan was more worried about the paintings.

"Where's the car?"

"In the garage."

"Good. Don't use it. It's stolen. If you get stopped—"

"Why didn't you tell me that before?"

"Stay in the cottage until I get there. I need to see the paintings before I talk to the insurance officials."

"When are you coming?"

"Soon. And the paintings better be there."

A click sounded in his ear. Nicholas pounded the kitchen counter with his fist as murderous thoughts raged in his mind. Stefan was giving him orders again. After he got the money, he'd kill the bastard. Stefan's blood would flow like a river. The death of a thousand cuts!

He flung open the cellar door and pounded down the stairs, inhaling the odor of gasoline and oil and grass clippings. Opposite the stairs a 250-gallon oil tank stood between an oil furnace and a gas-powered lawn mower. Jagged cracks split the basement floor, and cobwebs draped the wood beams overhead.

The Lacemaker, *The Milkmaid* and the Rembrandt *Self-Portrait* were stacked against the wall beside a workbench cluttered with tools. Stefan hadn't said when he was coming, but he lived in Boston. It would take him at least an hour to get here.

A bare bulb with a pull-chain dangled over the workbench. He turned on the light and studied the tools: claw hammers, screw drivers, a rusty hand saw, jars of nails and a metal tape measure. One by one he carried the paintings to the workbench, measured them, and jotted the measurements on a slip of paper.

The Milkmaid was 16 inches wide, 18 inches tall. *The Lacemaker* was smaller: 8 inches by 10 inches. The Rembrandt Self-Portrait was the largest: 15 inches wide, 24 inches tall.

He raced upstairs to the bedroom, dumped the contents of his gray-fabric suitcase on the bed and measured the suitcase: 25 inches by 30 inches. Without the frames, the canvases would easily fit inside it. He took the suitcase downstairs to the workbench and got to work.

———

In his office at Global Interpreting, Gregor closed the cellphone, trying to quell his anger. Kwan, saying the paintings were in a safe place.

Did he really think he would get away with this?

Rage clogged his throat. He had conceived the perfect plan, but Kwan had betrayed him. Kwan had the paintings, but the idiot didn't understand how fragile they were. Centuries old, they required the proper temperature and humidity to maintain their condition. He had to get them away from that miserable ...

Unable to think of a suitably vile epithet, he splashed more Remy Martin into a brandy snifter, gulped it down and felt the fiery liquor burn his throat. The cognac should have been his reward for a difficult job well done, but Kwan had double-crossed him.

His punishment for ignoring one of his rules. Trust no one.

After leaving the storage locker in Revere, he had driven to the apartments he'd leased for Kwan and Valerie. The paintings weren't in Kwan's apartment. No surprise there. They weren't in Valerie's apartment either, but her belongings were gone, which meant she had been there since the heist. From there he had driven to Global Interpreting. He had taken a long hot shower to erase the stink of the corpses. This soothed his aching muscles, but had not quelled his fury.

He lit a cigarette and sipped his cognac. Where was Valerie? During their phone conversation he had asked her twice, but she hadn't told him. He had been deliberately vague when he asked about the paintings. Valerie said she had put the Vermeers in the van. He had said nothing about the other two. Nor had she. Maybe Valerie had not conspired with Kwan after all.

He puffed the Gitanes and blew smoke. Marta would have a fit if she knew he was smoking in here, but to hell with Marta. She had no key to his office. It wasn't as comfortable as he would have liked, but large enough to hold a good-sized desk and a royal-blue sofa that converted to a pullout bed. And the adjoining bathroom had a shower stall.

He flicked ash from the Gitanes into the glass dish on his desk and massaged his temples. Every instinct told him to drive to Providence now and force Kwan to tell him where the paintings were. But stress had sapped his energy. Lack of sleep, Kwan's knife against his throat, eluding the police. Worst of all, the fury that consumed him

184

when he discovered the paintings weren't in the van. He needed to rest and plan how to deal with Kwan.

One thing was certain. He couldn't go there tomorrow. The cottage was in a residential area and the neighbors would be home on a Sunday. They might hear Kwan's screams.

Gregor studied the angry red scars on his hands. In London he had spent years coaxing information out of people. He could not recall a single instance in which he had failed to get what he wanted. He was looking forward to torturing Kwan. The rat-bastard would suffer before breathing his last.

By the time he finished with him, Kwan would be begging to die.

Kwan was too impulsive to negotiate with the insurance companies. Even if they agreed to pay, the process could take weeks, and Kwan was a hothead. Impatient. Anxious to flee the country.

Damn Kwan to hell! Not since he'd been in prison had he felt such rage and hate. In prison he had lived by his code. Always be in control. Always take revenge. Trust no one. His fatal error.

And that wasn't his only problem. Marta never came here on the weekend, but on Monday she would. By then the Gardner heist would dominate the news. Marta might suspect he had a part in it. He would deny it, of course. And there was another problem. The cop who had come here asking to speak to Gregor Kraus. Marta said she had told him nothing, but eventually she might crack. He had to get rid of her.

And if some cop was looking for him here, using his office as a crash pad was no longer safe. He took a final puff and stubbed the Gitanes out in the ashtray. He would sleep until noon. Then he would pack his belongings, lock the office and find somewhere else to stay.

Valerie's apartment had a television set with a cable connection. He would sleep in Valerie's bed. Too bad she wouldn't be there.

But he had more important things to do. On Monday he would go to Providence and get the paintings from Kwan.

———

Natalie shut off the TV and drank some bottled water. Before talking to Gregor and seeing the news report, she'd been ready to fall asleep. Now she was wide-awake, her mind reeling. When she'd told Pak Lam she intended to return the paintings to their rightful owners, she'd meant the two Vermeers. But four paintings had been stolen from the Gardner, and she had no idea how to find them.

Pym had ordered her to steal the Vermeers, but she doubted that he'd told Gregor to kill her. It now seemed clear that Gregor intended to double-cross Pym. A dying man, if she could believe what Gregor said. She glanced at the clock. 4:45 A.M. in Boston, 9:45 A.M. in London. She turned on her cellphone and dialed Pym's number.

He answered on the second ring. "Valerie, what's happening? I haven't heard from Gregor. Did everything go as planned?"

"No. The insider guard tried to kill me. Was that part of the plan?"

"Valerie! How could you think such a thing? Are you all right?"

"I am now. When he attacked me, I ran away."

"What about the Vermeers? Tell me what happened!"

"Gregor was supposed to pick me up after I left the Gardner, but the insider guard told me to put the Vermeers in a van that was parked in the courtyard. I did, but then he came at me with a knife. I managed to get away, but I don't know what happened to the paintings."

There was a long silence. "Hold on a moment."

She heard a series of harsh coughs. Finally, Pym came back on the line and said, "Sorry, Valerie. My cough is acting up again."

"Gregor told me you were ill. Is that true?"

"Gregor told you this?"

"Yes. He said you were—" Should she tell him? Why not? Things couldn't get any worse. "Gregor said you were dying."

"Well, we're all dying, aren't we? But I'm going to die sooner rather than later."

"I'm sorry. I didn't realize you were so ill."

"No reason you should. But I'm angry that Gregor told you. How did he find out?"

"I don't know," she lied. "Has he called you?"

"No, he hasn't. You have no idea where the Vermeers are?"

"No." She took a deep breath. "Jonathan, they stole four paintings, not just the Vermeers."

"Four?" Pym said, his voice full of outrage. "And Gregor has them?"

She hesitated. Gregor might not have them, but he wouldn't rest until he got them back. "Maybe. Or maybe the guard has them. I get the feeling they're working together."

Another silence. More coughing. At last, Pym said, "Valerie, I'm dying. The only thing that has kept me alive is knowing that I would be able to savor those two glorious Vermeers before I die."

Puzzled, she frowned. "You? What about the collector?"

A soft chuckle. "I am the collector, my dear. The paintings are here in my basement museum."

Stunned, she tried to make sense of it. The stolen paintings were in Pym's mansion? The idea sickened her. The incredible risks she had taken, stealing priceless paintings and killing two men, all for the pleasure of Jonathan Pym. How dare he?

"After I die, the paintings will be returned to their rightful owners, the museums or the private collections from which they were stolen."

"All of them?"

"Every single one. I'm going to make you an offer, Valerie. Hear me out before you respond. I'm a dying man but I might yet live to see the Vermeers. Gregor should have called me, but he hasn't, which means he intends to keep the paintings and sell them on the black market. I know your distaste for violence, Valerie, but I will pay you handsomely to find Gregor, kill him and ship the Vermeers to me as soon as possible. If you agree to this, I will wire a million dollars into your bank account."

She thought about it. One million dollars was a magnificent sum. All she had to do was find the Vermeers, ship them to Pym and kill Gregor. It didn't take long to make her decision. After the Ashmolean heist she had vowed never to kill another person as long as she lived and she intended to abide this. Not that she felt any sympathy for Gregor. But she wasn't going to kill him.

She wasn't going to ship the Vermeers to Pym, either. She didn't know how many paintings he'd stolen, but it sickened her that he had done this for his own selfish pleasure. She would do her best to find the Vermeers and the other two paintings. When she did, she would return them to their owners.

"Well?" Pym said, impatiently. "What do you say, Valerie? If you agree to my proposal, I'll wire half the money into your account today. To prove that I'm serious."

"And after you die all the paintings will be returned to their owners?"

"Yes. I've already added a clause to my will. Every single painting will be returned to its owner. Valerie, you've been a fine companion for two years. Please do this one last thing for me. You won't regret it, I promise. Say yes and I'll wire a half million dollars into your bank account right now."

"All right, Jonathan. I'll do my best to get them." That was no lie.

"Thank you. Call me when you have them and I'll tell you how to ship them to me."

"All right," she said and ended the call.

She didn't feel the least bit guilty about implying that she had agreed to his proposal. Why should she?

For two years Jonathan Pym had been lying to her about far more serious things.

CHAPTER 30

Frustrated and angry, Frank sat in a police car parked in front of the Gardner. He hadn't smoked a cigarette in years, but he wanted one now. The sky was still dark, the moon hidden behind a blanket of clouds, but lights blazed inside the Gardner.

Four paintings had been stolen, which confirmed his theory. Natalie Brixton and Gregor Kraus had been planning an art heist in Boston.

And he had failed to stop them.

Hank Flynn had called at 3:15 AM to give him the bad news. Frank drove to the station and one of Flynn's detectives drove him to the Gardner. When they arrived, Flynn was outside on the sidewalk, arguing with a grim-faced woman with long dark hair, the Assistant Special Agent-In-Charge of the Boston FBI office, as it turned out. The FBI would lead the investigation. After a testy exchange, the ASAC had waved Flynn into the museum.

But Frank Renzi had to stay outside.

Unable to sit still, he got out of Flynn's cruiser and jogged across the street. No traffic on the Fenway. The street had been blocked off to divert cars away from the museum. The rain had stopped but the air was hot and muggy, not a hint of a breeze. He paced the sidewalk, berating himself. He should have warned the Gardner security director. If he had, it might have prevented the robbery.

Maybe he should call DCI Stanford. 4:45 AM in Boston, 9:45 AM in London. But he had no information, dammit. He had to wait outside like some lowly civilian while Hank Flynn viewed the crime scene. He wanted in on the investigation, but that wasn't likely to happen with the FBI running it.

At the corner of Palace Road, a uniformed officer stood beside one of the cruisers that had been stationed outside the museum overnight. Another guarded the cruiser on Evans Way. According to the detective who'd driven Frank to the Gardner, the cops had failed to make their all-clear calls at 2:00 AM. No call from the security guard, either.

The first responders had found both cops in their cruisers. One was dead. The other one was unconscious and had been taken to Boston Medical Center.

Frank paced the sidewalk, assembling the pieces of the complicated puzzle. Four paintings missing from the Gardner. Ursula, a Global Interpreting translator, also missing. Stefan Haas was the Global Interpreting manager, allegedly, but Frank believed Gregor Kraus was the person who had killed Stefan Haas in London and stolen his ID.

Stolen art. Stolen identities. The common thread? Gregor Kraus, the man who wasn't there.

He visualized *The Milkmaid*, the Vermeer he'd seen the night of the gala. It was gorgeous, light glinting on the woman's goldenrod yellow blouse and a loaf of crusty bread. That reminded him of the curious incident at the reception, his feeling that someone was watching him, catching a glimpse of a woman in a gold lamé dress leaving the room with a man in a tux. With gloves on his hands.

It hit him like a flash-bang. DCI Stanford said Gregor Kraus had burn scars on his hands. If Kraus was at the gala to case the museum, he would have worn gloves to hide the scars.

Cursing himself, Frank clenched his jaw. How could he have missed it? That was Natalie at the gala with Gregor Kraus. If he had chased them, he would have caught her.

Hank Flynn came out of the Gardner and gave him a shout.

When he got in the cruiser, Flynn said, "Sorry it took so long. I'll fill you in later. Right now I need coffee."

He had a million questions, but he wanted coffee, too. They stopped at a Dunkin' Donuts for coffee and pastries. When they got to the office, Flynn sank onto the padded chair behind his desk and massaged his temples. He looked beat, sallow skin, bags under his eyes. "I can't believe this happened now," he said. "Two months from retirement and I gotta deal with a major case like this."

Frank took the visitor chair and sipped his black coffee. "Thanks for not telling the FBI woman about my interest in the London art heists."

With a grim smile, Flynn said, "When the FBI gets involved, I tell them as little as possible, especially Georgette. She's been a pain in the butt ever since they promoted her to ASAC two years ago. If she solves this case, she'll be running the Boston office."

"When the shit hits the fan, let her take the heat."

"We're gonna catch heat, too." Flynn sipped his coffee and bit into a cinnamon cruller. "My phone will be ringing off the hook, reporters looking for an inside scoop."

"What about the security guards?"

"No sign of them, but there was blood all over the place. A lot of it was in the Dutch Room on the second floor. That's where they stole the Rembrandt Self-Portrait."

"Blood, but no bodies. Maybe one of the guards put up a fight. Any bullet holes?"

"No, but there was blood in the hall and in the elevator. None in the Blue Room on the first floor where they stole the Manet. Someone shut down the security system at 1:05 AM and took the discs with the feeds from the security cameras. The CSI techs found tire tracks in the courtyard behind the museum. They're taking casts of the tracks."

"It might not do much good," Frank said. "I hate to harp on the London heists, but that gang used stolen getaway cars and put stolen plates on them."

Flynn yawned and massaged his bloodshot eyes. "This is gonna be a huge, a media circus. Ten years after the other heist? We're in for it." His phone rang and Flynn grimaced. "See what I mean?" He took the call and smiled, suddenly animated. "Hey, Marty, what have you got?"

Frank assumed he was talking to a detective and ate a bite of his blueberry muffin.

When Flynn ended the call, he said, "The doctors are about to discharge Officer Sweeney. They found Taser marks on his neck. He told Marty he remembered seeing someone with a Dunkin' Donuts bag, nothing after that. Hold on a sec." Flynn used his radio handset and told one of his officers to check the trash bins near the museum for a Dunkin' Donuts bag. Then his eyes widened. "No kidding. Good work! Get it in here. We'll have the lab process it." He set the handset on his desk. "When they towed the cruiser on Palace Road, my guy spotted a drug syringe on the pavement under the car."

"After the cops called in the all-clear at one o'clock, they drugged them."

"Looks like it, but who? This was a team, not a lone robber."

Frank's cellphone rang. He checked the number and said, "Kelly's calling me from New Orleans. I'll take it in the hall, let you get on with your work."

He stepped into the hall, punched on and said, "What's up, Kelly?"

"A heist at the Gardner Museum, that's what. It was the lead story on Good Morning America. They said four paintings were stolen! Did you know about it?"

"Yes. I'm at the station right now, outside Hank Flynn's office. We just got back from the Gardner."

"You were right," she said. "It's got to be Natalie, just like you said."

He smiled. Quite an admission from his ladylove. "That's what I think, but she didn't do it by herself. What else did they say on Good Morning America?"

"They said a police officer died. Is that true?"

"Yes. One of the cops in the cruisers outside the museum, but the other one is okay. Hank just got word that he might have been drugged. And there were Taser marks on his neck."

"What about the security guards?" Kelly asked.

"All three of them are missing. I didn't get into the museum, but Hank did." He glanced in the office and saw Hank signal him. "Gotta go, Kelly."

"Geez, Frank, aren't you going to ask me what I'm wearing?"

A running joke between them. Grateful for a bit of levity in an otherwise grim day, he smiled and said, "If you just got out of the shower, I'll be right over." Kelly laughed. "Call you later," he said, and went back in Flynn's office.

"The museum director just emailed me the information on the overnight guards," Flynn said.

"Lay it on me. If this is related to the London art thefts, I figure one of them was in on the heist."

"Charles Lawson was the head guard. Age fifty-five, lives alone in an apartment in Brookline, worked for the Gardner for twenty-two years." Flynn handed him a printout, a black-and-white copy of Lawson's driver's license and a brief work history.

He studied the photo. "Nothing stands out. Who are the other two?"

"Anthony Falcone, age twenty-two, lives with his girlfriend on Symphony Road. He went to Berklee for a year but dropped out. Here's a red flag. He got the job at the Gardner three years ago while he was still at Berklee."

"The two guards working the overnight during the 1990 heist were Berklee students."

"Exactly, and Anthony's a big fella." Flynn handed him the printout.

"Six-three, two-forty? Maybe he killed the other two guards and helped steal the paintings."

"I like him for it better than Lawson." Flynn handed him the third printout. "Daniel Leone, age twenty-eight, lives in an apartment on Mission Hill. The Gardner hired him six months ago."

Frank studied the photo. "I thought the name sounded familiar. He was guarding the Special Exhibit the night of the gala. Daniel Leone. Not an Asian name, but he looks Asian to me."

"As I recall," Flynn said, "so does Natalie Brixton."

"True. And I might have seen her at the Gardner gala." He described the well-dressed couple he'd seen and explained the significance of man's gloves. "Bottom line, I'm pretty sure it was Natalie Brixton and Gregor Kraus."

"I like it," Flynn said emphatically. "Maybe this time we'll catch her."

Lack of sleep and his failure to prevent the theft set his temper off flair like a rocket going into orbit.

"Fuck maybe! Natalie stole those paintings and I'm going to get her."

———

Looking pleased, Doctor Wu put a fresh bandage on her arm and said, "The wound is healing well. No infection. I have put butterfly tape over the wound, but it may leave a scar."

Relieved, she leaned back in the chair beside her bed. "Thank you so much, Doctor Wu. You have taken such good care of me."

"It was my pleasure, but I must see you again in one week." He studied her for several seconds, his brow furrowed in a frown. At last he said, "Why did you cut off your hair?"

"Mountain Man wants me to hide from the man who cut my arm."

She didn't want to tell him the real reason.

Doctor Wu nodded, but his expressionless was dubious. "See you next week," he said, and left the room.

She hoped not. By next week she wanted to be out of Boston, better still, out of the country. This morning, after getting the first passport photo taken, she had returned to her hotel room and chopped off her long black hair with scissors, flushing clumps of hair down the toilet. When she saw her image in the mirror, she wanted to cry. After spiking her hair with gel for a punk look, she had gone to a different store for the second photo. Before Doctor Wu arrived she had given both photos to Pak Lam.

She heard him outside her room, thanking Doctor Wu. Moments later he entered her room and said, "Madame Li has completed your passports." He handed her two U.S. passports.

They looked very authentic, blue covers with a gold seal. She opened one and saw her photo, the one with long glossy black hair. Her new name was Ling Lam. Her birth date was August 22, 1978.

The dated surprised her. She had been born the same year.

She opened the other passport and studied her photo, short spiky hair and a blank expression, no smile. Would it get her through a security checkpoint? Maybe, if she bound her breasts, wore a loose shirt and dressed like a man. Her idea to pose as a man had been an act of desperation, but now, seeing the photograph, she thought it might be possible. Her name would be Liang Lam.

Then she noticed his birth date: August 22, 1978.

The exact same date as Ling Lam. Two passports, one female, one male, with the same birth dates. And the same last name.

Her scalp pricked and her heart began to race. She had been so intent on studying the passports, she had forgotten that Pak Lam was standing beside her chair, watching her.

She looked up at him and said, "Are these your … ?"

"Yes," he said, stone-faced, but his dark eyes had a haunted look about them. "My twins."

"But how can I use their passports? They might need them."

"They will not need them." He gestured at a photograph on the bureau, similar to the one in his office, two small children and a beautiful woman, smiling into the camera. "The twins were six when this photo was taken. A month later a rival gang murdered them."

"No!" she gasped, shaking her head. "No!"

Time seemed to stand still. She would never forget the day the policewoman came to her house. Mom dead, murdered in a hotel room. Twenty-two years ago, but the memory was sharp and clear. The pain and anguish she'd felt was just as vivid.

She had lost her mother, but Pak Lam had lost his wife and his children. No wonder his eyes always bore a hint of sadness.

Fighting back tears, she said, "What happened?"

"My wife took them to the waterfront to see the tall ships. On their way home, three men ambushed them. They shot my wife and both of the twins."

"That is monstrous. How could they do such a thing?"

Expressionless, he said, "Ruthless people do monstrous things."

She took hold of his hands. "I am so sorry. I cannot even imagine the pain this caused you."

Something flickered in his eyes. "Natalie, you have told me the story of how you avenged your mother's murder. I too had my revenge."

Tentatively, she reached out and touched his cheek. "Was that how you got this scar?"

"Yes," he said tersely.

"Please," she said, "tell me about the twins. Your son and your daughter. If I am to use their passports, I want to know about them."

Lam remained silent for a moment. His eyes had a faraway look in them. "Ling was very musical, singing all the time. When she was four, my wife had her take Suzuki violin lessons. She loved it. Ling was very talented. Soon she was playing melodies for us every night on her violin. Liang was not musical but he was an outstanding athlete." Lam smiled. "The best pitcher on his Little League team. Maybe he would have pitched in the big leagues someday. For the Red Sox, perhaps."

He grew silent and his smile disappeared. Then, like a disintegrating iceberg, his face crumbled. Abruptly, he turned away.

Her heart ached for him. The reason for the ever-present sadness in his eyes was now clear. His wife had been murdered, and his hopes and dreams for children had been dashed, snuffed out by a rival gang.

He turned to her, his face impassive. "But we must not dwell on the past. I have given this considerable thought." He bent down and kissed both of her cheeks. "Now you are my adopted daughter."

Unable to speak, she rose from the chair and hugged him. "Thank you so much. I am honored to have you as my adopted father. I will try to make you proud of me."

Lam brushed tears from her cheeks. "I am sure you will. Feng is waiting outside with your car. Do your best to find the paintings and return them to their owners. If you are not able to do this, despite your best efforts, so be it. I wish you good fortune on your journey. Call me when you reach your destination and tell me how you are doing."

Overwhelmed with emotion, she bit the inside of her cheek to keep from crying.

But this was no time to show weakness, this was the time to show strength and determination. Gathering herself, she stood tall and gazed into his eyes.

"I will," she said. "I promise."

She would call him, of course, but her assertion referred to finding the paintings and returning them. Only then would she leave Boston.

CHAPTER 31

Sunday July 12, 2014 1:15 PM

Larry Ho sank onto his king-sized couch and let out a resounding belch. Sunday was his day off so he'd slept until ten. After a refreshing bath, he put on his black silk robe with the red fire-breathing dragon on the back. While his wife prepared dinner, he had passed the time with his father playing Go, the ancient Chinese game the old man loved, listening as his father spoke of the old country: the floods, the famine, the hardships. Larry had heard this before, but he listened politely. Some day he too would be an old man of ninety. This was hard to imagine—he was only fifty, in the prime of life—but when that time came, his son and daughter would listen to his stories.

Clatter from the kitchen interrupted his reverie, his wife cleaning up after dinner. She had outdone herself today: baked stuffed lobster, pan fried noodles, and oyster sauce for the pea pods and straw mushrooms.

His father was taking a nap. He had eaten only half of his lobster. Larry had eaten two.

A sudden pain stabbed his belly. He dug out a roll of Tums, ate one and used the remote to turn on his big-screen TV. A news bulletin was on, something about an art theft. He paid no attention at first—the local stations were obsessed with crime—but then he realized they were talking about the Gardner. Photos of the stolen art appeared on the screen.

He cared little for Western art—Chinese watercolors adorned the walls of his home—but the woman said they were worth hundreds of millions of dollars.

He popped another Tums, crunching the orange-flavored antacid as the announcer said, "The three overnight guards are missing and law enforcement officials believe the robbers may have killed them."

A commercial blared and he hit the mute button. Commercials were loud and distracting, and he needed to think. Gardner Museum. Stolen art worth a fortune. Guards missing. Was Nicholas one of them?

One thing was certain. If Nicholas was missing, he wasn't dead. He was in on the heist.

Larry mopped his brow with a handkerchief, recalling the day Nicholas had asked about Jamilla, his sudden interest when he found out she had once been a police officer. Larry did not believe this was a coincidence. But last week Jamilla had come in to tell him she was leaving Boston. The pain in his gut returned.

Ignoring it, he rose from the couch and headed for the door.

Forty-five minutes later he stood outside Jamilla's apartment, sickened by the odors in the hallway, burnt cooking oil, onions, greasy meat. A baby squalled in a nearby apartment.

"Open it up," Larry said, looking down at the bald head of Leroy Jones, a short squat black man with a gold stud in his ear, sweating inside his fancy suit.

Leroy pulled out a large key ring with many keys. "Dunno which one it is. Might take a while to find—"

Larry put a hand on his shoulder and squeezed. "Open the door!"

While the landlord tested keys in the lock, Larry studied the newspaper he'd bought at the 7-Eleven downstairs. *Gardner Heist Baffles Investigators*! Below it were black-and-white photos of the missing guards. One of them was Nicholas, but the caption under it said: Daniel Leone. Strange. He had asked the 7-Eleven clerk if he'd seen Jamilla lately. The clerk said he hadn't so Larry had called Leroy on the pay phone and told him to get his ass over here pronto. The shyster owned half the rat-infested apartments on the block and charged outrageous rent. Ripping off his own people.

He ate another Tums, recalling Jamilla's frightened expression when he asked if she knew Nicholas. She'd said she didn't, but maybe she did.

Leroy finally located the correct key and opened the door. Larry pushed him aside and stepped into a room with a worn-out sofa and a window with a tattered green shade. Toys were scattered over the floor, Hot-Wheel cars, crayons and a coloring book. "Jamilla," he called.

Not that he expected an answer, but he felt uneasy, being in her apartment uninvited. He went down a short hall, opened a door and saw a toilet, a sink, and a plastic shower curtain draped around a rusty tub with claw feet. He checked the medicine cabinet. Empty. In the kitchen across the hall dirty dishes stood in the sink, a coffee mug, two chipped plates, and a plastic glass with a Donald Duck sticker on it.

"Show me the bedroom," Larry said to Leroy, who was following him around like a puppy.

Leroy took him through the living room to the bedroom. The closet door was open. No clothes, just wire hangers on a wooden rod. Larry returned to the living room and noticed two suitcases standing against the wall behind the entry door. He hefted the larger one, set it on the sofa and unzipped it. Two pairs of jeans, cotton shirts, underwear and assorted toiletries, Jamilla's he assumed. He opened the smaller suitcase and saw kid's clothes.

"Looks like Jamilla be takin a trip," the landlord said.

Larry fixed him with a stare. "Did she tell you she was leaving? Give you notice?"

The landlord shrugged. "She paid through the end of the month is all I know."

Larry wanted to slap him, but what good would that do? Leroy didn't give a damn about Jamilla. Questions buzzed his mind like fruit flies. If Nicholas was in on the heist, maybe Jamilla was mixed up in it. But if she'd left town like she'd said she was going to, why pack two suitcases and leave without them?

The possibilities frightened him. Then he remembered the boy.

If something had happened to Jamilla, where was her son?

He popped another Tums. These questions with no answers were killing his digestion.

He stomped down the smelly staircase. When he got outside, he gulped fresh air and headed for his Lincoln Town Car, parked beside his restaurant. Halfway there, he stopped at a pay phone outside a barbershop, pulled out a scrap of paper, dropped in some coins and dialed.

"Special Agent Jeff Loring," a voice said. "Can I help you?"

Larry's stomach burned with acid. "I got information on that art heist."

"What sort of information?"

"I can't discuss it over the phone."

Smooth as a snake, the agent said, "Anything you say will be kept confidential."

Larry smiled at this absurdity. Then the agent said, "Could I have your name, sir?"

He blurted the first name that entered his mind. For years during his morning commute, he had listened to traffic reports, Joe Green whirling overhead in his helicopter.

"Joe Green. I got important information and I want to look you in the eye when I give it to you.

"Certainly, Mr. Green. What time would you like to come in?"

His stomach cramped and he almost hung up.

Then he remembered Jamilla's little boy.

"I'll be there at five o'clock," Larry said.

————

Frank got to the station at 2:35 and went straight to the interview room. A half hour ago Hank Flynn had called, saying he might have a lead. When he entered the interview room, Flynn did the introductions.

"Frank, this is Mr. Johnson. He called the station an hour ago. This is Homicide Detective Renzi, Mr. Johnson."

Johnson, mid-thirties, blond hair, blue eyes, didn't look thrilled about being here.

"Mr. Johnson drives a cab," Flynn said, by way of explanation. "Tell us what happened."

"The heist at the Gardner took up most of the news," Johnson said, "so I almost missed the story about the murder at the Mission Church. I dropped a passenger there early Saturday morning. A woman."

Frank's heart sped up. "What time was this?"

"Right around two A.M. I picked her up on Huntington Avenue, three blocks south of Ruggles Street. She asked me to drive her to the church, so I did. Didn't take long, ten minutes, tops. She didn't talk, just sat there in back seat, holding her arm. Like it was hurt, maybe."

"Can you describe her," Frank asked.

"Not really. It was raining. She was wearing a windbreaker and dark glasses."

"Was she tall? Short?" Flynn asked.

"Average. Five-six or seven, right around there."

"What color was her hair?" Frank asked.

"I don't know. The hood of the windbreaker covered it."

"How about her face?" Frank asked. "Do you remember what she looked like?"

Johnson shrugged. "I don't pay a lot of attention to my passengers, male or female. Plus, I wanted to go back to Copley Square, pick up a few customers leaving the bars, make some bucks and go home. Like I said, she wasn't on my radar screen until I saw the story about the dead veteran. You think she killed him?"

"We can't comment on that," Flynn said. "But this is good information. Very helpful."

Frank took out the composite sketch of Natalie Brixton and showed it to Johnson. "Was this the woman?"

Johnson studied the composite, frowning. "I don't know. She was wearing dark glasses so I couldn't see her eyes. It might have been her, but I couldn't swear to it."

Disappointed, Frank took the sketch and put it in his pocket.

"Can I go?" Johnson asked, ready to bolt from his chair.

"Yes," Flynn said. "We've got your phone number if we need to talk to you again. Thanks Mr. Johnson. You've been very helpful."

"You won't give out my name, will you? If she killed that guy, I don't want her coming after me."

"No need to use your name," Flynn said. "As long as you don't tell anyone what you've told us."

"Don't worry," Johnson said, rising from his chair. "I won't."

After Johnson left, Flynn said, "You think it was Natalie?"

"Yes, but I don't think she killed the guy in the church. Not her MO. She uses a gun, not a knife. But I think she was in on the heist."

"So do I. Hold on while I make a call. We might not have heard about the cab ride if this guy had called the tip line." Flynn dialed a number, waited, then said, "Hi Georgette, this is Lieutenant Harrison Flynn. Ten of my officers are assigned to the tip line. If a tip looks promising, they email me and copy it to you, but I don't get any emails from your FBI agents. Why is that?"

Frank wished he could hear Georgette's response. Nothing beat a pissing contest with the FBI.

Flynn looked at him and made his blue Irish-eyes go wide. "Georgette, you assigned three FBI agents to work the tip line, but I've got ten officers on it. Here's the deal. If your agents don't email me the promising tips they get, I'll pull my officer off the tip line and—"

Frank couldn't hear the ASAC's words, only her loud angry voice.

After a moment Flynn said, "Email me the leads or my officers will be working homicide cases, not the tip line." He cradled the phone and smiled. "That should do it."

"No leads from the FBI agents?" Frank said.

"No and I figure they must have gotten a few. So. Assuming Natalie Brixton was the woman the cabbie drove to the Mission Church, why did she go there?"

"Maybe she's got an apartment near the church. The security guard, Daniel Leone, had an apartment in Mission Hill. Did your detectives find anything at his apartment?"

"Dead end there. Just clothes and toiletries and a shitload of movie videos. The guy's a big fan of Sylvester Stallone. Dammit, Frank, we need a break."

"That was Natalie in the cab. But where is she now?"

"We've got the airport and the train and bus stations covered."

"All well and good, but she's clever at using disguises, wigs and hats and dark glasses."

"Frank, nobody's getting out of Boston with the paintings. We've got sniffer dogs at the airport. Anything suspicious, the State troopers will pull the person out of line and call in the dogs."

Frank fingered the scar on his chin. The cabby's tip was one more confirmation that Natalie was in Boston. And he was going to find her.

"First thing tomorrow I'm going to Global Interpreting and lean on Marta. This time I'll flash my NOPD creds. Maybe that will scare her into telling me where Gregor Kraus is."

"Want Marty to go with you? He's my best detective."

"Thanks, but Rafe tipped me off about Ursula. I'll take him with me." Frank smiled grimly. "Rafe and I love playing good-cop, bad-cop."

CHAPTER 32

Sunday July 12, 2014 3:30 PM

Nicholas stood at the kitchen counter, brewing a mug of green tea. The kitchen was a pigsty, bits of food crusted on the stove, rust stains in the sink. He had revised his theory about a little old lady living here with her cats. He didn't know where the cats were, but whoever had lived here was no old lady. Last night he'd found stacks of porn magazines in the bedroom closet.

Pictures of children having sex. Disgusting.

He took the tea in the living room. With the blinds closed, it was dark and gloomy, lit by a sixty-watt bulb in the ceiling fixture. A Sony 12-inch television stood on a black footlocker in front of the couch. Yesterday, after he'd stashed the paintings in a safe place, he had driven to Sears Roebucks and waited for the store to open at 9 AM. Then, using the cash Stefan had given him, he bought the Sony TV and a cowboy hat, a black Stetson with silver studs. It was expensive, seventy dollars, but he believed Sylvester Stallone might have worn such a hat. On his way back to the cottage, he had bought a box of green tea. Stefan had stocked the cupboards with coffee. He hated coffee.

The sound of screeching brakes sent his pulse racing. He ran to the window. A teenager in cut-off jeans and a muscle T-shirt got out of an old Ford Thunderbird and went in the house across the street.

Nicholas kicked the couch and dust motes rose in the air. Yesterday he had waited all day, but Stefan never arrived. Now the bastard wasn't answering his phone calls. Three times he had called, but Stefan didn't answer. He flexed his shoulders to relieve the tension. While he did not fear Stefan, he was not looking forward to their meeting.

The Manet was in the bedroom. Stefan would not be happy about the tear in the canvas. He would show him the Manet but not the others. Not until he got his money.

On the noon news a Providence TV station had run a special report on the Gardner heist. The stolen paintings were worth hundreds of millions of dollars. Hundreds of millions, and Stefan had offered him two. Then black-and-white photographs had appeared on the screen: Charles Lawson, Anthony Falcone and Daniel Leone.

His picture on the news!

He ran to the bathroom and studied his face in the grimy mirror. Could anyone recognize him from the picture on the TV? In the photo he had black hair and a thick dark beard. But the worst news had come at the end. An FBI agent said the insurance companies would not pay a ransom for the stolen art.

Murderous thoughts rampaged through his mind as he stormed into the kitchen. He took the Nakura hunting knife out of the leather sheath on the kitchen counter and touched the blade. After he got his money he would slice Stefan to ribbons. His blood would flow like a river.

The cottage was sweltering and his T-shirt clung to his back, damp with sweat. He slid the knife into the sheath, clipped it to his belt and pulled on his windbreaker. Stefan said the black Chevy was stolen, but Stefan lied. Stefan wanted to keep him a prisoner in this filthy little cottage. Screw that. Rigid with fury, he put on his cowboy hat, went in the garage, rolled up the garage door, got in the Chevy and drove off.

Five minutes later he parked at a small strip-mall with a Dunkin' Donuts on one end, a Store-24 at the other. When he went in the Store-24, a line of college students stood at the register. He took a bottle of iced tea from a cooler, tugged the brim of the cowboy hat down over his forehead and joined the line. When he paid for the iced tea, he added two dollars and asked for quarters. The clerk shoved the coins at him without looking up.

He got in the Chevy and headed for the payphone he'd seen yesterday behind a pizza shop, his mind raging with fury. The more he thought about Stefan, the more agitated he became.

But when he parked beside the payphone, a girl in a Brown University T-shirt was using it. He got out of the car and circled the booth. Oblivious to him, she played with her blond ponytail, laughing and talking. Couldn't the bitch see he needed the phone? He circled the booth again, unzipped his jacket and touched the knife. If she didn't leave in one minute, he would cut her.

His fingers curled around the handle of the knife as he counted the seconds. A pudgy middle-aged man in a polo shirt passed him, carrying a red-and-white pizza box. The man went to a tan Bronco and opened the door. But he didn't get in the Bronco, he stared at Nicholas, frowning.

Nicholas gripped the handle of the knife. Did the man see his photograph on the news and recognize him? Finally, the Bronco barreled out of the lot. Nicholas let out the breath he'd been holding.

The girl with the ponytail left the phone booth, beamed him a cheerful smile and walked away.

You're lucky I didn't slit your throat, bitch. He went in the booth, lined up eight quarters on the metal shelf below the phone, dropped in one quarter and punched the numbers. He heard the phone ring, but then a mechanical voice said: *Please deposit one dollar and forty-five cents.*

He dropped in more quarters. The phone rang three times before Stefan answered. "Yes?"

"My picture was on the news and the insurance companies won't pay a ransom!"

"Nicholas! Where are you?"

"At a pay phone. When I call you on my cell, you don't answer!"

"I told you not to leave the cottage."

"I want my money!"

"Your ex-cop screwed up. One of the cops died. That makes it harder for me to negotiate. When things cool down you will get your money."

"On the news it said they wouldn't pay—"

"Of course they will pay. But only if the paintings are in perfect condition."

Nicholas visualized the tear in the Manet canvas. "The paintings are fine," he said.

"I will believe this when you show them to me."

He ground his teeth. "Well? When are you coming to see them?"

"Tomorrow. Stay in the cottage until I get there."

Nicholas slammed down the receiver.

———

Larry sniffed the fetid air whipping through the window of the crowded MBTA train as it rattled along the underground track. An ebony-skinned man-child with dreadlocks sat on the opposite seat, oblivious to the clack-clack of the wheels, eyes shut, head bobbing to whatever came through the headset clamped over his ears. Intermittent bursts of sound leaked out.

To Larry, it sounded like electronic swarms of locusts.

He should have driven to the meeting, but downtown parking prices were ridiculous, seven dollars for a half hour. Vague discomfort stirred in his midsection. He popped a Tums.

Dealing with cops was bad enough; the FBI was worse.

The train jerked to a halt. Larry glimpsed the station sign: Copley. Four stops to Government Center.

The man-child with the dreadlocks departed, taking his electronic pestilence with him. Unfortunately someone equally unpleasant replaced him, an immense woman with pasty-white skin. A tent-like blue-flowered dress draped her bulging body. As the train left the station she removed a Styrofoam container from a McDonald's bag. The odor of greasy meat and onions filled the car. Oblivious to the disgusted glances of other passengers, she bit into what appeared to be a double-hamburger with cheese.

Larry dug out a crumpled roll of Tums—his second roll today—extracted the last one and put it in his mouth. Fascinated, he watched as the woman attacked the burger with furious concentration. Gobs of mustard and ketchup dribbled down her double chin. By the time the train rolled into Government Center, the burger was gone, though the odor languished in the car.

Desperate for fresh air, Larry lunged out the door. The escalator was out of order, so he climbed a steep flight of stairs. Short of breath and sweating profusely, he stepped out onto Government Plaza. A wave of dizziness hit him. He sank onto a cement bench and mopped his face with a handkerchief. Pain radiated up his arm to his neck. He patted his pockets, searching for another roll of Tums, but couldn't find one.

He massaged his left shoulder, then his neck. More than anything in the world he wanted to go home and lie down on his comfortable king-sized bed and rest. But he couldn't. He had to talk to the FBI agent.

Where was Jamilla's little boy? Where was Jamilla? She would never abandon her son. Larry mopped his forehead. He was certain Nicholas was involved in the Gardner heist, with some other scumbags, probably. He didn't care who, as long as it wasn't Jamilla. He knew where Kwan lived. He would give the FBI agent the address and tell him to go there and ask Kwan what happened to Jamilla. He'd tell him about that other guy, too, the foreign-looking man with the dead-fish eyes who'd asked about her at the restaurant. Joe Smith.

He levered himself off the bench. It was almost five o'clock and the FBI agent was expecting him. Another wave of dizziness staggered him, but he kept going, laboring up the redbrick stairs to Government Plaza. As he reached the top step, an excruciating pain exploded in his chest. For an instant he thought someone had shot him.

His knees buckled and he collapsed. His chest was on fire and he couldn't breathe. Fighting the pain, he rolled onto his side. He felt hot and cold at the same time, and a buzzing noise rang in his ears. He shut his eyes, but the loud buzzing noise continued.

Worst of all was the pain, pounding his chest like a sledgehammer. Distant voices mixed with the buzzing noise and his raspy breathing.

He tried to think. Meeting. He had to go to a meeting. He opened his eyes. A circle of faces hovered above him, but he couldn't speak, could only fight the terrible pain in his chest.

A great roar sounded in his ears, and everything faded to black.

One of the bystanders, an Asian medical student from Massachusetts General Hospital, performed CPR, and someone called an ambulance. The EMTs worked feverishly on the unconscious man, but by the time they rolled Larry into the MGH emergency room at five o'clock he was dead.

———

Natalie went to the coffee machine in her hotel room and used the hot water dispenser to fix herself a cup of tea. Exhausted by last night's ordeal, she had slept until noon. The king-sized bed was a soothing cocoon, crisp clean sheets and plump downy pillows. For the first time in weeks she felt rested.

Best of all, no one was looking for Lily Roberts.

No more calls from Gregor since their tense phone conversation, a conversation that had convinced her he didn't have the paintings. She hoped it had convinced Gregor that she didn't have them.

If Nicholas had the paintings—and it seemed clear that he did—Gregor would find him. Which meant Gregor would lead her to the stolen paintings. She checked her iPhone. No text messages.

She had analyzed his movements after the heist. According to the text messages on her iPhone, the Saab had left the storage building in Revere at 3:30 AM. From there it had gone to an apartment two blocks from hers in Mission Hill. Ten minutes later Gregor had stopped at her apartment. And found it empty, which was why he had asked where she was. Then he had driven to the garage at Global Interpreting. The Saab had remained there all night. Maybe Gregor was sleeping in the office.

But at one o'clock today the Saab had returned to Mission Hill and parked outside her apartment.

Creepy. Was Gregor staying at her apartment?

At that point she had put on her blond wig and her little black dress and left the hotel. Famished, she went to a French restaurant and devoured a Salmon Nicoise salad. Not as good as she'd eaten in Paris, but close, chilled poached salmon, fresh green beans, hard-boiled eggs and Calamari olives, served with a flaky croissant. Afterward she'd thought about doing her TKD workout at the gym. Her arm felt much better, hardly any pain. But caution had prevailed. Better to stay hidden in the hotel.

Now it was six o'clock. She sat on one of the blue-velvet easy chairs, turned on the TV and tuned in a Boston station. The news jingle sounded. The Gardner heist was the lead story.

The three security guards were still missing. The officer in the second cruiser had been released from the hospital. "Police believe he may have been drugged," the announcer said. "Results of the autopsy on the second officer have not been released."

No mention of the woman in the police uniform she'd seen in the mini-van. Murdered by Nicholas. Where was the van now, she wondered. Were the bodies of the other security guards inside it, too?

The anchorwoman introduced a clip of a noon press briefing. A grim-faced female FBI official said, "The insurance companies will not pay to ransom the stolen paintings. If the thieves are watching, we urge them to return the four paintings. Leave them in a safe place, call our tip-line and tell us where they are. No questions asked." An 800-number scrolled across the bottom of the screen.

Fat chance, Natalie thought. Gregor wouldn't return the paintings, nor would Nicholas. She doubted that Gregor had ever intended to ship them to Pym. Nor did Pym, apparently. Earlier she had checked her bank balance. Pym had deposited a half million dollars into it, just as he'd promised.

A new graphic on the screen caught her eye. **Murder at Mission Church**. "A Vietnam War veteran was found murdered early Saturday morning at the Mission Church," said the anchorwoman.

Footage of police vehicles outside the Mission Church appeared on the screen. "Robert McDermott, sixty-one, had been stabbed multiple times. Police ask anyone with information to call the District-Four station. One of McDermott's friends said McDermott had mental health issues and alcohol problems and had been homeless for years."

Natalie muted the TV. Goosebumps rose on her arms and her heart pounded. A man stabbed multiple times at the Mission Church, two blocks from her apartment. Would the cab driver remember her?

Nicholas had gashed her arm with a knife. Did he kill the man in the church? But why would Nicholas be in the church? Why kill a homeless veteran? Then she thought, the paintings. Nicholas must have hidden the paintings there and the man saw him.

An icy chill wracked her. Suddenly, she didn't feel safe.

She was certain Gregor had told Nicholas to kill her. Gregor didn't leave witnesses around to squeal to the cops. She should pack her things and leave Boston now. Pym had wired a half million dollars into her bank account. She had her new passports.

She rose from the chair, went to her duffel and took out the passports. Ling Lam and Liang Lam.

Her photographs were on the passports now, but all she could see were the smiling faces of Pak Lam's twins. His son, the Little League pitcher, and his daughter, the talented violinist.

Her eyes misted with tears and her throat thickened.

Rival gang members had murdered his adorable twins in 1984. For twenty-six years Pak Lam had kept their passports. Now he had given them to her, saying she was his adopted daughter. And he was her adopted father, a man she respected and cared for deeply. A man far more honorable and loving than her own father had ever been.

The thought of confronting Gregor terrified her, but she couldn't leave Boston now. She had promised Pak Lam she would find the stolen paintings and return them to their rightful owners.

Such a promise could not be ignored. It was a matter of honor.

CHAPTER 33

Monday July 13, 2014 9:20 AM

Frank jammed his fists in the pockets of his slacks and leaned against the door opposite Marta's desk. She was on the phone, scribbling on a yellow legal pad. "Certainly, sir. What time do you need her?"

Blah, blah, blah. The phone had rung nonstop ever since he and Rafe arrived ten minutes ago. Rafe was studying the art print on the wall above the sofa, could have been a connoisseur at an art gallery were it not for his size and his outfit, a large black man in a black running suit, packing a gun.

The instant Marta put down the phone Frank crossed the room and planted his palms on her desk. Before he could speak the phone rang again. "Leave it!" he barked.

Marta shrank back in her chair, as though she'd been cornered by a rabid dog.

"Twice I asked you about Stefan Haas. Both times you blew me off. Stop dicking me around. Tell me where he is or we'll get a search warrant and see what's in those file cabinets."

Marta tensed, her neck corded, frowning at him now. "I'd like to see some identification, Mr. Capone."

He flashed his NOPD creds. "Homicide Detective Frank Renzi, New Orleans PD. Detective Hawkins is with Boston PD. Tell us how to contact Mr. Haas."

"I can't. He's away on business."

"Gimme a straight answer!" Frank exploded. "Where on business?"

She raised a hand as if to ward him off. "I don't know! I don't have his itinerary."

He looked at Rafe, who picked up his cue.

"Ease up a little, huh?" Rafe said as he went to the desk. "I'd hate to see you get in trouble, Marta. We got no bone to pick with you. But we need to talk to Mr. Haas."

Vertical frown lines appeared between her well-groomed eyebrows. She swiped a wisp of blond hair off her forehead, picked up a felt-tipped pen and began doodling on her legal pad.

"You must have some idea where he is," Rafe said. "What airline does he fly? When's he coming back?"

"I'm not a secretary! Mr. Haas makes his own arrangements. I don't know when he'll be back. He's on a recruitment tour. We need more interpreters."

"What happened to Ursula?" Frank asked.

Marta said nothing, doodling on the legal pad, geometric shapes, angry black lines.

"Stefan Haas died in London," Frank said. "Gregor Kraus killed him and stole his identity."

Marta paled visibly, blood draining from her face like water down a toilet. "That is absurd!"

"Show us his picture."

Dots of pink appeared on her cheeks. "I don't have to show you anything."

"You're doing dynamite business," Frank said. "All those phone calls? You must have a brochure with a picture of Stefan Haas."

Marta scowled. Clamped her lips together. Drew another triangle on the legal pad.

"Where's Gregor Kraus?" Frank said.

"I don't know what you're talking about." She licked her lips. "Mr. Haas hasn't been in the office—"

"You must know how to reach him. What if there's an emergency?"

More doodles in thick black ink, a rectangle, then a trapezoid.

"Come on, Marta. Give us a phone number where we can reach him and we'll stop bothering you."

A muscle worked in her jaw. "I don't have one. Mr. Haas is ... difficult to reach."

He glanced at Rafe, got back a glum look.

"Okay," Frank said. "We'll get started on the paperwork for the search warrant. Maybe we'll have the IRS check your tax returns, have INS go over the immigration papers of the women who work here."

He saw a flash of panic in her eyes. He took out his business card and put it on the desk. "Tell Gregor Kraus to call my cellphone. If I don't hear from him by noon, we'll be back with a warrant." He jerked his head at Rafe and they left.

Inside the elevator, Rafe cocked an eyebrow at him and said, "Capone? What's that about?"

Frank grinned. "John Capone, Al Capone's nephew. I use it as cover when I want to throw my weight around. How come you were ogling the print?"

Rafe shrugged. "I liked it. The kid looked like he was having fun. Boy With Lute by Franz Hals."

"Jesus! Franz Hals? Someone stole a painting from the Franz Hals Museum in the Netherlands. The security guard was murdered later. Kelly and I talked to his widow in London."

"Huh," Rafe said, frowning. "You think that's the stolen painting?"

"No. But it's a strange coincidence."

Rafe looked at him, somber-eyed. "Ursula's dead and so is Stefan Haas. Marta's a tough nut to crack. Heavy duty shredder behind her desk, won't be finding anything useful in the Global Interpreting trash."

"Which means we better get in there with a search warrant before anything gets shredded."

"You really think we can get a search warrant?" Rafe said.

"I don't know, but I'll try. Marta's full of shit. There's no Stefan Haas and she knows it."

"You think Gregor Kraus will call you?"

Frank smiled grimly. "Yeah. When pigs fly."

———

Gregor sat at the kitchen table in Valerie's apartment, methodically squeezing his Iron-Man grippers. He should eat something but he had no appetite. He put down the grippers, poured a dollop of Remy Martin into his coffee and took a sip.

Planning the Gardner heist had been a challenge, but knowing the outcome would richly reward him had sustained him.

He slammed his fists on the table. His plan was brilliant. But he had left the execution to others. Valerie and Nicholas Kwan. Traitors, both of them. Kwan he would deal with today. But what about Valerie?

Where was she?

He could scarcely believe he had entertained the notion of sharing his triumph with her. Years ago he had celebrated with Marta but had quickly tired of her. Valerie was different.

Last night he had slept in her bed. Smelling her scent on the pillow was an exquisite pleasure, he had to admit. He closed his eyes and pictured her at the Gardner gala, her lithe body encased by the slinky gold dress he'd bought her, fueling his enchantment. Staying with her at the hotel in Dedham had increased his desires.

Desires that Valerie had rudely rebuffed. She didn't understand.

He wanted to share his success with her. Celebrate at an elegant hotel, share a cognac and watch her almond eyes light up in admiration as he detailed his audacious plan. Then he would take her to bed. His cock stirred, an insistent ache in his groin, fueled by memories of Valerie. Her well-toned arms and long slim legs as she worked out at the hotel fitness center. Her sexy dress that night, exposing her cleavage.

Glorious memories, interrupted by the chime of his cell phone.

His heart surged. Was it Valerie? He snatched up the phone and studied the number. Shit! Marta. "What is it?" he said.

"Gregor! That man came here again. This time he showed me his badge. He's a homicide detective from New Orleans. A Boston cop was with him. Merde! I knew he was a cop—"

"Calm down, Marta. Stop dithering. I'm busy."

"Gregor, you don't understand! The New Orleans cop knows about Stefan Haas."

His neck prickled. "What does he know?"

"He said Stefan Haas died in London. He said you killed him and stole his identity. You, Gregor."

He breathed deeply to calm himself. "He has my name?"

"Yes. Gregor Kraus, he said."

"How does he know my name?"

"I don't know! I didn't tell him. H-h-he just knew."

Gregor thought about it. This could be a problem. He had used Stefan's credit card when he'd registered at the Dedham hotel, and again when he'd rented the getaway car for Kwan.

"He left his card. Homicide Detective Frank Renzi. He said if you don't call him by noon, they'll get a search warrant to look at our files."

This was troubling, but obtaining a search warrant would take time. "They were bluffing. What reason do they have for a search warrant? If they come back, stonewall them."

"I can't!" Her shrill voice lanced his ear.

He heard her, breathing hard, awaiting his response. He forced a smile and used his persuasive voice. "Sure you can, Marta. You're the smartest woman I know." Except for Valerie.

"I saw the news about the Gardner heist," Marta said. "Did you steal those paintings?"

Just as he'd feared. Marta suspected him. "No, but I wish I had. They are worth millions."

"I know what they're worth," she snapped. "For God's sake, Gregor, do something about this cop!"

He massaged his eyes, considering his next move, and everything became clear. "I will, but we must plan our moves first. Meet me at the office tonight at seven o'clock."

He clicked off without waiting for an answer. But time was the enemy. Meet Marta at seven. But he had to get the paintings first.

He studied his hands, scarred but powerful. It wouldn't take long to persuade Kwan to tell him where they were.

———

Two hours later he parked the Saab in front of Burt's cottage in Providence. He got out and retrieved the groceries he'd bought to appease Kwan: fresh fruit and vegetables, cartons of milk and cream, packets of gourmet coffee. His snub-nosed Smith & Wesson was in a holster strapped to his ankle, readily available if Kwan pulled his nasty-looking knife. He'd worn a pair of gray slacks and a navy-blue blazer today. The loose-fitting jacket concealed the Taser strapped to his hip.

Carrying the grocery bag in one hand and a newspaper in the other, he went to the door and rang the bell. A full minute passed.

Irritated, he banged on the door. A slat in a window blind parted.

Seconds later Kwan opened the door. His beard was gone and his head was shaved, which emphasized the ugly scowl on his face.

"I bought you some groceries," Gregor said, "fresh fruit and vegetables, and gourmet coffee."

"Coffee," Kwan sneered.

The punk was wearing faded jeans and a white T-shirt, no sign of a knife. Of course not. Kwan had the paintings, a weapon more potent than any dagger. In the living room, a portable TV with a crude antenna stood on a footlocker in front of the sofa, and newspapers lay on the floor with Gardner heist headlines.

"When do we get the money?" Kwan asked.

"Where's the car?"

"In the garage. When do we get the money?"

"Show me."

With an angry hiss, Kwan turned and went in the kitchen. Gregor followed him and set the groceries on the counter. He'd forgotten how filthy the place was, and the stench of cat urine was overpowering in the sweltering cottage. He opened the door beside the refrigerator, peered into the garage and saw the rental car.

"How long do I have to stay in this dump? I need cash. I used all I had to buy the TV set. Because you tell me nothing, Stefan. You want to keep me in the dark!"

He shut the door to the garage and pulled out some bills. "Here's two hundred."

"That's not enough. I need more."

"Where are the paintings?"

An insolent smile appeared on the punk's face.

He peeled off five twenties and handed them over. "Where are the paintings?"

Kwan snatched the bills and leaned against the cellar door opposite the sink.

Were the paintings in the cellar?

"The Manet is in the bedroom," Kwan said.

"Show me." He followed Kwan to a bedroom with a single bed and a maple dresser. Propped against the wall beyond the bed was Manet's portrait of his mother, Madame Manet with her dour expression and implacable gaze. His heart jolted. There was a jagged tear in the canvas below her chin! He could never sell it in this condition and he couldn't very well hire someone to repair it.

A slow-simmering rage rose inside him. Kwan would pay for this.

"Where are the others?" he said in a quiet voice.

"Why should I tell you?" Kwan said, leaning against the doorjamb with a sullen look on his face. "The insurance companies won't pay to get them back."

"Of course they will." He waved the Boston Herald, the prop he'd brought to convince the punk. A photo of the Gardner was on the front page. "The cops were bluffing. The insurance companies are desperate to get the paintings back. They're waiting for us to contact them."

Kwan's sour expression softened and excitement appeared in his eyes. "When do we get the money?"

"Soon. But I can't negotiate with them until you show me the other paintings."

"Hsss! You take me for a fool. The paintings are worth millions and you offer me two."

Waving the newspaper to distract him, Gregor unbuttoned his jacket, circled the bed and slowly approached Kwan.

"Where are the other paintings?"

"Never mind. I will tell you when the insurance companies are ready to pay."

Holding the punk's gaze, he edged closer and slipped his hand into his jacket. "How much do you want?"

Kwan's eyes glittered with greed. "Ten million."

He whipped out the Taser and zapped 20,000 volts into Kwan's neck. Kwan's head snapped back. His body jerked violently, shuddered, then sagged.

Gregor shoved him down on the bed and zapped him again.

Kwan's lips twisted in a grimace and his eyes rolled up into his head.

Excellent. His persuasion kit was in the trunk of the Saab. It would only take a minute to get it.

CHAPTER 34

1:10 PM

Natalie fanned herself with a newspaper as the merciless midday sun beat down on the black Toyota Corolla. It belonged to Feng's brother, but Pak Lam had loaned it to her. She didn't know why Gregor had stayed at her apartment last night, but when the Saab left its parking spot this morning, she had followed it. Texts to her iPhone mapped its route out of Boston to Route 95 south to Providence. There, Gregor had stopped twice, once at a hardware store, then a grocery store.

Now the Saab was parked on a side street in front of a one-story cottage. Along the street, other cars sat outside other houses. She had parked at the corner, close enough to see Gregor enter the white cottage. But Gregor wasn't her only worry. The Gardner heist was all over the news. She had seen Frank Renzi twice, once at the Global Interpreting office and then at the Gardner gala. He hadn't seen her, but if he was still in Boston, she was in trouble.

Every instinct told her to leave town fast.

But first she had to return the stolen paintings. Gregor and Jonathan Pym no longer controlled her. For the first time in her life, she was going to do something positive. An exhilarating feeling.

She figured Nicholas had the paintings, which meant Nicholas was in the little white cottage a half-block down the street. Why else would Gregor go there? But all this waiting around was annoying. She took out a peanut-butter power bar, tore open the foil and took a bite. Lunch. Recalling a crime novel she'd once read, she smiled. It said police work was ninety-percent boredom and ten-percent terror. But male cops had an advantage. On surveillance they could bring along a container and pee into it. Women had to be wily.

While Gregor was in the grocery store she had bought a bottle of water at the coffee shop two doors down and used the restroom. To her relief, when she returned to the Toyota, the Saab had still been parked outside the grocery store.

She checked her hair in the visor mirror. To hide her short dark hair, she had styled her blond wig in a ponytail, pulled on the wig and put on her Red Sox cap. The one Gregor hated. A sobering thought.

The loaded Beretta was in the glove compartment, but if Gregor came out of the cottage with the stolen paintings, she couldn't just run up to him with the Beretta and say, "Hand them over."

Her breath caught in her throat as the door of the white cottage opened. Gregor hurried down the walk to the Saab. But he wasn't carrying the paintings. He took a satchel out of the trunk and returned to the cottage.

She finished the peanut-butter power bar and settled down to wait.

———

Gregor leaned against the workbench in the basement. The odor of oil from the furnace and gasoline from Burt's gas-powered lawnmower permeated the air. A 60-watt bulb above the workbench cast harsh light over Kwan's naked body, trussed on the cement floor, his wrists and ankles bound with picture wire. Another strand of wire connected them, effectively immobilizing him.

Although short in stature, Kwan was well muscled, a flat stomach above a mound of black pubic hair, nipples erect on his hairless chest.

Kwan groaned. His eyelids fluttered open and settled on the man he called Stefan. "Motherfucker!" Straining against the picture wire, Kwan tried to raise his arms, but failed.

"It didn't have to be this way, Nicholas. Where are the paintings?"

"Fuck you!"

Gregor planted a foot on his hairless chest. "Tell me where the paintings are."

"Never! You'll never find them!"

He took a pipe wrench out of his persuasion kit. In London, some enforcers used baseball bats to achieve their aims, but baseball bats were for amateurs. His persuasion tool weighed two pounds, eighteen inches long from the end of the cast-iron handle to the top of the wrench. A movable jaw provided additional possibilities. The maximum jaw capacity was 3 inches, more than enough for his needs.

"Where are the paintings?"

"Hssss! I will never tell. Your precious paintings will rot!"

Without warning, he slammed the wrench down on Kwan's right knee, pulverizing it. Writhing in pain, Kwan screamed, an agonizing screech that seemed to go on forever.

"Tell me."

"Never, motherfucker." Teeth clenched. Eyes glittering with rage.

Brandishing the wrench, he said, "Why do you make me hurt you? Tell me where they are."

He saw fear in the punk's eyes. Still, Kwan said nothing. He slammed the wrench down on Kwan's left knee and heard bone crunch.

"Motherfucker!" Kwan screamed. His chest heaved and tears of pain oozed from his eyes.

"Tell me where the paintings are."

Kwan began to scream, a wordless keening sound worse than a dentist's drill that went on and on. Fearing someone might hear, he took a roll of duct tape out of his persuasion kit, tore off two strips and knelt beside Kwan's head. Grasping Kwan's jaw, he clamped his mouth shut and slapped duct tape over his lips.

"Mmmmmmmmm!!" Kwan made guttural sounds.

He adjusted the jaw of the wrench, grabbed Kwan's right hand and inserted his ring and little finger into the jaw. He had to have the paintings. Unfortunately, violence was the only thing Kwan understood.

Kwan tried to pull his hand away, but his attempt was laughable.

Gregor used the Iron-Man gripper every day to insure that his hands remained strong and powerful. He tightened the jaw of the wrench, clamping Kwan's fingers inside it.

Kwan's eyes bugged out of his head.

He grasped Kwan's wrist with his left hand. His right hand tightened on the wrench. With a sudden jerk, he bent Kwan's fingers back toward his wrist, snapping them like sticks.

The guttural sounds rose to a high-pitched shriek, a sound so terrible it raised the hackles on Gregor's neck.

Tears ran down Kwan's cheeks and mucus dribbled from his nose.

"Six more fingers and two thumbs," he said in a quiet voice. "This can go on forever. Why suffer more pain?"

Kwan's chest heaved as he struggled to breathe, sucking air past the snot in his nose.

He ripped the duct tape off the punk's mouth. "Where are the paintings?"

"Not . . . here." A raspy whisper.

"Locker."

"Where?"

"What locker? Where?"

"Bus . . . station."

"A luggage locker?"

Kwan nodded.

Now they were getting somewhere. "Where is the key?"

"If I tell," Kwan moaned, "you will take the paintings and kill me."

He gripped Kwan's shoulder. His skin was clammy with sweat. "Tell me where the key is, Nicholas, or you will die a long, slow, painful death. I guarantee it."

Kwan closed his eyes, his chest heaving.

"You are testing my patience, Nicholas." The understatement of all time. He wanted to crush the bastard's skull and watch his brains spill onto the cement floor.

"The key is ... "

He thought his heart would stop.

"Garage ... cat litter."

Gregor raced upstairs. Burst into the kitchen. Flung open the door to the garage. Two bright-red Kitty Litter bags stood in the corner. Five-pound bags, one unopened, the other half full. Feverish with excitement, he grabbed the open bag and poured white pellets on the floor, dribbling out small batches and spreading them over the floor with his fingers to make sure he didn't miss the key.

When the bag was almost empty, a small brass key tumbled onto the floor. Stamped on the key was the number 227.

He returned to the cellar, sealed Kwan's lips with duct tape and made sure the bindings were secure.

"I found the key. If the paintings are there, I will let you go. You will get no money, of course. You have caused me far too much trouble for that. But you will escape with your life." He gestured at the pipe wrench. "If the paintings are not in the locker, I will kill you and take my time doing it."

Five minutes later he stopped at a traffic light at the bottom of College Hill, his heart thrumming his chest. Soon he would have his paintings. Three of them, at least. Thanks to his idiot helper, the Manet was ruined.

He glanced out the window. Sunlight dappled the redbrick sidewalks and the ivy-covered walls that surrounded a stately Victorian mansion. Two students in Rhode Island School of Design T-shirts rode by on bicycles. This didn't surprise him—the school was a block away—but the coincidence amused him.

Stefan Haas had attended RISD. Or so he'd said when Gregor struck up a conversation with him at a London club. Dark-haired, dark-eyed and handsome, Stefan was a rich American playboy. Their looks were similar and Gregor needed an alternate identity. Given Stefan's drug habit, coke being his drug of choice, it was easy. Stefan wanted a fix, so Gregor took him to a dark alley, strangled him, and stole his wallet and the keys to his flat. A cursory search had yielded Stefan's driver's license, passport and two snapshots to facilitate his disguise.

Posing as Stefan had been useful but according to Marta, some cop was onto him. Another problem to solve.

The light turned green and he floored the accelerator. Following the GPS instructions, he reached the bus station ten minutes later. He found a metered space in the lot across the street, fed the meter and hurried to the station, a one-story cement-block building with Trailways and Bonanza buses lined up along one side.

Inside, a dozen people queued up at two ticket windows. Passengers with suitcases or knapsacks waited on benches. Two little boys squealed with laughter as they raced past him. A dumpy woman in a blue dress—the mother, he presumed—yelled at them but they ignored her, darting around the benches.

Gregor scanned the room and spotted a sign: LUGGAGE LOCKERS. His pulse quickened as he pushed through a swinging door into a room with rows of gray-steel lockers. He took out the key and walked along the first row, scanning the numbered metal plates. The numbers ended at 200. Gripping the key, he rounded the corner and continued down a narrow aisle with lockers on both sides.

At last he came to locker 227. His heartbeat accelerated, pounding his chest. Were the paintings inside?

He inserted the key and opened the door. Inside was a gray-fabric suitcase. Suppressing the shout of joy that threatened to burst from his mouth, he pulled out the suitcase and returned to the waiting room. A sign to the right of the ticket booth pointed to the restrooms.

Yellowed porcelain urinals lined the right-hand wall of the restroom, which smelled of urine and disinfectant. A bald man in a baggy brown suit stood at one urinal. Lined up along the opposite wall were six green-enamel stalls.

Gregor strode past the bald man, entered the stall in the far corner and bolted the door. He placed the suitcase flat on the toilet seat and tried the metal clasps. They were locked. "Fuck!" he shouted.

A voice called: "You okay in there?"

He clenched his teeth. "I'm fine," he said. But he wasn't fine.

The fucking case was locked!

He could force the clasps, but not without tools. He counted to thirty and cautiously opened the stall door. The bald man was gone.

Carrying the suitcase, he rushed out of the station, hurried to the Saab and opened the trunk. A road-repair kit was in the spare-tire well. He checked the nearby cars. Seeing no one, he took out the tool kit, shut the trunk, got in the Saab and laid the suitcase on the passenger seat. He could hardly breathe, his heart churning in a jagged rhythm. Control. He had to control himself.

To maintain discipline, he counted to fifty. Only then did he remove a screwdriver from the repair kit and pry at one clasp. It didn't budge.

He wanted to scream.

Again he forced himself to remain calm. He removed a wooden mallet from the tool kit, set the screwdriver blade against the clasp and smacked the screwdriver handle with the mallet. The clasp sprang open. Exhilarated, he shouted, "Yes!"

He repeated the procedure with the other clasp and sat very still, feeling his heart thump his chest. The moment of truth.

He opened the suitcase, lifted a lime-green hand towel and saw *The Lacemaker*. Kwan had removed the frame, but the canvas backing was intact and the painting was in fine condition. He placed the Vermeer in the passenger foot-well and examined the next one. *The Milkmaid*, also in good condition. Reassured, he checked the Rembrandt *Self-Portrait* and stared at it, aghast. The bottom right-hand corner of the canvas was ripped off! His priceless Rembrandt, damaged!

Damn Kwan to hell! Rigid with fury, he clenched his fists. He had taken no pleasure in killing the insider guards in Europe. Or Ursula, for that matter. Only when she refused to satisfy his sexual appetites had he strangled her. As for Stefan, he had merely done what was necessary to obtain a legitimate alternate identity. But Kwan was different. Nicholas Kwan had damaged two of his paintings.

For this Kwan would die a slow and painful death.

———

Nicholas gnawed through the last strand of duct tape that covered his mouth and sucked in gulps of air. Straining against the wire, grimacing as it cut into his wrists, he tried to raise his hands to his mouth. Impossible, and even if he could, he couldn't chew through the wire that bound his hands together.

Stefan had hog-tied him, like a pig in a slaughterhouse.

The cellar was damp and chilly, but his body temperature had risen from the isometric exercises he had performed, hoping to diminish the pain. It didn't. Stefan had broken two of his fingers, and the pain in his knees was excruciating.

He pressed his cheek against the cool cement and focused his mind. He could not escape. He knew Stefan would kill him, but he would not beg for mercy. He would die with honor.

If only the motherfucker didn't hit him with the wrench again.

He shut his eyes and concentrated. Many times in the course of his twenty-seven years he had willed things to happen. He had not always succeeded, but this one thing he wanted badly.

He concentrated hard, visualizing Stefan's face.

Saw a round black hole appear in Stefan's forehead.

Saw Stefan's lips draw back and his tongue protrude.

Best of all was the torrent of blood streaming down Stefan's face.

CHAPTER 35

11:15 AM

Two days after the robbery Frank finally got to see the crime scene. The Gardner was closed until further notice and two police officers stood outside the entrance, but Georgette, the ASAC of the Boston FBI office wasn't there, nor were any FBI agents. Hank Flynn took him to the Blue Room on the first floor where the Manet had been stolen, then the Special Exhibit. On the walls were empty spaces where *The Milkmaid* and *The Lacemaker* had been displayed. Although the museum was closed, four armed police officers guarded the eight remaining paintings.

Then they went to the Dutch Room on the second floor. In 1990 thieves had stolen two paintings from this room, *The Concert* and *The Storm on the Sea of Galilee*, Rembrandt's only seascape. Frank hadn't been involved in the investigation, but he had visited the Gardner after it reopened. He stopped at a table by a window. Now brocade fabric filled the frame that had once held *The Concert* by Johannes Vermeer.

"Take a look at this," Flynn said, indicating a section of the room roped off by yellow crime scene tape. Dark stains marred the wood floor and more stains were visible on a faded carpet. "We figure one of the guards was killed here."

"A lot of blood," Frank said. "Looks like someone slit his throat."

"Before they stole the Rembrandt." Flynn took him to the wall adjacent to the interior courtyard. An antique chair stood below the space where the Rembrandt *Self-Portrait* had been. Bloodstains were visible on the upholstered seat, one of them a clear shoe print.

"Looks like the thief stood on the chair to get the painting off the wall," Frank said.

"The CSI techs took photos," Flynn said, "but I'm not convinced they'll help ID the thief."

"Right. Even if you ID the type and make of shoe, there could be thousands of them."

Flynn yawned and massaged his eyes. The first forty-eight hours after a crime of this magnitude, no one got any sleep, but Flynn looked exhausted, bags under his eyes, hollow cheeks, sallow skin.

"Let's go grab some lunch, Hank. You need a break."

"No can do. I need to get back to the office. I've got work—"

"No. I'm taking you out for lunch." Frank took his arm and pulled him toward the door. "My treat. You've done me a bunch of favors since I got here. I owe you one."

Ten minutes later they were sipping beers in a booth at a diner near the station. Frank studied his former boss. Something was wrong. During the years he'd worked for him, Hank Flynn had been a hands-on boss, a vigorous presence in his homicide investigations, tall, ruggedly built, muscular and fit. Now he looked thin and tired.

"What's up, Hank? You look exhausted. Are you okay?"

Flynn's blue eyes regarded him for several seconds. Then, with a faint smile, he said, "Very observant, Frank. You always were a great detective."

While the compliment pleased him, it also made him uneasy.

"I got a surprise a couple of months ago." Flynn picked up his beer mug and took a swallow. "I'd been feeling tired, no appetite, losing weight. Meredith made me see my doctor. Bottom line, I've got cholangiocarcinoma. Better known as bile cancer."

Stunned, Frank puffed his cheeks and blew a stream of air.

"Damn. That's a kick in the ass. I don't know much about bile cancer. What's the treatment?"

"There isn't one. Not in my case anyway." Flynn shrugged. "We all die sooner or later, but I've got a better idea than most about how soon it will be. That's why I'm retiring. Meredith and I are moving to California, to be with my daughter and her kids."

Frank fought the surge of emotion that threatened to overwhelm him, searching for words. Finally, he reached over and squeezed Hank's forearm. "Anything you need, name it and I'll be there. You were there for me when I needed you."

"Thanks, Frank. I appreciate it. Best thing you can do right now is help me solve the Gardner heist."

"You got it. I want to solve it as bad as you do."

"No one in the department knows about the diagnosis," Flynn said. "I'd appreciate it if you didn't say anything to anyone."

"I won't," Frank said. All of a sudden he wasn't hungry. Now he had more reason than ever to solve the Gardner case. And make sure Hank Flynn got the credit for it.

———

Providence

Gregor opened the five-pound Kitty Litter bag and poured the white pellets around Kwan's body. Kwan had double-crossed him. In the process he had ruined the Manet and damaged the Rembrandt.

A crackling funeral pyre would be his reward.

Wielding the power of life or death was not new to him. That was how he controlled people. Even hardened mobsters cowered in the face of death. Those who didn't capitulated when he threatened their loved ones. *Think how guilty you will feel after I kill your son or your wife or your lover.* Even the toughest criminal cared about relatives and lovers.

But love was a trap, one that would not ensnare him.

Kwan appeared resigned to his fate, lying on the floor, eyes closed, expression serene. Give the punk credit. The pain in his knees must be fierce, but Kwan didn't moan or cry out.

Gregor wondered what he was thinking. Not that he cared.

When the Kitty Litter bag was empty, he went upstairs to the bedroom. The implacable eyes of Madame Auguste Manet confronted him. A sudden realization hit him like a thunderbolt. Not the eyes of Manet's mother, his father's eyes. He studied the scars on his hands. For years Papa had burned his hands with merciless precision, withholding approval, denying him his love. To control him.

He had never been able to please Papa.

But Papa was dead. Now he was in control.

Seething with fury, he carried the Manet down to the cellar and propped it against the wall opposite Kwan's head. Using the container of gasoline that powered Burt's lawnmower, he sprinkled gas over the pellets. Trailing a stream of gasoline behind him, he went to the stairs and turned for a last look at Kwan.

The bastard was watching him, his eyes glowing with a fierce intensity. Kwan knew what was coming.

"Prepare to die, traitor. No one double-crosses Gregor Kraus and gets away with it."

He mounted the staircase, dousing the step below him with gasoline. When he reached the top, he set the container on the kitchen floor. Burt's cottage was about to go up in flames. The cops would know the fire was set, of course. They would identify the charred bones in the cellar, but they couldn't connect Kwan to him. Eventually, they would find out that Burt was employed as a driver for Global Interpreting. But he would take care of Burt tomorrow at JFK airport.

In the kitchen, he found a hand towel, folded it, and dropped it on the top step of the cellar stairs. He took out a Gitanes.

How long would it take for the cigarette to burn down to the filter?

Long enough, he decided.

He took a clothespin out of his persuasion kit, lighted a cigarette and sucked in a deep drag. The tip glowed angry red. He clipped the cigarette filter to one corner of the kitchen towel and visualized the orange-red flames licking at Kwan's body. A pity he couldn't stay and watch, but he had more important things to do.

———

Natalie mopped perspiration off her forehead with a tissue. Damp with sweat, her T-shirt clung to her back. The Toyota's front windows were open, but not a breath of air was stirring. She didn't dare start the car and run the air conditioner, fearing this would attract attention.

Earlier, she had followed Gregor to the bus station. Parked at the end of the row behind the Saab, she saw him hurry into the station. Twenty minutes later, carrying a gray-fabric suitcase, he came back to the Saab, took what appeared to be a small toolkit out of the trunk and got in the Saab. Five minutes later he put the suitcase and the toolkit in the trunk and drove off. Careful to keep her distance, she had followed him back to the white cottage.

This time she had parked on the other side of the street—the sunny side, unfortunately—in front of a blue ranch house. The window blinds were closed to keep out the sun, but her black Toyota had been parked here too long. If someone was home they might come out and ask why she was there.

She heard a high-pitched yip and checked the side mirror. A stout middle-aged woman in a sleeveless dress and a straw sunhat came around the corner, walking a small dog with short brown hair and a curly tail. The dog strained against the leash, tongue lolling from its mouth.

Natalie sank lower in the seat and watched the dog sniff at a maple tree and lift his leg. Willing the woman not to look her way, she grabbed the newspaper on the passenger seat, intending to hide her face with it. But the woman was intent on Fido. Tugging on his leash, she continued along the sidewalk without looking at the Toyota.

Relieved, Natalie straightened. Conscious of the time, she checked her watch. 2:15. She felt certain the stolen paintings were in the gray suitcase. This time Gregor had activated the car alarm before he went in the cottage. He'd been in there almost twenty minutes.

What was he doing?

The roar of a motorcycle startled her.

She checked the side-view mirror. Behind her, a brawny man with a full dark beard rounded the corner on a Harley Davidson. The noise was deafening. He wasn't wearing a helmet, just biker boots, torn jeans and a sleeveless T-shirt. Her palms dampened with sweat. She sank lower in her seat, but the biker didn't look her way, just roared down the street, parked the Harley in the driveway of the house across the street from the Saab and went inside.

Relieved, she sipped from her water bottle and leaned back against the headrest. A minute later, she jerked upright as Gregor burst out the door of the white cottage. The Saab's lights flashed and the alarm beeped. Gregor jumped in the car and drove away. She waited until the Saab turned the corner at the far end of the street, started the Toyota and pulled away from the curb. The hot air blowing on her face was a welcome relief after sitting in the car with the sun beating down on it.

Why was Gregor in such a hurry to leave the cottage? If Nicholas was in there, Gregor might have killed him. That would explain why he was in such a hurry. She slowed as she passed the white cottage and studied the windows. The window blinds were closed.

She increased her speed.

Then she heard a loud *whump* and the sound of breaking glass.

Startled, she hit the brakes and turned to look. Orange-red flames and thick dark smoke were spurting out the windows of the white cottage. Gregor had torched the place! Then she saw the biker come running out of the house across the street. She wanted to floor the accelerator, but she didn't. Attract no attention. Maintaining a moderate speed, she gripped the wheel, her hands damp with sweat.

After she turned the corner she increased her speed. The Saab was nowhere in sight. Gregor was probably heading for the nearest highway entrance. She pulled out her iPhone.

Five minutes later she got on Route 95 North. She still hadn't seen the Saab, but it was on the highway somewhere ahead of her. She settled into the traffic flow and gulped down half of her bottled water.

Now that Gregor had the paintings—and she was positive he did—where would he go?

———

Boston

They returned to Hank Flynn's office at 3:15. Still shaken by the cancer-diagnosis bombshell, Frank took the chair in front of the desk. He'd known Hank for years and considered him a good friend. He was convinced that Natalie was involved in the Gardner heist and he was hell-bent on catching her. Still, in the grand scheme of things, Hank's health was more important. But Hank wanted to solve the case too, had even asked for his help. It would be great to see Hank get credit for it.

Earlier he had told Hank what happened when he and Rafe grilled Marta, and Hank had given him the latest updates. They still didn't know who drugged the cops in the cruisers, and the security guards were still missing, but there was a bit of progress. Using the casts taken of the tire tracks behind the Gardner, the CSI techs had identified the make and model of the tires, most commonly used on Chevrolet Express mini-vans. Hank's top detective, Marty Talbot, was checking to see if any Chevrolet mini-vans had been stolen recently.

Now Hank was sorting through the pile of message slips that had accumulated while they were out.

"I told Marta I'd come back with a search warrant if Gregor didn't call me by noon," Frank said. "He hasn't called. There's a shredder in the office. If Marta calls Gregor and tells him we know Stefan Haas is dead, he might tell her to shred everything in the file cabinets. Can we get a search warrant?"

"What do we use for probable cause?"

"Gregor Kraus is using a fake ID. We know Stefan Haas is dead."

"True, but we don't know that Kraus killed him. I'm not sure a judge would go for it." Flynn's cellphone rang. He answered, listened for a moment, then said, "Good work, Marty. I'll put out a BOLO." Flynn closed his cell and said, "The night before the heist a brown Chevrolet Express mini-van was stolen from a used-car dealership in Mattapan."

"Was there a plate on it?" Frank asked.

"No. But whoever stole it could have stolen one and put it on the van. I'll have Marty check the files for any plates stolen a day or two before the heist."

"How's it going with Georgette?" Frank asked. "Did your tirade the other day help?"

Flynn smiled. "Indeed it did. Now I'm getting updates from her agents on any promising leads they get." His desk phone rang. Flynn grimaced. "Please don't let this be a reporter. I'm running out of excuses to get rid of them." He answered, listened for a while.

Then his mouth sagged open. "Jesus! Are you kidding?"

Frank knew something was up. His former boss might be gravely ill, but now he was smiling and his cheeks were flushed with excitement.

"Thanks, Georgette. See you there." Flynn rose from his chair. "That was Georgette. Providence PD got called to a house fire an hour ago. The fire chief found a body in the cellar and a charred painting. The fire chief has been following the Gardner heist. He thinks it's the stolen Manet."

Frank's heart beat a drum-roll inside his chest.

A house fire. A dead body. And the stolen Manet.

"What are we waiting for?" he said. "Let's go!"

CHAPTER 36

Providence, RI -- 5:15 PM

Lit by the orange rays of the setting sun, the one-story wood-frame cottage was a charred ruin. The white clapboard siding was dark with soot, the front door splintered by fire axes, the doorframe twisted. Electrical cords snaked through windows without glass. The attached one-car garage appeared to have less damage but the door gaped open.

Frank lowered his window and the acrid smell of smoke and scorched wood hit his nostrils.

Even with lights and sirens, it had taken them an hour to get here. Providence police cruisers blocked off the street. Hank Flynn dangled his Boston PD creds out the window, and a police officer moved a sawhorse to let them through. Television crews, reporters and photographers with telephoto lenses stood behind the sawhorse, eager to get closer. A fire truck stood in front of the cottage, ready to extinguish any flare-ups. Flynn parked twenty yards behind it.

"There's trouble," Flynn muttered.

Three FBI agents stood in front of the burned out cottage. Georgette, the ASAC of the Boston FBI office, was talking to a police official. Flynn ducked under the yellow police tape strung across the driveway, and Frank followed, taking care to avoid the fire-hose water mixed with soot and ash that puddled the blacktop.

Georgette saw them and frowned, but put on a fake smile and introduced the Providence Police Chief, Roland DeNunzio, a beefy Italian with thick dark hair, a Roman nose and a pockmarked face.

"Any ID on the body?" Flynn asked.

"No." DeNunzio puffed his cheeks and blew a stream of air. "I saw some bad accidents on highway patrol that didn't make me sick, but this did. The guy was hog-tied, wrists and ankles wired up. Whoever did it is a sick-o. Burn somebody alive like that? The stench was unbelievable."

"What about cause of death?" Georgette asked.

"Other than being burnt to a crisp?" DeNunzio said sarcastically. "The forensic pathologist took a preliminary look. Didn't see any bullet wounds, but she's not done yet."

"Who lived here?" Frank asked. Georgette pursed her lips, clearly annoyed that some interloper was butting into her investigation.

"We're not sure," DeNunzio said. "We're still trying to contact the owner."

"Where was the body?" Georgette asked. "We'd like to see it."

DeNunzio glanced at Hank Flynn, a subtle look but the message was clear. Georgette was leaning on him and he didn't like it. "In the basement, but you'll have to ask the fire marshal, see what he says."

He called to the fire marshal, who joined them, a wiry man with leathery skin and watery blue eyes. "This is the Chief Fire Marshal, Lorne Bryant," DeNunzio said. "These folks want to go in the cellar."

"Okay," Bryant said, "but the inside stairs are shot. We'll have to use the bulkhead out back."

When Bryant walked away, Georgette told the other FBI agents to wait out front and followed him. Flynn followed her and Frank took up the rear. When they reached the back wall of the cottage, Bryant stopped at a twisted metal door and said, "Watch your step."

They followed him down a cement stairway. The cellar reeked of smoke and a sickly sweet odor Frank recognized as burnt flesh. He'd smelled the same odor at a house fire in New Orleans, a two-story duplex. A drug dealer lived on one side, a single mother with three kids on the other. The kids were upstairs when the fire started; the mother was downstairs, asleep on a couch. She tried to save them but the flames, fueled by an accelerant, were too fierce. They found the two younger kids hiding in a closet. The oldest, a boy of six, lay on the floor near a window. Frank had been there when they pulled out the bodies.

But this was no turf war over drugs, this was premeditated murder.

They waited at the foot of the stairs while Bryant turned on a set of portable lights to illuminate the cellar. The fire crew had pumped out the most of the water, but greasy puddles remained on the cement floor. A gas-powered lawnmower lay in the corner, its metal frame twisted and bent. A wooden workbench had caved in and metal tools were strewn over the floor.

"That's where they found the body," Bryant said, indicating a chalked outline surrounded by blackened cement. "It was a major flashpoint. Someone put something flammable around the body. You can see the guy tried to roll, but it was hopeless, tied up like he was." Bryant shook his head. "Gives me the creeps."

"Where was the painting?" Frank asked.

Bryant pointed to a chalked outline on the wall. "It's a miracle I noticed it, the body freaked me out so bad. The Manet was propped against the wall."

"You were sharp to pick up on it," Flynn said.

Bryant smiled, pleased at the compliment. "My wife's an art freak, drags me around to all the museums. I'm not wild about the modern stuff, but I saw the Manet at the Gardner once and when they showed it on TV, I remembered it. Why'd they burn it, I wonder. Didn't they know what it was?"

"Crooks aren't brain surgeons," Flynn said.

Maybe not, Frank thought, but Gregor Kraus was ruthless enough to kill to get what he wanted. Frank figured the corpse was the hinky security guard, Daniel Leone. Like the guards involved in the European heists, Leone was disposable. He didn't know why Gregor left the Manet to burn in the fire, but he was pretty sure Gregor now had the two Vermeers and the Rembrandt.

Frank studied the chalked outline of the body, then the chalked outline of the Manet. "You know," he said, "it's almost as if—"

The others turned to look, and he gestured at the chalked outlines. "The Manet was opposite the vic's head, as though the killer wanted him to look at it."

"Jesus," Bryant said. "A real psycho."

A psycho? Frank doubted it. This was a rage kill.

"Where's the Manet?" Georgette asked.

"Police headquarters," Bryant said. "The director of the Gardner Museum is headed there now, but she's not gonna like what she sees. Most of the canvas was burned, only thing showing was the woman's face. Follow me. I want to show you something."

Bryant picked his way through debris to a charred wooden staircase. "See the burn pattern? Someone used an accelerant. The top step appears to be the point of origin. In the kitchen we found remnants of a Kitty Litter bag and a metal gas container, the kind you'd use for a lawn mower. Kitty Litter burns like a sonofabitch if you douse it with a flammable liquid."

"Any chance the killer might have burned himself?" Frank asked.

Bryant scratched his jaw. "I dunno, but he would've had to be real careful. We haven't figured out how he got it started yet. Sometimes it's impossible, but we'll keep at it. The car in the garage was fully engulfed when the fire crew arrived. Providence PD had it towed to the state crime lab. Maybe they'll find something." Bryant said to Hank Flynn, "You think the dead guy stole the Manet?"

Frank glanced at former his boss, wondering what he'd say.

"Maybe," Flynn said. "But if he did, where are the others?"

———

Boston 5:15 PM

Seated in the Toyota, Natalie drank some bottled water, rolled the cool bottle over one cheek, then the other. The sun was a red-orange disc low in the sky, but it was still hot and humid, no hint of a breeze. When the Saab turned onto the street where her apartment was, she had stopped at the corner, watching to see what Gregor would do. He'd left the suitcase in the trunk, but before he went inside he had activated the Saab's security alarm.

Now she was parked around the corner on Tremont Street in the shade of a three-story tenement. She was certain the paintings were in the suitcase, but if she tried to get into the trunk, the alarm would sound and Gregor would be there in seconds, with a gun. To get the paintings she would have to catch him unawares, impossible in broad daylight in a busy neighborhood like this.

Belching smelly exhaust fumes, an MBTA bus stopped across the street and disgorged several passengers, workers headed home for dinner and two teen-aged boys with backpacks. They called out in Spanish to another teen on a skateboard and ran after him.

She took off the Red Sox cap, pulled off the blond wig and scratched her scalp. Wearing it in this heat was torture. To hell with the wig. She stowed it in the duffel and checked herself in the visor mirror. She still wasn't used to seeing herself with short spiky hair. No telling how long she'd have to wait for Gregor to make a move.

Time for a bathroom break. A small grocery store was right down the street. She took her iPhone and wallet out of the duffel, put on the Red Sox cap and left the Toyota. Eager to flex her cramped muscles, she stood beside the car and did two minutes of stretching exercises. The odor of grilling meat drifting from the tenement porch was making her hungry.

A steady stream of traffic passed her as she walked the two blocks to the store. Along the way she passed neighborhood residents chattering in Spanish as they headed home from work. The signs on the store window were also in Spanish. She stepped inside, nodded to the clerk behind the counter and spotted two coolers in the back of the store. A dark-haired teen-aged girl in white shorts and a pink halter top grinned at her as they squeezed past each other in the cramped aisle.

Natalie took a large bottle of water out of one cooler. Her stomach rumbled. All she'd eaten since her room service breakfast—a cheese omelet—was the peanut-butter power bar. Other than salsa, she wasn't that fond of Latino food, but the chicken tortilla in the adjacent cooler looked good. She put it in her basket and headed for the checkout counter. On the way she passed a shelf with fresh fruit. She added a red delicious apple to her basket and went to the register.

"Hot out today," she said, smiling at the clerk, a young Hispanic man with dark eyes.

The clerk nodded and rang up her purchases. She paid him and said, "Is there a restroom I could use?"

"Si," he said, pointing toward the rear of the store.

"Gracias," she said, which pretty much exhausted her Spanish vocabulary.

The restroom was a unisex one-seater, but clean. She used the toilet, washed her hands and face, thanked the clerk again and left the store.

Heat hit her like a blast furnace. Two blocks away, the spires of the Mission Church soared into the dusky sky. On the news this morning most of the stories were about the Gardner heist, nothing about the murdered man at the Mission Church. Had the cabbie who'd driven her there contacted the police? She hoped not. She had enough to worry about already.

She got in the Toyota, lowered the windows and stowed the bottled water and the apple on the passenger seat. Enjoying the spicy taste and the moist savory chicken, she devoured the chicken tortilla. Her hunger satisfied, she balled up the wrapper, put it in the plastic grocery bag and drank some water.

In five minutes, the six o'clock news would be on. Gregor was probably watching TV in her apartment, monitoring any updates about the Gardner heist. Would he sleep there again tonight?

She couldn't sleep here in the car. Maybe she should go back to the hotel. But not yet. She would wait until it got dark. She took a bite of her shiny red apple. Juicy and delicious, as promised.

———

Providence 5:55 PM

"Call the owner again," Georgette said, frowning as she gave the police chief a stern look.

"I just called her five minutes ago," DeNunzio said.

"Doesn't she have a cellphone?" Georgette asked.

With a look of disgust, DeNunzio walked away from Georgette and dug out his cellphone.

Twenty feet away, standing in the shade of the burned-out cottage, Frank murmured, "She's not endearing herself with the chief."

Beside him, Flynn said quietly, "No surprise there."

"You think the corpse is Daniel Leone?"

"Wouldn't surprise me," Flynn said, keeping his eyes trained on DeNunzio as he talked on his cellphone.

Five minutes later, DeNunzio shut his cellphone and approached them, ignoring Georgette, but she rushed over to join them anyway.

"I talked to the owner," he said. "Bertha Smolinski. She doesn't live here, but her brother does. Burt Smolinski." DeNunzio's lip curled. "He's a convicted sex offender, did time in New Jersey, got out ten years ago and came to Providence. God knows why."

"Any offenses here?" Flynn asked.

"One. He served two years. Way too little, but judges these days ..."

"Maybe he was involved in the Gardner heist," Georgette said.

Ignoring her, DeNunzio said to Flynn, "He's on probation so I called his control officer. Burt's supposed to check in once a week, but last week he didn't."

"Does he have a job?" Frank asked.

"According to the CO, he works for some outfit in Boston. Global Interpreting."

Frank wanted to kiss the guy. He glanced at Flynn, who wore his poker-faced look.

"Call them," Georgette said. "Maybe they know something."

Flynn nudged Frank and headed for his Ford Expedition, walking fast. When Frank got in the cruiser, Flynn was already dialing a number on his cellphone. "I'm calling Marty, get him started on that search warrant."

"Great. Mind if I call Rafe and get him in on the search?"

"Good idea. Tell him to meet Marty at the District-4 station. Hopefully, Marty will have the search warrant approved by the time we get there. We'll pick them up and go straight to Global Interpreting. Damn! We finally got a break."

Frank nodded, deadpan. "No sense sharing with Georgette."

Flynn looked over and smiled. "Exactly."

CHAPTER 37

7:20 PM

Marta outlined the triangle on her yellow legal pad in heavy black lines, then slammed the pen down on the desk. Damn Gregor to hell! He'd promised to meet her at seven. Now it was 7:20. He wasn't the one who had to deal with the cops. The black cop was bad enough, badgering her with questions. But Renzi was worse, threatening her, skewering her with his bloodsucking eyes, thrusting his chin with the jagged white scar at her. If the feds got into the files, it was all over.

"Merde!" she shouted, her voice bouncing off the oak-paneled walls.

She grabbed her bottle of Perrier and chugged half of it.

Ten minutes ago, she had called Gregor's cellphone. Knowing her voice was too shrill—Gregor hated that—but unable to control it, she said, "Aren't you coming? It's ten past seven!"

"Relax," he'd said. "I'm on my way." Which only infuriated her.

"The Gardner theft. It was you, wasn't it, Gregor."

But he had denied it, his voice an icy dagger in her ear.

She massaged her throbbing temples. Was he lying? With Gregor it was difficult to tell, especially when you couldn't see his eyes.

Dark eyes that could turn cold and ruthless in an instant.

A lone tear slid down her cheek. She had survived some painful ordeals in her thirty-nine years, but never had she felt as alone as she did now.

Gregor was no help. Gregor was the problem.

———

When Gregor entered the office, Marta was seated behind her desk, scowling at him. "Tell me about these cops," he said.

"The black cop is with Boston PD. I knew the other one was a cop the minute I laid eyes on him! This time he showed me his ID. Frank Renzi, New Orleans PD."

Gregor stood his briefcase on the floor beside the desk. "Why does he want to talk to me?"

"The first time he asked about Ursula. Today he said Stefan Haas died in London. He said you killed him and stole his ID."

Marta raked her fingers through her wavy blond hair, smoothed her slim black skirt, picked up a pen and doodled on the yellow legal pad.

He almost felt sorry for her. Her distress was obvious, hands fluttering from her hair to her skirt, then grabbing her pen. "Why so worried, Marta? It's not like you."

"Renzi said he'd have the IRS and INS investigate the business! Why won't you talk to him?"

He said nothing. Find out about the cops first, then make his move.

"Damn it, Gregor, answer me! What are you hiding? What happened to Ursula?"

"I don't know," he said quietly.

"You pulled the Gardner heist, didn't you." A statement, not a question.

"No, but I guess I'd better talk to this cop and see what he wants."

Her eyes searched his face and her rigid posture relaxed. "When?"

Maintaining his smile, he approached the desk. "Soon. I won't make you take all the heat."

Her eyes filled with tears. "Oh, Gregor ..."

She pushed back the chair and rose to her feet. He embraced her and stroked her hair, feeling her breath against his neck.

"Why can't things could be the way they were before?" she asked.

The way they were before? He studied her face, the deep lines around her mouth, the vapid blue eyes. *Because you bore me to death.*

He turned her around and brushed the back of her neck with his lips. Her body relaxed and she uttered a low moan. Gripping her head with both hands, he twisted it sharply and heard her neck snap.

She slumped to the floor. Marta would never know the answers to her questions. He hurried down the hall to his office, unlocked the door and went inside. He checked the bathroom to make sure he'd left nothing behind when he had packed his things and moved into Valerie's apartment. He opened the medicine cabinet. Empty. Nothing on the vanity, no incriminating towels.

With a satisfied grunt, he went to his desk, plopped into the high-backed executive chair and began opening drawers. He didn't expect to find anything. When he was living in the office, he had used the shredder to destroy any incriminating papers every night before he went to bed. He opened the bottom drawer and smiled. He'd forgotten his flask of cognac was there. He put it in his briefcase. No sense leaving it for the cops. He locked his office and returned to the reception area.

Marta lay on the floor beside the desk, eyes vacant and staring, her head tilted at an impossible angle. Poor Marta. She had been angry for a long time. Now her worries were over.

He glanced at the Franz Hals print mounted on the wall above the sofa. *Boy With Lute.* Marta's choice. Several years ago they had stolen a painting from the Franz Hals Museum in Haalem. Not this one. Pym had ordered a different one—*Laughing Boy—*

and probably got big bucks for it. But Pym would get no money from the Gardner heist. Every penny would go into the bank account of Gregor Kraus.

Grasping Marta's ankles, he dragged her into the hallway. Her linguistic skills had come in handy a few times, but she didn't have the proper temperament to steal art. Marta worried too much. She was fearful, unlike Valerie, who had nerves of steel. Where was Valerie now, he wondered. Unfortunately, he would have to leave Boston without saying goodbye to her.

He picked up his briefcase and shut off the lights. Cautiously, he opened the door and looked both ways. The hall was deserted. He shut the door, locked it, and left Global Interpreting for the last time.

———

Natalie extended her right leg into the passenger foot-well, flexed it five times and did the same with her left leg. Damn! She was tired of sitting in the car. At 7:15, convinced that Gregor would stay in her apartment all night, she had started the Toyota, intending to return to her hotel. But then her iPhone beeped. Gregor was on the move. A minute later the Saab had stopped at the corner behind her parking space, turned left and drove down the hill toward Huntington Avenue. After waiting a minute, she had done a U-turn and followed him.

Now she was parked in the alley opposite the exit from the Copley Place garage where he parked the Saab. She assumed he was in the Global Interpreting office, though she had no idea why. She sipped some water. During the ten-minute ride from Mission Hill, the AC had cooled the Toyota, but now it was stifling again. Even after the sun went down, the temperature remained in the eighties.

Unable to find a metered space on the street, she had backed the Toyota into the alley, a tight fit but she had no choice. If she had to leave the car, it might be a problem. She could only open the door a few inches. Enclosed in the alley, she could barely hear the distant sounds of traffic on the main street.

Willing the Saab to appear, she stared at the exit ramp ten yards to her left. What if Gregor stayed the night at Global Interpreting? She was certain he had the paintings. If he decided to leave town in a hurry, she had to be ready. It might be her only chance to recover the paintings. He didn't know she was tracking him, didn't know she had the Beretta. Now the tables were turned. She was the hunter, not Gregor.

A minute later the Saab barreled down the ramp, continued along the curved roadway to a stop sign and stopped. The Saab began to move forward but suddenly jerked to a halt.

She heard distant sirens, coming this way. The sirens grew louder and a large blue-and-white police vehicle, some kind of SUV, raced past the Saab with its lights flashing. Another car followed the SUV. That one had no police markings, but its siren was blaring and a blue light on the hood was flashing. Both cars were heading toward the entrance to Copley Place. The instant they passed the Saab, Gregor pulled forward, turned right and zoomed away.

———

Riding shotgun in Rafe's unmarked car, Frank saw Flynn's Ford Expedition screech to a halt outside the entrance to Copley Place. Rafe parked behind it and chortled, "Damn this is fun! I can't wait to see what Marta's got in those file cabinets."

Ten minutes ago when Hank Flynn had stopped at the District-4 station, Rafe and Marty Talbot stood beside Rafe's car, talking. Frank got out and rode with Rafe. Marty, with the signed search warrant in hand, had jumped into Flynn's Ford Expedition.

Curious passers-by exiting Copley Place gawked at Hank and Marty as they left the Expedition with its lights flashing and ran inside. Rafe opened the trunk of his car and took out a battering ram. "I'll carry the ram," Rafe said. "You take the slim-jim and the pry bar, we'll be set."

When they went inside, Hank and Marty were waiting for them at the elevator. Nodding his approval of their forced-entry tools, Flynn said, "You two lead the way. You've been there before."

The Global Interpreting office was closed up tight, no lights inside. Frank put the slim-jim and the pry bar on the floor and drew his SIG, thankful he'd brought it with him. Marty drew his Glock 9mm. Flynn pounded the door and yelled, "Police! Open up."

When there was no response, Flynn said to Rafe, "Open it."

Rafe jimmied the pry bar between door and the door-jam and gave a sharp yank. The door splintered.

Frank glanced at Marty, who said, "I got your back."

Frank kicked open the door, crouched and sprang inside, extending the SIG in front of him. Behind him, Marty and Rafe charged into the office. "Hit the lights!" Frank said.

The fluorescent ceiling lights flickered on. There was no one in the office, but it had a funky smell. Frank approached the desk and saw a body sprawled on the floor in the hall to the left of the desk.

"Whoa! That's Marta," Rafe exclaimed. He bent over her body, felt for a pulse under her jaw, straightened and said, "No pulse, but her skin is still warm."

Flynn shut the office door and the four of them clustered around Marta. Her blue eyes were open wide, opaque with death, and her neck was bent at an angle.

"Someone broke her neck," Frank said. "Gregor Kraus, probably. His office is down the hall, but the door is closed."

"You think he's in there?" Rafe asked.

"No," Frank said. "If he killed Marta, he's long gone."

"Let's open it up," Flynn said, striding down the hall.

Rafe used the battering ram. Two minutes later they entered the office. Nobody home. "Don't touch anything," Flynn said. "I'll call dispatch and get a crime scene team over here."

They returned to the reception area and Flynn got on his cellphone. "I need a homicide team at Global Interpreting, third floor of Copley Place. Send the CSI techs and alert the medical examiner." He listened for a moment, then said, "No, don't call the DA's office. This will be a hot one. I want to talk to the DA myself."

Flynn closed his cell and smiled tightly. "Georgette will be here soon. Let her argue with the DA."

"What now?" Frank said as he holstered his SIG.

Gesturing at the file cabinets lined up behind the desk, Flynn said, "What are you waiting for? Get going on those files." He took out a box of latex gloves and distributed them.

Marty took the cabinet labeled Clients and Employees. Frank took Utilities and Bank Statements. Grumbling about getting the leftovers, Rafe wound up with the cabinet labeled Miscellaneous. While they got to work, Hank got back on his cellphone, called the Suffolk County District Attorney and explained what was happening.

Frank sifted through the folders, found one for electric bills and set it aside. Another folder held bills for the telephone. Not what he wanted. He set it aside. Bank Statements was next.

"Yo!" Rafe exclaimed, waving a sheet of paper. "Dig this! It's a rental car contract for a Saab. Looks like Marta rented it. It's in her name."

"Is that the only one?" Frank asked.

"That's it."

"Give it to me," Flynn said. "I'll put out an APB on the Saab."

Frank returned to his designated file cabinet. A minute later he found what he was looking for. "Paydirt! I found cellphone contracts, two of them. One for Marta Ludwig, another for Stefan Haas."

"Who's Stefan Haas?" Marty asked. "I thought we were looking for Gregor Kraus."

"We are," Frank said. "But he murdered Stefan Haas in London and stole his identity."

"What wireless company did they use?" Flynn asked.

Frank checked the contract. "All-Tech. Can you get them to ping the Stefan Haas cellphone?"

"I can try." Flynn glanced at his watch. "You figure Gregor took off in the Saab?"

"Yes," Frank said. "Let's hope he's got his cellphone with him."

Flynn nodded. "And let's hope I can find out where he is before Georgette gets here."

CHAPTER 38

Maintaining a steady 55-mph, Natalie settled into the middle lane of the Massachusetts Turnpike. The Saab was in the high-speed lane several car lengths ahead of her. After the police cars passed the Saab, Gregor had taken off, weaving in and out through the heavy traffic at high speed, but she managed to stay with him. When he took the entrance for the Mass Pike on Huntington Avenue, she had followed.

At seven o'clock, she had caught a news bulletin on the car radio. This afternoon Providence police had found the stolen Manet, badly damaged in a fire. That was a shock. Why would Gregor leave the Manet in the cottage and torch the place?

If Gregor wanted to leave town fast, the Mass Turnpike, a toll road, was the best way to do it. But why the hurry? Was he afraid the cops were after him? Why would they go to the Global Interpreting office at this hour? Maybe Gregor knew something that she didn't.

Rush hour was over, but there was still a fair amount of traffic. If Gregor was worried about cops, he'd be checking his mirrors to see if they were chasing him. Her black Toyota was innocuous enough, but if he noticed it, he might get suspicious. And if a cop stopped him, he'd be in trouble. She was certain the other stolen paintings were in the Saab, equally sure Gregor was carrying a gun.

Now they were coming to a tollbooth. She slowed down, waiting to see what Gregor would do. He bypassed the Alston-Brighton exit on the right and continued to the Mass Pike-West tollbooths. Most of them were for cars with E-ZPass but two cash-only booths were open.

When the Saab got in a cash-only lane, she joined the line for the other one, pulled out her wallet and took out some bills.

When she reached the booth, she gave the man a five-dollar bill and waited for her change. One lane over, the Saab pulled forward and drove off in the high-speed lane. The toll taker dropped change into her palm and the barrier swung up.

She accelerated, passed several cars and spotted the Saab in the high-speed lane. Staying well behind it, she settled into the middle lane and pulled down the visor. Driving west into the glare of the setting sun hurt her eyes, but soon it would be dark. Where was Gregor going? She glanced at her gas gauge. Less than half a tank. If he was driving to New York, she was in trouble.

Ten minutes later she passed a sign for the Route 128-Route 95 exit. Ahead of her, the Saab slowed, merged into the middle lane, then the exit lane. Another tollbooth loomed. She took out her wallet. After paying the toll, Gregor would have to make a choice. Would he go north or south? She joined a different cash-only line, watching to see what Gregor did after he paid the toll. As she reached the booth, she saw the Saab veer onto the Route-128-South fork. She paid the toll and let two cars precede her before she entered the southbound ramp. A minute later she merged into the traffic on Route-128-South.

Was Gregor going to Providence? Why would he do that?

———

A shelf with a coffee maker and a fax-printer-copier occupied the right-hand wall of the Global Interpreting office. Frank and Rafe were leaning against the machine in the front corner, watching the turf war.

Right after Hank put out the APB on the Saab, Georgette had stormed into the office with two FBI agents. She lit into Hank, asking how he got here so fast and why didn't he wait until she got here before he broke into the office? Ignoring the question, Flynn said, "I posted three uniforms in the hall to keep out any unauthorized visitors." Then the District Attorney arrived and Georgette had pounced on him, loudly asserting her status as lead investigator.

Now Georgette and the DA were huddled in the corner opposite Frank. Hard to tell who was winning. Both of them looked angry, Georgette still yammering but quieter, the DA responding with emphatic hand gestures. Meanwhile, the fetid odor of death hovered in the air, Marta's bodily wastes. The medical examiner hadn't arrived but was on his way. The CSI techs were busy, taking photos, drawing diagrams, dusting for prints, vacuuming the carpeting, the usual bedlam at a homicide scene.

Rafe leaned closer and muttered, "Wish Hank would hurry up and get the cellphone location."

"Me, too," Frank said. "Every minute we lose is to Gregor's advantage. We almost got him."

"Body was still warm," Rafe said. "Only missed him by five or ten minutes."

Marty Talbot and Hank Flynn came through the doorway of the hall that led to Gregor's office. Flynn looked around, his blue eyes flinty. "There's too many people in here. Renzi and Hawkins, wait outside in your vehicle." He gave Frank a hard look. "Stay off your cell so I can call if I need you."

Frank suppressed a smile and nodded. "Will do."

After he and Rafe got in the elevator, Rafe said, "Hank's been looking old and tired these days, but now that we got a lead, seems like he's got his mojo back. I loved how he finessed Georgette, dumping her onto the DA. Hoo-ee, let the slug-fest begin."

Frank was tempted to tell him about the cancer diagnosis but decided against it. If Hank didn't want people to know, he would respect his wishes. Like Rafe, he was happy to see his former boss energized and excited. "He wants this one bad. So do I, for a lot of reasons, but it would be great to see Hank go out on top. If he solves the case, he should get the credit."

The elevator door opened and they hustled out to Rafe's car. Almost sunset but the heat and humidity were stifling, not a breath of air stirring. They climbed into Rafe's car and Frank took out his cellphone.

"You see that look Hank gave us? I think he's got something going with the cellphone company."

"That'd be my guess." Rafe opened a six-pack of bottled water, handed one to Frank, uncapped the other and chugged half of it. When Frank's cell-phone rang, Rafe smiled. "Bingo."

Frank answered, "We're here, set to go, what's doing?"

Speaking softly, Flynn said, "I had Marty guard the door of Gregor's office while I made some calls. All-Tech Wireless gave me a bunch of shit about privacy rights, said they needed a warrant to ping his cellphone. So I called in the chips with one of my contacts. The guy lives in Needham, near the All-Tech office. He's there now, should have the location soon so be ready. Soon as I get the location, you go."

Frank closed his cell and relayed the news to Rafe. Incredulous, Rafe said, "We got a dead body, we're after a killer, and these schnooks are talking privacy rights? Kill somebody, your privacy rights are history. Good thing Flynn's got a connection."

"Yes, but Gregor's got a head start, and it'll be dark soon."

"Too bad about Marta. Seems like she was just a pawn in the game."

"Don't feel too bad. If she'd told us where Gregor was, we might have nabbed him before he burned the Manet. Not to mention the guy who got burnt to a crisp. And don't forget Natalie. I figure Gregor's got the paintings. I don't know if Natalie was there when he killed Marta, but if she wasn't, he'll probably pick her up before he splits."

His cellphone rang. He answered and heard Flynn say in a soft voice, "Got it. The cellphone is currently located at 50 University Avenue in Westwood. Otherwise known as the Route-128 train station."

"Jesus! The Route-128 train station," he said. Rafe immediately slammed the car in gear and peeled out.

"We're on our way, Hank. Any changes, let us know."

"Will do," Flynn said. "I'm sending three Boston PD cars to assist. Might get the Westwood and Dedham cops on it, too, but not until you're closer to the target. You two take charge."

"We will, but do me a favor. Find out if any trains stop there tonight."

"Damn," Flynn said. "I didn't think of that. Hold on, I'll have Marty check."

"Fuck speed limits," Rafe said as he slewed around a corner.

"Go for it," Frank said, and heard Flynn say, "Only one Amtrak train stops at the Route-128 station tonight, rolls in at 9:50 PM, destination Penn Station in New York City."

———

Gregor backed into a space on the third level of the Route-128 parking garage, shut off the motor and leaned back against the headrest. Finally, he could relax. He hadn't seen any cops following him, but the police cruisers outside Copley Place had unnerved him. Still, they could have been going there for some other reason.

If they went to the office they would find Marta, but so what? Marta wouldn't be telling them anything, and they would find nothing incriminating there. Well, his fingerprints perhaps, but by the time they identified them he would be on his way to Europe.

This afternoon at Valerie's apartment he had watched the six o'clock news. The top story: Providence police had found the Manet that had been stolen from the Gardner Museum. To his utter disgust, a photograph of the Manet, in pristine condition, appeared on the screen. The reporter said the Manet had been badly damaged in a fire. The fire marshal had found it in the basement of a burned-out cottage and recognized it, having seen news reports about the Gardner heist. Cursing his mistake, Gregor had screamed obscenities at the television set. He should never have left the Manet there. But when the reporter described the charred body that had been found at fire scene, he had smiled in satisfaction.

Kwan, the traitor, had died a horrible death. Even now this gave him great satisfaction.

Gregor arched his back and flexed his shoulders. Eventually the cops would discover Kwan's true identity, an Asian hood on the lam, hiding from the San Francisco cops. No big deal if the Manet had burned in the fire, but it hadn't. The Manet would connect Kwan to the Gardner heist and his body was in Burt's cellar. This was worrisome.

Had Burt seen the news reports on TV, he wondered. Doubtful. Burt was too busy fucking little boys. Yesterday he had called Burt and told him to meet him at JFK airport in New York tomorrow, his vacation was over. Burt wasn't happy about it, but screw Burt. Gregor had sent him the airline ticket, overnight Express. Eventually the cops would connect Burt to Global Interpreting, but tomorrow Burt was going to take a nosedive off the top level of a parking garage at JFK.

He stifled a yawn and surveyed the cavernous garage. Less than a dozen cars were parked on the third level, most of them a good distance away. He had parked the Saab three spaces away from the door to the staircase. He took out a pack of Gitanes, opened his briefcase and removed the flask of cognac. He didn't have to drive anywhere. Why not enjoy a cigarette and the cognac?

In an hour he'd be on a train to New York. The Business Class ticket had cost more than a hundred dollars but it had a reclining seat with a padded headrest. He'd sleep for four hours on the train, arrive at Penn Station at 2:15 A.M., pack the paintings in a container and ship them to Cologne. Eventually, the cops would find the Saab here in the garage, but by then he would be long gone.

He unscrewed the flask and took a healthy swallow of cognac. Never again would he take orders from Jonathan Pym. Or anyone else, for that matter.

Now he was in control.

He rolled down the window, lighted a Gitanes and smiled.

Two days from now he would be in Cologne to collect his million-dollar paintings.

CHAPTER 39

Natalie flattened her back against the door of the Level-3 stairway, her eyes fixed on the Saab. At last, after her interminable hours of surveillance, her opportunity to take the paintings away from Gregor had arrived. She felt jubilant, but also, she had to admit, fearful, her hands sweaty on the Beretta.

Five yards to her right, a fire-engine-red Jeep stood in the space closest to the door. Beyond it was a black SUV, then an empty space. Gregor's olive-green Saab was in the next slot, nose out, facing the car lane. If Gregor looked this way he would see her.

The Saab's window was open. Gregor was smoking one of his European cigarettes. She could smell it.

She had parked her Toyota on Level-2 near the stairs, nose out for a fast getaway. The spaces beside it were vacant. She waited a while to make sure no one was around, planning her moves. She had to take Gregor by surprise. Her short-sleeved maroon T-shirt was dark, but her white shorts were too conspicuous. She removed them and put on her black running pants. After chambering a round in the Beretta, she hid her duffel in the passenger foot-well, locked the Toyota and had crept up the stairs to the Level-3 door. But when she looked through the wire-mesh glass in the door, she couldn't see the Saab. Willing the door not to squeak, she had eased it open and slipped into the garage.

The shadowy garage was silent and still. The slightest motion might attract Gregor's attention. Ever so slowly, she lowered herself to a squatting position. Now she was hidden by the Jeep. Gregor couldn't see her, but if she made the slightest sound he might hear her. Holding the gun in her right hand, she braced her left hand on the cement floor, eased onto her knees and inched toward the Jeep.

Her heart was beating so hard she feared Gregor would hear it.

When her head bumped the door of the Jeep, she stopped. Let out the breath she'd been holding. Inhaled the odor of Gregor's cigarette. Gripped the Beretta in both hands. Keeping her head below the windows of the Jeep, she eased back into a squatting position. Slowly breathed in and out, to calm herself.

Another cloud of smoke spewed from the window. Then a cigarette butt, showering sparks as it bounced and rolled into the car lane.

Now or never. She sprang to her feet and sprinted to the Saab. "Put your hands on the wheel, Gregor. Up top where I can see them."

His mouth sagged open. "Valerie! What are you doing here?"

She aimed the Beretta at his head. "Hands on the wheel, up top, both of them. Do it! Now!"

A muscle jumped in his jaw. Slowly, he put both hands on the wheel at twelve o'clock and looked at her, frowning now. "What happened to you hair? Why did you cut it?"

"Never mind. Where are the paintings? In the trunk?"

Gregor gazed at her, his expression earnest, not pleading but almost. "Things did not go exactly as I planned, Valerie, but we can still be partners. The old man will soon be dead."

"Why did you burn the Manet?"

"So. You heard about the fire?"

"I didn't hear about it. I was there. I saw you run out of the house and a minute later the place was an inferno. Was that Nicolas in the basement?"

Clearly shocked, Gregor stared at her. "You saw me? How did you know I was there?"

"Never mind. Why did you burn the Manet?"

"Nicholas ruined it. There was a big tear in the canvas, impossible to repair. But the other three will bring a large sum of money, millions of dollars. I would be happy to share it with you, Valerie. After Pym dies, we wait a while, sell the paintings on the black market and split the money, fifty-fifty."

He looked at her expectantly. When she didn't respond, he said, "There is no reason why you and I cannot steal more paintings. There are plenty to be had. We make a good team."

A good team? The words sickened her. How could he think such a thing?

"No we don't. You kill anyone who gets in your way. You told Nicholas to kill me, but I got away."

Gregor smiled faintly. "This does not surprise me. You are very fit, Valerie. I took note of this at the hotel fitness center when you worked out on the machines."

"You got Nicholas to help you double-cross Pym and then you killed him."

Gregor said nothing, his dark eyes boring into her.

Her stomach plummeted in a free-fall of fear. Even though she was holding a gun on him, he still terrified her. She stepped back so he couldn't grab her and flicked the Beretta, a threatening motion.

"Give me the car keys, Gregor. Use your left hand. Slowly."

"Trust me, Valerie, the paintings are in the trunk."

"Trust you? You wanted me dead! Keep your right hand on the wheel. Give me the keys. Slowly, with your left hand. Don't make me shoot you. One wrong move and I will."

He clenched his jaw, his lips set in a grim line. With his left hand, he took the keys out of the ignition, extended his hand through the window and put them in her left hand.

She tucked them into the sleeve of her T-shirt. "Out of the car. When I step back, open the door. Slowly. Keep your hands where I can see them."

Gripping the Beretta in both hands, she aimed it at his head and stepped away from the Saab. He slowly opened the door, swung one leg out, then the other. "Stand up. Slowly. Hands over your head."

He eased forward, cleared the doorframe and stood there with his hands raised. She tried not to look at horrible scars on the palms of his hands. She motioned with the Beretta. "Stand over there in the vacant space. Keep your hands up where I can see them."

Moving slowly, he took three paces and stopped in the vacant space. With one foot, she kicked the door of the Saab shut. "Put your back against the black SUV. One wrong move and I will shoot."

He backed up to the black SUV and stood with his feet spread apart, watching her, his eyes wary. She studied his posture. He had on a short-sleeved royal-blue polo shirt and gray slacks. No gun visible, but he might have a small one tucked away somewhere.

"Put your feet together."

His eyes grew cold. "Valerie, stop giving me orders."

She aimed the Beretta at his center of mass, as she had been taught, midway between his bellybutton and his heart. "Shut up and do it, Gregor. Feet together."

Glaring at her, he put his feet together. "There. Happy now?"

She didn't answer. Training the Beretta on him with her right hand, she retrieved the car keys, opened the trunk and saw the gray-fabric suitcase. Just as she'd thought. The paintings were in the suitcase. Although this filled her with joy, she did not miss the sudden motion, Gregor bending down, reaching for his ankle, pulling out a gun …

She shot him in the kneecap.

"Arrrgh!" he screamed. He dropped the gun and the snub-nosed semi-automatic clattered to the cement. Gregor bent over, clutching his right knee with both hands, grimacing in pain. "Damn you! See what you've done to me." Blood was seeping through his gray slacks, leaking through his fingers.

She kicked the short-barreled gun away from him. "Back away from the SUV and sit on the ground."

Favoring his right leg, he hobbled away from the SUV, his face screwed up in pain. "Help me," he said. "I cannot bend my knee."

"No. I don't trust you. Sit on the ground."

Giving her a malevolent look, he bent his left knee, braced his hands on the cement and lowered himself to the garage floor. His chest heaved and beads of sweat dotted his forehead and upper lip. Gritting his teeth, he clutched his right knee with both hands.

Convinced he was no longer a threat, she sidestepped to the trunk of the Saab and opened the suitcase. Her heart soared. The Lacemaker!

She glanced at Gregor. He was watching her, teeth clenched, eyes full of fury. "They are all there," he said. "Two Vermeers and the Rembrandt, which Nicholas also damaged, a rip in the lower right corner. But this is not significant. You will get plenty of money for it."

She checked to make sure the other two paintings were there and slammed the trunk shut. And heard distant sirens.

Gregor heard them too. "Police," he said in a quiet voice.

Natalie whirled and ran toward the sound. It was coming from the opposite side of the garage, the side facing the highway. Ten seconds later she stopped at a low cement wall below a wide opening supported by thick cement pillars. It was pitch dark now, but from here she had a panoramic view of Route 128.

On the southbound side to her left, four lanes of vehicles with bright headlights were passing the train station. But off to her right on the northbound side, vehicles were swerving into the breakdown lane to let a speeding police car with flashing blue lights pass them.

A visceral jolt stabbed her gut. But why would they be coming here? Maybe there was an accident on the highway. And maybe there wasn't. If they came here, she was in trouble. She turned and ran back toward Gregor and the Saab, weaving through rows of parked cars.

Blam. A slug ripped into the cement pillar beside her, showering her with bits of cement. Her heart slammed her chest. Despite the shattered kneecap Gregor had retrieved his gun. Or maybe he had another one.

She ducked behind a car, twenty yards away from him. Holding the Beretta in both hands, she rose to a crouch, sighted over the car hood and fired at Gregor. And missed.

Braced awkwardly in a seated position, Gregor was shooting at her one-handed, using his uninjured knee as a gun rest. He shot at her again, but now she was moving, running at him as fast as she could. She stopped one row away, took careful aim and shot him in the left knee.

"Bitch!" he screamed. He dropped the snub-nosed semi-automatic and grabbed his left knee, screaming obscenities at her.

"I told you not to move!" She ran to him and kicked the gun away from him. It spun away and skittered across the car lane and stopped when it hit a low cement wall.

The sirens were closer now, more than one siren, she realized.

"Valerie," he said in a low voice. "We could have been partners. I have always admired you. Your courage, your nerves of steel."

She didn't believe a word of it. "You had an odd way of showing it."

He gazed at her with a haunted look in his eyes. "It is true, Valerie. All true. But now the police are here." He raised a hand in entreaty. "Do me one last favor. Finish the job."

"No. I'll let the cops take you. You and the paintings."

She sprinted to the stairs, raced down one level to the Toyota, unlocked it and jumped inside. But she would never escape in a car. The cops would stop her. With trembling hands, she shoved the Beretta into the duffel and took out her iPhone and the two passports.

Hope for the best, plan for the worst.

The sirens were very close now, turning into the roadway that led to the garage. If she was lucky and ran like the wind, she might be able to escape on foot.

———

Waves of pain washed over him, excruciating pain, worse than he'd ever felt in his life, worse than when Papa held his hands over the gas flame. Damn Valerie to hell!

But why didn't she take the paintings? She could have sold them or collected money from the insurance companies. Millions of dollars.

Drenched in sweat, he stared at his bloody fingers. If only the pain would stop. He knew it would not, but he knew how to manage it. He shut his eyes and concentrated, just as he'd done as a child. Put the pain away in a small box in the back of your mind.

Sweat rolled down his nose. He opened his eyes and brushed it away with his sleeve. The cops were here. He could hear the whoop of sirens outside the garage.

Just as he knew how to deal with pain, he knew no one would help him escape. When he was a boy of twelve, someone had shot Papa. He had been on his own ever since. Over the years, no one had helped him. So he had done what was necessary to take control.

Tonight was no different.

He gritted his teeth, lay back on the cement and rolled over.

Agonizing pain stabbed his knees. It took his breath away. Panting, he lay still and wiped his face on the sleeve of his polo shirt. He looked at the gun. Twenty-five feet away. An impossible distance, but he would not allow that to defeat him. Using his elbows, he dragged himself toward the gun, every inch an excruciating milestone, willing himself forward like a climber approaching the peak of Mount Everest.

If Kwan had not double-crossed him, he would be celebrating his victory tonight in New York. But in the end he had made the bastard pay for his treachery.

Ignoring the terrible pain, he inched forward, eyes fixed on the gun.

Valerie had betrayed him, too. He had as much as told her to kill him. But she hadn't. Because of her stupid code. Nerves of steel, but she didn't want to kill anyone. What good was that?

She didn't understand the power of life and death. And the control it conveyed.

Panting, he stopped to rest. If the police captured him, he would spend the rest of his life in prison.

He couldn't face that. Not again. Fighting off right-wing Aryans and black supremacists. And now he was a cripple. He would never walk normally again.

With grim determination, he fixed his eyes on the gun.

Now it was only fifteen feet away.

CHAPTER 40

9:30 PM

Frank stood beside Rafe's unmarked car in the pickup/drop-off garage adjacent to the train station. Holding his SIG in both hands, he surveyed the area, alert for any telltale sound or activity. Bigger than a football field, the shadowy cement structure was eerily silent and hot, not a breath of air stirring. He mopped his brow with his sleeve. Even the stubble on his chin was damp with sweat.

Somewhere inside the massive four-story parking garage adjacent to the drop-off zone was a rented Saab. He presumed Gregor and Natalie were in the Saab with the stolen paintings. An Amtrak train was due to arrive in twenty minutes. The clock was ticking. He wanted to search the parking garage and find the Saab, but Rafe was inside the station, making sure the civilians were safe.

Rafe burst through the glass double-doors of the station and ran up to him, his Glock in his hand. "The station is secure," he said, adding with a faint smile, "Nothing stirring, not even a mouse."

Black humor to ease the tension. "Where are the passengers?"

"Two of Hank's District-4 detectives put the station workers and the people in the waiting area into a conference room," Rafe said. "They'll stay with them. You ready to hit the parking garage?"

"Yes, but I better call Hank first and see what's happening at Global Interpreting."

"Go for it," Rafe said. "I'll keep an eye on things."

Frank hit his speed dial. Flynn answered right away.

"My contact says Gregor's cellphone is still there," Flynn said. "No response on the APB. What's your situation?"

"Six cruisers—three from Westwood PD, three from Dedham PD—are blocking the entrances and exits to the station, nobody goes in or out. The station is secure. Two of your detectives are guarding the civilians. Rafe and I are in the drop-off garage near the station entrance. Some taxis were here but we made them leave. Pissed off the drivers, but we told them they wouldn't get any more fares tonight."

"Good work. I convinced the Amtrak officials to contact the engineers on the 9:50 train and tell them not to stop there." Flynn chuckled mirthlessly. "It wasn't hard. I said there might be gunfire, wouldn't want any of their passengers to get hurt."

Frank gave Rafe a thumbs-up and said to Flynn, "I'm assuming Natalie and Gregor are in the Saab. We came in with sirens, so they know we're here."

"They're probably armed. Plenty of cover in a garage if they want to ambush you. Ask Rafe if he's got any vests in his car."

"Rafe," Frank called, "you got any vests in the car?"

"Got two or three," Rafe said.

"He does," Frank told Flynn. "What's doing with the federales?"

"I took the DA aside and explained the situation. He's fine with Boston PD doing the takedown. He's got enough problems dealing with Georgette. She knows Burt Smolinski was working for Global Interpreting, and she wants to take control of the crime scene, probably figures she'll find something here that will help her solve the Gardner heist. But she's got no clue about Gregor."

"Good. Rafe and I are set to go after him." And Natalie.

"Okay, but use the vests. Keep me informed."

Frank punched off and told Rafe, "Flynn says go, but he wants us to use the vests."

"No problem." Rafe opened the trunk of his car, held out a Kevlar vest and said with a sardonic smile, "Big one for the big fella, medium one for the point guard."

Frank holstered his SIG and took the vest. Facing the station entrance, he held the vest against his chest and adjusted the Velcro straps on each shoulder. About to adjust the straps on the side of the vest, he saw the door to the stairway beside the station entrance open.

The hairs on the back of his neck prickled. No one should be roaming around the station. All the civilians were in the conference room. But Gregor and Natalie weren't.

He dropped the vest and drew his SIG.

Fifteen yards away, a slender figure edged through the door, saw them and took off running. "Stay here," he said to Rafe. "It's Natalie."

She disappeared around the corner of the station. Frank sprinted to the corner and caught a glimpse of her as she darted onto a gravel path that ran alongside the train tracks. Pumped with adrenaline, he ran to the path, zigged left and saw her, thirty yards ahead of him.

To his right, a tall wire-mesh fence kept people away from the tracks. To his left, Halogen security floodlights on the upper levels of the garage gave off an eerie yellow glow, illuminating the path. Thick shrubs lined the wall of the parking garage. But Natalie wasn't looking to hide.

Fifty yards away at the end of the gravel path, a narrow tunnel ran underneath the highway. Above it, headlights flashed as cars zoomed along on Route 128. He had to stop her before she got through the tunnel.

He assumed she was armed. If she reached the other side of the highway, she might take a hostage in a nearby house or hijack a car.

"Stop or I'll shoot!" Not to kill, maybe, but he intended to stop her. Whatever it took.

She kept running, arms pumping, loping along, the same long-legged stride he'd seen in New Orleans. He saw no weapon in her hands, but that didn't mean she didn't have one. Breathing hard, thighs burning, he lengthened his stride. Now she was fifteen yards away. He was closing on her. She was ten years younger than he was, but his legs were longer and he was motivated. This time she wasn't going to escape.

Summoning every ounce of energy, he put on a burst of speed.

She glanced over her shoulder, still running but slower, looked like she was running out of gas.

"Stop," he shouted. "You're surrounded."

She slowed to jog, then stopped and turned to face him, panting for breath, her chest heaving. Beads of sweat dotted her forehead. She gazed at him, her almond-shaped eyes luminous in the moonlight. She had on a maroon T-shirt and black running pants. No sign of a weapon, but he wasn't taking any chances.

"On your knees, hands on your head!"

"I'm not armed," she said. "I have no weapon."

"Don't tell me what you've got. "Both hands on your head." Watching her eyes. If she intended to bolt, he'd see it there.

She raised her hands and put them on her head.

"Get on your knees. I'm going to frisk you."

Her lips quirked in annoyance, but she sank to her knees, a graceful fluid motion. She was in good shape, Frank observed, probably worked out regularly. Holding the SIG in his right hand, he stepped behind her and patted her down, shoulders to waist first, then her arms. No weapon, but a flesh-colored bandage, two inches by three inches, was taped to her right forearm.

"Okay, stand up and keep your feet apart."

In another effortless motion, she rose and stood still with her feet apart. He ran his left hand over her hips, then her legs, inside and out. No weapon. He took her arm and turned her to face him.

"Where are the paintings?"

"In the trunk of Gregor's car."

The ready admission surprised him. "The Saab?"

Her eyes widened slightly. "Yes. It's in the parking garage on Level-3, near the stairs."

He studied her face and realized why she looked different. "You cut your hair."

Her lips parted in a faint smile. "Yes. You like it?"

He almost laughed. After hunting this woman for two years, he had finally caught her, and she wanted to know if he liked her new hairstyle.

"You stole the paintings."

Her smile disappeared. "I stole the Vermeers. Not the others."

"Who stole the others, Gregor Kraus?"

"No, one of the guards. But he double-crossed Gregor and kept them."

And paid with his life, Frank thought, recalling the charred outline in the basement of the cottage in Providence. "Where's Gregor?"

She drew a deep breath and let it out slowly, staring off in the distance. At last she locked eyes with him and said, "I was going to return the paintings. But Gregor didn't want me to. He shot at me."

"Where is he?"

"In the garage near the Saab. Can I put my arms down? I'm not armed and—"

"No." He motioned toward the station. "Move. I'm right behind you. We'll talk later."

When they entered the drop-off garage, he marched her to Rafe's car. Rafe was waiting. "She says the Saab is on the third level," Frank said. "The paintings are in the trunk."

Before Rafe could say anything, Natalie said in a soft voice, "Detective Renzi, can I give you something?"

Startled that she had addressed him by name, he said, "What?"

"The keys to the Saab. You'll need them to open the trunk."

"Show me."

She lowered her arms, held out her right hand and opened her fist. A set of car keys lay on her palm.

He took them and glanced at Rafe, who looked at him, bemused.

"When I heard the sirens," Natalie said, "I knew you would be here soon. I didn't want Gregor to get away so I shot him in the knee."

"Ouch," Rafe said.

"I had already made him show me the paintings in the trunk."

"Where's the gun?" Frank said. "The one you used to kneecap him?"

Avoiding his eyes, she muttered, "I got rid of it."

A problematic answer, but he would question her about that later.

"Cuff her and put her in your car, Rafe. I'll get some D-4 detectives to guard her. Then we can go to the parking garage and get Gregor."

"Be careful," Natalie said. "He has a gun."

————

Stressed-out and angry, she slumped against the seat. Her worst fear had come true. Frank Renzi had captured her. His partner had handcuffed her and put her in the back seat of an unmarked police car. Now two policemen stood beside it with their guns drawn, to make sure she didn't escape. As if that were possible. A wire-mesh partition separated the back seat from the front, all the windows were shut, and there were no door handles. Not a breath of air and not a drop to drink.

She was hot and sweaty and her throat was so dry she could barely swallow. She shifted in her seat, trying to get comfortable. Her shoulders ached and her wrists hurt from the handcuffs that bound them together behind her back. She didn't want to think about what would happen next. Renzi had patted her down, but he hadn't found the iPhone or the passports hidden in the crotch of her underpants.

Passports she would never get to use. Tears misted her eyes. She might never talk to Pak Lam again. Her adopted father, a man she had grown to love. Rather than flee Boston as every instinct urged her to do, she had tried to do the honorable thing and return the paintings. When she tried to explain this to Renzi, she could tell he didn't believe it, gazing at her, expressionless, a skeptical look in his dark penetrating eyes. And how could she blame him?

She should not have stolen the paintings. This was her punishment.

We'll talk later. Soon Renzi would come back and interrogate her. A terrifying thought. Then she remembered something and smiled. In high school she had joined the drama club. She loved acting, pretending to be someone else and playing the role. It was easy. She had done this most of her life. Before a big performance, her drama couch always gave the actors a pep talk. "Don't be scared. Walk out on that stage and act confident. Act like you're having fun."

Fun. While Renzi interrogated her? She couldn't imagine it.

———

Guns drawn, they crept up the cement stairs, Frank on the right, Rafe on the left, their eyes sweeping the cement stairwell above them. They reached the first landing and started up the next set of stairs.

Frank pointed at the door to the third-level garage and whispered, "There's a window. Might be able to spot him."

Rafe nodded, his eyes fixed on the door as they reached the top of the stairs.

Suddenly, there was a gunshot. Instinctively, they flinched and ducked their heads. Rafe crept to the door and peered through the window. Moments later, he waved to Frank and said, "There's a body lying in a pool of blood."

When they entered the garage, a twenty-foot trail of blood near an olive-green Saab drew them to a body near a low cement wall beside the car lane. Gregor Kraus lay in a pool of blood from the gunshot wound in his head. Beside his head, a snub-nosed Smith & Wesson lay on the cement.

"He ate his gun," Frank said. "Put it in his mouth and pulled the trigger." They would get no answers from Gregor.

"Check out his bloody knees," Rafe said. "Must have hurt like a sonofabitch."

Frank turned to the Saab parked nose out opposite Gregor's body. He took out the car keys, went to the Saab and opened the trunk. Inside, a gray-fabric suitcase lay open on the floor of the trunk. On top of a green hand towel was The Lacemaker. Frank checked under the towel. To his relief, the other two paintings were there.

"We got them!" Rafe exclaimed, his dark-skinned face wreathed in a smile.

"Yes, we did." But he wasn't ready to celebrate yet.

He took out his cellphone. "I'll give Hank the good news. Then I'm going down and talk to Natalie."

CHAPTER 41

When Frank told the two District-4 detectives guarding Natalie that Gregor was dead and the stolen art was in the Saab, Hank's detectives were jubilant. They wanted Hank to get the credit, too. Frank sent them upstairs to guard the Saab. As soon as they left, he said to Rafe, "I want to talk to Natalie. Alone."

"I got no problem with it," Rafe said, expressionless. "But other people might."

"Two years I've been waiting to question her."

"Better make it quick," Rafe said. "The federales'll be here soon."

Frank's heart thrummed in his chest. At last, the moment he'd been waiting for, the confrontation he'd fantasized about for two years, a face-to-face meeting with Natalie Brixton.

He opened the back door, got in the car and shut the door.

Natalie gazed at him, her eyes wide and unblinking. Some said the eyes were a window to a person's soul, but Natalie's eyes revealed nothing. For someone about to be charged with felony art theft and murder, she appeared calm and collected. If she was scared, she was hiding it well.

"That day in the alley," he said. "You could have killed me but you didn't. Why?"

"I didn't want to kill you. I never wanted to kill anyone."

"You killed Tex Conroy and Arnold Peterson and Chip Beaubien."

"I didn't want to shoot Tex, but I had to. I was afraid he'd tell someone I was in New Orleans before I could find Chip."

"And kill him."

"He deserved it. Did you listen to the tape I sent you?"

"Yes. But Chip Beaubien didn't kill your mother."

"But he used women, just like his father. He took me to that cheap motel and tried to rape me. Even after I played the Peterson tape for him, he wouldn't admit his father murdered her." A muscle worked in her jaw. "He called my mother a cheap whore. What did he know? She needed the money. Bobo paid her for sex and when she wouldn't do what he wanted, he put his hands around her neck and strangled her."

"What about Oliver James? You killed him, too."

Natalie stared into space, a vein pulsing in her throat. Then she looked at him and said, "How did you get that scar on your chin?"

"I got another one on my leg where you shot me. Want to see it?"

"I'm sorry. I'm sorry I stole the paintings, too. What did Gregor say?"

"Gregor's dead. He shot himself."

Natalie's lips parted in a silent gasp. At last she said, "Gregor was an evil man. He planned the heists, but Jonathan Pym paid him to do it."

Finally, he was getting some answers. "Pym masterminded those art heists in Europe?"

"Yes. How did you hear about them?"

"Never mind. How did you get mixed up with them?"

"Jonathan Pym recruited me. I met him when I was working for an escort service in London. I thought he was stealing the paintings for wealthy collectors, but he wasn't."

"How do you know?"

She flexed her shoulders, trying to get comfortable, he assumed. Or maybe she was buying time to get her story straight.

"It's complicated," she said. "Pym wanted me to steal two Vermeers from the Special Exhibit at the Gardner, but Gregor was in charge." Her lips tightened. "Gregor was always in charge. He hired Nicholas, the insider guard. I didn't know it, but Gregor told him to steal two more paintings and kill me after I stole the Vermeers. Gregor was going to keep the paintings and sell them after Pym died."

"But Nicholas kept the paintings. So Gregor killed him."

"Yes. Everyone was lying. Pym, Gregor and Nicholas."

"Well, they say there's no honor among thieves."

She regarded him for several seconds, unblinking. He wondered what she was thinking, but her eyes revealed nothing.

At last, she said, "After Nicholas tried to kill me I called Pym and told him Gregor was going to double-cross him. That's when I found out Pym had been lying to me all along. He was stealing paintings for himself, not some wealthy collector. They're in his mansion in London."

"In his mansion?" Frank said, dumbfounded. "All of them?"

"Yes. Pym said he was dying. He wanted me to find the Vermeers and ship them to him. He wanted me to kill Gregor." Her eyes bored into him. For the first time they showed a hint of emotion, a silent plea for understanding. "I could have, you know, instead of shooting him in the knee. But I had no intention of killing Gregor. I wasn't going to ship the paintings to Pym, either. I wanted to return them to their rightful owners. That's why I left them in the Saab. So you could do it."

She gazed at him, her almond eyes large and dark and compelling. He saw no signs of deceit in them. Maybe she was sorry for stealing the paintings. Now that he'd caught her. Maybe she thought she could work a deal to avoid prosecution, and jail time. Not if he could help it. "What happened to the Manet?"

"Gregor said there was a rip in the canvas, so he left it there."

"Gregor set the fire?"

She hesitated, then shrugged. "I guess so. Nicholas killed the other guards and a policewoman. He told me to put the Vermeers in the rear compartment of a Chevrolet mini-van parked in the courtyard behind the museum. So I did. But I smelled this horrible odor, the odor of death. A dead woman in a police uniform was on the front seat. Then Nicholas attacked me with a knife. He gashed my arm, but I escaped."

Which explained bandage on her arm. Frank wished he had a tape recorder. Natalie seemed eager to tell him what she knew. But it would never hold up in court. He hadn't given her the Miranda warning.

"Where's the van?"

"It might be in a storage facility in Revere. Gregor drove me there once. I stayed in the car, but he might have rented a storage unit." She licked her lips. "Could I have some water? I'm very thirsty."

"Sure, hold on." She had cooperated so far. No reason not to reward her with a drink.

When he got out of the car, Rafe said, "How's it going?"

"Singing like a canary, but she's thirsty. Can you get me a bottled water?"

———

She felt to her stomach. Now that she was in a cruiser, speeding down the highway, lights flashing, siren wailing, the grim reality of her situation had finally sunk in. Talking to Frank Renzi at the train station, mesmerized by his dark penetrating eyes and his deep melodious voice, she had forgotten what lay ahead.

Telling him the story—most of it anyway—had been a relief. This time when she told him she had intended to return the paintings, it seemed as though he believed her. Maybe. A little bit anyway. But in the end it didn't matter. He had given her a bottle of water, put her in this police cruiser and told the cop to take her to the District-4 station and put her in a holding cell.

Her stomach cramped, a violent spasm. She'd seen enough cop shows on TV to know they would strip-search her.

Then they would find the iPhone and the passports. Game over.

Tears blurred her vision. Thirty minutes from now she would be in a jail cell. For the rest of her life, probably. The Boston cops would charge her with the murder of Oliver James. Premeditated murder, which meant life without parole in Massachusetts.

She studied the man behind the wheel, a young cop with a baby face, light-brown hair and a blackhead on his neck. Every so often he checked her in the rearview. What did he think she was going to do? She couldn't get out of the car. There were no door handles and she was handcuffed. But not like before. Renzi had removed the handcuffs and cuffed her hands in front so she could drink the water.

An image of Oliver James blindsided her. You killed him, too. Renzi's accusation. Her stomach heaved and bile rose in her throat, filling her mouth with a sour acid taste. She choked it down.

But the hideous taste gave her an idea. She concentrated hard, tensed her stomach muscles and thought about disgusting things, maggots crawling on spoiled food, slimy okra, her most hated vegetable.

Bile spewed into her throat. This time she didn't swallow, she spit up on the floor. "Pull over," she moaned. "I'm going to throw up."

The cop frowned at her in the rearview mirror and eased into the middle lane.

"Hurry," she said. "I can't hold it." She forced up another stream of bile and spat on the floor. The smell was disgusting, remnants of the chicken tortilla she'd eaten this afternoon.

The cop pulled into the breakdown lane and shut off the siren. She waited tensely, planning her moves. He was six feet tall, but she was wearing her black pumps with the steel-reinforced heels. If she focused hard and used her acting skills, she might be able to disable him.

He got out, circled the car and opened the back door, frowning at her. "Get out," he said. "I don't want my cruiser smelling like a toilet."

Moaning piteously, she swung her legs out of the car. The cop took her arm and helped her out. She staggered forward onto the grassy area beside the breakdown lane, fell to her knees and vomited, spewing out the disgusting contents of her stomach. She waited a moment, gathered her strength, then struggled to her feet, wiped her mouth on her sleeve and gave him her sad-look.

"I'm sorry I puked in your car. Can I have some water to rinse out my mouth? There's a bottle of water in the back seat."

"Okay. Wait here and don't move." The cop went to the rear door and leaned into the cruiser. As cars on the highway sped past them at 65 mph, she concentrated on what she had to do.

The cop backed out of the cruiser, holding the bottle of water in his hand. Focusing her energy, she executed a Taekwondo spin move and kicked him in the head with every ounce of energy she could muster.

He fell to the ground beside the cruiser. She pounced on him, squatted beside his head and located the Dokko point below his ear. Many sensitive nerve endings lay below the skin, but her Taekwondo teacher had said too much pressure on this Dokko point could kill, and she didn't want to kill him. She made a knuckle fist with two fingers and pressed it against the Dokko point, but not too hard.

The cop's eyes rolled up in his head and his body went limp. But she wasn't free yet. People in the cars on the highway couldn't see him lying on the ground beside the cruiser, but someone might come along and wonder why a cop car with flashing lights was parked at the side of the road. And she was wearing handcuffs.

A distant siren sent her heart racing. She crouched beside the fender of the cruiser and surveyed the highway. Off in the distance a police car with flashing lights was coming this way. She returned to the cop. A set of keys was attached to his belt. One of them might unlock the handcuffs. Unfortunately, she had no idea which one.

And now the flashing blues were closer. Her heart beat her chest like a moth at a 100-watt bulb.

Frantic, she dragged the cop away from the cruiser and rolled him into a gully. Gasping for breath, she ran around the cruiser and got behind the wheel. Although her hands were cuffed together and shaking badly, she managed to release the handbrake, put the gearshift in Drive and eased the cruiser into the travel lane.

The lights on the light-bar were still flashing. Miraculously, cars moved out of her way. Could she really get away? She accelerated, got in the middle lane, then the high-speed lane. The police cruiser with the flashing lights was still behind her, but not gaining on her.

She stomped the accelerator and the needle on the speedometer surged to seventy then eighty. Unwilling to celebrate, scarcely daring to hope, she concentrated on the road.

Suddenly, a voice said, "Officer Brennan, what's your twenty?"

Her heart slammed her chest. The police radio!

If they kept calling Officer Brennan and he didn't answer, they might send a cruiser to find him.

She had to get off the highway and call the Mountain Man.

CHAPTER 42

"Where is he?" Frank said as he stormed into the District-4 lobby. "The fucking idiot that lost my prisoner. Where is he?" Several heads turned. He knew he was losing it, but he was too angry to care.

Behind him, Rafe grabbed his arm and said in a low voice, "Cool it, Frank. Wrong time, wrong place. The boss just got off the elevator."

He turned, saw Hank Flynn and strode over to him. "Where's the sonofabitch that lost her? I want to talk to him."

Stone-faced, Flynn said, "Come up to my office and I'll tell you."

"You gonna tell me where she is? You gonna tell me how to find her?"

Flynn's blue eyes grew cold. "Zip it, Renzi. Get in the elevator. We'll talk in my office."

Seething, Frank set his jaw and stabbed the call button. The elevator doors opened and he went inside. His cheeks were red-hot and his heart was pounding his chest like a Force-5 hurricane. He put his thumb on the Door-Open button and stood there, fuming.

Outside the elevator, Flynn said, "Great work, Rafe. I put Frank in charge because we worked the Oliver James murder together, and I knew he was hot to find Natalie."

"Glad I could help," Rafe said. "Frank and I go back a ways, played hoop on the D-4 basketball team for years." Rafe grinned. "I play center, clog up the lane, Frank played point guard and ran the plays. It works out. Well, most times it does, except, you know, when his Irish temper acts up."

Flynn clapped Rafe on the shoulder. "Let's talk tomorrow," he said, and got in the elevator.

Frank did nothing to ease the tense silence as they rode the elevator to the third floor and walked down the hall to Flynn's office. Flynn shut the door and locked it, went to a metal cabinet in the corner and took out two glasses. Too wired to sit still, Frank paced back and forth in front of Flynn's desk.

"Frank, I know you're pissed, but going postal doesn't solve anything. Have a seat." Flynn opened a desk drawer and took out a pint bottle of Glenlivet. He poured scotch into both glasses, set one in front of Frank and said, "Sorry. I don't have any ice."

He took a big gulp and felt the single-malt scotch burn down his throat. He was still furious, but it wasn't Hank's fault that Natalie escaped. "You're right, Hank. Sorry I lost it, but we had her. And now she's gone."

"We might get her. I put out an APB with the description you gave me, with the short dark hair." Flynn sipped his scotch. "Officer Brennan's in Boston Med Center with a helluva lump on his head. He's got a concussion so they'll keep him overnight. Marty's with him now. We found the cruiser in Dorchester, parked outside a mini-mall."

"I should have known she'd try to escape." Even now he could hardly believe it.

"She was locked in a cruiser in handcuffs," Flynn said. "The odds on her escaping were pretty slim."

Frank fingered the scar on his chin, thinking, Not with Natalie.

"Believe it or not, she was pretty cooperative at first. She said the paintings were in the trunk of the Saab, told me where it was and gave me the keys. She also told me who the mastermind was. Which reminds me, I need to call DCI Stanford in London."

He glanced at the clock. 11:05 P.M. Five hours ahead in London. 4:05 A.M. Not a good time to roust Len Stanford out of bed, but he had to tell him about the other stolen paintings. "Can I use your phone to call him? Put it on speaker so I don't have to explain twice?"

Flynn sipped his Glenlivet and smiled. "Frank. You recovered the paintings. Give me the number. I'll call him now, let you talk to him."

A minute later, Frank heard Stanford, obviously groggy with sleep, croak, "Hello?"

"Len," he said, "Frank Renzi. Sorry to wake you at this hour but I've got news and it's urgent. Just so you know, my boss, Lt. Colonel Harrison Flynn is listening in. That okay with you?"

"No problem," Stanford said. "What in blazes name happened? Before I went to bed I saw a bulletin on the news, something about a fire and the stolen Manet, but no details."

"Gregor Kraus and Natalie Brixton pulled the heist, same MO as your heists over there. Gregor hired an insider guard, but the guard double-crossed him and kept the paintings. Gregor killed him and took the paintings."

"What happened with the Manet?" Stanford asked.

"According to Natalie, Gregor said there was a big tear in the canvas, so he left it to burn in the fire. The fire chief said it was in bad shape."

"Bloody rotters," Stanford said. "What about the other paintings? Did you recover those?"

"Yes. We tracked Gregor and Natalie to a train station. Natalie claimed she wanted to return them, but Gregor didn't. By then we were at the station. She wounded Gregor so he couldn't escape and left the paintings in the trunk of his car. She tried to escape but I caught her."

He raised an eyebrow at Hank Flynn, who gestured with his hand. Get on with it.

"Bottom line, Gregor shot himself and we found the paintings in the trunk of his car. But here's the important part. Natalie said Gregor wasn't the leader of the art heist gang. Jonathan Pym was."

"You don't say!" Stanford exclaimed. "Blast it all! Pym was the mastermind all along!"

"Yes, but here's the important part. Natalie said she called Pym after the Gardner heist and told him Gregor was planning to double-cross him. Pym wanted her to retrieve the paintings and ship them to him in London. Natalie thought Pym was stealing the paintings for wealthy art collectors, but Pym admitted that he was stealing them for himself. The paintings are in his mansion."

"Jesus fucking Christ!" Stanford exclaimed his voice booming over the speakerphone.

Flynn raised his glass in a mock-toast and smiled at Frank. Frank nodded his agreement.

"Pardon my language," Stanford said, "but after all these months, searching for these wretched art thieves, and all along the paintings were right here in London. Bloody unbelievable. I'd best round up my detectives and get over there straightaway."

"The sooner the better," Frank said. "Pretty soon the news will break that we recovered the paintings."

Flynn got his attention, indicating he wanted to speak. "DCI Stanford, Hank Flynn here. Hate to butt in, but do you need probable cause for a warrant to search his mansion?"

"Pleasure to meet you," Stanford said. "Good point. Might take me a while to get it."

"I don't know the system over there," Flynn said, "but we found a murdered woman in Pym's Boston office. Global Interpreting. We believe Gregor Kraus killed her. Will that help?"

"Should do," Stanford said. "Forgive me, but I'm still in shock. Did Natalie say how many paintings were in Pym's mansion?"

"No," Frank said. "I don't think she knew. She never saw them."

"My thanks to both of you for letting me know," Stanford said. "I'd best be off."

"Good luck," Frank said. "Call me after you do the search."

Flynn ended the call and said, "So this guy Pym was running the art heist gang?"

"So Natalie said. We'll see what DCI Stanford finds at his mansion. Wealthy guy, he's probably got six lawyers on staff to defend him."

"Be tough to defend if they find a bunch of stolen art in his house."

Frank remained silent. He was happy they'd recovered the Gardner paintings, even happier that Hank Flynn would get credit for it, but the fact that Natalie had escaped was eating a hole in his gut.

Natalie was gone and they weren't going to find her.

He slugged down some Glenlivet, brooding as depressing images entered his mind. Natalie crossing the Canadian border in a rental car. Natalie on a train, wearing a blond wig. Natalie at an airport boarding gate, bound for who knows where.

Exhausted, he massaged his eyes and yawned. He needed sleep, but he wouldn't get any tonight. He was too angry. The physical symptoms—rapid heartbeat, flushed face, acid stomach—had lessened, but his fury was not going to go away.

Where's Natalie? For two years those words had been ever present in his mind. Now they were back with a vengeance.

———

London 5:45 A.M.

Jonathan Pym sank onto the leather recliner in his library and closed his eyes. He hadn't slept all night. After seeing the bulletin on the late evening news, how could he? One of the paintings stolen from the Gardner Museum had been destroyed in a fire. Not one of the Vermeers, but still. Manet's magnificent painting, burned in a fire.

How could anyone do such a thing?

His eyes snapped open. Gregor had done it.

In addition to the Vermeers, Gregor had stolen a Rembrandt and a Manet and kept them for himself. Waiting for Jonathan Pym to die so he could sell them and make millions. After all he'd done for the man! Giving him a place to live when he got out of prison, paying him handsomely to steal the artworks, and Gregor had betrayed him.

A sudden cough wracked him. He pulled out a tissue and spat into it, a bolus of phlegm tinged pink with blood. He glanced at the brandy snifter on the table in front of the recliner. Not his usual cognac, the special cocktail he had prepared.

Yesterday, he had gone to his solicitor and changed his will. Gregor was no longer a beneficiary. Valerie would get Gregor's share. He'd put the statement he'd written in an envelope, sealed it and had his solicitor notarize his signature on the envelope. Without mentioning Valerie, his declaration detailed Gregor's role in the art heists and the deaths of the security guards and included the photographs he had taken of Gregor.

His posthumous revenge.

A copy of the statement was on the table beside the cocktail.

The police had recovered the Manet, but where were the others?

He reached in the pocket of his dressing gown and took out a postcard. *Woman in Blue Reading a Letter.* The painting was in his basement museum, but he had no energy to go down and look at it. For years he had enjoyed the artistry of Vermeer's masterpiece. But no more. Tears filled his eyes. He loved all his paintings, but the Vermeer was his favorite. Imbued with a stillness that defied description, the painting was a mystery.

260

The whereabouts of the Vermeers Valerie had stolen was also a mystery. *The Lacemaker* and *The Milkmaid*, not to mention the Rembrandt *Self-Portrait*.

Valerie hadn't called him, and when he called her cellphone, she didn't answer. In the end, perhaps she had betrayed him, too. But the final insult would come after he died.

Gregor's penchant for violence would sully his reputation. Prior to the Ashmolean heist, no one had died during any of the robberies. But Gregor had ordered Valerie to shoot the security guard.

When his solicitor opened his will and released his dying declaration to the press, Jonathan Pym would be vilified. Scorned like his larcenous father. Reviled like Van Meegeren, the painter of fake Vermeers.

The police would dig up the dirt and discover his shabby origins.

His hard-earned reputation would go belly up. But there was nothing he could do about that.

Only one thing remained within his control. He leaned forward and picked up the snifter with the cocktail he had prepared.

Time to drink the hemlock.

Holding the snifter in both hands, he raised it to his mouth and drank every drop.

CHAPTER 43

Tuesday July 13, 2010 4:35 PM

"You think the boy will be okay there?" Frank asked. "Jaylen?"

Rafe didn't answer right away, sipped his beer, then said, "Seemed happy enough playing with Lateesha's boy. Probably the best place for him, his father currently in prison and all. Lateesha was all torn up about Jamilla. Worried about Jaylen, too. She'll look after him."

Frank took out his cell and put it on the bar beside his Heineken. He was expecting an important call and he didn't want to miss it. Lonny's Tavern, their usual watering hole near Rafe's house in Dorchester, was quiet now, but when people got out of work, it would get busy fast.

"Did you tell him about his mother?"

"Not me, man. Figured it'd be better if Lateesha did it, you know, pick the right time, the right place."

Based on what Natalie had told him, they had located the stolen Chevrolet mini-van in Revere. A brutal discovery, three bodies decomposing in the heat, the sun beating down on the storage locker. The security guards, Anthony Falcone and Charles Lawson, were easy to identify. Jamilla Wells was tougher. She had on a Boston PD uniform so they contacted Human Resources, identified her and found out she had a son. Rafe had taken it upon himself to locate the boy.

"Tough break for Johnny Perkins," Frank said.

"Yeah," Rafe said. "Had a wife and two kids and a bum ticker. Take twenty thousand volts from a Taser, heart attacks can happen. I figure Nicholas Kwan killed Jamilla Wells and the security guards. Had a history, you know, killed a couple of cops in San Francisco."

Frank nodded and yawned. He hadn't slept for two days. He checked his cellphone, willing it to ring, then said, "Gregor let him do the dirty work. Natalie stole the Vermeers. Kwan took the others."

"And Gregor burned him to death." Rafe shook his head. "Man, that guy gave me the creeps. Did you see his hands? Serious burn scars. Wonder who did it?"

"I don't know. According to DCI Stanford, his father was an enforcer for a London gang. Gregor joined the gang when he was twelve, took over his father's job a few years later and eventually wound up in prison. After he got out, he hooked up with Jonathan Pym and started stealing art for him."

Earlier, Stanford had called him from London. Pym had swallowed a cocktail laced with poison, but Stanford found a note directing them to his basement museum. Stanford and his men had found a dozen stolen paintings. Stanford was thrilled. Not only did it solve most of his art heist cases, he could return the paintings to their rightful owners.

"So they're all dead," Rafe said. "Pym, the mastermind, Gregor Kraus, the enforcer, and Nicholas Kwan, the insider guard."

"Natalie isn't," Frank snapped. "She's still out there, somewhere."

"She got a hold on you," Rafe said.

Frank looked at him, incredulous. "What, you think I'm in love with her?"

"No. Different kind of attraction. To you, she's a puzzle."

He sipped his beer and thought about it. Natalie was a puzzle all right, and their brief talk at the train station hadn't solved it. He'd read the diary she'd kept after her mother was murdered, but it left too many unanswered questions. She had a rough childhood, but plenty of kids who grew up in difficult circumstances didn't become criminals. What drove her to take revenge on her mother's killer? Why get involved with an art heist gang? And a zillion other questions he wanted to ask.

"She killed people," he said. "She should be in jail."

"So have I," Rafe said, his dark eyes somber. "And so have you. That nutcase down in New Orleans?"

"That was different. He was about to kill two people."

"It was a righteous shoot, Frank, no question. Mine was too, comes down to it. What I'm saying, you make your own prison. You kill someone, it's not something you forget."

Frank couldn't argue with that. Years ago a little girl had died when Frank and another detective had executed an arrest warrant on a drug dealer. If he shut his eyes, he could still see her face.

"Pretty resourceful," Rafe said, "planting a bug on Gregor's car so she could track him."

Irritated, he said, "Don't rub it in. We put her in a police cruiser, handcuffed, and she still got away."

"Not rubbing it in, man. Just saying." Rafe slugged down some beer and ate a pretzel.

"Someone's helping her. How'd she get the handcuffs off?"

"Who knows? Natalie likes to walk on the wild side, take risks like a certain homicide detective I know."

"Cut the psychobabble, Rafe."

"She could have killed you two years ago but she didn't. Didn't kill Gregor, either. We figured she rode to the station with Gregor, but maybe she had a car and followed him there."

Frank stared at him. "Jesus! Why didn't I think of that?"

Rafe grinned and mock-punched his arm. "I work the Gang Unit now, but I used to work Homicide, remember? We find the car maybe we can figure out where she's going. They re-opened the garage at five this morning so folks could retrieve their cars, but the security cameras will capture the plate numbers or the EZ-Pass numbers of every vehicle that left the garage."

Frank doubted this would help him find Natalie. She was gone. He wished Hank would hurry up and call. After the crime lab techs found the bug, Hank had called the tracking company, but they refused to tell him the client's name, address and, most importantly, the number of the cellphone where they sent the tracking information.

"I should have driven her to the station myself."

"Woulda, coulda, shoulda. Let it go, Frank. We got plenty of other crooks to catch."

His cellphone rang and his heart sped up. He grabbed it and said, "Hey, Hank, did you get anything?"

"Yes. The security company decided to cooperate when they found out their client was wanted for murder. Here's what I got so far. Name, Valerie Brown. Mailing address, a UPS store on Huntington Avenue. They're still sending information to her cellphone. Here's the number."

He took out a pen and wrote the number on a napkin.

"Better call her quick," Flynn said. "Georgette will have this information inside of an hour."

"Will do. Thanks a million, Hank." He shut his cellphone and said to Rafe, "Thanks, man. You helped break the case."

"Hey, we were a team for a while, working Homicide, playing hoop. You ever think about coming back? Point guard we got now is okay, but not as good as you."

Recalling the good times they'd had, Frank felt a pang of nostalgia. "I miss playing hoop and hanging with you was always great, Rafe. I miss Boston, too, but Kelly and I are pretty tight."

"Bring her with you, man. Boston PD could use another good detective."

Frank laughed. "We'll see. Kelly's got a mind of her own. Had fun when she was up here, though. But it's about time you came to New Orleans. Send the kids to Grandma's for school vacation in February, take a break from the ice and snow, you and Willow come down and stay in my condo. It's in the French Quarter, near the clubs on Frenchman Street. We'll listen to some sounds."

Rafe grinned. "Sounds like a plan. I'll work on it. Go call Natalie."

———

O'Hare International Airport, Chicago 3:52 PM Central Time

Natalie rolled her carry-on bag to the far corner of the gate area, set her duffel bag beside it and sank onto an empty seat. Still exhausted by her nerve-wracking escape, she yawned, replaying it in her mind. After leaving the highway in the cruiser, she had pulled over, shut off the flashing lights and called Pak Lam. Ten minutes later, Feng arrived and removed the handcuffs with bolt cutters. She followed him to a strip mall and left the cruiser there. Then Feng had driven her to the Royal Dragon.

Picturing Pak Lam's delighted expression when he opened the door, she smiled.

"Congratulations," he'd said. "I saw a news bulletin on TV. The police recovered the stolen paintings. You have fulfilled your promise. Not only that, you escaped your captors. You must tell me about this." Over soothing cups of jasmine tea, she told him what had happened. Then he had told her the plan he had devised. "In three hours Feng will drive you to North Station. The train to Chicago leaves at 7:10 AM."

The sound of high-pitched voices drew her attention. A slender young woman with two towheaded toddlers claimed seats on the row perpendicular to hers. The kids looked excited, bright eyes and smiling faces, talking in piping voices though she couldn't hear what they said. Maybe this was their first plane ride. The mother took out a package of Goldfish crackers and poured some into their tiny hands.

Natalie opened her duffel and took out the mathematics textbook Feng had bought to go with her Liang Lam disguise: short dark hair neatly combed, a gray sweatshirt with MIT on the front, stonewashed jeans and black loafers. Before they left for the train station, she had bidden Pak Lam a tearful farewell. He gave her two thousand dollars—a parting gift, he'd said—kissed her on both cheeks and wished her a safe journey. At the station there were police officers with dogs, but Feng acted like her big brother, chattering away as he walked her to the correct platform. "Do not worry about the Toyota. I will drive my brother there to get it." Before she boarded the train, Feng had smiled and said, "Your disguise is perfect. You look like a geeky grad student on break from his studies at MIT."

But at the airport security checkpoint, a man in a TSA uniform noticed her MIT sweatshirt and said, "Good school. My brother went there." The one factor her disguise couldn't alter was the pitch of her voice. Fearing it would betray her, she just smiled and nodded. The TSA officer had waved her through.

The long-sleeved sweatshirt concealed the bandage on her arm. The wound hardly hurt at all now, but her muscles were stiff from riding the train all day. She flexed her shoulders, then her neck. In forty minutes she would board the plane. Then she could relax. She might even be able to sleep. After she reached her final destination, she would let her hair grow back and live as Liang Lam's sister, Ling Lam.

Her iPhone rang. Assuming it was Pak Lam calling to bid her a final farewell, she took it out of the duffel. Then she saw the caller ID.

Her heart slammed her ribs. Frank Renzi.

How did he get her number? The phone chimed insistently. If she didn't answer, would he keep calling?

Slinging her duffel over her shoulder, she towed her suitcase out of the waiting area. The gate across the concourse was closed, the plane scheduled for a midnight departure. A handful of passengers sat in the row of seats facing the concourse, but the gate area was empty.

The phone kept ringing. She hurried to the far corner, took a deep breath and pressed Talk. "How did you get my number?"

After a brief silence, Renzi said, "You're resourceful, Natalie, but so am I. You got away, but I'll find you eventually."

She loved the sound of his voice, but his words sent icy chills down her neck. I'll find you eventually.

"Where are you? In an airport?"

Fearing he had somehow tracked her to Chicago, she anxiously looked around to see if anyone was watching her. But no one was paying her any attention. She was just a young guy in an MIT sweatshirt talking on a cellphone.

"I'm glad you found the paintings," she said.

"Pym's dead, did you know that?"

"No. But Gregor told me he had some kind of wasting disease."

"Maybe, but that's not what killed him. He drank poison."

That surprised her, but she felt no sympathy for Pym. Jonathan had always been into control.

"When you were in London did you ever date a guy named Stefan Haas?"

She frowned. What a strange question. "Not that I recall. Why?"

"Valerie Brown wears a blond wig sometimes, right?"

She gasped. How did he know her false name? Valerie Brown. Then she thought: *The iPhone account.*

"I've got a snapshot of you with Stefan Haas. He sent it to his mother in New Hampshire."

Stefan Haas. She frowned. That was the name on the credit card Gregor had used at the hotel. "I may have met him when I was working as an escort, but I never remembered their names."

"Gregor killed him and stole his identity. He had a credit card with Stefan's name on it."

She gnawed her lip. If the police knew that, they would find her clothes at the hotel in Dedham. But she would be in Europe by then. Besides, there was nothing incriminating in her belongings.

"If he did," she said, "I had nothing to do with it. I told you Gregor was ruthless. I'm done with killing. I told you that yesterday and I meant it." She hesitated, then said, "Frank, I'm sorry I shot you in New Orleans. I'm sorry I stole the paintings too. I can't change that now, but I won't be stealing any more. Don't try to find me and don't call this number again because I won't answer."

She ended the call and stood there, unable to move. Her hands were shaking and so were her legs.

She put the iPhone in her duffel, walked across the concourse and returned to her seat near the mom and her toddlers. They were adorable, not twins but close in age, one a three-year old perhaps, the other a year or so older, dashing to the window to peer out at the tarmac, then back to their mother.

She didn't plan to have children, but she liked them. After she settled into her escape-hatch city, maybe she'd get a job working with kids. Teach them how to speak English, perhaps. Maybe she'd be a librarian. That might be fun. She loved libraries and books. Once a week she could gather a group of small children around her and read them an adventure story. She'd had a few adventures.

Reading about them was safer. She wouldn't have to carry a gun. Or kill anyone.

The woman at the boarding gate announced that first-class passengers and people with small children were free to board. The young mother gathered her luggage and her two children and headed for the gate.

On impulse, Natalie took out her iPhone and composed a text.

Dear Mountain Man, plane is boarding. Thank you for all your help. Will call you soon. She hesitated for a moment, then typed: *You are a wonderful father. Love, Natalie*

After she hit Send, she dashed across the concourse, popped the SIM card out of her iPhone and dropped it into a trash container. Renzi might eventually trace her to the airport, but by then the SIM card would be at the dump. And she would be in Europe.

A sense of exhilaration swept over her. At last she was free!

Gregor was dead and so was Pym, so they couldn't pursue her. Adjusting to another big city would be difficult, but she had done it before. New York. Paris. London. And now she had a family.

This time she would have someone to talk to. This time she could call her adopted father.

The Mountain Man would always be there for her.

#####

Susan says . . .

Thank you for purchasing Natalie's Art. If you enjoyed the book I would very much appreciate an honest review on Goodreads and/or whatever Amazon site you purchased it.

To receive an email alert when my next book comes out, sign up at

http://eepurl.com/ExkX9 I'll never use your email for anything else.

ABOUT THE AUTHOR

For many years award-winning novelist Susan Fleet played trumpet professionally in the Boston area. While teaching at Brown University and Berklee College of Music, she began writing crime fiction. The Premier Book Awards named her first novel, Absolution, Best Mystery-Suspense-Thriller of 2009. The Feathered Quill Book Awards named her third novel, Natalie's Revenge, Best Mystery of 2014.

Susan lived in New Orleans for nine years and now divides her time between Boston and the Big Easy, the settings for her Frank Renzi crime thriller series. Visit her at http://www.susanfleet.com Send her an email; she would love to hear from you!

Crime novels by Susan Fleet

Absolution

Diva

Natalie's Revenge

Jackpot

Non-fiction by Susan Fleet

Women Who Dared: Trailblazing 20th Century Musicians
Violinist Maud Powell and Trumpeter Edna White

Dark Deeds, Vol. 1: Serial killers, stalkers and domestic homicides
Dark Deeds, Vol. 2: Serial killers, stalkers and domestic homicides

ACKNOWLEDGMENTS

I can still remember my shock and dismay when thirteen masterpieces, including The Concert by Vermeer and Rembrandt's only seascape, The Storm on the Sea of Galilee, were stolen from the Isabella Stewart Gardner Museum in 1990. I sincerely hope there will never be another robbery there.

Since the fictional heist in Natalie's Art in 2010, significant changes have come to the Gardner. In January 2012, a new wing opened, with a concert hall, greenhouse, gallery, gift shop, restaurant, and space for educational programs. It now serves as the new entrance on Evans Way. Sadly, the art works stolen in 1990 have not been recovered and the thieves have not been found.

Long before this book was a twinkle in my eye, I visited the Gardner Museum many times, before and after the 1990 robbery. This facilitated my descriptions of this beautiful museum and some of its art works. In my research I consulted several books on art theft. *Stealing Rembrandts: The Untold Story of Notorious Art Heists*, Anthony M. Amore and Tom Mashberg; *Priceless: How I Went Undercover To Rescue the World's Stolen Treasures*, Robert K. Wittman; *Museum of the Missing: A History of Art Theft*, Simon Houpt.

My thanks to Blair and Waundolyn, who work at the Route 128 train station. Their information and suggestions helped me write the final scenes. Members of the crimescenewriters group explained how car-tracking devices operate. My law enforcement consultants prefer to remain anonymous, but I greatly appreciate their expertise. However, Natalie's Art is a work of dramatic fiction. Any errors or inaccuracies are mine alone.

Additional thanks go to Diana Hockley, Carolyn Wilkins and Jaimie Bergeron for suggestions on early drafts. Special thanks to John Amaral for his invaluable editorial suggestions and line edits.

Last but not least, my heartfelt thanks to you, my readers! I would love to hear from you. You can contact me via my website: www.susanfleet.com

www.ingramcontent.com/pod-product-compliance
Lightning Source LLC
Chambersburg PA
CBHW070327260626
47160CB00003B/970